MINOT-SLEEPER LIBRARY
Bristol
New Hampshire

(603) 744-3352
- LIBRARY HOURS -

Monday	10AM - 6PM
Tuesday	1PM - 8PM
Wednesday	10AM - 6PM
Thursday	1PM - 8PM
Friday	10AM - 6PM
Saturday	10AM - 2PM
Sunday	Closed

LOAN PERIOD
Books- Two Weeks
Audio Books- Two Weeks
Magazines- One Week
Videos- One Week
RENEWALS
Upon application the materials
may be renewed unless reserved for
another patron.

If a patron materially injures library
property, he shall make good the loss or
damage in such way as the Librarian may
direct.   Failure   to   pay   fines   or
assessments for loss or damage shall
debar a patron from the use of the library.

BEFORE I SLEEP

ALSO AVAILABLE IN BEELER LARGE PRINT BY
RACHEL LEE

AFTER I DREAM

BEFORE I SLEEP

RACHEL LEE

BEELER LARGE PRINT
Hampton Falls, New Hampshire, 2000

Library of Congress Cataloging-in-Publication Data

Lee, Rachel
Before I sleep / Rachel Lee.
  p   cm
  ISBN 1-57490-302-0 (alk. paper)
    1. Large type books. I. Title

PS3562.E3596 B4 2000
813'.54—dc21   00-062096

Published in Large Print by arrangement with
Warner Books, Inc.

BEELER LARGE PRINT
is published by
Thomas T. Beeler, *Publisher*
Post Office Box 659
Hampton Falls, New Hampshire 03844

Typeset in 16 point Adobe Garmond type.
Sewn and bound by
Sheridan Books in Chelsea, Michigan

To Helen Breitwieser,
for working so hard to give wings to my dreams.
Your friendship is priceless.

Sincere thanks to newsman Roger Schulman for an inside look at the studios of WFLA Radio in Tampa, and for generously answering so many of my questions.

Deep appreciation to my beloved spouse Cris, who once hosted as Rick Burbage, for vetting my talk-radio scenes, and for giving me so much insight about what it's like behind the microphone.Before I Sleep

BEFORE I SLEEP

PROLOGUE

JOHN WILLIAM OTIS TOOK THE NEWS WITH HIS USUAL calm. He had been on death row for nearly five years, and all his appeals had failed. It wasn't exactly a shock.

But it filled him with a great sorrow for opportunities lost, and he sat for a long time thinking about the things he would never be able to do now. He sat thinking about the people who had died, the only people on earth who had loved him. And thought about the fact that everyone believed he had killed them. He hadn't killed them, but everyone else thought he had, and he was resigned to his fate.

He picked up a battered copy of *A Tale of Two Cities*, and read his favorite lines, on a page he had turned to so often that its edges were worn off almost to the print. "It is a far, far better thing I do, than I have ever done; it is a far, far better rest that I go to, than I have ever known."

He thought about that, too, for a long time, then reached for his Bible with its torn, cracked cover, and opened to another of his favorite passages. "Greater love hath no man than this, that a man lay down his life for his friends."

They fed him meat loaf for dinner, and he ate, though it seemed pointless now. They took him to the yard for a brief walk, giving him a cherished taste of the evening sun on his skin, watching him carefully because now that it was final, they feared he might do something stupid. But they were nice about it. He liked his guards, and they him, and at times it seemed as if they were all members of a select fraternity. He would miss their camaraderie.

Back in his cell, he picked up a composition book on

1

which he had carefully lettered: *The Poems of John William Otis.* He looked at it for a while, thinking what a poor legacy it was to leave behind, and thinking of all the poems he would now never write.

Then he opened to a blank page, picked up the stubby wooden pencil they let him use, and began to write.

"Today I Heard"

Today I heard that I will die,
and then I went to dinner.
It should be more, somehow.
Solemn, ponderous, thunder,
Pomp, circumstance, flourish,
Marking the moment of enforced
mortality.

But no.

It might have been mail call,
with a letter from my brother,
whom I will never see again,
Or the library man,
with a book of Keats,
which I will never finished,
Or the laundry man,
with fresh, clean sheets,
which I will stain with sweat by
morning.

But no.

Just a quick visit from the warden.
And three weeks hence, more visits,

another dinner,
fresh clothes,
a haircut,
a shave,
a short walk,
And then I will be no more.

But no.

They will ask me to repent,
To say that I am sorry,
and I am sorry,
for everyone who hurt.
But I will never speak of this,
for love is sacrifice,
and I must prove my love.

But no.

Today I heard that I will die,
and then I went to dinner.
Meat loaf, potatoes, carrots, corn
bread,
And icy cold milk were my
counselors.
Marking the moment of enforced
morality.

But no.

CHAPTER 1
22 DAYS

"YOU JUST DON'T GET IT," SAM FROM CLEARWATER SAID.

Carissa Stover smothered a sigh and leaned back a little from the microphone. Outside, the night was dark, and on the windowpane beside her she could see the silvery shimmer of rain. She was getting very tired of this particular discussion on her show.

"No," she said to the caller, "*you* don't get it. You can't buy an acquittal in the criminal-justice system. No way."

The caller wasn't going to surrender that easily. "But a ten-million-dollar defense—"

"A ten-million-dollar defense comes close to buying a level playing field," she said forcefully. "So what if the defendant had five lawyers and six investigators working for him. The state had the entire city police force, the state police, the state crime lab, a whole staff of state-paid prosecutors—and a lot more than ten million dollars to spend on the prosecution. In fact, the state outspent the defense in this case by two to one."

"But—"

"No," Carissa said flatly. "Jonas Bellows did *not* buy an acquittal. He bought a level playing field." She punched the button that cut off that caller and continued to speak into the microphone. "Come on, folks, we've beaten this horse to death every night since the verdict came down. Let's talk about something new before I go home.

"You're listening to the Talk of the Coast, 990 WCST, Tampa Bay's number one talk radio station. This is Carey Justice, and our subject tonight, and every night, is the law. How does it affect you and me? When does it screw

4

up? When does it do right? If you've got a story to tell, we want to hear it. Our phones are open right now, and taking calls at 555-9900 in Hillsborough, 559-9900 in Pinellas, and toll-free at 1-800-555-9990."

She punched the next blinking green button as she read from the screen in front of her. "Sarah from Largo, you're on the air."

"Carey?" a woman's voice said uncertainly.

"Yes, this is Carey. You're on the air, Sarah."

"Oh. Well, I saw in the paper that that twelve-year-old boy who skinned that dog alive is going to get probation. Why can't they just send him to jail?"

"They could, actually. For maybe five years. And I kind of agree with you, Sarah. This kid sounds like a serial killer in the making to me."

"Yes. Yes, he does! And how anyone could do that to a poor little dog . . ."

"But he's still a kid, Sarah. A juvenile. We like to believe that kids are still young enough to learn from their mistakes. We like to give them second chances to get their act together and grow up. Don't your kids ever make mistakes, Sarah?"

"Well, of course they do, Carey. But nothing like this!"

"I agree this kid's a monster. But I don't see how sending him to prison is going to make him any better. Do you?"

"It might scare him into behaving."

"If he's scarable, this conviction and probation ought to do the job." She cut Sarah off and continued on a subject that was sure to light up her phone lines.

"Think about it, folks. It's easier to do prison than probation and community control. You think not? Try it sometime. See how long you can go without being able to run out to the store to get ice cream or a six-pack. See how

5

long you can behave if you're allowed to go out of the house only to go to work, and if you detour for fifteen minutes on the way home to get gas and milk . . . the next thing you know your probation officer is charging you with a violation and dragging you back into court.

"I'm telling you, probation and community control are set up to make people fail. And when they fail they go straight to prison. Caller, you're on the air."

A few minutes later she cut to the news and commercials, which gave her a much-needed breather. She leaned back in her chair and stared at her reflection in the dark, silver-streaked glass of the window.

She saw the shadowy face of a pretty enough woman with dark hair and hazel eyes. The face of a woman who was as disillusioned as it was possible to be.

Rising from the chair, she took off her headphones and allowed herself a full-body stretch that made her spine pop. Then she went to hunt up a can of soda. Caffeine. She needed caffeine if she was going to make it through the next hour.

She pushed change into the vending machine down the hall from her studio and opened the drink, downing half of it in one thirsty gulp. When she was on the air, she drank bottled water, but right now she wanted to get hyped on caffeine and sugar. It meant that when she went home in an hour she probably wouldn't be able to sleep, but what the hell. There was no reason to get up early in the morning.

The newsroom intern joined her. Dale Jennings was a pretty young woman of about twenty-four, with blond hair and blue eyes big enough to sail a destroyer in. She seemed to live and breathe radio the way Carissa had once lived and breathed law.

"The phones are hot tonight," Dale remarked.

"Everyone seems to want to talk about Bellows, though."

Carissa shook her head. "A half million listeners, and every one of 'em wants to put in their two cents about that case. It wouldn't be so bad if they weren't all saying the same thing."

"They believe Bellows is guilty."

"Too bad. The jury said he's not."

"I know." She was holding a piece of paper, and now she passed it with shy eagerness to Carissa. "Here's something that just came in on the news wire. I figured you could use it to shift the topic to something else."

"Thanks." Carissa took the paper and scanned it quickly.

Then she froze. Her heart slammed, then seemed to stop beating altogether.

The governor had signed the death warrant for John William Otis.

Hot honey.

Those were the words that always came into Seamus Rourke's head when he heard the low, smooth voice of Carey Justice coming out of his radio.

And he heard it every weeknight, unless he was working. Tonight he walked through his front door, ditched his shield and his gun on the coffee table, then yanked his tie off with one hand while he turned on the radio with the other.

"You're listening to the Talk of the Coast, 990 WCST, Tampa Bay's number one talk radio station . . ."

Sometimes he heard those words in his sleep. Sometimes he heard Carey's voice in a silent, empty room in the dead of night. Even after five years, she still haunted his dreams.

Listening to the radio with only one ear, not really

7

caring what she said, or what her callers said, just wanting to hear the soft, sweet honey of her voice, he walked into the kitchen and pulled a bottle of water out of the fridge. It used to be beer, but he hadn't touched alcohol since the accident.

He jerked his thoughts back sharply from that precipice, knowing how steep the fall was on the other side. There was a whole area of his memory staked out with a warning sign: *There be dragons.* He skated around it as often as he could, sometimes teetering right over the brink. Tonight he couldn't face it. Tonight he refused to let his past poison his present.

Not that it was much of a present. He could almost have laughed at himself, a thirty-eight-year-old police detective whose entire life consisted of work and an evening radio talk show. It wasn't always that way. There'd been a time when he'd actually had a whole goddamn life.

He looked at the bottle of water in his hand and figured the only thing missing from this dramatic, self-pitying self-image was a beer or a shot of whiskey.

Carey had gone to commercials and the news, so he turned the radio down to cut out the blabber and annoying jingles. Nor did he want to hear the news. He saw entirely too much news on the street, when it was happening or had just happened.

The doorbell rang. Seamus stared at it in disbelief. His doorbell almost never rang anymore. Figuring it had to be some kid trying to sell him the local paper, he flung the door open with as pleasant a smile as he could muster.

The smile died when he saw his father standing on the threshold.

"Seamus," said Danny Rourke.

"Dad," Seamus said, his eyes traveling from the old

man's face to the duffel bag he held in one hand. "What's this?"

Danny regarded him from bloodshot eyes. "The IRS took my boat, boy. They took my boat and every damn nickel I had. I got no place else to go."

Seamus probably should have been more surprised than he was. Mostly all he felt was a sense of inevitability. Life had a way of rubbing your nose in the very things you most wanted to avoid. "It's the drinking, Dad."

Danny sighed. "I know. I know. Believe me, if there's any place else I could go . . ."

"Fuck it. Get in here. But if you want to stay, you're by God going to go to AA."

"Yeah, yeah," said his father, dropping his duffel on the floor beside the door.

Seamus closed the door behind him and locked it. Danny smelled like a brewery, which was hardly surprising. He'd probably spent whatever money he'd had left in his pocket in some bar while he tried to figure out how to avoid turning to his son for help.

"I was just going to make dinner," Seamus said when the silence seemed to grow too long, WCST was still reading the news, and rather than chance hearing it, he reached over and turned off the radio. The silence took on depth and breadth, filling the room until he felt he almost couldn't breathe.

"I could do with a bite," Danny said finally. "I'll help."

"Why'd the IRS seize your boat?"

Danny shrugged. "I don't know for sure. I maybe forgot to file a return? All I know is they sent me a bill a few months back. I ain't been making money the way I used to, boy."

Of course not, Seamus thought. Not when two beers in the evening had turned into an endless all-day drinking binge.

9

Danny shook his head. "They say I owe 'em damn near thirty thousand dollars in taxes and then there's penalties. No way I got that kind of money. So, they took the boat."

"The boat's worth a lot more than that."

"I don't reckon they care."

"Well, go put your stuff in the guest room and take a shower while I make dinner. You know where everything is."

There'd been a time when his father had been an honored guest in his home. No more. He'd be more willing to pull a wino off the street and invite him in. At least the wino wouldn't have a history he couldn't forget.

Danny shuffled down the hall, looking shrunken and weak compared to the big, burly man Seamus remembered from his childhood. He ought to feel some sympathy, but he couldn't. He couldn't feel anything at all except the one fleeting, angry thought that Edgar Allen Poe must be writing the script for his life.

He cast a glance toward the radio, but left it turned off. No more hot honey tonight. Christ, when had he become such a masochist?

The thought seemed to clear his head, and he marched into the kitchen to pull some chops out of the fridge.

One of these days, he told himself, he had to find a way to get his head out of his ass.

Carissa stepped out the station door into the parking lot and felt the heat and humidity hit her like a fist. It was eighty-six, drizzling, and as utterly miserable as Florida could get.

She always wore jeans and sweaters to work because the station was air-conditioned to iciness, probably on the theory that people would stay more alert. Or maybe it was just that Bill Hayes, the station manager, liked it cold.

Either way, the contrast always hit her hard.

Her sweater was plastered to her skin in moments, from sweat more than rain, and it prickled like a hair shirt. She could hardly wait to get home and rip it off. Usually she wore a T-shirt beneath, so she could shed the sweater when she left, but tonight she'd been late leaving for work and had forgotten it.

She climbed into her car, a bright red Jeep, turned on the ignition, and put the air-conditioning on high. The rain beat a steady, lonely tattoo on the canvas top. The radio was on, as always, tuned to WCST. Tonight, she reached over and switched it off.

The show following hers was run by Ted Sanders, a right-wing Rush Limbaugh wanna-be, and she didn't want to hear Ted spouting about the joys of the death penalty and how Old Sparky was the first line of defense against evil in society. Carissa wasn't dead set against the death penalty, but she figured electrocution was about as enlightened as burning at the stake.

She hadn't mentioned John Otis on her show. When she'd walked back into the station after her break, she had planned to, but the words wouldn't come out of her mouth. Instead she'd spent the last hour talking about lawsuits.

Everybody had an opinion on the law, and everybody thought they understood how things really worked. And when it came to lawsuits, everybody wanted tort reform— until their own ox was gored. It had turned out to be a pretty lively discussion, thank God.

But now she was alone, and John Otis might as well have been sitting in the seat beside her. She didn't want to think about her role in putting him on death row, but she had a feeling she wasn't going to be able to avoid it.

Instead of going home, she headed for a club where

11

some of her friends hung out. Maybe she wouldn't go home at all tonight. Almost anything seemed better than being alone with her thoughts.

She had a moment of sanity, a moment of pure clarity when she realized she was going to have to face the Otis thing all over again, whether she did it tonight or she postponed it for twenty years. What she really ought to do was drive around the darkened streets and let memory pummel her until sleepiness caught up with her. It was going to pummel her anyway, and she might get deadened to the pain if she just let it have its way.

She turned around, intending to circle the bay. Crossing the Howard Frankland Bridge to Tampa and coming back by way of the Courtney Campbell Causeway was always a calming drive at this time of night, as long as motorcycles weren't drag racing on the Causeway. Or maybe she could head south, over the Sunshine Skyway, and for a few minutes be several hundred feet above it all on the soaring bridge that looked as if it leapt aloft on golden sails.

But the Jeep seemed to have a mind of its own. It took her to Roof's Place anyway, and pulled into a parking slot before she'd even made up her mind about which way to go.

"Traitor," she said to the steering wheel.

But she hadn't eaten all day. One thing or another seemed to have gotten in her way since she awoke that morning. Her stomach rumbled, reminding her that while John William Otis might be on death row, she was very much alive, and Roof's made great club sandwiches and chicken wings.

Giving in, she turned off the ignition, climbed out into the suffocating mugginess of the night, and went inside.

The music and noise was deafening after the quiet of

the night outside. The jukebox was playing a country tune about some guy whose wife had left, taking the dog and the pickup truck. Apparently the singer was missing the dog and truck more than the woman.

"Hey, Carey!"

She wasn't happy to see Kel Murchison and some of the others from the station. Talk radio in America these days was a right-wing occupation in which Carissa stood out like a sore thumb, being slightly left of middle.

There was no way to escape them, though, without being rude. She made her way to their table and exchanged greetings. Kel had the afternoon drive-time show, just before hers every weekday evening. Ed Ulrich, who went on air with the name of Ed Rich, was the news anchor. The station's two biggest guns. With them were lesser lights, a couple of producers.

Ed had a radio voice and a radio face. In other words, his voice was great but his face looked like the backside of a mule. Too many years sitting in front of a microphone had given him a potbelly. Kel, on the other hand, was built like a greyhound, with a long face and lantern jaw He ate constantly and burned it all off on weekend bicycle trips. The joke around the station was that anytime Kel wasn't talking, he had food in his mouth.

"Join us," Kel said.

Carissa looked at the two of them and saw something in their expressions that reminded her of birds of prey. They were going to beard her on the Otis thing, and if they did, she was probably going to spend the night in jail for battery. She was that close to the edge.

Then she spied another friend sitting alone at the table in the corner. "Thanks," she said, "but I'm meeting a friend."

She started to move away, but Kel stopped her. "You

going to do Otis on your show?"

She looked down at him, hating him. "I'll think about it."

"It'd be a great topic for you," he said. "Ed and I were just discussing it. You have the inside story."

"I'll think about it."

"If you don't, I will."

She nodded, leaving it at that, and walked as fast as she could over to Barney Willis's table.

She knew Barney from Legal Aid, where she donated ten hours every week helping the poor deal with their legal wrangles. In a society where nearly everything was controlled by the law, there were an awful lot of people who couldn't afford help for even the simplest thing, like a dvorce.

Barney was a lawyer, too, a man with twenty years of experience under his belt, and a thriving law practice. Like most lawyers, he was one of the beautiful people, attractive and fit. Carissa had first noticed that in law school years ago. She couldn't remember more than one or two homely people in her entire class.

Barney had been volunteering at Legal Aid for nearly two decades, and from things he'd absently let drop from time to time, she gathered he did a lot of pro bono work in his private practice, too. Barney was one of those attorneys who just couldn't let an injustice go by without taking up his sword to straighten things out. Carissa didn't know whether she admired him or thought he was a fool. In her experience, most people who had legal troubles were at least partly responsible for them.

But she *did* like him.

"Can I join you?" she asked.

"Anytime," he replied with a smile. His teeth were perfect, professionally whitened.

She pulled out a chair and sat. "Angie still hasn't come back, I take it."

He shrugged, but the hurt was visible in his dark eyes. "I'm a workaholic. I can't blame her."

"So, she should have gotten a job. Then she'd have had a life, too."

"Things aren't always so black and white, Carey."

"Actually, I see things in shades of dingy gray." She looked up at the waiter who'd just arrived, pad at ready. "Club sandwich, please. Light on the mayo." She hesitated, then thought, what the hell. "And a beer. Whatever's on tap." She turned back to Barney. "Speaking of shades of gray, aren't you seeing it all in black and white when you take the blame?"

"I recognize my faults. Working sixty or seventy hours a week isn't exactly good for family life."

"Show me a lawyer who doesn't work sixty hours a week."

"There are a few." He sipped his drink. "Most of them do wills and trusts."

She had to smile at that. "Dead people are easy. They don't call in the middle of the night."

"The only good client is a dead client, is that it?"

Wrong subject. She felt the fist squeeze her heart again and looked away. Where was that beer? She wanted it.

"You look . . . out of sorts tonight, Carey."

She shrugged and dragged her thoughts away from the mire. "Long day."

"Me too." He sighed and leaned back in his chair, looking around the room.

People moved continuously in swirling splotches of color, voices were raised to be heard over the music pouring through speakers around the room. There was a lot of laughter, but most of it sounded off-key to Carissa.

Great, she thought, looking at Barney again. This is a wonderful time to get depressed.

The beer took the edge off her nerves, so she had another one. By the time she finished her sandwich, she was on her fourth. She wasn't used to drinking, though, and she was definitely beginning to feel rubbery.

Barney said something about a case he was working on, but she couldn't concentrate on it. Freed by the alcohol, her mind was determined to go in only one direction.

Finally she pushed back from the table. "I have to make a call."

Barney nodded, then called the waitress to bring more wings.

Crossing the room seemed harder than usual, but Carissa didn't care. She found the pay phone near the rest rooms and punched in a number she hadn't dialed in five years.

Seamus was standing with his hands in dishwater when the phone rang. He reached for the dish towel immediately, figuring something important had come up in one of his cases. His beeper was on his belt, but turned off since he wasn't supposed to be on call tonight.

When he got to the living room, his dad was putting the receiver down beside the phone on the end table.

"For you," Danny said.

Of course it was for him, Seamus thought. It was *his* phone. He shook himself as he reached for the receiver, trying to lose his irritable mood. Having Danny in the house wasn't helping.

"Rourke," he said into the phone.

"Who was that who answered?"

He recognized the voice. How could he not? But what he didn't expect was the sinking sensation in the pit of his stomach and the way shock made him grip the phone until his fingers ached. It shouldn't rattle him like this, he thought. He listened to her every night on the radio. It shouldn't affect him at all to hear the voice. "My dad," he said finally. "Hello, Carissa."

"I didn't know you had a dad."

"Most of us do." He waited, wondering why the hell she would call him, but not wanting to ask. He didn't want to give her even that much.

"Yeah," she said. "I guess most of us do."

He picked up on her tone, on the slight slurring of her words. "Have you been drinking?" She never drank. That was one of the things that had attracted him to her in the first place.

"Just a . . . just a couple of beers."

He heard noise in the background, figured she was out somewhere. "Don't drive yourself home," he cautioned. "Call a cab."

"I'll do what I damn well please."

"Carey—"

She cut him off. "I'm not your problem anymore, Rourke."

He felt the bite of an old impatience. "So why'd you call?"

She was silent for a long time. In the background, he could hear voices laughing and talking, and some sad country song wailing.

"Carey?" he said finally. "Why'd you call?"

"Did you hear?"

"Hear what?"

"The governor . . . the governor signed the death warrant for John Otis today."

He let her words echo for a minute. They'd argued over this one until it had become the last straw in their

17

relationship. The last straw among a hundred other straws they hadn't been able to weave together. "So?" he asked, forcing himself to be brutal. "That's not news. It was coming sooner or later."

"Yeah." She paused, and he could hear her draw a long shaky breath. "Yeah. We knew it was coming. So how does it feel, Seamus?"

"How does what feel?"

"How does it feel to know you're responsible for a man's death?"

Christ! If he could have gotten his hands on her just then, he might have shaken her until her teeth rattled. No, he wouldn't have. He never would have touched her. But, by God, he wanted to.

"I did my job," he said flatly. "So did you."

"Yeah." She gave a strangled laugh. "Yeah, I did my job."

"He killed his foster parents! He slashed them to death with a razor. He's getting exactly what he deserves."

Her voice grew quiet. "Maybe. Maybe not. But I'll tell you one thing for sure, Seamus Rourke. It might as well be you and me flipping the switch on him in three weeks. So how does it feel to be an executioner?"

He closed his eyes, angry and not wanting to be angry. Hurting for her and not wanting to hurt. It should have been dead and buried by now, but her call was raising a zombie from the grave.

"Look, Carey," he said finally, "the system did what the system does. You didn't hand down that death penalty. The jury did."

"Yeah, right."

"Carey, you need to get someone to drive you home." He was more worried about her driving drunk than anything else, he realized. In this mood . . . "Carey?"

18

"Just mind your own damn business!" She snapped, and slammed the phone down.

He stood a minute listening to the dial tone, then hit the automatic callback code. A man's voice answered.

"Where's that phone located?" he asked.

"Um, Roof's Place, man. You need to talk to somebody?"

"No thanks."

He hung up and looked at his dad, who was watching a late-night movie. "I need to go give a ride to a friend," he said. "I don't know when I'll be back."

Danny looked at him and nodded. "Sure, son. Sure." Then his bleary eyes jumped back to the TV set.

Seamus wanted to smash the set. He wanted to throw his father out. He wanted most of all not to see Carissa Stover again.

So he picked up his gun and badge and headed out. He wouldn't need the gun, but he was a cop. He never went anywhere without it. Besides, much as he hated his dad, he didn't want to have to deal with his suicide. One had been more than enough. Two would probably kill him.

And right now, he didn't trust any of the people in his life not to do something stupid.

CHAPTER 2
22 DAYS

THE STEADY RAIN HAD BECOME A THUNDERSTORM. Seamus drove down Thirty-fourth and watched red, pink, and blue lightning leap across the sky, watched the clouds glow from within in a dazzling array of colors. The Tampa Bay area was the lightning capital of the world, and late summer was the height of the display. There had been a

19

time when he had loved the wild storms that often blew through. These days he hardly noticed them except as an inconvenience.

He drove into a patch of heavier rain, and not even at top speed could his wipers keep up. He slowed down and tried to restrain his irritation. He didn't want to think about what might happen to Carey if she tried to drive in this mess in her current state.

Cars and booze. They had turned his life into a living hell.

He reached Roof's Place at last and pulled into the parking lot, spraying water in every direction as he hit the flooded gutter and then a deep puddle. He was just wondering where to start looking for Carey when he saw her Jeep in the side lot. It was the same vehicle she'd bought when she'd worked at the State Attorney's Office. He pulled up behind it and parked so that if she managed to slip past him, she wouldn't be able to pull out.

Leaving his emergency flashers on, he climbed out into the downpour and felt water swirl around his ankles. Damn the woman anyway. She'd been nothing but a pain in the butt since he first set eyes on her.

He started to dart past her car to the protection of the roof overhang, when he caught sight of movement in the driver's seat. Pausing, he looked through the plastic window and saw Carey sitting at the wheel with her head tipped back and her eyes closed.

He rapped on the door, but she didn't respond. Muttering an oath, he tried the door and found it unlocked. He flung it open.

"Jesus Christ, woman!" he said. "Have you lost your mind? Sitting in an unlocked car in a dark parking lot this late at night?"

Her eyes fluttered open, and she mumbled something.

It was useless. He reached for her arm. "Come on. I'm taking you home."

That seemed to wake her fully. Suddenly she was glaring at him. "No! Get lost, Rourke."

With a huge effort of will, he reached for some shreds of patience. "I'm not leaving you here," he said flatly. "If you don't get raped or robbed, you'll get busted."

"Busted! I'm not doing anything wrong!"

"You're' drunk and you're sitting in your car. Hey, you're the lawyer! You don't need *me* to tell you about being in actual physical control of a vehicle when you're drunk."

"I only had a couple of beers!"

"Thats what they all say." He leaned toward her. "Look, here are your choices. You can climb into my car and let me take you home, or I can arrest you for DUI. Either way, you're not going anywhere alone, because I'm parked right behind you."

She turned her head and recognized his aging gray Taurus. "Fuckin' cop," she said.

The Carey he knew hadn't done much swearing. That word coming out of her mouth shocked him a little. It was the alcohol, he reminded himself. But one thing for sure—he didn't like what he was seeing.

"Come on, Carey," he said impatiently. "I'm getting soaked to the bone."

She looked at him, then surprised him by touching the tip of his nose and wiping a raindrop from it. Then she laughed, a slightly hysterical sound. "You're all wet, Rourke."

"At least I'm not drunk."

"I'm not drunk!"

He looked away for a moment, reaching for another shred of patience. "Wanna take the Breathalyzer and see?"

21

That shut her up. She looked down at her hands and the keys in her lap. "I don't want to leave my car."

"It'll be okay. You can get a cab in the morning and come back for it. Come on."

She started to climb out, and he had to snatch at her keys so they didn't fall to the ground. She took an unsteady step toward his car, then reached out to brace herself against the side of the Jeep. He used the opportunity to grab her small handbag from the passenger seat and lock the car. Then he took her elbow in a steely grip and guided her around to the passenger side of the car. He buckled her in and slammed the door.

When he climbed into the driver's seat, the air-conditioning felt icy. He was nearly soaked to the bone, but so was Carey. He flipped the knob from cooling to heating, and was grateful when the warmth started to seep in.

She didn't say anything, and her head was tipped over toward the side window, so he thought she'd fallen asleep. Thank God for small favors, he thought as he pulled back out onto the street. Lightning streaked down from the sky, followed rapidly by a boom of thunder. The lights along the street flickered and went out, and the night was suddenly as dark as a tomb.

"You still living in the same place?" he asked, wondering if she would wake up enough to answer. If not, he could check her driver's license.

"No."

So she was awake. "What's your address?"

"I've got a place in Feather Sound."

All the way up there. He sighed. "I guess radio pays better than prosecuting."

"Yeah, a whole lot better." Her head rolled against the headrest, and she looked at him. "I always figured it was weird that you could spend seventy thousand dollars going to law school and only be worth twenty-five when you got out."

"Nobody said working for the state was the way to get rich."

She laughed again at that, but there was still that hysterical sound to it.

He let it go, hoping he got her home before she came apart. He took Thirty-eighth across to I-275, figuring it was the fastest way to go, even at this time of night. He wondered if she was living with somebody now, and then wondered why he should even be interested.

Their relationship had been dead for five years, long enough that if it had been a body, it would be nothing but bleached bones. Of course, if you buried the body, it could last a lot longer. And maybe that's what he'd done with this mess with Carey. Maybe he'd buried it when he should have left it in the open and let the carrion animals pick it clean.

"Rourke?"

He wished she'd just go to sleep. "Yeah?"

"You killed somebody once you said."

That was one of the things he'd always disliked about her, the way she would use things he told her to pick away at his defenses. It was like being cross-examined on the witness stand.

And right now he had the feeling that she was going to use that little bit of knowledge to open a doorway to hell.

"So?" he asked gruffly.

"How do you sleep at night?"

"Christ!" He slapped his hand against the steering wheel. "Jesus, Carey, the guy was shooting at me! How do I sleep at night? By remembering I'd be dead if I hadn't managed to kill him first!"

23

She was quiet again for a while, and he turned on the ramp for the interstate, hoping she'd get the message and just shut up.

She didn't. "Why are you so angry?"

He drew a long breath before he answered, trying to moderate his tone. "Oh, I don't know," he said finally. "How about that I haven't had any sleep in thirty-six hours, that I ought to be in my bed right now catching up instead of being out in the middle of a stormy night rescuing a drunk ex-girlfriend who's suffering from some kind of existential angst."

"You don't feel anything about John Otis?"

Christ. It wasn't going to go away. "Look, the guy was convicted of the brutal murders of two people. He deserves what he's getting."

"But I don't think he did it."

"There sure as hell wasn't any evidence that he didn't. And it wasn't your decision anyway. I collected evidence. You presented it in court. But it was the *jury* that convicted him. It was the *judge* that sentenced him."

"That's an easy way to deny responsibility."

Yup. He hated her. He was sure of that now.

"People shouldn't get the death penalty in circumstantial cases."

"Take it up with the legislature."

"It was a lousy case, too. As thin as I've ever seen."

He sighed, forcing himself to let go of the anger. "It wasn't thin. He'd done it before to his father. In exactly the same way. Then he had an argument with his foster parents, and they turn up slashed to death. You're not going to convince me that it was just a coincidence that his father and his foster parents were all slashed to death with a razor."

She stirred, waving a hand as if she were trying to

24

silence him. "You don't get it, Rourke. He killed his father to protect his brother. In all the years that bastard abused those two boys, Otis didn't kill him to protect himself. He did it to protect his brother. And that's a whole different thing from killing his foster parents over a stupid argument."

"In the first place, that argument cuts both ways. Otis *said* he killed his father to protect his brother."

"The abuse those kids suffered was never in question."

"So? That doesn't mean that's why he killed his old man. If that was really his motive, why didn't he do it sooner? Maybe—just maybe—Otis is a born killer. And maybe he figured that since he got away with it the first time, he could get away with it again."

"I don't buy it."

"The jury sure as hell did."

She fell silent then, her moment of clarity apparently lost in an alcohol-induced haze. At least for now.

When he'd first met Carissa Stover, he'd loved having this kind of discussion with her. She was a brilliant woman who knew how to argue substance without taking it personally. Their disagreements had exhilarated him.

Until they started arguing about Otis. Their disagreement over that case and its aftermath had brought out in harsh relief all the flaws in their relationship. And the arguments had grown personal. Too personal.

As the case had wound toward its conclusion, Carissa had become increasingly stressed and impossible to live with. She flared over every little thing, and he was already too bruised to take any more of it. He whipped himself enough. He didn't need her to whip him too.

He shook his head now, not wanting to remember how ugly it had become.

At sixty-five, the Taurus ate up the miles to Feather

Sound. Finally he had to speak to her again, much as he would have preferred to drop her off without saying another word.

"Carey?"

"Mm."

"What exit do I take?"

"Clearwater."

"Okay."

She sat up straighter, and when it came time, she directed him into the entrance of her development. She had one of those fancy new town houses that he'd read about recently in the paper. Radio sure did pay well. This place was above his touch as a cop.

Her town house was one of the smaller ones, though. She had probably paid ninety to a hundred grand for it. Not extravagant, he decided. And maybe radio didn't pay all that well after all.

"You wanna come in?" she asked.

"Why?" He told himself he wanted to get home and go to bed. He told himself the last thing on earth he wanted to do was spend another minute with Carissa Stover. But he found himself climbing out of the car into the pouring rain and walking around to help her out. He justified it by reminding himself she was drunk. He had to make sure she got safely inside.

She'd begun to sober up, he realized. She was steadier on her feet as they walked toward her door. She couldn't manage the key herself, though, so he snatched it out of her hand and shoved it into the lock.

Thunder boomed, rolling in from a long way away. Lightning flickered, for an instant overpowering the yellow glow of the porch light, illuminating her face in harsh relief. What he saw was painful to behold.

"Christ!" he said under his breath, and shoved the door

open, pushing her through it ahead of him. He was glad to close the night and the storm outside. He didn't need it to play any more tricks with her face. He didn't want to feel anything for this woman, not even pity.

She was already walking away from him, toward a winding staircase, pulling her sweater over her head as she went, giving him a breathtaking view of her slender back and the white of her bra.

"Damn thing prickles like a cactus shirt," she muttered as she climbed the stairs, dropping the sweater on the first riser. "Make some coffee, Rourke."

He just stared at her, disbelieving. What the hell had happened to the sometimes shy, always modest woman he had known?

Life. The word floated into his mind like a curse. Life. Just the way it had happened to him. She'd been little more than a girl back then. Now she was a woman. Maybe even a virago. Life had a habit of twisting people in the damnedest ways.

Dragging his eyes from her before she rounded the bend in the stairs and gave him a sideways view of her full breasts in the white cradle of her bra—a view that he knew would confirm he still craved her—he turned, trying to figure out where the kitchen was stashed.

He found it at the back of the entryway, through a door that opened just beneath the upper landing of the stairway. It was a nice kitchen, not too big but not too small. He remembered how she had often complained that architects had sacrificed the kitchen to the needs of people who dined out five nights a week. This kitchen was meant to be cooked in, and even had a cozy little breakfast nook with a bay window.

So, he thought, she had her kitchen. He wondered if she ever used it. Because all the while she'd complained

27

about tiny kitchens in modern construction, she'd complained just as loudly about how miserable it was to cook for one.

The coffeemaker was on the counter, and beside it the same glass jar she had always kept coffee in. He found the filters in the cabinet above. She had always been logical in her organization. That much hadn't changed.

As he spooned coffee into the machine, he found himself remembering how appalled she'd been by the utter lack of order in his home. He'd told her that he used it all up on his work, and didn't have any left over for his house. She'd laughed then. He wondered if she would laugh now.

Then he told himself he didn't care.

The coffee was almost finished by the time she reappeared in dry clothes, white slacks and a navy blue top. She'd brushed out her damp dark hair and caught it up in a clasp on the back of her head. He had to keep himself from sucking air at the sight of her slender neck. For some reason, that had always turned him on.

She sat at the table and put her head in her hands. "God, I've got a headache."

"Hangover."

"Already?"

"Yup. Where's the aspirin?"

"In the cabinet over the sink."

He brought her three, along with a glass of tap water.

She tossed them off like a shot of whiskey. "So tell me about your father."

"What's to tell? He's my father. I have one like most of the rest of the world."

She looked at him from hazel eyes, eyes that had always seen too damn much. He'd once fancied that when she cross-examined witnesses, they felt as if she could see

28

straight to their souls—which was probably why so many of them blurted out things that their attorneys wished they'd left unsaid. "You're evading the question, Rourke."

"Damn straight, Stover."

"So, another big, dark secret from your past?"

"I didn't say it was a secret, dark or otherwise. It's just none of your damn business."

She threw up a hand, as if to say, Have it your way.

He pulled out a couple of mugs and filled them nearly to the rim with steaming coffee. He was going to need the caffeine just to get home.

She took the mug from him with a nod of thanks, and he sat across from her, blowing on his coffee and waiting to see if she was going to try to push any more of his buttons. If he hadn't wanted the coffee so badly, he'd be out of there already.

She surprised him, though. Instead of staying on the attack, she sighed and wrapped her hands around the mug as if it were a warm fire on a cold night. Which maybe it was. Steamy as it was outside tonight, inside the air-conditioning was chilling him through his wet clothes.

She averted her face, staring off into space as if she couldn't bear to look at him. "I ought to be able to drop it."

"Yup."

"I thought I had until I saw the bulletin from the AP wire tonight."

"It'll go away again. But I'll tell you one thing—drinking isn't going to help a damned thing. It's a bad way to go, Carey. One way or another, it'll mess up your life."

She looked at him with those X-ray eyes of hers. "It messed up your life, didn't it. A drunk driver killed your baby."

God, the woman had an absolute talent for throwing

his past in his face, for raking up things that shouldn't be raked up. It might have made her one of the best young prosecutors in the State Attorney's Office, but it sure as hell made her intolerable to live with. What was she trying to do? Hurt him as bad as she was hurting?

Well, he thought, taking a swig of coffee, she'd succeeded, but he was damned if he'd let her know it.

"I wasn't going to drive," she said, apparently oblivious of her transgression. "I was going to sleep it off."

"Mm." He didn't trust himself to speak.

"I'm not that stupid, Seamus. Honestly. I've seen victims, too."

Maybe she had, maybe she hadn't. He wasn't going to argue it. What he wanted was to finish his coffee and get the hell out of there.

She rose and went to get the coffeepot, returning with it to top off both their mugs. "I'm sorry I wrecked your evening," she said as she put the pot back on the warming plate.

His evening had been wrecked from the minute he'd opened the door to see his dad standing there. What did one more drunk matter? "I listen to your radio show sometimes," he said, wanting to change the subject *now*.

"Yeah?" She resumed her seat and gave him a pinched smile that didn't reach her eyes. "Crusader for truth and justice, that's me. Holding back the abysmal tide of ignorance about our justice system with a broom."

He shrugged and sipped coffee. No subject was safe with her tonight.

"I'll bet it really chaps your hide when I talk about how cops lie."

He sucked air through his teeth. "Nope."

"Really? I thought you were a crusader for truth and justice, too."

"I'm a crusader for justice. There isn't any truth."

"Ahh. So lying is okay?"

"I didn't say that." He could feel his temper heating again. "And this isn't your goddamn talk show, so don't get smart with me. Evidence is all we have. The truth is unknowable."

He shoved back from the table, deciding he'd had enough of her. "Have a nice life, *Ms. Justice.*"

He headed for the door, and heard her following him. The sweater, he noticed, was still lying on the first stair, abandoned and forgotten.

As he opened the door, he turned his head and saw her staring at him, her eyes wide and hollow-looking, her arms folded tightly across her breasts as if she were cold to the bone.

"Don't you get it, Rourke?" she said softly. "Without truth, there is no justice." Exactly the words she had spoken when she had told him she was quitting the prosecutor's office.

He didn't even say good night. He stepped out into the warm, muggy air and felt the raindrops pick up where'd they'd left off. If he never saw her again, it would be too damn soon.

Carey stood where he'd left her, listening to the slam of the car door and the roar of his engine as he drove off.

Finally, moving as if through molasses, she got her coffee mug from the kitchen and went to the living room where she turned on all the lights, put some quiet music on the stereo, and collapsed in the recliner. It had once been her dad's chair, and she still found comfort sitting in it.

But tonight there was little comfort to be had. The storm battering her windows didn't come close to the storm battering her mind.

John William Otis was going to die.

She forced herself to face it, to turn the idea around in

31

her mind, much as she wanted to shy away from it. He was going to die, and it was going to be as much her fault as anyone's. She wondered if she'd feel any different if she were absolutely convinced of the man's guilt but she had no way of knowing. Otis had been her first and last death-penalty case. All she could know was that she had done her job despite her feelings about the case, and a man was going to die. Because of her.

Stupid of her to have thought that Seamus might be the one person on earth who could understand how she felt. He'd always had a simplistic concept of the justice system. If the jury said it was so, it was so. He even seemed able to accept that when the verdict went against him.

To hell with it, she thought. She'd been running around in circles on this for years, and she was fed up to the gills with the whole question.

John William Otis was going to die, and there wasn't a damn thing she could do about it. Seamus Rourke didn't give a damn about it, and she couldn't change that either.

He had looked older, she thought suddenly. Five years had added some gray to his dark hair, and lines to his face. Even his gray-green eyes looked older, as if they had seen almost too much to bear. He looked tired. Haggard.

And impatient. She didn't remember him being so impatient, at least not until the end, when they had seemed to be fighting all the time.

She sighed, and felt the aspirin drive out the last of the headache. The alcohol fog was fading, too, leaving her clear-headed, wired on caffeine, and all too aware of her shortcomings.

She wasn't happy with herself, but there was nothing new in that. It had been a long time since she had been happy with herself.

Life, she thought, was an absolute bitch.

32

CHAPTER 3
21 DAYS

THE BLAZING AFTERNOON SUN FILLED THE AIR WITH moisture from last night's rain. By the time Carey completed the short walk from her car to the station door, a sheen of perspiration already covered her face, and her hair clung damply to the base of her neck. It was a relief to step into the chilly air of the small reception room.

Becky Hadlov, the receptionist, sat at her desk, talking cheerfully on the phone. Becky had once cherished the hope of becoming a TV news anchor. She had the blond good looks for the job, but not the voice. Disappointed dreams, Carey thought. The world was full of them.

A young couple sat in the chairs before the front window, talking in quiet voices while they waited for someone. Nervousness crackled in the air around them. Job interview?

Carl Dunleavy, the afternoon host, was on his way out, heading for his second job in his own business as an auto detailer.

It was a sad fact that radio didn't provide job security. Most everyone here had some kind of backup job, or worked for more than one station. Carey considered herself lucky in that her ratings and the syndication of her show on a hundred other stations gave her a nice income. But all of it could dry up as fast as she could say "ratings."

She paused to talk to Carl. He was a tall, lean man with a runner's build and a Renaissance man's knowledge. She hadn't yet found a subject he couldn't discuss intelligently, and, like a good talk host, he had an opinion on every one of them.

She liked him probably more than anyone else at the

station. Carl was happy with what he was doing, and happy to be doing it. He never stabbed anyone else in the back, and was always quick to lend a helping hand. And unlike some other people here, he had been quick to help her in a lot of ways during her first days on the job.

But he, like everyone else, wanted to know the same thing.

"Are you going to do the Otis death warrant?"

Carey shrugged. "I haven't made up my mind."

"You ought to. If you don't, someone else will, and the death penalty is always one hell of a topic. Ratings, Carey. Ratings. The only reason everyone else is waiting to see if you do it is because you have the inside scoop on the trial. Nobody wants to shoot off his mouth only to have you come on the air and say it isn't so." He flashed a charming smile. "For once you've got the upper hand. Enjoy it."

She had to smile back. Somehow she had wakened today with a feeling of calm. She hoped it would last.

"And," he said, "You missed the meeting.

"Oh, shit." She'd forgotten all about it.

"Bill isn't real happy with you." He was referring to the station manager. "So he set you up to do the mall opening next Saturday. Lucky you, you get to hand out bumper stickers and prizes from two until six."

Carey groaned. This was her least favorite kind of public appearance. She didn't mind giving speeches. She even enjoyed riding in the float for Guavaween. She *loved* going to schools to talk to classes about her work. But she loathed sitting in malls and handing out prizes.

Carl laughed. "That's what you get for not being there to defend yourself. Where were you, anyway?"

"Sleeping off a really bad night."

His expression suddenly became serious. "Otis?"

"You could say that."

"I was thinking about that. I can't imagine what it must be like to know you helped put the guy there. Not that I think anything is wrong with it, but I can sure see how it might bother you."

At last, she thought, somebody who actually understood she might have negative feelings about this. "Thank you for understanding, Carl."

He nodded and started to pass by. "The thing is," he said, pausing, "you didn't really put him there. He put himself there. Do the crime, do the time."

And then he was gone, having totally missed the real point. But what could she expect? He, like all the rest of the world, figured the conviction settled it.

She passed by the broadcast studio and glanced in to see Kel Murchison busy talking to some caller. He was also looking up every few seconds toward his producer in the next booth, obviously getting ready to cut away to commercial. When he looked in her direction, she waved, but kept walking.

As she came around the dogleg in the hallway, she could hear what he was saying coming out of the speaker high on the wall.

"But people on minimum wage jobs don't get cost-of-living increases," he said to the caller. "So why should social security recipients?"

"People making minimum wage can look for better jobs," the caller responded. "I can't."

Carey tuned it out, and made her way to the news anchor's office, where she could scan the AP wire for interesting tidbits to use on her show. Ed was across the way in a recording booth, talking into a microphone. She waved to him through the window as she ducked into his office, then called up the index on the computer.

Ten minutes later she'd printed out a half dozen

bulletins that she thought would make great conversation starters on her show: a federal appeals court decision, a Florida Supreme Court decision, a local lawsuit against a cellular phone company, and a couple of other items.

Ed had apparently finished recording his newscast, because he came into the office behind her. "Are you going to talk about Otis?" he asked. "It's been on every newscast I did today, and it headlined in the papers this morning. The phones will light up like Christmas."

The phones, she thought. Always the phones. All that mattered was that people were listening and calling.

"Yeah," she said, making up her mind. "I'll do it." If it was all over the news, callers were going to want to talk about it anyway. She might as well deal with it.

But the decision made her stomach feel like lead.

She stopped to talk to Bill Hayes about the meeting she'd missed and avoided complaining about the mall assignment. He'd enjoy it too much if she let him know how much she disliked it, and she refused to give him the satisfaction. He gave her hell about missing the meeting, and she just nodded her way through it, knowing his rant was meaningless as long as she didn't argue with him. With Bill, all you had to do was let him have his say, and he'd forget about it.

"You going to do the Otis thing?" he asked finally.

"Gossip sure gets around," she remarked.

He shrugged. "Kel remembered that you worked on it when you were a prosecutor."

And of course Kel couldn't keep that to himself. She began to wonder if he'd brought it up deliberately in order to pressure her into doing a show about it. But why? She couldn't think of a good reason—unless he wanted her to do the topic first, so he could tear it all to shreds on his show.

"I'm doing it," she told Bill.

"Good. Good. It'll be hot."

She took some time to sit down with her laptop computer and try to organize her thoughts for a monologue to start the show with. It wasn't easy. Her mind had found its current calm by avoiding any real thought about Otis. Every time she tried to focus on the topic so she could decide what she wanted to say, her mind shied away like a frightened deer. Coming to grips with this wasn't going to be easy.

An hour later, the laptop screen was still blank. Finally she went to get a cup of coffee, then sat down in the snack room at a table and started doodling absently on one of the legal pads she carried everywhere with her for recording ideas and things she learned.

It was strange, she found herself thinking, how she couldn't forget it and couldn't think about it all at the same time. It was hovering there at the edges of all her thoughts like a cloud of doom hanging over her head, but she couldn't really look it at, as if it were sliding away, always staying on the periphery. And she was never going to learn to live with this if she couldn't get a handle on it.

She glanced down at her pad and felt a shiver of shock run through her at what she had written.

Twenty-one Days, Twenty-one Years.

And suddenly she knew what she was going to say in her monologue.

"Good morning," she said into the microphone. "This is Carey Justice, and you're listening to the Talk of the Coast, 990 WCST."

Her stomach was growing heavier by the minute, and her mouth was drying out. She didn't want to do this. She licked her lips and forced herself to go on.

"I don't want to do this show," she said, ignoring the startled look from her producer who was in the next booth, watching through a window. "I'd rather go back in time and see if I could undo some of the things that happened. I wish I could make it all better. But I can't do that. None of us can. All I can do is pick over the bones and hope I—we—learn something from it.

"This is a story about twenty-one years and twenty-one days, the twenty-one years of John Otis's life before the crime that got him the death penalty, and the twenty-one days he has left to live."

The phones were already starting to light up. She ignored them and forced herself to continue.

"I don't know how many of you remember the first time John Otis was tried for murder. He was a twelve-year-old boy then. For the first twelve years of his life, he was subjected to some of the most appalling abuse that can be heaped on anyone, adult or child. I wasn't much more than a kid myself then, but I remember the stories that were in the press, and I remember finding it almost impossible to believe that any child could survive such horrible treatment.

"Maybe you don't think it's relevant to what's going on now, but I do. If John William Otis really did kill his foster parents, then maybe we need to recognize that we helped make this child what he became.

"What do you think happens to the mind and soul of a child who is sodomized by his father from the age of two? What do you think happens when he's chained in a dark closet like a dog for weeks on end with almost nothing to eat, and just barely enough water to survive? What do you think happens when he's beaten bloody and drenched with water and chained naked outside on the coldest nights of the year? What do you think happens to him when nobody steps in to help him because they're all afraid of his father?

"And what do you think happens when he sees his little brother being abused in the same way?

"Thirteen years ago, a jury took pity on this boy, and said that he killed his father in self-defense. What do you think about that?

"Five years ago John Otis was convicted of killing his foster parents on the slimmest of circumstantial evidence. I was a prosecutor on the case, and I'm not convinced he did it. Not one witness saw him do it. There was no physical evidence linking him to the crime. No confession. Nothing at all. Nothing at all *except* a neighbor who heard him arguing with his foster father, and the fact that the wounds were similar to what happened to his real father, nine years before.

"That was it. That was all we had to sell. And we sold the hell out of it. Yes, there was another prosecutor on the case. I was just riding second chair, doing the detail work, questioning a few witnesses. But I don't want to hide behind that little fact. I was part of the team that sold a jury on the idea that an overheard argument and a similarity to past events equals proof of premeditated murder beyond and to the exclusion of every reasonable doubt.

"But you were there, too. Oh, you probably weren't in the courtroom. Not that day. But you'd been clamoring for the death penalty, more executions more often, justice swift and sure. We heard you, in the prosecutor's office. And that jury heard you. So we're all in this together. This is what we've done.

"John William Otis has twenty-one days left to live. Twenty-one days. Because you and I decided to kill him.

"Our number in Hillsborough . . ."

39

She rattled off the phone numbers for each county, and the cellular line, and the WATS line, even though she could see that those who'd taken the time to listen to her monologue would be getting busy signals for a while. Then she set her hook.

"In twenty-one days, we're going to get together and kill someone. What do you think about that?"

She cut away to her first commercial break, with calls already backing up. She looked through the window at Marge, and saw her producer engaged in the frantic tasks that were her job during the breaks, loading the commercial, news, and weather carts for the next round while the first group played.

Well, she thought, with a surprising depth of bitterness, she'd done her job. She'd started her show with a monologue that was bound to keep people listening through the commercials. And that was the whole point of talk radio, to get those listeners so involved that they didn't want to miss a word, so they'd listen to all the ads.

Marge was giving her the countdown through the window now, using her fingers. Ten seconds. Five.

Looking at the screen where the callers were listed, Carey saw she had her pick, and even recognized some of them as regulars. She decided to go with someone she thought had never called before. Reaching out as the commercial ended, she punched a green button.

"This is Carey Justice, and you're listening to 990 WCST. Della from Tarpon Springs, you're on the air."

"I don't know why you're talking like the death penalty is wrong, Carey," said the querulous voice of an older woman. "It's an eye for an eye."

"That's the Old Testament, Della. I take it you don't believe in the New Testament?"

"Well, of course I do! I'm a good Christian woman.

But what that man did—"

"Leaving aside the question of whether he really did it—and I'm not sure he did—I seem to remember the New Testament says we ought to turn the other cheek."

"But what this man did—"

"What this man did, if he actually did it, was a horrible, heinous crime."

"Yes it was!" Della said fervently.

"But what good does it do to kill him?"

Della was silent, apparently unsure how to answer.

"Della?" Carey repeated, making sure her voice wasn't confrontational. "What good do you see being served by killing him?"

"He's a monster, and he has no right to live!"

"Well," Carey said, pitching her voice to be sympathetic, "I guess that's what the jury thought when he killed his real father. That the old man was a monster and didn't deserve to live."

"That's right. And he was."

"But what about now, Della? You're a good Christian woman. What if I tell you that John William Otis has been saved? That he's not the person he was when he was twenty-one."

"Well. . ." Della trailed off uncertainly. "Has he?"

"I don't know. I'm just speculating here, but I tell you what, Della. I'm going to find out. But for now, just suppose he *has* been saved. Do you still think he should die?"

"Well . . . yes. Yes I do! We have to make the streets safe for God-fearing people."

"I agree with you. Nobody should be at risk from a criminal. But couldn't we make the streets safe just as easily by keeping John William Otis in prison for the rest of his natural life?"

41

"I . . . I suppose. Yes, we could, if he really stayed in prison for life."

"We can do that, Della. We have really good maximum-security prisons these days. And if you pay any attention to what the legislature is doing in Tallahassee, you know we're spending lots of money on prisons. We can keep him in jail for the rest of his life."

"I guess so."

"So what's the point in killing him?"

Della fell silent, and Carey cut her off, going to the next caller.

She had spent more time on Della than she ordinarily would have on such a pallid, uncertain caller, but she had done so purposely to set up the question. What she wanted, what she needed, were passionate kooks and people with really well-thought-out opinions who could argue interestingly. Anybody who thought that talk radio was the public's forum didn't understand that it was entertainment before all else.

To her relief, she saw that one of her favorite lunatics was on hold, a man she could always count on for wild and inflammatory speeches on any subject. He was definitely out in the ozone.

"George from Bradenton, you're on the air."

"What, are you crazy?" George demanded without preamble. "What the guy did was a horrible crime, and it doesn't matter whether we can keep him in prison forever. He deserves to die, just like those people he killed! We can't be letting murderers get away with this! And all this talk about how the electric chair is cruel and unusual punishment—I'll tell you what's cruel and unusual! What he did to those people is worse than anything Old Sparky will do to him!"

"You think so, George?"

"I know so! What's the matter with you? Did you lose your stomach for it?"

"This isn't about me, George. This is about a man who's going to die."

"Yeah, right. I heard what you said about all of us killing him. He's killing himself because of what he did. And I'm not going to feel a damn bit guilty about it."

"Good for you, George," she said acidly. The guy was trying to bait her into a personal argument, and she wouldn't allow it. Within the limits of talk radio, she tried never to let discussions become personal pissing contests.

George was on a roll, though, and hardly heard her response. "And what's all this crap about protecting society anyway? This isn't about protecting society! This is about retribution. This is about punishment. Nobody can give those people back their lives, but we can sure as hell take his to get even for it!"

She started leading him on. "We oughtta make that sumbitch pay, huh, George?"

"Damn right, counselor."

"Make it painful, too."

"Yep."

"As bad as it was for them."

"You got it."

"And you'd be willing to pull the switch?"

She knew she'd taken a risk; he might back away, and she was due for a break in less than a minute. She wanted to do a "hot break," cutting into the commercials directly from the conversation, with no warning. She couldn't afford for George to get reasonable now. But she'd judged her quarry well.

"Damn right I would," he said, his voice rising. "And I wouldn't just throw the switch, either. I'd tease him with it. A little jolt here, another there. Let him know exactly

43

what's coming. Let him sweat and hurt. Just the way he did to them."

She punched off his line at the end of the sentence and stepped in as if he'd finished.

"That's what we call justice," she said, and stabbed the white button that started the commercial break.

The rest of the hour went just as well, most of the callers disagreeing with George, whether or not they disagreed with the death penalty. And she had no doubt that George would call back, because he was now the topic of conversation, and he loved nothing better. Good old George, a host's dream.

At the top of the hour, she left the booth for a ten-minute break while news, weather, and commercials played. She headed straight for Bill Hayes's office and was relieved to find him still there.

"Show's going good, Carey," he said, absolving her of her error in missing the meeting.

"Yeah, it's hot. But it's not about Otis."

"What do you care? It's good radio."

"Right." She tried to keep the sarcasm out of her voice. "Can I bum a cigarette?"

"You don't smoke."

"Now I do."

Most of the time she had the feeling that Bill didn't really see anyone except as cogs in the wheel of this station, but right now the look he gave her said he was seeing *her*, Carissa Stover. He pulled a pack of cigarettes and a lighter out of his desk drawer and passed them over. "If you close the door, you can smoke in here. I won't report you to the air police. Otherwise, get the hell out back with the cat."

"Thanks. I'll bring them right back." She turned to leave.

"Carey?"

She looked back at him, waiting.

"If you want, you can pull the topic back to Otis. I know you can. But if it's too . . . difficult for you, just let the show go the way it's going. It's all right. Nobody said you *had* to bare your soul for ratings points. Okay?"

She felt the sudden burn of tears in her eyes, and blinked rapidly. "Thanks. I'll think about it." Then she turned and headed for the back lot, where she could smoke her first cigarette in fourteen years and talk to a cat that couldn't talk back.

The cigarette made her feel light-headed and sick, and after thee drags she dropped it to the dirt and ground it out under her heel. She stayed only to pet the station's cat.

Pegleg, as the three-legged ginger tomcat was called, had turned up a couple of years ago in bad condition with tattered ears and an infected leg. Someone had taken him to the vet, who had amputated the bad leg and nursed him back to health. Apparently Peg figured that meant the station was home, and he'd stuck around ever since. There were bowls for cat food and water that someone always kept full near the weathered picnic table, and Peg seemed to like lounging on the table near the microwave antennas. He let all the station personnel pet him, but ran from strangers.

Tonight he was feeling particularly friendly, and as soon as Carey put out her cigarette and sat at the table, he jumped into her lap, purring loudly.

Carey scratched him behind his ears, realizing that her show was avoiding the subject of Otis because she was letting it, and she was letting it because she didn't really want to go there. And what was more, she was going to let it keep going its own way because she wasn't ready to do anything else.

Her mind made up, she placed the cat gently back onto

45

its perch, then went to take the cigarettes back to Bill. He was involved in a phone conversation, and merely wagged his fingers at her when she put the pack and lighter on his desk.

The next hour went pretty much the same as the first. She began to feel she was almost running on automatic, safe and secure in the knowledge that people were arguing among themselves about the death penalty, and she didn't have a whole lot to do except keep the ball rolling. The plight of John William Otis was secondary in the minds of her listeners, and for now she was content to leave it that way.

But then she saw a new caller pop up on her screen, and the subject tag that Marge had typed in made the hackles on the back of her neck stand up: *Otis didn't do it.*

She interrupted a caller in the middle of a diatribe about lethal injection versus the electric chair, cut away to commercial, and stared at the glowing phosphor words. *Otis didn't do it.*

She punched the button that let her talk to Marge. "This guy who said Otis didn't do it. Did he say anything else?"

Marge was busy loading carts, but she took time to answer, sounding a little harried. "I hate it when we have a string of short commercials. I didn't give him a chance to say anything else. Do you know how many calls I've been answering?"

"Did he sound wild or weird or anything?"

"I don't remember."

"Thanks."

Marge gave her the one-minute signal, and she nodded, staring again at the words. It was just her imagination, but they seemed to glow brighter than all the others. Bob from Gulfport. He wasn't a regular caller, but if he turned out to be some doped-up freak who didn't really have anything to say, she could disconnect him in an instant. She decided to go for it, even though it meant returning the show's focus to Otis.

At Marge's signal, she punched the button. "Bob from Gulfport, you're on the air."

"Carey?"

"Yes, this is Carey." She had to smother a sigh, but resisted the temptation to disconnect him. People who started this way rarely tended to be good callers. "What do you want to say?"

"John Otis didn't do it."

She felt a stirring of impatience. You couldn't just drop something like that and let it go. It made for bad radio. "Didn't do what?"

"He didn't kill his foster parents."

"Were you there? Did you see what happened?"

The caller went silent. She reached for the disconnect button, but just before she hit it, he spoke. "I know he didn't do it. And I'm going to prove it."

"How are you going to do that? Don't you think his defense attorney tried to do that? The problem here, Bob, is that there wasn't any real evidence one way or the other. Otis was registered in a hotel in Vero Beach the night the murders happened, but nobody could remember seeing him. There was no evidence at the scene to suggest that someone *else* had done it. Do *you* have evidence?"

"No, but I'm going to prove he didn't do it. I will. You'll see!"

He hung up before she could disconnect him, and she heard the dial tone. Instead of cutting it out of the broadcast, she left it, deciding to use it.

"Well," she said to her listeners, "I can't imagine how he's going to prove it without evidence, and I guess he can't either, or he wouldn't have hung up.

"But you know, that was another thing that always bothered me about this case. John Otis registered at a hotel in Vero Beach on Friday night, the day before the murders. And he checked out on Sunday afternoon and came home.

"Now folks, why would a guy go to Vero Beach, drive all the way back here to commit murders like that, drive back to Vero Beach, then come home the following afternoon to be arrested?"

But no one tried to answer the question. No one really seemed interested in the man on death row.

Maybe that was the whole problem, she thought as she drove home that night. Nobody gave a damn about John William Otis.

And maybe it was time someone did.

CHAPTER 4
18 DAYS

SEAMUS ROURKE LOOKED ACROSS THE BREAKFAST table at his father, and figured there was little in the world he less wanted to see.

Danny had been with him three days now, and Seamus was beginning to feel as if his life was coming apart at the seams. The old man was a constant reminder of things he absolutely didn't want to think about.

Worse, after three days the old man still smelled like booze. Seamus, who'd always considered himself a reasonably tolerant man, was discovering there was something he couldn't tolerate at all.

"Did you go to AA yet?" he asked.

Danny looked up from his plate of bacon and eggs, his

eyes still reddened and bleary. "Nope."

"Look, Dad, I told you that was a condition of staying here."

"And I said I'd do it."

It was the voice of an annoyed father speaking to an importunate son. The thing was, it didn't work anymore on this son.

Seamus pushed his plate aside, his breakfast half-eaten. "I told you how it's gonna be. That's my final word on the subject. I'm sure as hell not going to live with a drunk."

He stomped out of the kitchen, grabbing his jacket from the chair where he'd laid it. His gun was already holstered on his belt. He pulled his car keys off the peg beside the door without sparing a backward glance for the man he held partly responsible for turning his life into a living hell.

As he walked out the door, he heard his father say forlornly, "I wasn't drunk that night, boy. I wasn't drunk."

But he'd been drunk every night ever since, Seamus thought bitterly. He slammed the door, then slammed the car door after he climbed in. Fuck him, he thought. Fuck him anyway.

He peeled out of the driveway with a squeal of tires, and left rubber when he had to brake for a stop sign. "Dammit!" He slapped his hand on the steering wheel and forced himself to calm down. Little in this world could make him as angry as Danny Rourke—or Carissa Stover.

But he didn't want to think about her either. Christ, what was she doing, turning her show into a John William Otis marathon? The last three nights she had opened with a monologue about the guy, and the ensuing discussion had revolved around the death penalty and whether society was responsible for making monsters like Otis. He was thinking about not even tuning in tonight.

Because she made him listen. This time he couldn't just soak up the liquid honey of her voice. No, he found himself listening to her arguments, and getting madder than an angry wasp. Four times last night alone he'd had to stop himself from picking up the telephone and giving her a piece of his mind. Just what did she think she was doing?

He sure as hell didn't like the way she was making him think about John Otis as a man. He didn't like the creeping sense of guilt she was giving him over what that murdering son of a bitch had been through as a child. Hell, he was a cop. When somebody brought something like that to his attention, he did his damnedest to put an end to it. But nobody had told anybody about what was happening to that boy. Why should he feel guilty about something he hadn't even known about?

Finding that thoughts of Carey were only making him angrier, he wrenched them away from her and thought about the old souse, otherwise known as his dad. He was just barking when he threatened to throw Danny out if he didn't go to AA, and he knew it.

That was the worst of it. He couldn't throw the old man out. He'd seen what happened to people like Danny when they had no one to turn to anymore. They wound up living under highway overpasses or in cardboard boxes in alleys, going hungry and spending whatever money they could find or beg on a bottle of cheap wine.

Well, he wasn't going to have that on his conscience, too. His conscience was already overloaded.

By the time he pulled into the police-station parking lot on First Avenue North, he had a grip on his temper.

It was a beautiful day, he told himself. The last of the rain had dried up, and for once the air was clear of the heavy humidity. A warm breeze blew, stirring the leaves on the trees, and it was as perfect an August morning as he could have asked for. And while he was working, there would be no room in his thoughts for Danny and Carey.

These were small blessings for which he decided to be suitably grateful, especially since there was little else in his life to be grateful about right now.

He took his place at the table in the robbery-homicide squad room, which was really two rooms that used to be one. Some of the guys still groused about how the other room had control of the air-conditioning for both, but Seamus didn't much think about it. It was one of those "what's the point?" issues in his life.

He scanned his mail and discovered that a defense attorney had subpoenaed him for a deposition next Thursday in an attempted-murder case. He couldn't remember whether it was the domestic violence case or the hit-and-run that had turned out to be deliberate. He made a note on his calendar, notified the State Attorney that he'd be there, and wrote a note to himself to review the file to refresh his memory.

Gil Garcia slid into the chair beside him. A good-looking man of forty, Gil had inky black hair dashed with gray, the weathered face of a man who'd seen it all, and a warm, disarming smile. The wisdom in the squad room was that Seamus was a bulldog who wouldn't let go of a case, and that Gil could charm anyone into talking.

Gil's charm hid a tough, life-hardened cop who seldom took anything at face value. He wasn't cynical, the way some cops got, but he wasn't quick to trust.

Which wasn't a bad thing in a cop, Seamus thought. People lied, and sometimes they lied without any good reason to do so. What's more, if you had two witnesses to an event, you were likely to get two entirely different stories out of them. Hell, they wouldn't even agree on what the perp was wearing.

Gil had a theory about that, which was probably why he hadn't become cynical. He believed that people didn't really remember events. "They remember their emotional impressions of what happened," he liked to say. "The brain fills in the details, and as often as not they're wrong."

Seamus was inclined to agree with him, which meant there weren't any really good witnesses, there were only people who appeared to be good witnesses. Which meant there wasn't any such thing as truth, just something that appeared to be true. Seamus wasn't sure he liked the implications of that, but it was another of those "what's the point?" issues.

Gil checked his own messages, made a couple of calls, then turned to look at him. "Ready to get to work on the Mayberry case?"

Seamus patted his pocket to make sure he had his notebook, then shoved himself back from the table. "Let's go."

The Mayberry case had been assigned to them just two days ago, when the original detective on the case had had a heart attack. They'd spent the last couple of days getting up to speed from a file review, and from the stricken detective's young partner.

Three weeks ago, a young man named Doug Mayberry had been shot to death riding his bicycle through a quiet neighborhood. One of the strangest elements of the crime was that no one had seen or heard a thing, even though it had happened in broad daylight and most of the residents were retired people who were home a lot of the time. The young man had bled to death in the street before he was discovered.

Seamus quite frankly didn't believe that no one had seen or heard anything. The gunshot had to have been audible, even with windows closed and air conditioners running. Surely some retiree had been out working in his yard. Dogs must have barked. The young man had probably cried out for help.

Equally striking was that the victim seemed to have no enemies. Everyone seemed to like him, and both his girlfriend and his parents said he hadn't been in any fights or arguments in recent memory.

Consequently, Seamus was convinced that *someone* was lying. Probably even several someones. And that meant that people were scared. He wanted to know why they were scared every bit as much as he wanted to know who had killed Doug Mayberry. This kind of fear didn't arise from having heard gunshots or shouts. Terror came from knowing something that could get you hurt.

It was Gil's turn to drive, so he slid into the passenger seat and rolled down the window to let out the heat that had built up in the car.

They drove north on Forty-ninth, to an area populated by stuccoed cinder-block homes that had been built in a time when land was still relatively cheap and available. The yards were spacious and mostly well cared for, boasting manicured lawns despite the area's water shortage. People who moved here from the Northeast just couldn't imagine a yard without grass and found it perennially difficult to believe that in a place where it rained so often, a place surrounded by water, there could be a shortage.

Here and there, though, were signs of the coming reality: xeriscaping with native plants, and yards that sprouted palm trees and were covered with white gravel.

The neighborhood was upscale enough that it hadn't

suffered from the blight that was gradually creeping into some older, less well-to-do neighborhoods as retired householders died. In this area, new retirees kept moving in to replace the ones who had passed on. There was even evidence that young families had moved in: bicycles, swing sets, and wading pools.

But there was a population shift going on in the entire county, with more young people arriving and fewer retirees moving in. St. Petersburg, which had been nicknamed God's Waiting Room, was gradually growing younger, and with that reversal came a concomitant increase in crime.

In short, Seamus didn't think he'd be looking for a new line of work anytime soon.

It was the same day of the week as the murder, and about the same time of day. Gil and Seamus figured that by knocking on doors they'd have a decent chance of finding out who had most likely been at home at the time of the killing, and maybe they could get them to talk.

Gil pulled the car over and parked against the curb, but he didn't immediately turn off the ignition, preferring to let the air conditioner keep them cool.

"Quiet," Gil remarked.

"Yeah." No one was outside, no one was walking down the street, and as they sat there and watched, there weren't even any other cars.

Seamus scanned the houses, and the blank eyes of windows stared back at him. Some had their blinds or curtains drawn against the heat, others appeared to be black mirrors. Nothing and no one stirred. He kept waiting for a curtain to twitch, or some nosy neighbor to peer out to see who was parked at the curb, but the houses might well have been devoid of life.

"So maybe nobody did see anything," Gil remarked.

"Somebody would have heard something."

"Maybe this is the only neighborhood in the world where nobody peeks through the curtains to see what's going on when they hear a loud noise or shouting."

Seamus nodded, scanning the houses and street again. "It's like a scene out of some science-fiction movie," he remarked finally. "I could see this kind of quiet if everybody in this neighborhood worked."

"But they don't." Gil sighed and rubbed his chin, his palm rasping on the fastest-growing stubble in the department. "Well, let's give it a little while. We got a two- or three-hour window on the actual murder anyway."

They didn't have to wait long. Five minutes later a green-and-white St. Petersburg patrol car pulled up beside them. Gil rolled down his window and the cop car rolled down its passenger side window.

"Hey, Rico," Gil called to the man in the green-and-white, "how's it going?"

"Hey," Rico Minelli replied. Resting his left forearm on the steering wheel, he leaned toward them. "You wouldn't be the call I got about suspicious strangers in a parked car, would you?"

Gil and Seamus exchanged quick looks.

"Ain't nobody here but us ducks," Seamus said. "We've been sitting here maybe ten minutes. What time did that call come in?"

"Less than five minutes ago."

"Bingo," said Gil. "You wouldn't happen to have the name and address of the caller?"

"Sure. It was a Mrs. Hatcher, at 4201. Right there on the corner." He pointed. "I'll just go tell her you guys are cops."

"Wait," said Seamus. "We'll go with you."

"Oh, definitely," agreed Gil. "We want to commend

the neighborhood watch." He switched off the ignition, and he and Seamus climbed out. Seamus glanced quickly around again, sure that curtains ought to be twitching madly now. After all, there was a cruiser on the street, a cop was questioning two strangers in a parked car, and now the strangers were getting out of their car *Somebody* ought to be taking note.

And sure enough, two doors down at 4206, he saw the white curtains move. "Another one," he said to Gil. "Isn't it amazing what a little patience will do?"

Gil flashed one of his hundred-watt smiles. "Remember the Kitty Genovese case?"

"You mean the one in New York where the woman was stabbed to death and not one of her neighbors intervened or called the cops?"

"The same. Do you suppose Genovese's neighbors moved down here? To this very neighborhood?"

"It's beginning to look like it."

"Yeah."

"In fact," Seamus remarked, "this neighborhood is beginning to have a very strong 'I don't want to get involved' feeling to it. Remind me not to shop for a house around here."

"What are you guys talking about?" Rico asked. Having parked his car against the curb, he joined them now. He had the beefy build of a weight lifter and wore the light green shirt and dark green shorts of the standard summer uniform. Some folks complained that the St. Pete cops didn't look like cops in those shorts, but those folks didn't have to work outside in this heat all summer.

"We're talking about neighborhood uninvolvement," Seamus explained.

"This is a good neighborhood," Rico protested. "The Mayberry killing is the first murder we've ever had here.

We don't even get many domestics."

"Probably because the neighbors don't report it when they hear screaming," Seamus said drily.

Gil spoke. "Do you get many calls from around here like the one you just got?"

"From time to time." Rico shrugged. "Not much happens here. And it's not even a through street, so there isn't much traffic."

"A little corner of paradise," Seamus remarked, trying to keep the sarcasm out of his tone. He'd always had mixed feelings about neighborhoods like this, where life was smooth and realities of the street were far away, probably because he'd grown up the hard way. It especially galled him when people with all this privilege failed to do their duty as citizens. "This kind of thing just doesn't happen here."

Either he succeeded, or Rico chose to ignore the sarcasm. "No," said the younger cop. "It doesn't. The worst that happens around here is an occasional B and E."

Breaking and entering. Mostly teenagers, no doubt, looking for a thrill and a little loose cash.

"'Hark,'" said Gil. "'what light through yonder window breaks?'"

Seamus turned in time to see curtains moving in another window, in a different house. "Verily, I perceive the light of concern.

"Aye, there's the rub," said Gil, rocking on his heels.

Rico looked at the two of them. "You guys always talk weird?"

"Always," Seamus assured him. "It's a sign of the emptiness of our heads. Let's go reassure Mrs. Hatcher before she has kittens."

"Or a cow," Gil said. "She *could* have a cow."

"You guys are crazy," Rico decided.

"No, just Gil is crazy," Seamus replied. "I'm the sane one."

Rico laughed.

When they reached Mrs. Hatcher's stoop, Seamus stood with his back to the door, watching the neighborhood as Rico hammered twice on the door with his fist, in the best police style. Hammering instead of knocking had two benefits to a cop. First, it could be heard throughout the entire house, so time wasn't wasted. Second, it was authoritarian and strong, making it clear to whoever was inside that the cop was in charge.

It also had the benefit of being audible around the neighborhood. Seamus was rewarded with the sight of a pale face in an upstairs window across the street. The face pulled back from the window as soon as the person realized Seamus was looking his or her way. Very interesting.

Mrs. Hatcher answered the door She had the look of an aging soccer mom in her khaki slacks, polo shirt, jogging shoes, and short gray hair If asked, Seamus would have bet that at one time she had either taught physical education or coached girls' sports. All she needed was a whistle hanging around her neck.

"Hello, Officer Minelli."

So this neighborhood, that never had any trouble, knew the officer by name? Seamus made a mental note to look into that. He was sure Minelli's name wasn't on any of the reports of the murder Another cop had answered the initial call, and others yet had conducted the initial investigation.

"Hi, Mrs. Hatcher. I just wanted you to know that the strangers you saw are actually police detectives."

Mrs. Hatcher, far from looking grateful or relieved, said disapprovingly, "Detectives? I suppose they're here about the murder."

Gil gave her his most charming smile. "Unfortunately, yes."

Mrs. Hatcher pursed her lips. "Well, I've said all I have to say about that."

Seamus didn't even bother to smile. "I realize this is very inconvenient for you, ma'am. It was certainly inconvenient for the young man who was killed."

"Don't you dare imply that I don't care about that young man! But I already talked to the police. At length. I didn't see or hear a thing, and I resent being questioned as if I were lying."

"Of course you do," Gil said sympathetically. "Don't mind my partner. He sometimes forgets that the living are as much victim of the crime as the dead."

Mrs. Hatcher sniffed, glaring at Seamus, then smiling at Gil. Rico had stepped aside. "Well, I just don't know anything. If I did, I'd certainly tell you. And that's what I told the other policemen."

"Just when exactly did you become aware that there had been a murder, Mrs. Hatcher?" Gil asked pleasantly, as if he were having a casual conversation.

"When Maudeen Cleary started shrieking." Mrs. Hatcher shook her head. "That woman didn't stop screaming for ten minutes."

"She must have been very upset," Gil said with concern.

"I suppose she was! We all were, and we didn't scream our heads off."

"No, of course not," Seamus said. "You weren't alone when you first saw the body"

Mrs. Hatcher started to take umbrage, but Gil forestalled her. "Don't mind his rough edges, ma'am. He has a lot to learn. So the Cleary woman's screams were the first you knew of it?"

"Didn't I just say so?"

"Were you home all day?"

For the first time, Mrs. Hatcher hesitated. "Yes," she said finally. "I believe so. At least that's what I told the other policeman, so it must have been true. But it's been three weeks . . ."

As if such details wouldn't now be engraved on her mind, Seamus thought. She certainly didn't strike him as having Alzheimer's.

"Of course," Gil said encouragingly. "Things do get a little dim with time for all of us. Now about the gun-shot . . ."

"I didn't hear a thing," Mrs. Hatcher said firmly. "Not that I remember, anyway."

"Really?" said Seamus. "But you heard the Cleary woman scream, and the gunshot must have been just as loud."

The woman frowned. "I *didn't* hear a thing. I told you." She averted her face and looked at Gil. "I already said everything I intend to."

Seamus was relentless. "You noticed we were parked out there within a few minutes of us getting there. You must look out your windows quite a lot, Mrs. Hatcher. I notice you don't even keep your curtains drawn."

She stiffened, and Gil intervened. "What my partner is trying to say in his unpolished way, is that we figure you for a good neighbor. It would be my guess that nobody in this neighborhood has to worry about a truck backing up to their house in broad daylight while thieves load it with all their possessions."

"Well, I hope if I saw something like that that I wouldn't ignore it."

"Of course not," Gil said smoothly. She smiled.

"So," said Seamus, "you expect us to believe that the better part of an entire day went by and you never once glanced out a window and saw that man lying there bleeding to death?"

Mrs. Hatcher backed up, her face paling. "I tell you, I didn't know a thing until Maudeen screamed."

"Of course you didn't, Mrs. Hatcher," Gil said pleasantly. "Thank you for your time. I hope we won't have to trouble you again."

Mrs. Hatcher barely nodded before she slammed the door on them. Gil and Seamus walked back to their car, Rico on their heels.

Rico said, "You guys do good cop, bad cop really well."

Seamus and Gil exchanged looks. "What's he talking about?" Seamus asked.

"Beats me."

"You know," Rico said. "The way you were talking to that lady One of you being the heavy, the other one being the nice guy."

"Oh," said Gil, shrugging.

Seamus looked over his shoulder. "Hate to disappoint you, Rico, but that's just our normal personalities."

Gil stifled a smile.

"Oh." Rico thought about it. "What was that all about? The questions with Mrs. Hatcher. Why did you ask her again? She must have been questioned two or three times already."

Not too swift, this guy, Seamus thought. "Just verifying the woman's story. Basic police work, Rico. You always go back to make sure they haven't remembered something new."

"Always," Gil agreed. "And she didn't remember anything new."

"Not a thing," Seamus echoed.

They stood by their car, watching as Rico drove away.

Seamus looked at Gil. "She knows something."

Gil nodded.

"She also knows Rico's name. Seems kind of odd in a

61

neighborhood that almost never needs the police."

Gil nodded slowly. "Maybe she had a B and E at one time, and he responded."

"Could be."

Gil looked at Seamus.

Seamus looked back. "And cows fly," he said finally.

"So I've heard."

Together they walked toward the next house.

"Well, you were right," Gil said late that afternoon as he and Seamus returned to the squad room and took their seats at the table. "There's a conspiracy of silence in that neighborhood."

"So loud it's almost deafening."

Gil rubbed his ear with a knuckle and grinned. "Did you say something?"

Seamus's phone rang, and he reached for it. He hoped it might be one of the neighbors they'd spoken to that afternoon, claiming to have suddenly remembered something. After all, he and Gil had done their best to leave those people with the impression that they could expect to be questioned by the police every few days until they died unless something broke on the case.

"Seamus," Carissa Stover said, "I've got to talk to you."

His stomach lurched, leaving him feeling almost seasick. What, was the woman developing ESP now? Had she somehow realized that he'd decided he never wanted to hear her voice again, even on the radio? "I'm at work, Carey. Try me at home later." *But I won't be there.* If he had to stay out all night to avoid her, he would.

Then he decided he was being a chickenshit about a woman he'd broken off with five years ago. It didn't matter anymore. Not at all. Right? Right.

"I'm at work, too," she said, her voice tight. "But this *is* about work. About your work. I want to talk to *you, Detective.*"

He remembered that edge in her voice. In or out of the courtroom, it cowed most people. "About what? Is it urgent?" And then he realized she had just cowed him. He swore silently. He was making futile gasps of resistance. Christ!

"I need to talk to you. Privately. About police business. And face it, Seamus, you're the only *honest* cop I know."

He wondered if her mouth had finally gotten her into serious trouble. Curiosity, of which he had always had entirely too much, reared its head. "Okay. When?" And there went number six or seven of his nine lives, he thought with resignation.

"Here, if you want. At the station. I don't go on the air for a couple of hours, but I've got some stuff to do."

Neutral territory, he thought. She wanted to talk to him about as much as he wanted to talk to her. The realization didn't ease his queasiness any. Taking her home the other night when she was drunk had managed somehow to make five years ago seem like only yesterday. His body, he thought, craved hers the way addicts craved cocaine. That's all it was, a craving. A physical addiction. He didn't actually care about her anymore, he just wanted her.

And that was something he was sure he could deal with.

Feeling better suddenly, he said, "Sure. Give me thirty minutes. I've got some paperwork to take care of first."

"Great. And Seamus . . . thanks."

Thanks? Carissa Stover didn't thank people for anything. She asked for it, then accepted it as her due. And for some reason he didn't like the idea that the years might have changed her. It renewed his uneasiness.

"Hot date?" Gil asked when he hung up.

63

"No. Business." He was being short, but he didn't want to get into it.

"Was that Carey Stover? Didn't you used to date her?"

Seamus's eyes suddenly felt hot in his head, and he wondered if flames were leaping out of them as he looked stonily at his partner. "Ancient history."

"Right," said Gil. He let the subtext hang in the air between them.

The hell of working with Gil Garcia, Seamus thought as he started to write his report, was the way the guy could crawl into his head.

He wondered if it was too late to pull up the drawbridge, close the windows, and lock the doors.

He had the feeling it already was.

CHAPTER 5
18 DAYS

CARISSA WAS HOLED UP IN AN EMPTY RECORDING booth with papers scattered all around her, giving a damn good imitation of being deep in preparation for her show. She still had to figure out the thrust of another monologue on the Otis case to kick off with tonight, but she didn't have a foggy idea what tack she wanted to take. Right now, waiting for Seamus to arrive, she didn't seem to be able to think about anything at all except the reason she had called him.

The back of her neck was tingling, and hadn't stopped since she'd talked to Evan Sinclair at the Prosecutor's Office about a story Ed Ulrich had mentioned to her. The harder she had tried to shake the feeling, the more persistent it had become. Finally, she had called Seamus, even though she knew full well what he was going to say about this.

Finally the half hour was up, and she went out to the lobby to see if he was there. His car was just pulling into the parking lot under leaden skies. Gray, wispy fingers were reaching groundward from the rapidly moving clouds, almost touching the tops of the palm trees at the entrance to the parking lot. The palm fronds and the live oaks around the edge of the lot were being tossed by the strong wind looking silvery in the strange greenish light.

Tornado weather.

"Looks nasty out there," Becky Hadlov remarked.

"I love this kind of weather." It was a pleasant change from the burning sun and baking heat of this time of year, as long as she didn't have to drive in it.

"You would."

Carey glanced over her shoulder. "Meaning?" She was careful to make the question pleasant.

"You like excitement."

"True enough." Why else would she have dragged Seamus Rourke, whom she would have been happy never to see again, all the way over here on a mere wisp of intuition?

She turned back to the windows and saw Seamus walking up with his usual, insouciant stride. That was the very first thing she had noticed about him, she remembered: that walk. That "I'm comfortable in my body and with my maleness' walk that had caused an instantaneous sexual reaction in her.

He still had the walk, and she still had the reaction. Great. Wonderful. Like she needed this?

He was wearing a lightweight dark blue suit, white shirt, and tie. She recognized the slight bulge at his hip that was his gun, and remembered watching him strap it on his belt in the mornings, an action that had always somehow left her feeling that they couldn't possibly be on the same side. She had carried a badge, too, back then, but not a gun. That gun had marked a major difference between them.

Or so she had thought. But what was the difference? she asked herself now *He* could shoot a perp if necessary. *She* had sent one to the electric chair. Maybe it had been realizing that there really was no difference that had been the final straw for her.

He reached the door and pulled it open, letting in a gust of warm, moist air that was laden with the sound of the wind, clattering palm fronds, and passing traffic. He stepped through, and the door closed, shutting out the mixed sounds of nature and civilization.

"Hi," he said.

"Come on back." Carissa turned and led the way to the booth she'd commandeered. When she closed that door, no one would be able to hear what they were saying.

She pointed to a stool and he took it. Then she rounded the console and sat on the other side, facing the familiar array of buttons and slides. They grounded her somehow and, with Seamus this close, she needed to be grounded.

"So what's up?" he asked, unbuttoning his suit jacket and letting it fall open.

All of a sudden her intuition seemed flimsy, and she wished she had never called him. What did she have, after all, except a time proximity between two events that were probably totally unrelated?

"Carey?"

His tone was impatient. She recognized it from the days when she had been battling through an endless crisis of conscience, and he had started to get tired of her unending talk about the law, justice, and her job. He'd even called her a one-trick pony. Maybe she was. She was still talking about the same things on the radio.

"Carey?" This time there was no impatience, but instead genuine concern. She looked into his gray-green eyes but couldn't read them. He'd always had unreadable eyes—when he wanted to. "Did something happen to you? Did somebody threaten you?"

She shook her head quickly. "No. Sorry. I'm sorry. It's just—you're probably going to laugh at me."

"Since when does that bother you?"

She wanted to tell him she didn't care what he thought about *her,* but even as she opened her mouth to say so, she realized that wasn't strictly true. "I just . . . well, I want you to give me a full hearing, okay? Somebody's life could depend on it."

He sighed. "Otis."

"Yes, Otis!" Her temper was close to snapping, and she had to force herself to remain calm. She was not ordinarily so close to the edge, but the whole idea of a man being executed in part because of things *she* had done was eating her alive—especially since she had always harbored a belief that he was probably innocent. "You're not going to tell me that you want this man to be executed if he's innocent?"

"He's not innocent. He was convicted of murder."

"And for you it ends there?"

He nodded. "For me it ends when I make my testimony in court, counselor. It *has* to end there, whether the suspect is convicted or not. We've been over this a thousand times, Carey. Christ, maybe a million times. It sure felt like it."

The reference to the last days of their relationship struck her as almost brutal, but she forced herself to ignore it. "Seamus—"

"Is that why you called me? To argue about this again?

67

Jesus, Carey, there's nothing left to say that we both haven't said."

"But there *is* something more. Maybe."

She had to give him credit. His face didn't shutter, the way it had too many times in the past. He grew still, attentive, listening.

"The other night on my show I got a call from someone who said that John Otis didn't do it, and that he was going to prove it."

"So? Anybody could say that. All it takes is one crackpot."

"I know that. I deal with crackpots all the time in this job. And that's all I thought he was. I even poked fun at him a little."

He nodded slowly, waiting.

"Did you hear about the break-in at Tricia Summers's house the night before last?"

"The Channel Five news anchor? I heard something about it on the news. So?"

"Ed Rich, our station news anchor, asked me about it yesterday. He wanted to know if I could get any inside information out of one of my friends since the Sheriff's Department isn't saying very much."

"Hardly surprising. Summers probably doesn't want to be a news item."

"I thought so, too. I mean, maybe she had some sex toys stolen, or some sexy photos. That's what I told Ed, but I agreed to check it out anyway and see if I could find some little thing that would give him a scoop."

Seamus sighed. "God, I love how the media work."

There wasn't much she could say to that, since at one time she'd felt pretty much the same way. But the remark put her on the defensive. "I wasn't going to give him anything scandalous," she said. "But it wouldn't hurt to see if there was something he could use."

"Yeah, right."

She wanted to bean him, but decided it wasn't worth one-to-four for battery. "Anyway, I got in touch with a friend at the State Attorney's Office, and he looked into it for me."

"And what lovely, scandalous little detail did you turn up?"

"It's not scandalous, Seamus. It's frightening. Somebody went to all the trouble to break into her house and circumvent her alarm system to do just one thing: slash a nightgown with a razor blade."

"Maybe he got interrupted before he could do anything else. It may be sick, Carey, but it doesn't have anything to do with Otis."

"Possible not. But maybe you've forgotten. Tricia Summers was the legal reporter for Channel Five during the Otis trial. She did a live segment from the courthouse every day on the evening news."

"I remember So?"

"Do you remember how slanted her reports were? Do you remember her standing there after the verdict came in and telling all her viewers that it was a good day for the Tampa Bay area and a triumph for the justice system? The other stations were more matter-of-fact about the verdict, but she was practically cheerleading."

"Okay, so she was connected. A lot of other people were connected, too. It doesn't mean anything."

"The nightgown the guy slashed was pink silk."

"So?"

Carissa stared at him, her insides rolling as her mind recalled images she would far rather have forgotten. She could still remember the feel of the plastic evidence bag in her hands as she showed the nightgown to the jury.

"Maybe you've forgotten. The nightgown Linda Kline was wearing the night she was slashed to death was pink silk."

"It was so blood-soaked I . . ." He trailed off and shook his head. "Coincidence, Carey. I'm sure a lot of women have pink silk nightgowns."

"That may be. But Tricia Summers doesn't. The nightgown that was slashed didn't belong to her."

Thunder boomed outside, and not even the soundproofing of the booth could entirely muffle the sound. It seemed to echo in Seamus's head as Carey's words sank home. He felt a shift, like an earthquake, inside himself.

And immediately he started scrambling to put his world back together again. "Anybody could have found out the color of Linda Kline's nightgown. It was in evidence, for Chrissake. It was probably mentioned in the news reports."

She nodded. "Eighteen days, Seamus."

He didn't have to ask what she meant. He knew about her countdown on the radio. "Slashing a nightgown isn't the same as slashing a person. The color might be coincidental, or it might be deliberate, but even so, that doesn't tie it to the original crime. And the guy who called you might just be some kind of weirdo who wants to capitalize on the Otis execution and get himself in the papers."

To his surprise, she just nodded. But those hazel eyes of hers said something else entirely.

He sighed inwardly and tried once again to remind her of the logic of the Otis case. "Look, you know we considered other perps. And *nobody else* could have committed the crime." He started to tick on his fingers.

"First, you need motive. Otis was the only one with a motive—he had a knock-down, drag-out fight with his foster

70

father the night before the murders. Two, you need opportunity. Nobody else could have gotten into that house without breaking in. It had to be somebody with a key. That left John Otis. And he didn't have an alibi that stood up."

"He was in Vero Beach."

"Nobody saw him there, from the time he checked into the hotel until the time he checked out. Plenty of time to drive back here and commit a couple of murders. Opportunity, Carey."

She nodded woodenly, and his exasperation began to grow again.

"The case is closed," he said. "You know that. And no slashed nightgown is going to reopen it."

"Probably not."

"So what the hell did you call me for?"

"I don't know," she admitted finally. For a moment she looked away.

"You're obsessed."

She nodded.

"It's not healthy. You had a job to do, and you did it. You did what was right."

"Did I?"

"Jesus." He shook his head and rubbed his chin, and tried to look at anything at all except the woman who faced him across the console. "You've got to get over it."

"You're one to talk."

He felt an impulse to violence so strong that he actually had trouble quelling it. "Don't go there," he said through his teeth.

She had the grace to look ashamed. "I'm sorry. I guess we both have our obsessions. But mine is one I can do something about, Seamus. This is bothering me. Seriously bothering me. Something about this slashing is making my hackles rise."

71

"You're just clutching at straws."

She sighed. "Okay, I'm clutching at straws. But I thought. . ." She trailed off.

Ah, he thought, at last. The real reason for her call. "You thought what?"

She shrugged one shoulder, looking as if she were hunching for a blow. "I thought maybe you could check it out and see if there are any other similarities to the Kline killings."

"It's out of my jurisdiction."

"You know people in the Sheriff's Department. You could find out more than I can. I still have friends in the prosecutor's office but. . ." She shook her head. "You could find out a lot faster than I could. And time is of the essence."

"If there are any similarities, someone would—"

She ruthlessly interrupted. "If there are any similarities, no one's going to be looking for them, and you know that as well as I do," she said sharply. "The Kline case is closed, and John Otis is on death row. Nobody's going to be looking, and cops are as shortsighted as anyone when it comes to things like that. It'll never occur to any of them to see what might be right under their noses!"

He hated to admit she was right. "I've got a full caseload—"

"Damn your caseload! Why don't you just for once consider that instead of catching a killer, this time you might be able to prevent a killing!"

"Not on the basis of a slashed nightgown."

She apparently had no answer for that. He rose from the stool and buttoned his suit coat. The meeting was over. "See you around," he said, and turned toward the door.

"Seamus? I'm going to Raiford to interview Otis."

He looked over his shoulder at her. "You really are a glutton for punishment, aren't you." Then he walked out.

Carissa sat at the console for a long time, feeling close to tears and close to anger, and unable to settle on one or the other. Talking to Seamus had always been like talking to a brick wall, she thought. His mind-set was so fixed.

But so was hers, she admitted wearily. So was hers.

Bill Hayes caught her at the nine o'clock break. She was taking the time to slip out back and smoke a cigarette from the pack she'd bought yesterday. She told herself that if she only smoked a couple a day, she could quit at any time, but the fact was, after an hour of talking with callers about Otis, the death penalty, and abused children, she would have crawled on her hands and knees for a nicotine fix.

She was standing out back on the rain-slick pavement, halfway through the cigarette when Bill stepped out to join her. The rain had stopped temporarily, but the cat was nowhere to be seen.

Bill lit a cigarette and took a couple of drags. "You've got to get off the Otis thing," he said.

"Why?"

"Advertisers are getting nervous. They're worried your ratings will fall off if you stick with one subject."

She shrugged. "The phones are still ringing like mad, and people have plenty to say about it. I don't force them to talk about it, Bill. I just do my monologue. If they want to discuss something else, they can."

"You know the phones don't matter, Carey You know perfectly well all that matters is how many people are listening, and most of them don't call. You can light up the phone lines with only a handful of listeners."

She didn't respond.

"Work with me, Carey. No advertisers, no show."

She sighed and took another puff on her cigarette. Upping her head back, she looked up at the night sky.

"Besides," he said, "you're nationally syndicated. How many folks outside Florida give a shit about Otis?"

"They care about the death penalty."

"Maybe. But do they care enough about it to listen to it being discussed every night for three weeks?"

She couldn't honestly argue that they did. Tossing away her butt, she pulled another cigarette out of the pack and lit it. So much for just a couple a day.

"You know," Bill continued, "I can understand why you care so much about this. But talk radio is entertainment, Carey. You've got to be careful of using it as a soapbox."

"Limbaugh uses it as a soapbox."

"Wrong. Limbaugh is an entertainer who plays to a conservative audience. His mistake was beginning to believe in his own *shtick*. He's not as big as he used to be."

"There are twenty million ditto-heads."

"Maybe. But there aren't thirty million, and there never will be. But even so, he never plays one issue to death day after day. He plays a variety of them. He's smart enough to keep grabbing on to new stories as they come up."

"And?"

Bill tossed his cigarette away and faced her. "You can continue your countdown, but don't make it the only focus of your show. Because if you do, in eighteen days your show is going to be as dead as John William Otis."

He went back inside, leaving her to finish her cigarette.

Seamus got home late, a little after ten. He'd been called out to visit a murder scene that had turned out to be an open-and-shut case of domestic violence. Three neighbors had seen the ex-husband, who was supposedly out of town for a week, drive up and drive away shortly before the victim had come crawling out her front door covered in blood and begging for help.

Case closed.

The words seemed to echo in his head, drawing his thoughts back to his meeting with Carey. That woman was bound and determined to find something on which to hang her belief that John Otis was innocent.

Shaking his head, he stepped through his front door into his living room, and nearly reeled at the overpowering stench of beer. The first thing he saw was his dad, sprawled on the couch, snoring loudly, with a heap of empty beer cans on the floor beside him.

"God damn it!" he said, and slammed the door.

Danny Rourke wasn't in a coma. He pushed himself up on his elbow and looked in his son's direction. The nystagmus of Danny's eyes was obvious to Seamus, who'd done plenty of field sobriety tests in his day.

"I told you I wasn't going to stand for this," he told his father.

"I know," Danny mumbled. "I know." He pushed himself into a sitting position. His head lolled almost like a rag doll's, before he managed to steady it. "I quit, son. I really did."

Seamus kicked the beer cans. They rolled a short distance across the carpet. "What's this, then?"

"I couldn't . . ." Danny trailed off and tried again. I got the shakes, son," he said in slurred tones. "I got 'em bad."

"Christ." Seamus dropped onto his easy chair and stared at his father, feeling a mixture of hate, anguish, and love. "You need detox."

Danny managed an exaggerated nod.

"Shit." He couldn't do it for the old man, and the old

man couldn't do it for himself. And if his alcoholism was this bad, he really did need professional help. How in the hell was he going to afford it? But did he have any choice?

"IRS wrote me," Danny said. He pointed to a crumpled piece of paper on the end table.

Seamus picked it up and smoothed it out. It had apparently been forwarded from Danny's old address. And it was not the kind of news that was likely to help the old man stay sober. They wanted to know where he was hiding the business equipment that he'd previously taken deductions for.

"Where's the business equipment, Dad?"

"Sold it."

It was just about what Seamus had figured. He'd probably sold everything that wasn't nailed down in order to pay for his booze. "Do you have any idea how long they've been after you?"

Danny shook his head.

"Judging by this, I'd say you've been ignoring their letters for a long time."

"They wanted some money and I didn't have it."

"But how long ago was that?"

"Don't know."

Of course not. Danny had been living in an alcoholic haze of forgetfulness for some time. "How'd you buy the beer?"

"Ten bucks," Danny said thickly. "I had ten bucks."

"Do you have any more?"

"No."

"Good. I'm slamming your butt into detox tomorrow, Dad. Like it or not, you're going to dry out and stay dry. Do you hear me?"

Danny managed a limp nod.

"I'll find someone to handle this IRS business for you, but you've got to promise me you're going to stay dry, Dad."

"Promise."

"Now get to bed and sleep it off."

He watched his father stagger down the hallway to his bedroom, and tried not to remember the father he had had as a child. Tried not to remember how he had once believed that Danny Rourke knew everything about everything, and that his father could always keep him safe. Tried not to remember just how much he had once loved that old man.

What the hell was he going to do about the IRS? At this point, Danny probably needed more than an accountant; he probably needed a lawyer, and lawyers weren't cheap.

In fact, between a lawyer and detox, Seamus figured he could kiss off all his savings, and probably a good portion of his disposable income for the next five to ten years.

But what else could he do?

He might want to hate the old man, but Danny was still his father. He couldn't just throw him out and forget about him.

But even as he sat there, nursing his anger and resentment, telling himself how much he hated his father for the way he had blighted so many lives, Seamus found himself remembering.

He remembered thirty years ago when everything had seemed possible. He'd been baseball mad back then, and had dreamed that he was going to grow up to be a major-league pitcher. He'd wanted so bad to go to a spring training game at Al Lang Field. He'd been begging since he got old enough to have his own baseball glove, but there'd never been a good time. Danny had been working himself half to death on his shrimp boat, trying to support his young family, and time off to go to a baseball game just didn't seem possible. Nor did the cost of the tickets, only a few dollars, but a few dollars more than Danny

Rourke had had to spare at that time, while he was struggling to pay off his boat and make all the ends meet.

But Danny had never told his son no. He'd always said, not yet, son. Not yet. Someday.

"Someday" had finally arrived. Danny had come back a day early from a shrimping trip. Closing his eyes, Seamus saw his father coming up the front walk, dirty and grungy from hard work, burned by the merciless sun, stinking of shrimp and the sea.

"What are you doing back so soon?" Seamus's mother had asked, her voice full of delighted laughter.

And Danny had looked down at his son and grinned. "It was a profitable trip," he said, "and I've got a boy to take to a baseball game."

The boy had shrieked with excitement. The man he had become sat with his eyes closed and burning, and his throat so tight from unshed tears that he could hardly breathe.

What had become of them all?

CHAPTER 6
18 DAYS

CAREY STEPPED OUT OF THE STATION SHORTLY AFTER eleven. She carried her sweatshirt, her laptop computer, and a half-empty bottle of water, and she had only one thought on her mind: getting home and getting to bed. The last couple of nights her sleep had been interrupted by terrible nightmares, dreams she forgot as soon as she opened her eyes. Last night she had slept with a light on to dispel the shadows in the corners of her bedroom, but it hadn't helped. Even light couldn't hold back the oppressive sense of impending doom that was dogging her steps.

A shadow detached itself from one of the trees, walking toward her, and her heart slammed as she recognized a male figure. She turned, ready to dash back into the station.

"Carey! It's me."

Seamus. Her flight response instantly converted to fury. "What the *fuck* are you doing?" she demanded.

He stopped a few paces away. "You never used to swear," he said.

She was about to give him a demonstration of just how much she *could* swear when something stopped her. The tone of his voice hadn't been accusatory, she realized. It had been almost—wistful. "You bring out the best in me," she finally said, her tone slightly acid.

"I always did." The same acid laced his words.

"What do you want?"

"To talk. Come on. I'll buy you breakfast, and we'll do a little horse trading."

She hesitated, reluctant to expose herself to any more of this man. Five years ago he had cost her a lot of heartbreak; as angry as she had been with him, she had still drowned her pillow with tears. It would be awful to discover she was still susceptible. But that wasn't likely, she decided. Whatever hadn't been torn out by the roots during their breakup had certainly withered and died during five years of neglect.

Besides, horse trading meant he had something to offer her, and she couldn't pass up the possibility that he'd changed his mind about looking into the Summers slashing case.

"Okay," she said. "The Pancake Place?"

They had once eaten a lot of midnight breakfasts at the Pancake Place. Both of them had worked long hours in their jobs, and had gone through periods where the only time they could find to sit down to a meal together was in the middle of the night. Seamus had been fond of breakfast at any time of the day or night, and, before long, Carey had developed a taste for it herself. To this day she sometimes made herself French toast or pancakes when she got home from work.

But coming to one of their old haunts might not have been a bright idea, Carey thought as they entered the restaurant. The decor hadn't changed one bit; it was still brightly lit with overhead fluorescents, and the tables, chairs, and booths were still the same beige Formica and brown Naugahyde, a little worse for wear.

She could feel the years peeling away, leaving nerve endings exposed.

But the waitress was different, and time stopped ping-ponging between then and now. The menus were different, too, freshly printed on white stock and inserted in brand-new plastic covers. But the items on them were the same, and she heard herself ordering her favorite strawberry pancakes and decaf. Seamus ordered steak and eggs with an extra side of English muffins. She recognized the signs: He hadn't eaten since breakfast.

The coffee came in a carafe, and Seamus filled both their mugs. She watched him stir cream into his, and wondered if his stomach was bothering him, since he usually drank it black. Then she wondered why she should care. It was not her business anymore.

"My dad," he said, then fell silent.

She waited, but when he said no more, prompted him. "What about your dad?"

He sighed and stirred his coffee some more. The spoon clinked steadily against the side of the cup. "My dad has some problems."

She almost asked what that had to do with her, then

reined in her impatience. It was one of the things he had always complained about, the way she could never just let a story unfold but had to go after it with questions. The lawyer in her, he'd called it. But she'd always been that way. She was like a bird with a seed, pecking away to get at the kernel as quickly as possible. It was part of what made her such a success on her show, and part of what had made her a good trial attorney; but it was her nature, not something she had learned.

It was also something she was learning to control when it seemed wise, and right now it seemed wise.

He looked tired, she thought, tired and . . . very unhappy. But his being unhappy was nothing new, she reminded herself. That was one of the things that had driven her crazy about him, the way he never permitted himself to just *enjoy* anything.

"My dad," he said again.

She couldn't help herself. It just slipped out. "Right. Your dad. I got that part."

He looked up sharply, almost as if he were going to snap at her, but then surprised her with a short laugh. "My dad," he said again. "It's a subject I don't want to discuss. But I guess you can tell that."

"I do get that feeling. However, if you don't get around to it, we might be here all night."

He gave another laugh, this one actually humorous. "You know how hard it is for me to talk about personal things."

"I seem to remember commenting on it a few times."

This time he smiled at her. "With justification," he admitted. "Okay. My dad. The bane of my existence."

"I thought that was *me*," she said lightly.

"You've been superseded."

"That's good. I think. I never quite saw myself as a

81

bane. On the other hand . . ." She trailed off, dropping the forced lightness, and reached out to touch the back of his hand. It was wrapped tightly around his coffee mug, telling her clearly how difficult this was for him. "It's okay, Seamus. Just do it your own way."

"I don't have a way," he reminded her. He turned his head, looking at the dark window beside them. There were no other customers in the restaurant, and the parking lot outside was almost invisible. It was like being cut off from the rest of the world.nnnn

"My dad," he said, "is an alcoholic. I'm going to put him in detox in the morning."

"I'm sorry." She didn't know what else to say. She assumed this had to be painful for him. But he surprised her.

"He needs it," he said bluntly. "He's ruined his life with his drinking, and I'm not going to live with a souse."

"I can understand that."

"He has nowhere to turn but to me. If I throw him out, he'll be living on the street." He looked at her. "I made it a condition of staying with me. He has to dry out and stay dry."

"You don't really have any alternative."

"I don't think so. But there's more."

Just then they were interrupted by the waitress, who brought their platters of food. Seamus was hungry enough that he let the conversation lag until he'd eaten more than half of his twelve-ounce steak and most of his, home fries.

"Anyway," he said, picking up where he'd left off, "in the process of running his business and his life into the ground, he got into some trouble with the IRS."

"That's never fun."

He shrugged one shoulder, as if to say it didn't matter whether it was fun, it just was. He didn't waste breath railing about things that couldn't be changed. "Whatever. The point is, he's in trouble, and I don't even know how much trouble. He can't remember when they started coming after him or how much they want. He said it was thirty thousand plus penalties. I do know that they confiscated his fishing boat, which is worth more than the thirty thousand dollars he owes them, but then he got a letter today asking him the whereabouts of the office equipment he'd claimed deductions for. Apparently he sold the stuff to support his addiction."

"Not good."

"Nope."

"He'll owe taxes on whatever money he got for the stuff in addition to the claim they're already making."

"Yup." He cut off another chunk of steak and chewed it. Then, with an impatient movement, he pushed his plate aside and reached for his coffee cup.

"You need to finish eating," she told him. "You haven't eaten since early this morning, right?"

"I lost my appetite. Danny has that effect on me."

"Danny?"

"My father."

"Oh."

"When he first told me what was going on, I figured confiscating the boat would settle it. To judge by the letter today, it's not going to be that easy. Apparently whatever he owes is more than the boat's worth—athough I have to tell you, Carey, I just can't figure it. He never made enough money to run up that kind of tax bill."

"Penalties and interest. They add up really fast."

He nodded slowly and sighed "I'm not even sure he owes all this money. He hasn't been working much, if at all, because of his drinking. He couldn't have made more than a pittance in the past five years. And he can't remember the last time he filed a return."

"So maybe they're taking this action based on estimated income for the years he didn't file."

His brows lifted. "I didn't think of that."

"Well, I'm not a tax attorney, but it wouldn't surprise me if they did something like that, and as long as they don't get other information, they're going to go on the assumption that he just quit filing but is still working the same as he always has. Of course, I don't have the foggiest idea if that's even legal or possible. There might be something else going on."

"Well, I honestly can't figure out how he came to owe so much. But like you said, it could be penalties and interest."

"You need to get somebody to look into it, Seamus."

"That's what I thought. And that's where we get to the horse trading."

"I'm not a tax attorney," she reminded him. "I took one course on tax law in school, and that's all outdated now."

"But you're an attorney. You know how to talk to people, how to find things out, and how to negotiate. You're also extremely bright. I have no doubt you could find out what you need to know."

"You'd do better to hire someone who really knows what she's doing."

"Maybe. But I doubt it. And the other part of my problem is that paying for Danny's detox is probably going to clean me out."

"You shouldn't have to pay for that! He's an adult. There must be some program . . ."

He shook his head. "Danny's my responsibility. I'm not going to foist him off on taxpayers."

"But you're perfectly willing to ask *me* to do a favor."

"No. I'm not asking for a favor. I said horse trade and I

meant horse trade. You scratch my back, and I'll scratch yours. Good old-fashioned barter."

"And just what do I get in exchange?"

"I'll look into the Summers case for you."

One corner of her mouth lifted. "Damn you."

He shrugged and smiled. "Trade."

"It won't take you more than a few hours to check into the Summers case. It might take me years to straighten out Danny's mess."

"I'm not asking you to straighten it out. I'm asking you to find out what's going on. Then I can decide what I need to do about it. Just find out the parameters of the mess, so I can get a handle on it. Right now, I don't even know where to start."

"Probably by calling the phone number on the letter he got today," she said drily.

"If they'll even talk to me. I'm just his son, remember. They might not tell me a thing."

It was true. Taxpayers did have some privacy protection.

She sighed and looked down at her hardly touched plate. She didn't really have a choice. She would never sleep easily again if she passed up this opportunity. She'd been tormented for five years by the feeling that stones had been left unturned in the Otis trial, so how could she leave a stone unturned now, when there were only a few days left to correct the situation?

"Okay," she said. "I'll do it. But you have to get the information on Summers fast."

"I know."

"And Danny has to agree to my representing him. I can't just dive in on this on your say-so, Seamus."

"He'll agree. Come home with me right now, and I'll wake him up out of his drunken stupor."

85

"Fair enough." But she had the feeling she was going to get a lot more than she bargained for.

Seamus still lived in the same modest bungalow. Pulling into his driveway behind him was like déjá vu, Carey thought, worse than the Pancake Place. She switched off her ignition and waited for her emotions to settle.

The night was windy, and the royal palms in Seamus's front yard were tossing wildly. Low clouds scudded across the sky, yellowed by the city lights below Tall live oaks grew on either side of the house, old trees that spread their sheltering branches over the roof In the daylight they provided cooling shade. At night they seemed to swallow the house in a dark cavern.

She shivered with an inexplicable sense of unease and found herself reluctant to get out of the car. Ghosts, she thought. This place was full of ghosts.

Seamus came back to her and opened her car door. "Come on in:' he said. "I don't want you sitting out here while I wake the old fart."

She climbed out and watched him close her car door. "You don't have a lot of respect for your father," she remarked."

"Not anymore.

How sad, she thought, following him up the driveway and along the walk to the front door She also found herself wondering how she could have lived with this man for six months and not heard one mention of his father. "Has he always been alcoholic? That would explain a lot."

"No." But he offered no additional information, leaving her to wonder what the story was behind this.

A solitary lamp was lit in the living room. He didn't turn on any others. "Wait here. I'll go wake him up."

So she waited, looking around a room that had once

86

been familiar to her. It looked the same, but in the past it had never reeked of beer.

She turned as she heard him coming back down the hall. This time he had an old man on his arm. Danny Rourke was a little unsteady on his feet, bent and old-looking, far too thin to be healthy. But what Carey really noticed was the way Seamus held his father's arm. Regardless of how he might talk about Danny, Seamus loved him.

Seeing Carissa, Danny shook off his son's arm and tried to stand straighter. His eyes were bloodshot and red-rimmed, and he swayed a little as he stood on his own, but there was pride there, under the alcoholic veneer, and she felt herself responding to it.

"Dad, this is Carissa Stover. She's an attorney. I asked her to look into your trouble with the IRS. Carey, my dad, Danny Rourke."

Carey walked over to the old man and offered to shake his hand. His grip was strong, and he gave her a smile as he mumbled a greeting. Long ago, he had probably been a very attractive man.

"Mr. Rourke," she said. "I told Seamus I'd look into the problem, but I can only do it if *you* want me to represent you."

"I can't pay you."

"Seamus is paying me, Mr. Rourke."

"That's not right." Danny looked up at his son. "You shouldn't do that."

"Don't worry about it," Seamus said shortly. "Just tell the lady you want her to represent you. All she's going to do is find out what the hell is going on, so I can figure out what we need to do about it."

"It's my problem," Danny insisted, his voice only slightly slurred. "I'll get what's coming to me."

Seamus shook his head. "It's *my* problem, Dad. You made it my problem when you turned up on my doorstep. Now say yes to the lady so she can get home to bed."

Danny's eyes reflected hurt and humiliation as he looked at Carey. "Yes," he said. Then he turned and shuffled back down the hall to bed, steadying himself against the wall.

Neither Seamus nor Carey said anything until they heard the door close behind him.

Carey spoke first. "He's got a lot of pride."

"Not enough to stay away from the bottle."

"Don't you think you're being a little hard on him?"

"Hard?" He repeated the, word disbelievingly. "Nobody pours the booze down his throat except him."

"Alcoholism is a disease."

"Sure. One that can be cured by refusing to bend the elbow."

Carey thought of the pack of cigarettes in her purse and figured she wasn't so very different from Danny Rourke. Crutches could be very difficult to get rid of.

"Come on," he said. "I'll walk you to the car."

"But I need some information if I'm going to get to work on Danny's case."

He looked embarrassed. "Oh. Yeah." He picked up a crumpled piece of paper from the end table and handed it to her. "This is the letter from the IRS. It's all I've got. God knows what happened to his business records. If he didn't lose them, they were probably on the computer he sold—or on the boat the IRS confiscated."

"There's probably enough information here to get started," she said after scanning the letter. "At least enough to find out exactly what they want."

"A gallon of blood and a pound of flesh," he said. "And how they expect him to make any money to pay them back when they've taken his boat beats the hell out of me."

"How old is he?"

"Fifty-nine."

Carey shook her head. "I would have guessed seventy something."

"The sun and the bottle will do that to a person."

He walked her out to her car and opened the door for her. She didn't climb in immediately, though. Instead she leaned against the side of the car, folded her arms, and let the wind whip her hair around.

She was reluctant to break the tenuous thread between them, she realized. She didn't want to drive away and go back to her lonely, empty life and thoughts of John William Otis. What she wanted was just a few moments of escape from all the burdens that seemed to weigh on her.

"What?" he said finally. The streetlights cast strange shadows on his face.

"My station manager told me to stop focusing solely on the Otis story," she said. She wasn't sure what made her tell him that, but as soon as she spoke she knew she was seeking some kind of validation. And from exactly the wrong person, she thought unhappily. Seamus had already told her she was obsessed.

"Did he say why?"

"The advertisers are getting nervous. They think people will stop listening."

"Do you think that's a legitimate concern?"

"What I think doesn't really matter, I guess. If the advertisers are getting nervous, they'll stop buying time on the show."

"Self-fulfilling prophecy, in other words."

"That's one way of putting it."

"So what are you going to do?"

89

She had forgotten how well he could listen. Toward the end, neither of them had been listening, and both had been doing a lot of shouting. "I'm not sure."

"Did he say you couldn't do Otis at all?"

She shook her head. "He just wants me to do some other stiff, too."

"Well, that's reasonable."

"I guess. But it's weird."

"What is?"

She waved a hand. "How little there is to say about a man's life. How little there actually is to say about taking a man's life."

He turned and leaned back against the car beside her. The rustle of the wind in the treetops and the clatter of the palm fronds was a soothing sound, like the rushing of water in a river. "What would you have people say?"

"I don't know. It's just that—well, it seems so momentous to me. We should at least face the enormity of what we're about to do."

"I don't think most people consider it an enormity. They consider the crime that got him there to be enormous."

"I suppose. And, of course, most of them are safely removed from direct contact with what's going to happen."

"I don't think it's as simple as that, Carey."

"No, probably not. Nothing is ever that simple." She shook her hair back from her face. "Maybe I'll use that for a monologue."

"What?"

"That our hands are as dirty as Otis's."

He gave a short laugh. "That'll sure make you popular."

"Well, it's true. Whether we vocally support the death penalty, or just give it tacit approval, we're conspiring to commit cold-blooded murder."

He pushed away from the car and looked down at her. "That'll be sure to thrill your advertisers."

She shrugged.

"Look, Carey. You're very involved with the case. But you're also a good lawyer, and you know how to look at all sides of an issue. Before you go out there and accuse John Q. Citizen of conspiring to commit cold-blooded murder, maybe you ought to consider that John Q. Citizen is merely trying to wrench justice from an impossible situation."

"It won't give the Klines back their lives."

"No, it won't. And that's why the penalty is so severe. No amount of restitution can repair the damage. All we can do is exact a penalty commensurate with the crime."

He reached out and touched her cheek gently. All of a sudden, she found it impossible to breathe, impossible to move. The night wind whispered in her ears as his fingertips whispered over her skin, making her feel more alive than she had felt in a long time.

"I'm sorry," he said.

"For what?"

"That it didn't work out for us. That it got so ugly at the end."

"Breakups tend to be ugly, Seamus."

"But neither of us is an ugly person. I said things—well, I've regretted them ever since. If you happen to remember them from time to time, just tell yourself I didn't mean them. Because I didn't."

"We just weren't suited."

"No. I guess not."

They stood there looking at one another in the poor light from the streetlamps, and Carissa felt as if the night were suddenly hushed with expectancy. She waited. He waited.

And nothing happened.

Finally, she turned and slid into the car. Seamus watched while she dug her keys out of her purse, then reached out to close the door. He paused.

"When are you going to see Otis?"

She looked up at him, wondering why he should even care. "I'm going to drive up to Starke Sunday afternoon. I'll see him early Monday morning, then drive back in time to do my show."

He nodded. "I'll drive up with you."

Shock caused her heart to slam. An overreaction, surely. "Why? They won't let you see him."

"I don't want to see him."

He slammed the door without offering any explanation for why he was going with her. She hesitated, wanting to question him, but finally deciding she probably didn't want to hear his answers.

She switched on the ignition and backed out of his driveway. As she drove away, she glanced into the rearview mirror and saw him still standing there, all alone in the night.

CHAPTER 7
17 DAYS

CARISSA AWOKE IN THE MORNING FEELING WORSE than when she'd gone to bed just after two. Her eyes itched as if they were full of sand, her muscles felt leaden and achy, and her mouth felt as if a colony of moles had taken up residence. She hadn't slept well again; anxiety and fear had woven themselves into the few unpleasant dreams she had managed to have.

And Seamus. Of course, Seamus. His voice was in her

ears when her eyes opened as if he had been part of the dreams that had dogged her. He probably had been. Seeing so much of him after having convinced herself that she hated his very guts had unsettled her.

It unsettled her even more when she realized that she was looking at the lump of the pillow beside her and wanting to cry because it was just a pillow and not a shoulder. Not Seamus's shoulder. Her throat grew so tight that it hurt to breathe.

"God!" Throwing back the covers, she forced herself to get up.

Staggering across her bedroom in a body that didn't want to obey, she decided to take a run to get the blood flowing. She pulled on her shorts, sports bra, and a tank top, clipped her hair back, and headed downstairs, making up her mind that tonight she was going to take an antihistamine to help her sleep. Enough was enough.

She grabbed a bottle of water from the fridge and swallowed half of it on her way to the door. When she opened the door, the late-morning Florida heat poured over her, washing away the dregs of her energy. The sun glared, hurting her eyes, and she stood there on the threshold trying to get up the will to step out into it.

The newspaper was on her doorstep, wrapped in clear plastic, and it suggested a good excuse to stay in. She could scan it for stories for tonight's show.

She settled for the paper, deciding that in this heat she'd only drop before she ran two blocks. She picked it up and turned to go back in. That's when she saw her door.

How she had missed it when she opened it, she couldn't imagine, except possibly the sun's glare had distracted her. But facing it now, she felt herself go suddenly light-headed with anger.

Someone had spray-painted the carved wood in screaming red with the words *BLEADING HEART*.

There was a sound in her head like a dry twig snapping, and suddenly she was gasping for breath, overwhelmed by fury and fear. She didn't even reach out to see if the paint was still wet. She ran inside, closing the door with a bang and locking it.

She leaned back against it, trying to catch her breath.

It was just paint, she told herself. Graffiti. It meant nothing.

But it meant something. It meant that someone had found out who Carey Justice was, and had gone to the trouble to find out where she lived.

And that made the blood in her veins run cold.

The Pinellas County sheriff's deputy who responded to her call was pleasant, polite, and not very helpful.

"Do you know if any of your neighbors are mad at you?"

She shook her head. "I don't think so. I don't know any of them really well. We work different hours."

He made a note in his notebook. "Anybody else who might have it in for you?"

"Oh, anyone of a half million listeners to my radio show."

"You do radio?"

"Talk radio. WCST."

He looked up. "You're Carey Justice."

She nodded.

He made a note of that, too. "I listen to you sometimes."

"Anyway, I think this is linked to the shows I've been doing lately on the death penalty and John William Otis."

When he looked up again, his eyes had grown opaque. "I heard what you're doing. Stirring up a real hornet's nest."

"That's my job."

He made another note. "I guess that would explain what the 'bleeding heart' means."

"It was the first thing I thought of."

He nodded. "Well, to be quite frank, there's very little chance we'll ever catch who did this. I'll talk to your neighbors, find out if anyone saw anything, but if they didn't . . ." He shrugged. "Like you said, it could be any one of a half million people who think Otis ought to fry."

She managed to stifle a sigh. "Look, I'm not worried about the paint. I can have the door fixed. What I don't like is that someone made a connection between me and my radio persona, and they found out where I live. How would someone do that? The radio station doesn't let that information out."

He nodded, closing his notebook. "You might've given that away when you told everybody you'd worked as a prosecutor on the case. Somebody might have gone to the trouble to find out your name."

She hadn't thought of that. Damn, she hadn't thought of that.

"And of course, somebody could have followed you home from the station."

That thought gave her chills. "Not last night."

"It didn't have to be last night," he pointed out. "All I can tell you is to keep your windows and doors locked, and be cautious. If anything else happens, let us know. In the meantime, we'll try to find out something about the graffiti, but I wouldn't get your hopes up."

She nodded. "I know."

"And you might consider doing something else on your show. If you've attracted some kind of nut, that might put him off."

95

That only made her angrier. There was a little issue here called free speech.

She walked the deputy to the door. After he stepped out, he turned to face her. "Otis should fry," he said. "It's what he deserves for killing those people."

She couldn't even reply. Her face felt as stiff as if it were carved from wood.

She watched him walk out to his car, a young, swaggering buck in the white shirt and green pants of the Sheriff's Department. Like most cops, he walked as if he owned the world.

Well, she decided as she closed her door on the sight of him, maybe tonight she'd do a little show for him about police perjury and misconduct. She certainly had enough stories in her war chest to get that ball rolling.

And she could spend the evening imagining the smile being wiped off his smug young face.

The first thing she saw when she pulled into the station parking lot at a little after three that afternoon was the graffiti that covered the entire front side of the building.

Fry Otis and *Burn WCST* had been sprayed in vivid red paint across the wall, along with *Kill Justice* and *Fry Carey*. A TV crew was out front, filming the building, but she hardly saw them. She pulled into a parking slot, then sat staring at the vandalized building.

She started shaking, but not from fright. Anger filled her with white heat. If she could have gotten her hands on the people who had done this, she would have put the fear of God into them. And worse, she had the sickening feeling that this was going to be the final straw as far as the station was concerned. If Bill Hayes didn't order her to stop talking about Otis, the owners probably would.

She climbed out of the car with her laptop, her sweater,

96

and her bottled water. There was no hope of escaping recognition by the TV crew. The reporter, Adela Gutierrez, had worked with her on some promos together in the past, and of course a lot of the media people socialized at station Christmas parties.

But she *could* try to limit the damage. Before she came within camera range, she signaled to Adela that she wanted to have a private word with her Then she turned her back so that if the cameraman tried to catch her, he'd get nothing but brown hair and the back of her white blouse.

Adela wrapped up her segment, then told the cameraman to wait and not to film anything until she told him to. Hearing that, Carey turned and walked over to her.

Adela greeted her with a smile and a handshake. "You've really stirred it up this time, Carey."

"Looks like it."

"You'll give me a comment, won't you?"

"Well, that depends. I haven't talked to Bill Hayes yet, so I don't know what the station's position on this is going to be."

Adela nodded. "But you can still say what *you* think."

"On one condition. That you don't give my real name on air. I don't want some nut to know who I really am. It would be too easy to find me."

"That might be a little difficult, Carey. You have a personal tie-in to the Otis case, and you might put a lid on me, but somebody else will let it out. It's part of the story."

"The story is the vandalism."

She shook her head. "The story is that you're a former state attorney who prosecuted the case, and you still have doubts about it, doubts that you're bringing up on the air

97

to run a marathon about Otis. The vandalism is just a sidebar."

Carey's stomach sank. She hadn't thought her shows about Otis were newsworthy. And that was really dumb, she realized, because she had had the subjects of other shows turn up as news in print or on television; there was no reason she should have assumed that the media wouldn't be interested in this story.

Now she was facing a reporter who wanted a scoop for tonight's five o'clock news. If Adela was right about the thrust of the story here—and she probably was—then even if Carey refused to speak to her now, it would be all over the papers in the morning anyway.

"All right," Carey finally said. "I'll answer just one question, as long as it isn't about the station."

Adela hesitated, then nodded. "Fair enough." She pursed her lips a moment, then turned to stand beside Carey, microphone at ready. "Mike?"

The cameraman settled his minicam more firmly on his shoulder, made some adjustment and said, "Go ahead."

"I have with me WCST talk-show host Carey Justice. Carey, how do you feel about the graffiti? Are you afraid?"

"No, I'm not afraid, Adela. I'm angry. There's no need to vandalize private property. Whoever did this should have just called my show and spoken his piece."

"But what about the threats against you and the station?"

Two questions, Carey thought, but decided to answer anyway. "This is just an exercise of free speech. It goes to show that feelings run high on this issue. That's all."

Then, before Adela could ask yet another question, Carey ducked past her and headed for the door, aware that the camera followed her all the way. She could hardly wait to see how this turned out on tonight's news.

Inside, the station seemed perfectly normal. Becky Hadlov sat at the reception desk, talking on the phone. As Carey passed, Becky handed her a stack of messages, all of which were calls from reporters at area newspapers and TV stations. Great.

Becky put her hand over the mouthpiece of the telephone. "Bill wants to see you."

Of course Bill wanted to see her. He was probably going to read her the riot act. In fact, it wouldn't surprise her if he asked her to pay for repainting the front of the building. Anything seemed possible today.

"He's in the snack room," Becky called after her.

Carey switched directions and headed toward the back of the building. The snack room was usually empty at this time of day, but this afternoon it was crowded. A surprising number of show hosts were there along with Bill, as were some of the advertising and marketing people, a number of the producers, and some of the techies.

Carey stopped short. "Did I miss a meeting notice?"

Bill shook his head and pointed to an empty chair. "We're talking about the graffiti."

"Oh." She sat, putting her laptop, sweater, and bottled water on the table. She had the uncomfortable feeling that Bill was about to make an example out of her. Well, she told herself, she could always find another job.

"As I was saying," said Frank Villiers, one of the marketing people, "we're already getting ads yanked from Carey's show. National advertisers don't seem to be too concerned yet, but local advertisers are bailing out. If she stays on this topic, we'll lose an awful lot of revenue over the next few weeks."

"And it's impossible to tell how many listeners we're losing," said the marketing director. "We're not due for another ratings sweep for five weeks."

"She was topping the ratings in the last sweep," said Ted Sanders, a surprising ally from Carey's perspective. They were poles apart, politically. "I wouldn't be all that sure that a lot of people are turning her off. She's always discussed controversial issues from a liberal perspective. And the conservatives seem to love to argue with her."

Carl Dunleavy, the afternoon host, spoke. "I think we need to be reasonable here. Carey's been pushing an important issue into public awareness. And I think all of us who have shows have been seeing spillover into our programs."

Ted nodded, as did two of the other hosts.

"Which means," Carl continued, "that people probably aren't getting bored with the discussion. And if they're not getting bored, they're still listening."

The marketing director spoke again. "It only takes a few callers to light up the lines. I'm worried about the *listeners*, and so are our advertisers."

"So are the owners," Bill said. "They suggested that Carey find something else to discuss."

Only the advertising people looked happy about that. Talk radio might be entertainment, but most of the hosts and producers had strong feelings about the sanctity of their freedom of speech.

"Yesterday," Bill continued, "I was prepared to consider the cost in terms of revenue. Today I find myself considering the cost in terms of this station's automony, and our right to broadcast whatever we choose, within the bounds of decency."

Carey perked up, and looked attentively at him.

Bill waved a hand. "That graffiti really made my blood boil. I will not have our broadcast policies dictated by a group of cowardly scum who come in the dead of night to paint nasty slogans on our building. I will not have our policy decided by a few chickenshit advertisers who haven't got the gumption to support free speech."

"Hear, hear," said Ted. Carl nodded approvingly.

"So here's our policy henceforth. The graffiti will remain on the building. I'm not going to paint it over until the city threatens us with a code violation. Carey will continue to do her shows about Otis as long as she wants. And I want the rest of you to take the same tack on the air. We will *not* be silenced by cheap terror tactics."

Applause spread through the room.

"But," said one of the techies when the. applause died down, "what about safety? Especially, what about Carey's safety? These guys could get nasty."

"I've already thought about that. We're going to hire off-duty policemen to provide round-the-clock security. And if any more death threats get phoned in—"

Carey interrupted him. "Death threats?"

Bill suddenly looked uncomfortable. Carey's producer, Marge Stanton, shifted in her seat and looked apologetically at her.

"What death threats?" she repeated.

Marge spoke. "We got a couple of them last night when you were on the air."

"Why didn't you tell me?"

"I thought they were just some more crackpots. It's happened before."

"It happens all the time," Carl said reassuringly. "To all of us."

"But the station has never been vandalized before. And my home was vandalized sometime last night."

Bill looked concerned. "Your home?"

"Somebody spray-painted *bleeding heart* on my front door."

Bill's frown deepened. "We have a system that can track the phone numbers of all callers. We don't ordinarily use it, but we're going to start. That way if anyone calls in anything that sounds serious, the police can track it down, okay?"

Everyone nodded except Carey, who was beginning to feel as if she were out on a precarious limb. It wasn't the first time she'd had death threats; hell, she'd even had a few while she was a prosecutor. But never before had the threat come right to her front door. Suddenly the graffiti seemed more frightening than infuriating.

Bill looked at her, saying finally, "Your call, Carey. You can back down if you want to."

But she looked around at all the other faces, faces that were showing a surprising solidarity.

"If you don't back off, we won't," said Ted. "Hell, I'll ram it down their throats. That ought to take some of the focus off you."

"But you support the death penalty."

"Sure I do. But if you say there's a chance that John Otis is innocent, then I believe there's a chance. And while I support the death penalty, I don't ever want to see an innocent man executed."

"Me either," said Carl. A couple of the other hosts nodded.

"What's more," Ted said, "the issue is whether you have the right to have an opinion and voice it in a public forum. As some guy once said, 'I may not agree with what you say, but I'll defend to the death your right to say it.' I think most of us feel the same way. Hell, that's part of what talk radio is all about. And that's something I'm perfectly willing to go to the mat over. That's the real issue here, and I think every one of us is capable of running with it."

"That's it then," Bill said, clapping his hands to his thighs, indicating the meeting was over. "The station policy is that we will not back down from any issue. And I want each and every one of you to hammer on that, even if only for a few minutes at a time. As for our advertisers . . ." He looked at the marketing people. "You can offer them a disclaimer to be broadcast at our expense if they want it. Something to the effect that they don't necessarily support any opinions heard on the show, but that they do support the right of people to voice those opinions. Fair enough?"

Now even the ad people looked happier.

"Ed, you record the disclaimer. Carey, let me know your decision about whether you want to continue with the Otis thing."

He rose and left the snack room. The techies trailed after him, along with the advertising people until finally there were only hosts and producers left. Carey looked at them, and they looked at her.

"I'll understand if you want to drop the topic," Carl said. "*All* of us will understand. Especially since your home was vandalized. But I wish you wouldn't. Somebody has to hold back the forces of darkness."

Carey sat there after everyone had gone back to their work, thinking about it. It had seemed so simple when she started. She had wanted to be a voice of reason in a society that sometimes seemed to be maddened with bloodlust. She had just wanted people to take note of the fact that a man who might be innocent was about to die.

Now this.

Nothing in life was ever simple.

"This is Carey Justice, and you're listening to 990 WCST, Tampa Bay's number one talk radio station. Don't touch the dial, folks, and don't pick up the phones just yet. Tonight we're going to do something a little different.

"You've probably heard by now that the offices of WCST were vandalized. Apparently some people don't like the fact that I've spent the last four shows talking about John William Otis and the death penalty. Apparently some person didn't think it was enough that he could vote against me by switching to another station. He didn't think it was enough that he could call in and express his own views and argue with me.

"Instead he tried to frighten me, and tried to frighten the station into dropping the subject altogether.

"Well, you know what? John William Otis has only seventeen days left to live and I happen to think it's worth some public discussion when we, as a society, set out to take a man's life on circumstantial evidence. Now maybe you don't think so. Or maybe you think I'm crazy. That's your right, and all you have to do is pick up the phone and say so here, where everybody who's listening can hear you.

"But it's my right to speak my piece, and I'm going to speak it.

"And that's what this show is really about tonight. It's about free speech in this country, and whether we're going to give in to terrorists who want to silence us. WCST has decided that the station will not be silenced on this issue. I've decided that I won't be silenced on this issue.

"And with me tonight are three other WCST hosts and our station manager. They don't agree with my opinions, but feel just as strongly as I do that we can't allow terrorism to silence any of us.

"With me in the studio are Kel Murchison, Carl Dunleavy, and Ted Sanders, familiar to many of you from their popular programs. Also with us is Bill Hayes, our station manager. Bill, I believe you wanted to open this evening."

"Thank you, Carey. I want to make it perfectly clear to our listeners that WCST is solidly behind free speech on the airwaves. It is our policy that neither our hosts nor our station will give in to efforts of any kind to silence us on issues that we feel are of public interest. We most especially won't give in to cowardly public interest.

"It is the position of WCST radio that our entire purpose is to present a variety of opinions to the public. In fact, that's what talk radio is all about. If we start allowing a small group of people to dictate what is and isn't suitable subject matter, then we won't be talk radio anymore, we'll be *propaganda* radio.

"This station is not about to allow that to happen."

Carey cut straight away to commercial, and Kel looked over at Bill. "So that means I can talk about the poor quality of the pasties the girls at After Midnight wear?"

Bill rolled his eyes, and everyone else laughed, easing some of the tension that had inexplicably built.

During the next segment, each of the other hosts voiced his view about the vandalism in a give-and-take discussion among themselves. After the next break, the phones were opened.

The first two callers offered strong support for the station's policy. Carey found herself thinking that this was going to be an awfully boring show if nobody but cheerleaders called in. What she needed was one of her favorite wackos to call in and argue *against* the policy.

The third call woke them all up.

"Go ahead, caller."

"I'm gonna kill you, you fuckin' bitch!"

Carey hit the disconnect and the dump button at the same time, silently repeating the caller's words to tell the computer just how much to excise out of the tape delay. The listeners wouldn't even know something had happened, although the computer would now subtly slow down the broadcast until it had once again built up the delay.

As soon as she released the dump, she punched another call button. "Caller? Are you there?"

"Yeah, I'm here," said the familiar voice of one of her favorite wackos, J.D. from Lutz. "Y'know, all this high-falutin talk about freedom of speech is just a load of bull."

"You think so, J.D?"

"I know so! Freedom of speech is only to protect the citizens from government interference. It don't give no radio station any right to say anything if the people don't like it."

"The people can always change the station."

"Yeah, that's the same crap they say about television. Turn the channel if you don't like it. You ever tried to turn the channel, Carey?"

"I don't watch much, I'm afraid."

"Well, give it a try sometime. It's the same crap on every channel. People wearin' no clothes, people swearing and cursin' words I don't want my kids to hear. Put on a kids' show and you know what you find?"

"Afraid not, J.D."

"You find some Spic teachin' 'em all to talk Spanish, that's what. And it's the same with the damn radio. I change the stations and what have I got? That crazy music teachin' the kids to love the devil. Or that highbrow crap that sounds like a bunch of old ladies with a bellyache. Or some preacher trying to steal the last ten bucks off some widow."

Carey didn't dare look up. She could hear the stifled laughs from the others in the studio with her. "Gee, J.D., it sounds like you don't like very much."

"I'm particular about what I do with my time."

"I can see that. But is it really so bad if your kids learn a couple of words of Spanish?"

"I don't want them learnin' no furrin words! English is good enough for American kids. You start givin' them Spics an inch, and they'll take a mile."

"Well, they were kind of here before us, J.D. And there's an awful lot of them living here now. It would be neighborly to learn a few words of their language."

"Neighborly? What's that got to do with it? They're livin' in the U.S. of A., and we speak English here. They don't like it, let 'em go back to Cuba."

"Some of them have been living here longer than we have."

"So what? We own it now."

"You know, J.D., you're the kind that gives redneck a bad name."

"So I'm a redneck. And I'm damn proud of it."

"I know quite a few rednecks who don't feel the way you do."

"Well, I don't. You wanna live here, you gotta live the American way."

"But Americans come from all over the world, J.D. From every place you can think of."

"So? That don't mean they don't have to be American when they get here."

"So what you're saying is that you don't believe in free speech?"

"Oh, I believe in free speech all right. Course I do. That's the American way. But it don't mean some Goody Two-shoes like you can get on a radio station and tell us all the law is wrong."

"Why not? You're getting on here to tell us it's right, aren't you? Isn't that what free speech is about?"

"It ain't about criticizing the guv'ment or the American way."

"But if we never criticize, then we don't really have free speech, do we?"

"You just don't get it, do you? I'm tellin' you, love it or leave it. You don't like it here, move on. But don't sit there at your fancy microphone fillin' the airwaves with crap about how the law is doing somethin' wrong. Otis murdered those people, and if the state don't fry him, I might get a mind to go huntin' him with my shotgun. Scum like him don't deserve to live."

"On that score, I think a lot of people agree with you, J.D."

"Course they do. That's why we got the law."

She cut him off and moved on to the next caller. To her relief, the show picked up after that, and the issue had become free speech and whether she had a right to exercise it about the Otis case. It put an interesting spin on a subject that even she had realized was apt to wear thin before long.

It helped, too, that the other hosts joined in, giving a different direction with their divergent opinions. At the first news break, Bill rose to leave and told them all to keep it up.

"It's hot," he said. "It's really hot. Good going, guys."

"I thought you were going to stay," Carey said.

He shook his head. "I'm going to find out about that caller who made the threat."

"It was just a crank," she said. But the truth was, she didn't quite believe that. Not when she had graffiti on her front door.

"Maybe. But somebody's gonna put the fear of God into him."

"He's right, Carey," Carl said after Bill left. "Somebody

should at least check into it. It won't hurt."

"If somebody really wants to kill me, I don't think they're going to announce it on the radio."

Kel gave a snort of laughter. "Hey, you used to work with criminals. You're not going to tell me they weren't stupid enough to do just that."

Carey wished she could disagree with him, but she couldn't. In her experience as a prosecutor, she'd learned just how dumb some criminals could be.

The thought was enough to keep her from going outside to have a cigarette.

CHAPTER 8
17 DAYS

WHEN SHE EMERGED FROM THE STATION THAT NIGHT, the first person she encountered was the off-duty cop Bill had promised would be there. The next person was Seamus Rourke.

He was leaning against his car, wearing white shorts, a black polo shirt, and Top-Siders. He had the sexiest legs she'd ever seen on a man, and if she hadn't known better, she might have wondered if he was wearing those shorts on purpose.

"What's up?" she asked as she approached.

"Oh, a little of this and a little of that. I heard about the death threat you got tonight. I also heard that it hasn't been the first one."

"Who the hell told you that?"

He flashed a smile. "Ve haff eyes everyvhere."

"Right."

"So okay. Your station manager called to report the threats, and a little birdy mentioned it to me."

"No secrets in the St. Pete Police Department, huh?"

"Nary a one. We have the best grapevine this side of prison. Anyway, I don't like the idea of you going home alone tonight. I figured I'd ride shotgun. Especially since your place was vandalized last night."

She put her hands on her hips. "Just when did I become the major subject of discussion on, the police grapevine?"

"Along about the time you started saying maybe John Otis was innocent. Come on, Carey, you had to know you were going to get attention with this stunt."

"It isn't a stunt."

He shrugged. "Bad choice of word. My point is, when a former prosecutor starts saying the system screwed up, a lot of people get interested. Cops. Prosecutors. Assholes with a kink. You name it. You made the five o'clock news, the six o'clock news, and the ten o'clock news tonight. Your name seems to be on every tongue. Which helps lubricate the grapevine."

"Well, I can look out for myself. I've been doing it for a long time, Seamus."

"Yup. And I'm a male chauvinist pig who thinks a guy with a gun is better protection than an attitude. So sue me. And cut out the bravado. If you've got half a brain in your head—and I know you do—you ought to be relieved that you don't have to go home alone tonight."

She hated it when he was right. So she looked him over, as if making an assessment. "I don't see your gun."

"It's in the glove compartment."

"I feel ever so much safer."

"I knew you would. I'll follow you. Just don't try to lose me. It aggravates me when people do that."

"Aren't you going to check out my car first?" she asked, with an exaggerated bat of her eyelashes. The worst of it was, as annoyed as she was at him for scaring her by taking

110

the threat seriously, he was still making her want to laugh.

"I already did, Counselor. Let's go."

She *did* feel a whole lot better knowing he was behind her as she drove up I-275. Much as she had been refusing to face it, the fact was that dread had been steadily building in her since the threatening phone call. She'd been playing mind games, tying to pretend she didn't care, but the tightness in every one of her muscles told her that her body wasn't listening.

Of course, she would rather have hit her thumb with a hammer than admit that to Seamus. In many respects he was a caring, sensitive, modern man, but in others he was a definite throwback to the caveman. Heaven forbid she should pander to his male ego.

Twenty minutes later, they pulled into her driveway It was getting near midnight, but it was Friday night, and some of the lights in the houses around were still on. As she pulled up into the carport, she glanced at her door and wondered with an uneasy lurch of her stomach what was all over It now. it looked like a bunch of white rectangles.

She climbed out and waited for Seamus to join her on the sidewalk. He was carrying his gun now.

"Maybe I'd better go first," he said.

"Why? You think a bunch of nastygrams is going to kill me?"

"You don't know what might be written on them."

"They're not sticks and stones," she said, referring to the old nursery rhyme.

"Maybe not, but words can do a damn fine job of scaring you."

"Just how far are you going to carry this protection business? You want me to climb into a bell jar you can put on the mantlepiece?"

"I don't have a fireplace." He shook his head. "Okay,

okay, but don't say I didn't try to spare you."

"I'd rather know what I'm up against."

When they got to the stoop, they could see that a variety of envelopes were taped to the door with cellophane tape. None of them had anything written on the outside.

"We shouldn't touch them," Seamus said. "Fingerprints."

"Now I need the St. Pete PD to open my mail? I think not."

"Carey, you of all people should know better than to ruin potential evidence."

Just then the door of the next town house opened and her neighbor, Julius Blandford, stepped out.

"Are you all right, Carey? I heard voices."

"I'm fine, Julius. This is Seamus Rourke, with the police." The last thing she wanted was to have her neighbors gossiping about the fact that she'd brought a man home at midnight.

"Oh. That's good. We're all kind of worried about you. We saw your door."

"Ugly, isn't it? Anyway, we're just trying to decide what to do about all these envelopes. Do you have any idea who put them here?"

"Sure. Folks from around here. Maybe something from the property owners' association about getting the door fixed." He chuckled. "You know how they are. No violations allowed."

"Well, the insurance adjuster can't get out here until Monday morning, so they'll have to wait at least that long."

"Like it's a crisis or something. If you need anything, just holler. We're all trying to keep an eye out for you."

"Thanks, Julius. Thanks an awful lot."

"It's the least neighbors can do. I just wish one of us had seen the guy who did it." He said good night and went back inside.

Carey reached for the envelopes and pulled all ten of them off the door. "I think that settles the fingerprint issue."

"Probably."

They stepped inside and Carey dumped her laptop and sweater on the lowboy beside the door. "Decaf?"

"In a minute. Call me paranoid, but I want to check out the house first. You just wait here by the door. If you hear anything suspicious, run like hell."

She didn't think he was being paranoid, though she didn't say so. Truth was, it made her feel good that he was going to look around before he left her here alone. She didn't even mind that he was going to be looking into the private places of her life.

He was back in less than ten minutes, gun holstered. "Everything looks fine. Windows are locked, closets are empty, no bogeyman under the beds."

"Thanks." She carried the envelopes into the kitchen, where she tossed them on the table, then set about making a pot of coffee. She was hungry, too, not having eaten since a light meal just before she left for work, so she pulled out the griddle, whipped some eggs and milk together, and began to make French toast.

"So tell me," Seamus said, "how do you get it to brown just right? I never do."

"What? The toast? I don't know. Patience, I guess. How many slices do you want?"

"Four. Five. I'm starved."

She melted butter on the griddle, then slapped the first four slices of soaked bread on, sprinkling them generously with cinnamon. By then the coffee was done, and she carried a couple of mugs to the table, where she sat and began to open the envelopes.

One by one she read the brief notes, and one by one she passed them to Seamus. By the time she finished, her eyes were damp. Ten of her neighbors had taken the time to pen her notes telling her they were sorry her door had been vandalized, assuring her they didn't share the opinion of the vandal, and promising to keep an eye on her property.

"Nice neighborhood," Seamus remarked as he set the last one aside.

"It's sure a pleasant contrast to what I found on my door this morning."

"I'm working a case in a different kind of neighborhood now. Everybody swears they didn't see a thing, and I don't believe them."

"The one where that young man was shot while he was riding his bicycle?"

"The same. You know something about it?"

"Only what was in the papers."

She went to flip the toast, then leaned back against the counter. "Did you find out anything about the Summers case?"

"Nothing you didn't already know. The nightgown that was slashed didn't belong to her. Somebody broke in through glass patio doors in the back of the house, out of sight of any neighbors or passersby. No prints left behind. They're still checking out the carpet sweepings, but it probably won't help much. She entertains a lot."

Carey snorted. "Yeah. A lot from what I hear."

"So it was probably an angry ex-boyfriend. Summers thinks it was something to do with her—and I quote—'hard-hitting investigative series about the local drug trade.'"

"She would."

He gave her a crooked smile. "Why do I get the feeling you don't like her?"

"Because she's a blond bimbo who mistakes poorly thought-out opinion pieces for being real reportage."

"Ouch. The claws are out tonight."

"At least I have the sense to realize that what I do is entertainment."

"You could have fooled me the last few days."

She shrugged, not liking him very much at the moment. "So I picked up an issue I care about. I wasn't deluded enough to think that was news."

"It's news now."

"Not my fault."

He leaned back in his chair and sipped his coffee, regarding her steadily. "It is your fault," he said finally. "You're never going to convince me you don't know exactly how much power you wield when you get behind that microphone. On any night of the week, you have a half million listeners. There aren't many people who can claim that kind of podium. When you pick a topic of major public interest, your *show* becomes news."

"A sidebar. All I do is provide a forum."

"You've been doing more than that the last few days. And you know it as well as I do, Carey. You've picked the issue, and you've campaigned for it. You didn't just throw it out for public discussion. You had an agenda."

"So?"

"So it's news when somebody with that big a podium starts campaigning on a particular issue. If you were talking about people who insist on passing someone who's just put his turn signal on, that might not draw a whole lot of attention. But you're talking about how the death penalty is applied in this state, which is a screamingly hot political issue, and you're using all the might of your microphone to do it. You become the news along with the issue, and I don't for one moment believe you thought you were merely being entertaining."

She gave up the battle and put the French toast on a plate. She put another three slices on the griddle to brown, one more for Seamus and two for herself. He was right, of course. And more than once she had used her show in ways that didn't have solely to do with entertainment. Much as she liked to believe herself a cynic, she often came uncomfortably close to playing Don Quixote.

"You can't make the whole world play fair, Carey."

She felt her shoulders and neck stiffen with resistance. "I know that."

"Do you?" He sighed audibly, and she heard his chair scrape on the floor as he moved. "I think you keep *trying* to tell yourself that."

She didn't want to look at him. Seamus had always had an uncanny knack for finding the parts of her that made her most uncomfortable.

It was a minute or so before he spoke again. "You never told me exactly why you resigned from the State Attorney's Office. Was it because of the Otis verdict?"

She wanted to say that it had been, but that wouldn't have been truthful. There had been a time when she had cared enough about Seamus's opinion of her to shade the truth, but not anymore. He had hurt her as much as he could hurt her, and had told her what he really thought of her, and it didn't matter anymore. She couldn't *let* it matter.

"The verdict was the next-to-last straw," she said, watching steam rise from the griddle as the toast cooked. "But at the time . . . at the time I was confused about it. I wasn't really certain that I was right. I mean . . . wiser heads than mine thought Otis was guilty. So. . ." She trailed off and tilted her head back a little, drawing a deep breath. "So I doubted my own feelings about it. And I was a chicken."

"Chicken? What more could you have done?"

"Just about anything!"

"What do you mean?"

"I mean I could have made some of those arguments I drove you crazy with to someone who could have done something about them!"

When he at last spoke, he sounded almost tentative, like a man who knew he was stepping into a minefield. "You. . . didn't share those arguments at work?"

"I not only didn't share them, I never even mentioned that I had doubts!" Her voice was sharp with anger, grief, guilt, and self-loathing. She sounded like a woman on the edge of hysterics and maybe she was.

"I thought . . ."

She knew exactly what he thought. Night after night she had come home and dumped her doubts, arguments, and objections on him. Why wouldn't he assume she was making the same case at work?

"Actually," she said, her voice thick, "I never said a word."

"Why not?"

"Because! Because it was my first death-penalty case! What the hell did I know about it? I was a gofer, go here, go there, take a deposition, check a story, answer a motion with a specified argument—I had no autonomy! Worse, I'd bought into the prosecutorial mind-set. Charge and try, charge and try, to hell with what kind of case you've got, just put it in front of a jury. Let the jury decide. Let the judge decide. Our job was just to make sure we charged everybody and tried everybody. It wasn't our job to decide who was guilty. That was somebody else's burden. Our job was just to do our damnedest to make everybody else think the guy was guilty."

"I . . . see."

"No, I don't think you do. Do you know how many cases get settled by plea bargain when we know damn well we don't have a case strong enough for conviction? Loads of them, Seamus. Put a weak case in front of the prosecutor, and he or she will play a game of poker with the defendant, and win more often than not simply because the defendant isn't willing to take the risk that the jury might convict him anyway, and he might get a worse sentence. We play God with people's lives every single hour of the day, and count on them being too scared or too poor to really fight us. Finally, we even have ourselves convinced that they wouldn't plead out if they weren't guilty.

"Well let me tell you, that's one of the biggest delusions in the legal system. But the biggest delusion of all is the one the judge and jury have, that the defendant wouldn't be in court if he hadn't committed the crime. The nicest part of that one is that a prosecutor can tell herself that the judge or jury wouldn't have convicted if the guy weren't guilty. It's an easy, comfortable way to look at the system and you get to buying in to the whole idea that where there's smoke there must be fire. The guy was arrested, so he must have done something."

"Most of the time that's probably true."

"I'm glad you're so sure of that, because I'm sure as hell not." She turned and faced him. "Then comes the Otis case. I'm already believing the idea that if the guy was arrested, he probably did it. But the case was so weak, we tried a plea bargain. Did you know that? But the defense attorney said we didn't have a leg to stand on, John Otis said he didn't do it and wouldn't say he did, and the media got so hot to trot that the State Attorney figured he'd never get reelected if he didn't go to trial for the death penalty."

Seamus nodded, saying nothing.

"So we go forward with the prosecution. From the instant that decision was made, no word of doubt was allowed. Why not? Because the jury would decide. It would be on the jury's head. And honest to God, Seamus, I never thought any jury would send a man to death on that lousy case. I got through the entire pretrial and trial periods by believing that twelve honest men and women couldn't possibly execute a man based on circumstantial evidence, not without one scintilla of real physical evidence to link the man to the murders. God, I was so wrong!"

"Carey . . ."

But she turned her back on him and flipped the French toast with angry movements. She didn't want to look at him right now. "And all the way through that, I'd come home at night and express my doubts and you'd argue with me. You'd tell me I was thinking with my heart, not my mind. You'd tell me I wasn't being logical. You'd tell me I was *wrong*! Well, I was twenty-nine years old, with only four years as a lawyer under my belt, and I honest to God didn't have enough confidence to stand up and object when the whole damn world was telling me just how wrong I was.

"And for that I am never, ever going to forgive myself!"

"Jesus." He spoke the word softly, almost prayerfully.

She suddenly felt tired, beaten. When she spoke, her voice was heavy. "Worst of all, I was just simply afraid of losing my job."

His chair scraped again, and the next thing she knew, his hands were on her shoulders, squeezing gently. "I'm sorry."

119

She couldn't even make herself answer. There wasn't enough air in the room to fill her lungs. She tried to draw a breath, and her diaphragm refused to budge. Her throat tightened until it hurt, and not even to save her life could she have made a sound.

"I'm sorry," he said again, and turned her around. He pulled her gently against his chest, wrapped her in his strong arms and held her close, as if he wanted to shelter her from all of life's outrageousness. "I'm sorry. I didn't understand. . . ."

She refused to cry. Much as it would have eased the tightness in her chest and the ache in her throat, she refused to give in. She had cried her eyes out for many nights when she and Seamus had split, and she hadn't cried once since then. She wasn't about to start now, and she wasn't about to do it in his arms. Ever.

But she couldn't force herself to draw away from the haven he offered, a haven she needed more than she had realized. Her self-image of a competent, independent, cynical, tough, hard-nosed entertainer had just been stripped away, and she wanted to hate him for it.

But she couldn't.

He had touched the throbbing nerve that had been torturing her since word of the death warrant had reached her, and the pain had blossomed into an all-consuming agony. None of the words she so easily tossed about had really expressed what it was that was hurting her.

She had helped sentence a man to death, and she hadn't done one little thing to prevent it. She hadn't once spoken up where it might have counted. She hadn't even refused to be a party to the case. Instead she had gone along in cowardly cooperation, always reassuring herself that at some point the system would see what she saw, and John Otis would not be sent to death. For the last five years, she had promised herself that one of his appeals would triumph.

Instead, his death warrant had been signed, and now, when it was too late to save him, she didn't think she was going to be able to live with herself ever again. She was guilty of the worst possible crime of conscience, the crime of silence. The crime of going along. The crime of expecting others to do what she didn't have the gumption to do herself.

And there was no way to make it better.

"You can't blame yourself," Seamus said. He lifted a hand and stroked her hair gently. "Sweetie, even if you'd shot off your mouth until you got fired, the case would have gone forward. You're right, it was a political hot potato. No amount of protest would have kept it from going to trial. What you did or didn't do had no effect on the outcome."

She sucked in a large gasp of air and pulled her head away from his shoulder. She couldn't stand him right now. Rationalization was an ugly thing, and no matter how he rationalized for her, there was no escaping the fact that she had failed in her ethical duty as a lawyer and her moral responsibility as a human being.

She turned away and tossed the French toast onto the plates, then switched off the stove. When she turned again to face him, with a plate in each hand, her face was as composed as a stone sculpture. "You like syrup, don't you?"

He nodded, watched her closely, as if he were afraid she was going to explode into a million pieces of screaming, deadly shrapnel.

She carried the plates to the table, set them down, then moved briskly to get silverware and more coffee for them. When at last she sat facing him, she spread her napkin on her lap and kept her eyes fixed on her plate.

"Delicious," Seamus remarked several mouthfuls later. "Thank you."

He used the edge of the fork to slice off another piece of toast. "So," he said slowly, "what was the *last* straw?"

She looked up. "What do you mean?"

"You said the verdict was the next-to-last straw."

"Oh." she turned her head to the side, looking at the bow window, wishing it weren't night so she could see the small garden that always gave her a sense of peace. "Well, it was nothing, really. I was assigned a felony case. The charge was battery on a law enforcement officer."

She glanced his way, giving him a wry smile. "Around the courthouse, do you know what the conventional wisdom is about Batt-LEO? They say it means the cop used excessive force and is trying to cover it up."

He grimaced. "I won't say it never happens."

"Oh, it happens all right. And I had a case of it. The defendant was covered with bruises that competent medical authority said could only have happened if he'd been hit by a heavy, blunt instrument, or dropped from a height of six feet. The cops said they never touched him, that all they did was wrestle him to the ground. They said the bruises were already there, and that the defendant complained about them when he got out of the car, even though a half dozen witnesses testified he'd been just fine a couple of hours before. After the beating the guy couldn't even walk. It was so bad they took him to the emergency room.

"What's more, the defendant's companion backed up his story that the cop just started whaling on him. Nor were the cops trying to arrest the guy. He'd merely been a passenger in a vehicle stopped for speeding. So why would this guy get in a fight with the cops?"

"It happens."

"Maybe. But it also turns out the cop and the defendant have a long, unpleasant social history."

He nodded. "Not so good."

"That's what I thought. Anyway, the cop was adamant the guy was drunk and hit him, but insisted he never hit back. The cop's partner was so vague on what happened that it was downright suspicious. So I refused to prosecute the case."

"And then?"

"They turned it over to someone else and the guy got four years for hitting the cop. So I quit. I couldn't stomach it anymore. Cops lie and juries believe them. I've seen it time and again."

"It happens," he said. "I won't deny it. Cops are just people, and some are more ethical than others."

"Yeah." She shook her head. "The problem is, they're supposed to be *better*. They're supposed to be upholding the law."

"I won't argue with that." He stirred a piece of French toast around in a puddle of syrup, then put his fork down. "I can see why you got disillusioned."

She shrugged a shoulder and pushed her own plate aside. Her appetite had died somewhere during her discourse on the Otis case. "My fault. I was too damn idealistic when I got out of law school. I should have known that human nature would get in the way. So how's your dad? Did he get into treatment?"

"By eleven o'clock this morning. He actually seemed glad to go."

"Maybe he was. Living with your disapproval isn't easy."

He winced, and the look he gave her was pained. "I suppose you know all about that."

"I suppose I do."

He sighed and shoved his plate away. "I guess I deserve that."

She shrugged again.

"So you see me as a self-righteous son of a bitch?"

"I wouldn't say self-righteous. But you are always *right*."

"Same difference."

She shook her head and lifted her coffee mug, cradling it in both hands.

"Look, I was wrong, the way I reacted to your doubts about Otis. I'm not saying the guy wasn't guilty as sin. I'm just saying that I was wrong how I responded to you. I assumed you were making all those arguments at work, for one thing. And I assumed the reason you were making them to me was that you wanted me to bolster your belief that the guy was guilty. I thought I was being supportive."

She looked at him in disbelief.

He held up a hand, as if to say, *I know it sounds stupid.*

All of a sudden she gave him a sad smile. "I wonder how many other times one of us was guilty of bad assumptions.

"Damned if I know."

Carey continued to look at him feeling a terrible ache for what might have been. Too late. So many things in life came too late. "I'm sorry, but I didn't get through to the IRS today."

"Doesn't matter. Whenever is probably soon enough. The old man is so deep in shit right now, he needs a snorkel."

"Why are you so angry with him, Seamus? Just because of his drinking?"

"Isn't that enough?"

She cocked her head. "I wouldn't have thought so. I'd have expected you to feel pity for him, not this kind of anger."

He looked down, visibly hesitating. Then he said, "Well, he was driving the car when my daughter was killed."

Carey felt a current of shock run down her spine. It was as if the world suddenly went still and cold. "I thought—I thought there was a drunk driver. I thought your wife was driving when they were hit."

He shook his head. "Danny was driving. He was visiting for the weekend, and she asked him to drive because Seana was having convulsions from a high fever. Mary didn't want to be driving because she couldn't watch the baby in case she stopped breathing."

She nodded. "It makes sense." She waited for him to say what he always said: *I should have been there.* But Seamus had been on a stakeout, and matters had apparently happened so rapidly that Mary hadn't even tried to get ahold of him. He blamed himself for that, and had never stopped blaming himself for it. His constant, heavy burden of guilt had been one of the things to come between them.

But he didn't say he should have been there. Not this time. Instead he continued. "Danny had had a couple of beers earlier. He always had a couple after he finished work. The blood test showed he wasn't legally drunk at the time of the accident but . . ." He looked away.

"But maybe he could have reacted faster," she supplied for him. She could understand how that might plague him.

"Mary didn't put Seana in her car seat," Seamus continued. "I guess she was in too much of a hurry to go, and didn't want to pull it out of her car. I don't know."

And suddenly, for the first time, Carey understood why Mary Rourke had hanged herself a few short weeks after the accident. The woman had blamed herself. The baby

125

had probably died only because she hadn't been in the car seat when the drunk driver had hit them. The child had probably been flung violently around in the car, ripped right out of her mother's arms, most likely. Maybe even thrown through the windshield. Danny and Mary had walked away with minor injuries, but the baby had died. And then Mary had killed herself.

She reached out suddenly, covering Seamus's hand with hers and squeezing, trying to convey her sympathy. For the first time she understood the full magnitude of the load he was carrying. It was far more complicated than Seamus's previous explanation that his child had died in a car accident caused by a drunk driver, and that his wife had hanged herself from grief. And all of it might have been avoided if Seamus had been home that night. No wonder he felt so guilty.

And now *she* felt guilty, too. How different might things have been if she had just once asked him for details about what had happened to his family? But she hadn't dared ask, because she had feared treading in places where she wasn't welcome. Because she had feared raking up the cooling ashes of his grief. Because she had feared causing him more pain. Because she had known him to be reserved about things he felt deeply, and she had feared his reaction to her curiosity. God, what a fool and a coward she had been!

So she had never really understood what he was suffering, and because she hadn't understood, she had come to resent it.

"I'm so sorry," she said, speaking the inadequate words because there was nothing else she *could* say.

His face had taken on a tension she recognized. He was struggling with strong emotion. "It was bad enough aboutthe baby," he said, his voice thick. "Bad enough. But

I didn't realize—I was so wrapped up in my own grief—if I had just known—" He shook his head. "I should have realized she was suicidal."

"Did she tell you she was? Did she say anything at all about it?"

"I don't know. That's what's so goddamn awful about it, Carey! I don't know. I was in a fog, and I just don't know!" He stood up suddenly.

"I'd better go. You'll be okay, won't you?"

"Yes, of course . . ." She rose with him and followed him to the door, feeling a desperate need to do something to help him, but she didn't know what. "Seamus? Will you be all right?"

He paused at the door and looked down at her. "I'll never be all right again. But I've survived these seven years, so I guess I'll just continue surviving."

He opened the door and stepped out. "I'll pick you up on Sunday morning to go to Starke, okay?"

"Okay."

She watched him walk to his car, then closed the door, locking the night out. It was a symbolic gesture, and it didn't do a damn bit of good.

CHAPTER 9
16 DAYS

THERE WERE TIMES WHEN JOHN WILLIAM OTIS WAS convinced that he was the only sane person in the world. He'd felt that way throughout most of his childhood, a period he refused to remember because it only brought pain. He had lived in an insane world where he had been tortured and starved by the man who had given him life. He figured no amount of thinking was ever going to make him understand that irony, so he just left it alone.

He also figured one of the sanest things he'd ever done in his life was kill his father. As he'd approached manhood, as his body had started to change, he'd seen the way his father was beginning to look at his baby brother.

He'd worried about it, trying to figure out what he could do to protect Jamie, but after all the abuse he'd suffered, he hadn't grown strong or big, and there was no way he could have bested the man in a fight. So he'd thought and thought, and no answers had come to him. It had never occurred to him that he might turn to a teacher or a neighbor for help. At some point in his childhood, he'd begun to believe that all the adults in the world knew exactly what his father was doing to him and to Jamie, and that they approved. It had seemed the whole world was on his father's side.

Of course, he knew better now, but by the time he had learned that he was wrong, it had been too late. He'd already killed the man, and he had never once regretted it because he had saved Jamie once and for all. Never again had he needed to throw himself between his father and brother to spare Jamie the blows of the fists and belt. Never again would he have to draw his father's wrath onto his own head to save his baby brother. For that he would gladly have gone to the chair.

Nobody had been more surprised than young John Otis when he had been acquitted of murdering his father.

For a while, during the years that he had lived with Harvey and Linda Kline, the rest of the world had seemed to become sane. For the very first time in his life, he had had someone to look after *him*, someone who really seemed to care about him.

Then they had been killed, and the world had gone insane again. Not that he thought his conviction had been crazy. No, if the jury really believed he had done it, then the death penalty was the sanest choice they could have made.

It didn't even strike him as insane that he'd been convicted of a crime he didn't commit. It was his own fault he'd been convicted, anyway. He could have placed the blame where it really belonged, but he refused to. He let them think what they would, and had no one to blame but himself.

But the world was going crazy again, and he found himself watching it happen with a kind of detachment. His guards watched him constantly, afraid he might try to kill himself.

The thought never entered his mind. He wasn't afraid of Old Sparky. He heard death by electrocution could be painful, and sometimes the chair didn't work right, but he wasn't really worried about it. He was a sane man, after all, and it seemed to him that being electrocuted had to be a lot quicker than hanging himself, or stabbing himself with that little stub of pencil they let him have, and quicker was better, any way you looked at it.

Nor was he afraid of the pain. He'd stopped being afraid of pain in early childhood, when the whole world had been a haze of pain, both physical and emotional. Pain was something he could endure, and he figured there was no way that Old Sparky could be any worse than having your father burn you again and again with a hot iron.

What he was afraid of, really afraid of, was dying. Pain or no pain, he couldn't make it happen any sooner am it absolutely had to. Sometimes at night, when he lay sleepless on his cot, fear made his skin crawl as if a thousand bugs were running over him and he'd have to jump up and pace his shadowy cell. The daytime was easier, because there were a whole lot of things he could do to distract himself, but in the night there was nothing but the quailing of his mind and the companionship of death. Sometimes it was all he could do not to scream out that he didn't want to die.

It didn't help that the preacher told him he'd go to heaven where everything would be beautiful because he wasn't sure of that. He'd killed a man. He'd killed his own *father,* and not even in the deepest moments of self-examination had he been able to find any honest regret over that.

So he was an unrepentant sinner, and God was just another father who might torture him for eternity. Sometimes, in the dead of night, he even thought he could smell the approaching fire and brimstone.

But they still thought he might try to kill himself sooner anyway, and they never let him out of their sight for long. He wondered why they couldn't see the absurdity of it. He was sentenced to die, so it really should make no difference whether it was by his own hand or by theirs, but they evidently thought it made a great big difference. After all, if he killed himself, he would escape his punishment. That was such a crazy way to look at it that he was apparently the only person in the world sane enough to see it.

They wouldn't even let him see Carissa Stover alone. They were nice though. When he said he wanted to see her in his cell, they agreed, instead of insisting he go to one of the visiting rooms. He wondered if they understood his attachment to his cell. Probably not. They couldn't understand that it was the only home of his own he'd ever had. That it was as familiar and comfortable to him as their living rooms were to them. That he needed the security of his few possessions because he had nothing else in the world he could call his own.

Nor did he especially care whether they understood. All that mattered was that, within the limits set on them by his being a prisoner, they were doing their best to make his last few days on earth as pleasant as possible.

Except for the constant watching. He felt it starting to grate on his nerves, but he let go of the irritation. Life was definitely too short to let something so minor shadow his last hours.

He figured he'd been born to die young. It was his fate. Why else had all his appeals failed so swiftly when there were men here on death row who'd been awaiting execution for much longer? Hell, one of them had been here ever since John Otis had been eight years old.

Fate had carried him through the process faster than any of the rest of them, so he had decided it must be God's will, just retribution for his sin of patricide. But just or not, he ached for all the things he would never see, all the things he would never do, all the poems he would never write.

He loved life, though there had been little in his life to love. And now it had all come down to this, that a visit from a woman who had helped put him on death row should seem welcome, as wonderful as a present on Christmas morning.

He cleaned his cell, making sure it was spotless. It had been a long time since he'd had a visitor, Even his attorney had seemed to have forgotten he was still alive.

But Carissa Stover hadn't forgotten. He remembered her in the courtroom during his trial, a young, trim woman in a no-nonsense navy blue suit, with soft brown hair and wide hazel eyes that had kept darting his way as if she were looking for something. He'd always wondered what it was she wanted. Maybe she had expected him to sprout horns or start vomiting pea soup? Maybe she'd been scared of him? He didn't think so.

And today he was going to ask her. The other lawyers had never really looked at him. The jury had never really looked at him. At times during the trial, he'd honestly believed he was invisible, except to Carissa Stover.

And depending on what she said today, he might even show her his poems. For now he tucked the book under his mattress, out of sight. If she had come just to get something sensational for her radio show, he wasn't going to let her see it, that was for sure. It was too private, too personal. After he was dead he wouldn't be able to hide it any longer,, but while he was alive it was for him to say who could come into that private place.

Breakfast, eggs and grits, wouldn't settle in his stomach. He was nervous, he realized. It had been a long time since last he'd felt this nervous. Of course, this was the first time since the trial that he would come face-to-face with someone who had helped put him here.

Given that, he thought she must believe him to be some kind of monster, because only a monster would kill the only two people in the whole world who had really loved him.

So why was she coming to see him?

Then, with patience he had learned the hard way, he settled down to wait.

The guards were nice enough, Carey thought. They searched her thoroughly, but they let her take a microcassette recorder with her into John Otis's cell, after they checked it out. They'd probably search him from head to foot, and turn his cell inside out after she left, to make sure he hadn't managed to get something from her that he shouldn't have. She wondered if he'd gotten used to that indignity. If anyone could get used to it.

Seamus had hardly said a word to her since he picked her up yesterday. His silence had added to her uneasiness, making her wonder if he disapproved of this visit, then making her wonder why she should care. His opinion didn't matter anymore.

But he did that sometimes. She remembered all too well how he would go into these silent periods, brooding and saying nothing. It might have nothing at all to do with her, and everything to do with memories he had raked up on Friday night. They were certainly memories better left buried.

She was wearing navy blue slacks and a cool cotton blouse, and she refrained from looking into other cells as she passed. And, unlike the movies, no one called out anything to her as she passed by in the company of a guard. No one said anything at all. This building, crowded with people who were the dregs of society, felt as empty as a tomb. It was as if the eyes of ghosts were on her.

John Otis looked very much as she remembered him. He was slight, barely taller than she, with a face prematurely old. His light brown hair was cut very short, and his prison clothes bagged on his slender frame, as if he had lost weight, or as if they had nothing small enough to fit him.

His sleeves were short, and his arms still bore the scars of burns and lacerations from his childhood. From what she had read of his past, she imagined most of his body was covered with similar scars.

But his blue eyes were bright, almost childlike and warm as he smiled at her.

"I never expected to see you again," he said. He didn't approach her, as if he thought she might be frightened of him. So she crossed the small space and offered to shake his hand.

He looked down at her hand, as if he had forgotten what the gesture meant, but then, almost hesitantly, he reached out and clasped her fingers.

"No touching," the guard said from beyond the cell.

Carey stepped back and dropped her hand. Otis did the same. But she saw in his eyes that he appreciated the civilized gesture.

He pointed to the one chair. "You sit there. I'll sit on my bed."

"Thank you." She wondered if the chair was there just for her, or if he always had one.

She looked around, noting the worn Bible and the paperback copy of *A Tale of Two Cities*. There were also a couple of other books, and she leaned forward to see what they were. *Leaves of Grass* by Walt Whitman, and a Robert Frost anthology.

"I brought a tape recorder," she told him. "Do you mind?"

"What are you going to do with it?"

"I just want to remember what we discuss without getting it all mixed up in my head."

"You won't play it on the radio?"

"Not if you don't want me to."

He nodded. "Okay. Turn it on."

She did so, holding it in her hand facing him. "I'm sorry about the death warrant," she said awkwardly.

He cocked his head. "Really? I thought you wanted this to happen."

She shook her head. "No, I don't."

"Why not? You prosecuted me."

She could feel her cheeks heating. She didn't really want to get into this with him, because she couldn't see what good it would serve. She finally found something noncommittal to say. "I no longer support the death penalty."

He nodded. "It's different when you know you're responsible, isn't it?"

She started, and stared at him, wondering if he was reading her mind.

"That's okay," he said quietly. "You were just part of the system. If it wasn't you, it would have been somebody else."

"That's a very generous view to take."

He shrugged. "I've got nothing else to do anymore except take a philosophical attitude."

She found herself starting to smile, and caught her breath when he smiled back. His smile seemed to light up his whole face.

"So what do you want?" he asked. "Do you want to know what it's like to have only a few weeks to live? I'm not sure my experience would be meaningful to anyone else. I might feel a whole lot worse about it if I were outside. Then I'd have a lot more to lose."

She was taken aback, and hardly knew how to answer. "I suppose so."

"Not that it's really so bad in here. My guards are nice. I don't have much to worry about. Nobody beats me up or anything. It could be a lot worse."

And had been. The unspoken words seemed to hang on the air. "I hear prison is awful."

"Well, of course it is. There isn't any freedom. And sometimes things happen. But overall, I don't have much to complain about."

As compared to what? His childhood? She supposed he wasn't the most objective judge of the horrors of prison life.

"Anyway," he said, "I suppose you want to ask me if I did it, and want to know if I'm sorry for doing it."

She nodded slowly, wondering why it was she seemed unable to take control of this interview.

135

"I said all I had to say about that before the trial," he answered. "There's nothing more to say now. It's all decided."

She sat there looking at him, and an understanding washed over her in icy waves. Shock held her rigid as she looked into his bright blue eyes. She couldn't say how she knew, but she knew as surely as if the message was written on his face. "You know who did it, don't you? And you're protecting someone."

He shrugged. He might as well have agreed.

"My God," she said, "why don't you speak up? It's still not too late!"

But he shook his head. And deep in the depths of his blue eyes, she saw the flicker of fear, the flicker of pain he would never admit.

"John, this isn't right!"

He ignored her. "You know, during the trial you kept looking at me. You were the only person who did. And I always felt there was something you wanted to say. Something you wanted to know. What was it?"

Lead had settled into her heart and stomach, and she could only stare and try to draw a deep breath. Finally, she managed to say, "I just found out."

"Oh." He nodded as if he understood, but admitted nothing at all.

She tried again. "I kept thinking that you wouldn't kill because of an argument. Everybody said you'd done it to your father, so you did it to your foster parents, but I didn't believe it. You killed your father to protect your brother. That's not the same thing at all."

He smiled then, a quiet smile, as if he appreciated what she was saying, but he still didn't answer.

Finally, gathering her control, she began to steer the conversation, hoping that if she got him talking, she might get him to let slip something that would help him. The horror that had been riding her since she heard the death warrant was signed had dug its icy claws into every corner of her soul. She could not let this happen.

But John William Otis was not about to help her help him. Every time she tried to come back to the Kline murders, he turned the conversation elsewhere.

Time was getting short. Instead of trying to get him to talk about what *had* been, she decided to ask him about what *might* have been.

"If they let you out of here tomorrow, what would you do, John?"

He smiled, and a dreamy look seemed to come over his face. "I'd go to New England."

"New England? Really? Why?"

"I've always wanted to go there. Ever since I read my first Robert Frost poem."

"Which one is your favorite?"

He pointed to a paper hanging on the wall, attached there by a piece of tape. Rising, she went to look at it, and found a carefully hand-lettered version of "Stopping by Woods on a Snowy Evening."

Inexplicably feeling tears prickle her eyes, she read it aloud, her voice hushed, almost breaking as she read the last line: "And miles to go before I sleep."

"It's beautiful, isn't it?" Otis said softly. "I always wanted to see snow. Sometimes I dream about it, but it's not the same, you know? It's not the same as feeling how cold it is. I wonder if it's as soft as they say, and what it's like to have a snowflake fall on your cheek. I wonder what a handful of it would feel like, and what would happen when I squeeze it. I'd like to lie down in it and make a snow angel. I saw that in a movie, making a snow angel."

She turned to look at him, and saw that his head was

137

bowed. An overwhelming urge to touch him filled her, but she didn't dare, not under the watchful eyes of the guard.

After a bit, he drew a deep breath. "I guess I'll never see it."

Carey bit her lip and blinked hard, fighting down the sorrow that was suddenly threatening to choke her. Something. She had to find something to say, something to comfort him, but no words would come.

"Time," the guard said. He sounded almost reluctant.

John leapt up from his cot and turned, lifting the thin mattress and pulling out a composition book.

"Here," he said, thrusting it at her.

Carey looked down at it, her vision blurred by unshed tears. *The Poems of John William Otis.*

"Take it," he said.

"Why me?"

"Take it," he repeated. "You understand. You won't just throw it away or burn it. I couldn't stand for someone to throw it away."

She lifted her head, looking at him, feeling helpless and hating herself for it.

"You have to leave now, Ms. Stover," the guard said. He was opening the door.

"Please," said John Otis. "It's all that matters now."

The prison officials let her keep the book. They searched it first, to make sure Otis wasn't sending some kind of illicit message, and they discussed the propriety of it, then decided to let her have it.

"He'll just leave it to her in two weeks anyway," the warden said. "It doesn't matter."

But it did matter.

Clutching the book tightly to her breast, Carissa stepped out of the gray atmosphere of Raiford Prison into

138

the blinding sunlight and high temperatures of the first day of September and wondered how the world could look so unchanged.

"What's that?" Seamus asked as she got into the car.

Settling into her seat, she looked down at the notebook she clutched. "Poems. Otis gave them to me."

He looked at her a moment. "Fasten your seat belt."

She put the notebook on her lap and reached for the harness, buckling it with a click that somehow sounded final. Seamus backed out of the parking space, then headed them toward home.

"I figured we'd get some lunch along the road," he said presently. "Fast food, or should I look for something better?"

"Fast food is fine."

"Okay."

She looked down at the notebook in her lap, wishing Otis hadn't given it to her. God knew what she'd find in there, but she somehow suspected it wasn't going to help her sleep any better.

Worse, it felt like a trust. Regardless of what was inside it, she was going to feel as if she had to guard it for the rest of her life. How could she not?

Finally, she dragged her gaze from it and looked out the window at the passing countryside, but she didn't see the trees or the houses, or even the growing line of thunderheads before them.

They were so close to Jacksonville that she was tempted to ignore her need to go to work tonight, and instead head for the east coast. There was a tiny little motel in Neptune Beach, high on the dunes overlooking the Atlantic, that she loved to stay in. What was it called? She couldn't remember the name.

"Are you going to be okay?"

The sound of Seamus's voice startled her, and she realized they were coming into Gainesville. "I'm fine. I didn't sleep much last night."

"I'm not surprised."

He took them to a burger place, but rather than eat inside with a busload of excited, noisy children, they took their food with them. Carey ate hers absently as they drove south on I-275, but it tasted like sawdust. Finally, she stuffed the remains of her burger back into the bag and drank the diet soft drink instead.

"How'd it go?" Seamus asked.

She figured he deserved some kind of answer since he'd been sitting on the question for nearly two hours. "It was okay. He seems nice."

"A lot of them do. That's why people make the unfortunate mistake of trusting them."

For all she considered herself a cynic, she hated Seamus's cynicism. "I know that," she said finally. "But it was something else. He wasn't practiced. He wasn't doing a con. I think I can tell the difference. I met enough of them in State Attorney's Office."

He nodded, saying nothing.

So that's how he was going to be, she thought wearily. Silent. Noncommittal. The way he had been on the trip up here.

But then he surprised her. "Do you feel better or worse, now that you've seen him?"

"Worse. He's not guilty, Seamus. I'd stake my reputation on it."

"Did he say so?"

"No. Actually he wouldn't talk about it at all. But I'll tell you something. Not only did he not kill the Klines, but he knows who did."

Another five miles passed before he spoke again.

140

"Sweetheart—"

"Don't call me that!"

"Sorry. Look, I have a problem with mind reading. If he didn't say that, how can you know that?"

"It was something about the way he looked. And the way he didn't deny it when I suggested it."

"That's not very helpful."

"No, it isn't. And he knows that." She closed her eyes against the sun and the headache that was beginning to grow in her forehead and neck. "He's protecting somebody."

"That only happens in the movies. Real live people don't go to the electric chair to protect somebody."

Yesterday she would have agreed with him. Today she couldn't.

"At the risk of having you tell me again what a son of a bitch I am, I gotta tell you, Carey, I'm beginning to wonder if you aren't—" He broke off.

"Delusional?" she asked. "It's possible, I guess. Although under the circumstances it'd be a whole lot more helpful if I believed John Otis was a rotten s.o.b. who killed the Klines in cold blood."

"Maybe. And did you ever consider that if he knows who did it, he's an accomplice?"

A shiver ran through her. No, she hadn't thought of that.

"I mean, if he is protecting someone, then he was part of it anyway, and he's getting what he deserves."

In an instant they passed from bright sunshine to the gloom beneath the line of thunderheads. The day darkened, turning greenish.

"I hope we make it back in time for your show," Seamus said as the first large raindrops spattered on the dusty windshield.

141

Carey discovered that she didn't care one way or the other.
Something inside her, stressed too far, had shut down.
Opening the book of poems, she began to read.

CHAPTER 10
16 DAYS

"They Tell Me Snow"

They tell me snow is white and soft
And downy fluffy on the ground.
That where it lays on earth and trees
It mutes and humbles every sound.

They tell me snow is bright and wet
And scrunchy hard when packed in balls.
That snow forts shield the worst of blows
While children's happy laughter falls.

They tell me snow is gray and slick
And slipp'ry slidy on the street.
That people slide and cars collide
When snow and our impatience meet.

They tell me snow is gay and free
When giddy happy people play.
They lie and wave their arms and legs
Leaving angels where they lay.

They tell me snow is all these things,
And hopeful longing I concede
That all these snowy things seem real,

Yet somehow, doubting, I still need

To hear the silence in the air,
Feel the wet cold in my hair,
Step so lightly, not to fall,
And leave my angel, most of all.

They tell me all these things of snow,
But 'til I see it, I won't know.

Carey finished reading the poem into the microphone, and let a moment of silence go out over the air. "And that," she said finally, "was a poem written by John William Otis. Ted Sanders follows the newsbreak. Stay tuned."

She cut away to commercial then, glad that her time was over. Pulling off her headset, she stood up and stretched hugely. Sitting at the mike didn't seem to be growing any easier with time.

Ted walked in, giving her a big smile. "Great show tonight, Carey."

"Thanks." At least it had been different. She'd started with a mention of the countdown to Otis's execution date, and then had gone on to discuss other things for the full three hours, coming back to Otis only at the very end when she read his poem. She figured she could make her point without devoting the entire show to it.

Besides, after seeing Otis that morning, she couldn't bring herself to talk about him. The whole mess had become even more personal than it had been before.

She should never have gone to Raiford, she thought as she walked out into the steamy night. It hadn't clarified a thing except her conviction that Otis was innocent. It certainly hadn't given her even the tiniest lever to use to prevent his execution.

"Carey!"

Ted's producer was leaning out the door.

"Carey, get back to the studio, now!"

Turning, she ran back to the building. Ted was in the studio, talking into the microphone. He waved her to come in.

"She's here," he said into the microphone. "It's okay, Bob, she's here." He pointed to another set of headphones on the conference table.

Carey put them on and at Ted's gesture spoke into the mike in front of her. "This is Carey Justice," she said.

"Carey," said a voice that was somehow familiar. "I called last week about Otis."

"I'm sorry, I don't remember."

"I'm the guy who called and said he didn't do it."

Now she *did* remember. "That's right."

"You didn't believe me."

"Well, to tell you the truth, I don't believe John Otis killed Linda and Harvey Kline."

"You don't?"

"No." She looked at Ted questioningly, wondering why he had called her back in for this. This was the kind of caller a host usually cut off right away.

Ted spoke. "Bob said he has some information about the break-in at Tricia Summers's house, but he said he wouldn't tell anyone except you."

"Well, I'm listening, Bob. What about the break-in?"

"I thought it would convince everyone that John didn't kill the Klines. But nobody's paying any attention."

A chill began to creep along Carey's spine. She looked at Ted, who was frowning, then at Ted's producer, who was back at her post on the other side of the window. "I'm paying attention," she said into the mike. "I thought there were similarities."

"The police aren't paying attention."

Get his number, Carey mouthed to the producer, who shrugged that she didn't understand.

"Tell me about it, Bob," she said into the microphone. As soon as the guy started talking, she reached for the pad and pen Ted had beside him. Quickly she scrawled, "Tell Lucy to get his number!" and passed it back to Ted. He nodded and pressed the button that would allow him to talk privately to Lucy.

"I thought the pink nightgown would let them know," Bob was saying. "They're stupid! They're all stupid!"

"Well . . ." Carey wasn't quite sure how to handle this. She wanted more information, but she didn't want him to hang up before they had his number She had no idea how the computerized tracking system worked, and whether any time was needed.

"It was so obvious a fool could have seen it," Bob said, his voice rising. "But I guess they're even stupider am that. So it's their fault, Carey! It's their fault!"

"What's their fault?" She looked toward Lucy and saw the woman making an "OK" sign and waving a piece of paper.

"It's their fault I had to kill somebody!"

"Wait!" Carey felt as if her heart had stopped dead. Everything else seemed to fade away except the microphone in front of her. "You don't have to kill anybody, Bob. Just talk to me. Make me understand so I can make them understand."

"They won't understand. It was the nightgown! It was the same damn nightgown the other woman was wearing."

"How do you know that, Bob?"

"Tell 'em to check it out. But it's too late anyway. John

145

didn't do it. I did."

There was a click followed by a dial tone, suddenly the scariest sound in the world to Carey. She couldn't think of anything to say. She looked at Ted and saw he was equally at a loss. Lucy, however, was quicker than either of them. She cut them away to a commercial, covering the dead air.

"Jesus Christ," Ted said when he realized nobody would hear him except Carey. "Jesus H. Christ."

Carey's brain ground back into action. "When you go back on the air, don't say anything about it, Ted. There's no way you can discuss that call without taking the chance you'll piss this guy off enough to make him actually do something."

He nodded. "You're right. What are you going to do?"

"Call a friend at the police department."

He looked grim. "Sounds like a plan. Christ. I can't believe this! I've had people threaten to kill *me,* but I've never had anyone threaten to kill somebody else. It gives me the willies!"

Carey knew exactly what he meant. It was worse somehow. Maybe because when the threat was against you, you didn't really believe it. But when it was against some poor, innocent bystander . . .

She let the thought trail away, unable to deal with it. Leaving the studio, she went to get the phone number from Lucy and ask her to save the tape in case the police wanted it, then hunted up a phone she could use.

Seamus wasn't at home, so she called the police station.

"Detective Rourke is out on a case, ma'am," said the detective she was finally put through to. "Maybe somebody else can help you."

She tried to remember the names of other detectives she'd known in her days as a prosecutor, and found herself drawing a blank. "I'm a radio talk-show host," she said finally. "I just had someone call me claiming knowledge of the break-in at Tricia Summers's house last week. He also said he killed somebody."

"Lots of jerks call and tell us the same thing, ma'am," the voice on the other end of the line said. "Did he offer anything useful?"

"I've got his phone number."

"Well, give it to me, and I'll have somebody look into it." *When they get around to it,* his tone implied.

Carey was suddenly furious. She wasn't used to being treated this way by cops. Of course, a state attorney had a hell of a lot more clout with the police than a mere radio personality. Her voice took on a jagged edge of ice.

"Look, Detective, just have Seamus Rourke call me ASAP. My name is Carey Stover, and my number is 555-3214. And if he doesn't get this message, I'll call him at home at 5 A.M. Got it?"

There was a pause on the other end of the line, and she could imagine the guy tying to decide whether to give her hell or let it go. Wisely, he decided to let it go. "What's your number again?" was all he asked.

She repeated it, then hung up the phone.

Slug! She wondered how much important information vanished in the depths of the ignored heaps on that lamebrain's desk.

Then she went home, because there wasn't another damn thing she could do.

People shouldn't live alone, Seamus thought. It made such a mess when they died and weren't discovered right away.

He stood in a well-appointed living room in a small condo not too far from where Carey lived, although there was no significance in that. The criminal court and the State Attorney's Office were conveniently nearby. The prosecutor who lay dead in his bed had probably chosen

147

this place for its location.

The smell of death had filled the condo, permeating the paint, the rugs, the upholstery. The violence, however, had been limited to the bedroom. Whoever had slashed the man to death had come upon him in his sleep and taken him by surprise.

The crime scene technicians, however, were checking this room out as thoroughly as the murder scene. Black fingerprint powder layered every surface. The vacuuming was already done, and the latents were being lifted, item by item.

Gil came out of the bedroom. "Weekends," he said.

"Yup."

"They figure out how he got in?"

"Sliding glass door out back."

"Too easy."

"I'll never have one."

"My ex wanted them."

"And?"

Gil shrugged. "I told her I wasn't going to mop up the blood."

Seamus shook his head. "What did she say?"

"That I had my mind in the gutter, and I ought to get real."

"That's pretty real."

"That's what I thought. Done?"

Seamus nodded. "I found some footprints out back near the patio, so they're making casts. Maybe they'll match the ones in the blood on the bedroom rug."

Gil shrugged. "It'd be nice if he was wearing size fifteen hand-made Italian loafers."

"Be still my beating heart."

They walked out together. The night was almost over, and what little they could do at this point was done. Now they had to wait on forensics and the medical examiner.

At their cars, parked on the street several houses down to make room for the forensics vans and patrol cars, they paused.

"Ideas?" Gil said finally.

"You're not gonna like them."

"Try me anyway. It's 4 A.M., my head's spinning, and any theory is better than no theory."

"Well, it was probably an angry girlfriend or somebody he put away."

"That's usually the way the ball bounces."

"And the cookie crumbles."

Gil rocked back on his heels and looked up at the night sky. "Christ, I hate this job."

Seamus knew what he meant. There were times when this job was just too damn much. He knew the guy lying on the bed in there. Or what was left of him.

"Okay," said Gil after a moment. "Enough pissing for one night. I heard a 'but' in what you just said."

"Well . . ." Carey was getting to him, Seamus thought. She was getting to him, and Gil was probably going to tell him he needed to be committed. "There is the fact that this guy was the lead prosecutor on the John Otis case."

Gil looked at him. "You've been listening to the radio too much."

"It isn't the radio I've been listening to. This guy was killed the same way as Linda and Harvey Kline, and he was involved with the Otis case."

"And unless they're letting death row inmates out on furloughs right before execution, Otis couldn't have had anything to do with this. Are you getting a fever?"

"I didn't say Otis had anything to do with this."

Gil leaned back against his car. "Maybe my ears aren't working."

"No, it's just your brain. Nobody's brain works well at

149

this time of night. Forget it. I want to think some more about this. I'll talk to you in the morning."

"It *is* morning," Gil reminded him. "However, we'll talk about it whenever we drag our asses out of bed and get to work. Say noon?"

When Seamus climbed into his car, he automatically pulled out his cell phone and called in. "I'm going home," he told the detective on duty, "and I won't be in until noon. Any messages?"

"Yeah," said Sid Markovitz. "Some crazy woman called, said she was a talk-show host with some info, and if you don't call her she'll call you at 5 A.M."

"I'll call her."

"Let me give you the number."

Seamus was about to say he had it, when he realized he didn't. She had moved since their days together, and probably had an unlisted number. He scratched down the digits on the notepad, he kept clipped to his dash.

"Thanks, Sid. And by the way, she's only partly crazy."

Then he dialed Carey, taking some nasty pleasure in the fact that he was dragging *her* out of bed.

"What's up?" he said, when he heard her groggy voice.

"Seamus?"

He remembered her saying his name just that way in the middle of the night, and he remembered what always followed. His entire body sprang to unwelcome life, and that made him mad. "Who else would it be? You called the station?"

"Oh, yeah." She was waking up. He could hear it as her tone changed and her voice grew brisker. Already he was missing the sleepy, soft sound. "I had a caller tonight. From what he said, he did the break-in at Tricia Summers's house."

"So call the sheriff. It's their case."

"But there's more," she said, her tone becoming impatient. "He said John Otis didn't do it, that *he* did. And what's more, he said he killed somebody else."

The tumblers clicked into place. Seamus heard them, a quiet *snick* in his brain as it came together.

"I'm on my way over," he said. "I'll be there in ten minutes. Put the coffee on. I need it."

Put the coffee on.

Carey stifled the urge to commit mayhem and lay on her bed, staring up at the streaks of light from the streetlamps that had seeped past her curtains to make gashes across the ceiling.

Put the coffee on.

Man, she thought, there was nothing like a sense of male privilege. If she'd barged in on him at this hour of the morning, she wouldn't have told him to make her coffee.

No, that wasn't entirely true. In law school and in the years since, she'd adopted some of that male sense of privilege for herself. It had wound up getting her called pushy and abrasive.

So he's pushy and abrasive, she decided, and felt a small trickle of satisfaction. What was sauce for the goose was sauce for the gander. The knife cuts both ways. A whole bunch of aphorisms ran through her head, signaling that her brain was waking up, whether she wanted to or not.

She threw back the blankets and sat up. Only then did she realize why she was so irritated with him. Waking up to the sound of his voice had stiffed long-buried memories of awaking beside him, hearing his quiet murmurs and feeling the touch of his hands and mouth. Need was running along her nerve endings, a subtle irritation that was making her angry with him.

151

Stupid, she told herself. Stupid, stupid, stupid.

She pulled on a knee-length cotton kimono and headed down to the kitchen, where she started the pot of coffee. It was nearly 4 A.M., so she figured he'd probably been up all night on an investigation. She tried to resist the urge to take care of him—it certainly wasn't *her* responsibility any longer—but found herself putting strips of bacon into the electric frying pan, pulling the toaster oven out of the cupboard and a carton of eggs out of the refrigerator.

Wrong food, she thought as the bacon started sizzling. Protein wakes you up, carbohydrates help you sleep. She probably wouldn't be able to go back to bed now. Oh, well, maybe some protein would help him drive home in one piece.

The doorbell rang just as she was turning the bacon. She made him wait while she finished, then went to let him in.

"Smells good in here," he said as he stepped across the threshold.

"I'm making breakfast." And he looked awful, she thought. Dark circles under his eyes emphasized the fatigue that lined his face. The smile he gave her barely lifted the corners of his mouth.

"Thanks," he said, then utterly astonished her by bending to brush a gentle kiss on her cheek. "You always look cuddle-able when you first wake up."

Before she could think of a response, he was heading for the kitchen like a heat-seeking missile.

She followed, feeling as if something in the world had shifted, as if there had been some kind of earthquake that had displaced everything just a little, so that it seemed the same but wasn't.

And she wasn't nearly awake enough to be having heavy thoughts. She was as close to brain-dead as it was possible

152

to be while still moving around.

He poured the coffee while she checked the bacon and started making rye toast. When the toast came out of the oven, he took over buttering it.

It was like old times. When they had lived together, they had often worked like this in the kitchen, sharing the tasks comfortably. How she missed that! Her throat tightened, and she blinked rapidly, trying to hold back unwanted tears.

Her life had gone to hell when she and Seamus had parted ways, and she had never quite managed to put it back together again. There was a gaping hole at the center of her existence which she had been refusing to look at, but suddenly it was as obvious as the Grand Canyon.

Not now, she told herself. Not now!

They didn't talk until they were seated at the table with their breakfasts.

"Okay," Seamus said, "run the whole story by me."

She did just that, reciting the phone conversation as well as she could remember it, and finishing up by giving him the phone number.

He took it, looked at it, and stuffed it in the breast pocket of his shirt. "Any chance the station has a recording of the call?"

She nodded. "Lucy's saving it If you want it, you can get it when Bill comes in at ten., Otherwise, they'll probably record over it later today."

"Well, there went my plan to crash."

He wasn't just listening to her, she realized suddenly. He was paying close attention. The back of her neck prickled as awareness penetrated the remaining fog in her brain. "You believe me," she said.

He looked wearily at her. "I always believe you."

"That isn't what I mean."

"Come again?"

"I mean . . . you think this is significant. You're not brushing it off as a wacko caller."

He shrugged one shoulder. "It needs to be checked out. I'm reserving judgment. What time did the call come in?"

"A little after eleven."

He pulled his cell phone out of his pocket, flipped it open and punched in a number. "Dek, it's Rourke. I need you to check a phone number out for me." He read the number, then waited, drumming his fingers on the table. He looked at Carey. "You sure they'll have the tape?"

"I asked Lucy to save it."

"Don't they save them all?" But as soon as he spoke, he shook his head. "I guess not. It'd be too much."

"We'd be overwhelmed. We save stuff only long enough to get a good line off it to use in station advertising. Sometimes we save something that might be of particular interest later, or something that's historical. They've still got all the tapes of the first shows that were broadcast after the start of the Gulf War. But other than that . . ." It was her turn to shrug.

"But she *will* save this one."

"Sure. I asked her to. Besides, she heard the call. She knows it could be significant."

He nodded, then returned his attention to the phone. "Yeah? Okay. Thanks." He disconnected, turned off the phone, and put it away. "Pay phone over in Tampa," he told her. "It's useless."

"Seamus, what's going on?"

He looked at her, his gaze opaque. "The guy said he did the Summers break-in."

"And you could have just called the sheriff about it. It's their case. That's what you told me to do. Come on, give."

He hesitated visibly. "Oh, hell," he said finally. "Is there any more coffee?"

Before she could reply, he'd answered the question himself by looking over at the pot. The glass carafe was still half-full. He pushed back from the table and went to refill his mug.

She sat looking at him, frustrated to feel closed out of the loop. When she had been a prosecutor, she hadn't been closed out of any loop, but now she was nobody, just a bigmouthed member of the media, and he was going to shut her out. Frustration made her fingers curl until her nails bit into her palms.

"Seamus . . ."

He sighed and looked at her. "What the hell," he said. "You'll hear all about it in the news today."

"Damn straight."

He gave her a humorless smile. "There's been a murder."

"Oh, God." Her stomach turned over, leaving her feeling sick. "You think this caller is related."

"I have to check everything out."

"Of course. Was it . . . was it a slashing?"

"Maybe. The vic had been dead for a couple of days. You know how it gets . . . difficult."

"Yeah." She'd had to look at some of those bloated corpses. A shudder ran through her, and her stomach flipped over again.

"Anyway, it looks like it maybe was."

Blood, she thought. Blood everywhere and a messy corpse. There were guesses that could be reliably made even at the scene, even after a couple of days. Her stomach was rolling like a blender now, and she tried not to let her imagination produce gory images, but they kept popping up anyway.

155

"I have to wait on the M.E.," he continued.

"Of course." Feeling her gorge rise, she pushed back from the table. She had to get away from the sight and smell of the food remnants on the table. She headed for the living room.

He followed her.

"Otis," she said.

He made an impatient sound. "Just because the caller says—"

She whirled on him. ,You, re going to tell me it's a copycat?"

He held up his hands. "Easy, babe."

"I am not your babe!"

He stuffed his hands in his pocket. "Don't I know it."

For an instant, just the merest instant, she thought he looked almost wistful. Not now! Not with this murder hovering in the air around them. This was not the time . . .

But as fast as the look had come, it had vanished from his face and he was all exhausted business again. "Look, I can't be sure the vic was slashed. Nobody can until the M.E. checks it out. But it looks like it. It *could* be a copycat. It could be some sicko who's capitalizing on the publicity surrounding Otis's execution. And that's what I'm going to hear from my superiors if I start suggesting what you're thinking. So, at least for right now, let's just leave that aside, okay? First we have to catch this guy anyway. No phone call is going to be enough to convince anybody who matters that Otis didn't do the Kline killings. You know that, Carey. You know that."

"We've got two weeks, Seamus. Just two weeks! Christ!" She wrapped her arms around herself and tried to stop shaking. "How the hell are you going to feel if you catch this creep three weeks from now, after Otis is dead, and you find out he did the Klines, too?"

"Right now," he said heavily, "I'm not going to think about that. It'll just get in the way."

"No, maybe it'll light a fire under your butt! Maybe you better take another look at the Kline killings. Maybe something got overlooked in the rush to pin it all on Otis."

"I'll check out everything that's worth checking out!"

She shook her head and turned away from him. "You know, all the moral arguments about the death penalty are real nice philosophical discussions to have on a rainy evening over a glass of brandy. I've had them many times with other lawyers. But you know what really gets to me?"

"'What?"

"Morality aside, it all comes down to one thing, Seamus. The finality of it. Once John Otis is executed, if evidence turns up exonerating him, there's not one damn thing anybody can do about it. It'll be too late! And that's what's really wrong with the death penalty. It's something we can't ever take back."

He didn't respond. After a couple minutes, that began to bother her. Seamus always had a response. It was one of the things she had liked about him in the beginning, the way they could have lengthy discussions about almost anything. Never once could she remember him answering anything she said with nothing but silence. Finally, she turned to look at him.

"What aren't you telling me?" she asked.

He looked sadly at her. "I'm being a coward."

"What? Why?"

"I don't have to be the one to tell you." He sighed. "On the other hand, you'll want to kill me if you get it from the papers or the news feed."

A chill began to settle into her bones, and a blizzard

began to blow in her soul. Reaching out, she steadied herself on the back of a wing chair. "What?"

"The victim was Harry Downs."

"Oh my God. . ." The room seemed to go dark, and her vision narrowed until it was a tiny tunnel with Seamus a long way away on the other end. A loud buzzing filled her ears, and the cold in her bones turned to an unhealthy heat before becoming cold again.

The next thing she knew, she was sitting in a chair and Seamus was forcing her head down between her knees. Light came back to the world, and along with it a searing pain in her heart.

Harry. She squeezed her eyes closed and tried to absorb the incredibility of it, the pain of it. A fleeting prayer winged heavenward from her soul, asking God to forgive her for the way she had hated that cocksure son of a bitch, hated him as much as she had admired him. Could hate kill?

The craziness of that thought hit her like a bucket of cold water, clearing her head. Anger filled her. She snapped upright, shaking off Seamus's hand. "He was the lead prosecutor on the Otis case!"

Seamus's answer was a long time coming.

"I know," he said heavily. "I know."

CHAPTER 11
15 DAYS

THEY MADE ANOTHER POT OF COFFEE. SEAMUS GAVE up all thought of getting any sleep. He was worried about Carey. Hearing that someone you knew had been brutally murdered, even if you hated him, was tough to take. Maybe especially if you hated him. Hate, after all, was as strong a feeling as love, and more likely to cause a sense of guilt. He remembered all too well the strong antipathy Carey had felt for Harry Downs. She'd made no secret of it around Seamus.

She drank her coffee in silence, not even looking at him. Then she poured another cup. The first signs of a red dawn were beginning to streak the sky, and through the windows the shadowy shapes of the plants in her garden were just becoming visible. The dirty dishes were piled beside the sink, and he thought about washing them, just to have something to do. Fatigue felt as if it had seeped into his bones, though, so he let it go.

He sat and waited.

"He was the lead attorney on the Otis case," she said again.

"I know."

She looked at him for what felt like the first time in hours. "You're not going to ignore that!"

"No. I'm not going to ignore that."

"If you won't review the Kline case, I will."

"Fine." He waved a hand. "Help is always welcome."

"Don't patronize me."

"I'm not! But I don't think we're going to find anything there. If there was anything, we'd have found it back then.

159

An awful lot of us looked that case over, Carey. There wasn't a whole lot of anything to go with."

"There was enough to get the wrong man convicted."

He didn't bother arguing with her because, quite frankly, after tonight he was beginning to have some serious doubts himself. Maybe she was being irrational, thinking that something had been overlooked in a case that had been gone over with a dozen fine-tooth combs, but she was entitled to a little irrationality.

Besides, it made him feel better that she was getting into fight mode. That was a hell of a lot more hopeful than her sitting there in utter silence staring at nothing.

Caffeine was buzzing through his system, making him feel edgy, but not enough to cut away his tiredness. Finally, he said, "We both need to get some sleep. Neither one of us is going to be any good to anybody if we don't get some shut-eye."

She nodded slowly. "I guess."

He didn't like the way that sounded. Worry stiffed again. "How about I crash on your couch?"

"It's not big enough. You'll never get any decent sleep." She stood and went to empty her mug in the sink. "Come on, you can share my bed."

For an instant, his heart leapt but then it settled back down. He knew she didn't mean that. Not now. Not under these circumstances. And it wouldn't have mattered anyway because he was too damn tired.

They climbed the stairs together. She crawled under the covers of her king-size bed still wearing her kimono. He kicked off his shoes and stretched out beside her, on top of the covers, wearing his shirt and slacks. His gun and shield he put on the bedside table.

A king-size bed, he noticed, and wondered who she had shared it with. He brushed the thought aside. All that

160

mattered was that he would know if she stirred. Then sleep reached up and sucked him down into its welcome forgetfulness.

Carey found no such relief. For a long, long time she stared up at the brightening ceiling and tried to hold the demons at bay.

Strong arms held her, and Carey burrowed into their warmth, luxuriating in the hazy hinterland between sleep and waking. She felt safe and secure, and some deep-rooted longing was being satisfied by the arms that held her. Seamus. His body heat was like a warm fire on an icy night. It had been so long. . . .

But gradually her waking senses grew aware of other things. One of them was that he was awake, and trying gently to ease away. The other was that the faint, nauseating scent of death clung to him.

Harry Downs. Her heart slammed into high gear, and anxiety hit her, driving the last sleepiness away. She jerked her head up and found Seamus looking down at her, his eyes alert, though reddened from lack of sleep.

"I have to go get that tape," he said.

"I'll go with you." She rolled away quickly, not wanting to be close to him any longer. He was a promise of things he couldn't give. Hadn't she learned that the hard way?

She could feel his gaze on her back as she rummaged through her closet, trying to decide what she wanted to wear.

"I can't drive you back," he said. "I'm supposed to meet my partner at noon, and I need to shave and shower before I go in."

"No problem. I'll follow you."

They didn't even bother to make coffee, but left as soon as she was dressed.

Following him in her Jeep down I-275, Carey forced herself to focus on how thoroughly rotten she felt from lack of sleep. The last thing she wanted to remember was how good it had felt to wake up in his arms.

They made good time, pulling into the station twenty minutes later. Carey walked Seamus past reception, straight to Bill Hayes's office.

"Come in," Bill called in answer to her knock. She opened the door to find him on the phone.

He raised a finger, indicating he needed a moment, then raised his eyebrow when he saw Seamus. "It's all good PR," he said into the phone. "The more weirdos, the better. Listen, I gotta run. I'll get back to you on that."

He hung up the phone and waved to the chairs facing his cluttered desk. "Have a seat. What's up?"

Seamus waited until Carey was seated, then took the remaining chair.

"This is Seamus Rourke with the St. Pete PD," she said. "He wants the tape of the Ted Sanders show last night."

"I heard about that call." Bill looked Seamus over, as if trying to determine his caliber. "I believe in cooperating with the police, but this is station property, and we have our own uses for it."

Seamus's expression never changed. "I'm perfectly willing to get a warrant. From what I hear, something on that tape may be relevant to a murder that took place over the weekend."

Bill sat up a little straighter. "Really?" He rubbed his chin. "I suppose you want the original."

Seamus nodded.

Bill sighed. "Can I copy it first? I want to use part of it in a promo spot."

Seamus shrugged, smiling pleasantly. "That's fine by me."

162

"Can you give me a half hour or so?"

Seamus looked at his watch. "I'll be back in an hour."

Out in the hallway with Carey, Seamus said, "An hour is time for breakfast. Join me?"

She felt a remarkable lack of hunger, maybe because they'd had breakfast just six hours ago, or maybe because Harry Downs was dead. "I need to call some people, and I'm not really hungry."

"So have some coffee with me. We need to do a little brainstorming anyway."

That perked up her interest. "Okay."

At least he didn't pick a traditional breakfast spot. Carey thought she would vomit if she had to smell hying bacon. Instead he drove them to a bagel shop, where they both got bagels and hot coffee and sat at a corner table.

"How good are your friends at the State Attorney's Office?" he asked her.

She considered the question. "I've got some sources over there."

"Do you think you can get a look at the Otis file?"

"It's been five years. I don't know how much is left, other than public documents. But yes, I can get whatever they have. It might take a couple of days to get it out of storage, though."

"Worth a try. If you're willing, I also want you to take a look at everything they've got in the newspaper morgues."

"Really?" She wouldn't have thought of that.

"Well, it might tip us to somebody involved in the case who could have had a reason to pin it on Otis."

She nodded.

"And follow it up to the present. Any link to Otis at all. Besides, it'll give me a list of potential victims, if whoever killed Downs is really going after people involved with the case."

Carey felt the back of her neck prickle, as if a cool breeze had wafted over her. "*I* was involved in the Otis case."

His expression was grim. "Believe me, I haven't forgotten that."

He didn't say any more, but he didn't need to. Carey could connect the dots as well as he.

As soon as Seamus picked up the tape and left her at the station, Carey found a phone and called Evan Sinclair over at the State Attorney's Office.

"I can request the file, Carey," he told her, "but I can't let it out of my possession. You'll have to come over to my place to see it."

Evan had been hitting on her for years. She stifled a sigh and wondered what was the best way to handle it so that she wouldn't wind up offending him beyond hope. Of course, if she went to his house and had to fend off his advances, that would probably put paid to their relationship for good.

"I'll visit you at your office, Evan," she finally said.

"I deserve a little more than that."

"Okay, I'll buy you dinner. In a restaurant."

He laughed then, taking it in good humor. "Still hung up on that cop, huh?"

Was she? she wondered after she cradled the phone. She doubted it, but one thing she knew for sure was that she felt no desire to carry her relationship with Evan past friendship. No sparks there, at least not on her side.

Then, feeling a twinge of conscience, she called the IRS about Danny Rourke. This time she got through to a woman in the Problem Resolution Office, and soon had notes painting a bleak picture. Danny Rourke had stopped filing his income tax returns five years ago, but bank records showed he had still been making some money from his fishing business for the next couple of years. When all was said and done, the IRS was estimating that he owed well over sixty-five thousand dollars in back taxes and penalties.

"He's an alcoholic," Carey told the woman. "He's in a treatment center right now, and I can tell you he doesn't have a dime to his name."

"He's paying you, isn't he?"

"I'm doing this pro bono."

"Oh." Silence.

"I understand you've confiscated some of his property. A fishing boat, in fact."

"We'll have to auction it. I doubt we'll get that much for it."

Carey was well aware that these auctions didn't bring full value, so she didn't argue. "Well, you can't get blood from a stone. The man is ill and broke. I'm sure we can negotiate something."

"I'll have to talk to my supervisor."

"You do that."

After she hung up, Carey felt a little better. At least she had managed to accomplish something to help someone.

Sitting there, listening to the sounds of the radio station all around her, it suddenly struck her that it had been a very long time since she had felt she had helped anyone, except for her work with Legal Aid. Talk radio sure didn't give her the feeling that she was doing any good for the world. It didn't even give her the feeling that she was justifying her existence.

Whoa there, she told herself sharply. This was not a good way to think.

She had gone to law school with all kinds of idealistic notions and had managed to preserve them until working as a prosecutor had uprooted them one by one, leaving her cynical and wounded. Everybody had an ax to grind, and everybody lied, and all too often the cops weren't any better than the perps. She had watched political considerations be weighed into decisions that should have been made solely on the basis of the law. She had watched judges do back flips and act like prosecution stooges even though it meant ignoring the law or believing blatant lies simply because they had wanted to be reelected and feared being thought soft on crime.

And in the end, she had come out of the process feeling sullied and raw. The good guys, it seemed, were motivated by the same self-interest that the bad guys were. And while the bad guys might steal and rob and rape, the good guys could take away people's lives by locking them up or killing them. In the end, she had found the law to be almost as dirty as the criminals it was trying to punish.

But it had been five years, and during those five years, she had found satisfaction in her work with Legal Aid. The people who came to her there had relatively minor problems—divorces, landlord disputes, bankruptcies, employment problems—but the problems had been overwhelming them, and she had been able to offer an invaluable service. And in the process, some of her wounds had healed.

But the last thing she wanted to do was let go of the protective shell of cynicism that she had built. It was all that stood between her and the pain she had felt when she realized that there was no room for idealism in the world, that horse trading was the bottom line for nearly everyone.

There were exceptions of course, and she found herself remembering them now. Judge Greg Hanson, for one. He was considered a maverick and a wild card by the state attorneys, but he was a man who could be counted on to stand up for the law And there had been a couple of prosecutors who'd been around long enough to be able to stand up to the political pressures that weighed so heavily on their boss, the State Attorney.

And there had been Evan Sinclair, who had surprised her one day in court. A decree had come down from the higher-ups that the state's lawyers were not under any circumstances to accept downward departures from sentencing guidelines set by the legislature. The order had come through as the result of a newspaper investigative report that had recorded the percentage of downward departures being allowed in the county.

The departures hadn't really been all that shocking. Every case, after all, had its own set of facts, and judges were tying to weigh the threat to the public in their sentencing decisions, especially when prisons were crowded. Some people, it was reasonably felt, were not likely to err again, or to be a threat to anyone else. But the stats looked bad in the paper, so the prosecutors were ordered to oppose downward departures.

Then had come the case of a man who had rented a gold necklace from a rent-to-own place. He had pawned the necklace in the full expectation of being able to continue making his payments on it, and being able to get it out of hock within a week.

Unfortunately, he had been arrested for getting into a brawl in defense of his sister before he could recover the necklace. He didn't get out of jail again for three and a half years.

He was charged by the state for theft of the necklace, even though the rent-to-own place got the necklace back from the pawn shop for a hundred dollars. The man had been out of jail for six months when the cops picked him. up on the necklace charge. He scraped the money together, and paid the rental company everything he owed

167

them, but the state asked for twelve years anyway, because the score on his rap sheet demanded it.

The defense attorney made a persuasive argument for a downward departure, pointing out that what had happened had been beyond the defendant's control, and that the defendant was making large strides in getting his life together, was working full-time, paying child support, and had paid full restitution to the rental company.

The judge had looked at Evan, who was representing the case for the state, and asked what he thought of a downward departure.

Evan could have made an argument for twelve years as his bosses would have expected. Pawning the necklace had been a violation of the rental agreement, even if the defendant hadn't realized it. But instead all Evan had said was, "Your honor, the state is not permitted to agree to a downward departure."

It was as good as saying he would have, if he could have. Carey, who had felt that the prosecution was pointless once restitution had been made, given the facts of the case, had been surprised and pleased by what Evan had done.

Nor had the judge misinterpreted him. "I cannot," said Judge Greg Hanson, "in good conscience sentence this man to twelve years based on these facts."

So sometimes it did work right. And at times it occurred to her that if all the idealistic attorneys bailed out of the system, then only self-interest would remain. Sometimes she felt uneasy, as if she had betrayed a trust.

But she didn't want to think about that now. It was just a way to avoid thinking about Harry Downs and John William Otis.

She could deal with the hash she had made of her own life later. Right now, she had to save a man from death row.

She had a friend at the newspaper who occasionally fed her tidbits to use on her show. It was a two-way street, though, and Sally Dyer never forgot it.

"Yeah, I could get you everything from the morgue on Otis," Sally said, her voice hoarse from years of smoking. "What's in it for me?"

"Maybe an inside track on who killed Harry Downs."

Sally's voice sharpened. "What do you know about that?"

"Not much just yet. But there may be a link, Sally. I need to check it out. Word is, Harry was slashed to death. And he was lead prosecutor on the Otis trial."

"A lot of people could have wanted to slash Harry," Sally said, and coughed. "Christ, Carey, the man put some really tough dudes away."

"But the method may have been the same as in the Kline case. That's a little coincidental, don't you think?"

"Maybe. Do you know that for sure?"

"Not until the M.E. prelim is in. But for now, we've got two weeks until the Otis execution. I can't afford to wait for anything."

"You've sure been stirring up the stew on that, haven't you." Sally thought a moment. Carey could hear her pencil tapping nervously. "Okay, I'll do it. What exactly do you want?"

"Everything where there's a mention of John William Otis."

"That ought to be a trailerful or two."

"All the way back to his first murder trial, if you can get it."

"They're going to want to fire me in the morgue. Okay. Let me see what I can do. If I get it on floppy, can you read it?"

"I've got a laptop."

"Okay then. That might make things easier. Let me get on it."

"If necessary, I'll come over there and read everything, but I could sure work a lot faster if I could do it in every free moment."

"I figured that out already." Sally gave a dry laugh. "Why do I think you've got a tiger by the tail?"

"Time will tell."

"I get first dibs."

"Always."

And after that call, Carey felt a whole lot better—until she started thinking about poor Harry Downs again. Thinking of him drove her out back to smoke the first cigarette she had had in days.

Harry might have been a son of a bitch, but he hadn't deserved to die.

Gil pulled the earphones off his head and switched the tape player off. "Interesting. Especially the part about the nightgown."

"That's what I thought," Seamus agreed. He felt as if he were viewing the world from the bottom of a swimming pool, and his brain was full of cotton, "Carey noticed the similarity first. Linda Kline was wearing a pink silk nightgown, too."

"Shit." Gil rubbed his chin wearily. "It's hard to call it a coincidence when Summers didn't own the nightgown that was slashed."

"Yup."

"But that still doesn't mean this guy did the Klines. Maybe he just researched the case. That would even cover the connection between Summers and Downs and Otis."

"I know."

Gil reached for his coffee and grimaced when he found that it was cold. "Well, let's pull the Otis file anyway. No stone unturned, and all that."

"I've already requested it."

Gil tipped his chair back and looked up at the ceiling. "This kind of puts the pressure on."

Seamus nodded and rubbed his eyes with the thumb and fingers of his right hand. He usually did better than this on a few hours of sleep, but for some reason his brain was refusing to make connections without a lot of difficulty.

"Look," said Gil. "I don't make a habit of mother-henning, but get your ass home and get some sleep. We've got that interview tonight on the Mayberry murder, and it would be a great help if you were awake."

"I want to wait for the prelim." Among his messages this morning had been one from the M.E. promising a preliminary report by late this afternoon on the Downs killing.

"I'll get it and bring it with me tonight. A couple of hours isn't going to make a hell of a lot of difference, and you know it."

Seamus was past arguing. For whatever reason, he was on the edge of hallucinating. "Yeah, all right. See you at seven."

And all the way home, he tried not to feel guilty about all the cases on his desk, because Gil was right; he was next to useless in his present state.

And he was next to useless because he hadn't really gotten much shut-eye this morning. Lying next to Carey had made it impossible for him to sleep soundly. Every one of his senses had been acutely aware of her.

Shit. What he really needed was some kind of twelve-step program for people who were addicted to misery.

God knew, he wasn't any good at breaking the habit himself.

Like this morning. Why in the hell had he shared Carissa's bed? Even with covers and clothing between them, it had been an asinine thing to do, like picking at a scab on a barely healed wound.

It was hardly any surprise that he felt like he was bleeding from his soul all the time.

And that, he told himself, was a very sick state of mind. He slept until five-thirty. The September sun was still high, bright and hot, but in the shade of the live oaks that sheltered his house, he felt removed from the steaming world outside. Looking out his bedroom window, he saw shimmering heat waves rising from the pavement of the street, but they didn't reach into the shadows around his house.

Nothing reached into the shadows around his house.

He headed for the kitchen to make some coffee, and heard the air-conditioning click on. Moments later, cool air was stirring the warm, heavy air inside. He paused under one of the ducts, letting the chilly air wash over him until he felt more awake.

In the kitchen, he started the coffeemaker and hunted up some day-old bagels and a tub of cream cheese, all the while trying not to look out the back window.

His backyard had been a no-man's-land since his wife had hanged herself from the oak out back. He wouldn't even mow the grass anymore, but paid a company to come and take care of it every week.

But somehow, with a bagel in one hand and a mug of coffee in the other, he found himself standing at the kitchen sink, staring right out at that damn tree. He ought to have it cut down. For seven years he'd been telling himself to get rid of the thing, but he couldn't bring himself to do it. It was like a hair shirt, to remind him of his sins and failings.

He couldn't have found words to explain to anyone why he felt that he needed the tree as a reminder. It wasn't as if he would ever forget the awful events of that couple of weeks, or forget his part in them. Nor was it likely that if he didn't see the tree for a while, he might actually go a day without remembering.

He stood now looking at it, hating it, and admitting that a healthy person would simply have cut the damn thing down—or moved to another house.

Muttering a curse, he turned his back on the window and tried to eat his bagel. Even with cream cheese it seemed too dry, and wanted to stick in his throat. He washed it down with scalding coffee, accepting the discomfort as his due.

His wife, Mary, had been a beautiful, vivacious young woman. Somewhere in this house of pain, he had photo albums full of pictures of Mary, full of pictures of their daughter, Seana. He wasn't sure why he kept them, because he was sure he'd never be able to look at them again. He had no one to pass them on to, now that his only child was dead. Somehow he had come to a point in life where all the family he had was his father. And Mary had never had any family at all.

They had tried to build that dream family, the two of them. Maybe they had expected too much. Maybe that was why neither of them had been able to deal with the reality of tragedy. He sure wasn't dealing with it, even now, and Mary hadn't been able to deal with it at all. Sometimes he even had the stupid idea that he continued to draw breath only so that he could experience the suffering that was his due.

Sick indeed.

He threw the bagel in the trash and worked on finishing the coffee. Another cup, hot enough to burn, singed his tongue.

He'd only tried once to break out of the prison that tragedy had built around him, and that, too, had failed miserably because he hadn't been able to escape the confinement of his guilt. Carey had been right about that, when she had accused him of wallowing in it. He *did* wallow. And he was perceptive enough to feel disgust with himself.

What he needed, he decided, was a good, swift kick in the ass. Carey had suggested that, too, during one of their heated arguments about what was wrong with their relationship. She would still be right.

Feeling a weighted need to do something, he got the phone book out and called a company to come take the tree out of his backyard. He didn't even want a stump left.

Then, feeling he had taken a step in the right direction, he got ready to go back to work.

He might not be able to change the past, but he sure as hell could change the future.

You're listening to the Talk of the Coast, 990 WCST, Tampa Bay's number one talk radio station. This is Carey Justice, reminding you that John William Otis has just over fourteen days to live. Fourteen days before he will die for a crime he may not have committed. Have you thought about the fact that once we execute a man, we can never take it back? If, by some chance, fifteen days from now we discover that someone else killed Linda and Harvey Kline, we won't be able to give John Otis his life back.

Tonight our subject is the election of judges. The theory behind judicial elections is that by making judges accountable

174

to the public, the public will have a say how justice is administered in their towns and counties. Sounds good, doesn't it? But justice is supposed to be blind, and how blind can it be when it has to consider public opinion? We're going to talk about that tonight, but let me start with a story . . .

"Damn," said Gil, "that woman is something else. Her voice'll melt the socks right off you."

Even over the car radio, Carey's voice was hot honey, and reminded Seamus of the sleepy way she had sounded this morning. For some damn reason, in the back of his mind he was getting erotic images of all the things he'd like to do to and with Carey's body. "Yeah," he said, wanting to think about something else.

"She really intends to push this Otis thing right to the end, doesn't she."

"That's my impression."

Gil pulled over and parked in the lot of the Denny's where they were to meet the man who had called them. They climbed out of the car.

"Okay," said Gil. "It's hot enough to pass for a sauna and my brain is beginning to feel like the egg in that drug commercial. Suppose you bring me up to date."

"If you insist."

"Oh, I insist. Funny, but I hate walking blind into these things."

"You want to be bored?"

"Bore me."

"Sam Hollister. He lives in the neighborhood where Mayberry was killed. Want the address?"

Gil rolled his eyes.

"He called, says he wants to talk to us, but we have to meet him someplace he won't run into any of his neighbors."

"Well, Denny's is sure it," Gil said drily.

Seamus smiled wryly. "Hey, there's one closer to his home."

"Ah. So the ninety billion gray heads who walk through here in the next hour won't be gray heads he knows."

Seamus shrugged. "I won't ask him to do any undercover work for us."

"Wise decision."

But it wasn't really a bad meeting place, and they both knew it. Especially at this time of evening. Most of the elderly customers would have dined earlier and long since left. As it was, there were enough windows to ensure that if anyone that Sam Hollister recognized approached, he could duck into the men's room and pretend he was there alone.

Which was exactly what Seamus told him when they took a booth by a window back near the rest rooms.

The advice made Sam's rheumy blue eyes sparkle with excitement. The excitement was short-lived, though, and was replaced almost immediately by fear. The thin, elderly man sank lower in the booth, almost as if he wished he could crawl under the table.

"Let me get us some coffee," Gil said. "What do you take, Mr. Hollister?"

"Decaf with cream and sugar."

"Want anything else?"

Sam shook his head.

Gil signaled for the waiter and ordered three coffees while Seamus dug out his notebook and pen from his breast pocket. They waited to begin the questioning until the coffee had been delivered.

"Sure has been hot out there today," Gil remarked by way of breaking the ice.

Sam gave an almost shy smile. "I don't suffer from the heat the way I used to. When my wife used to talk about retiring to Florida, I used to tell her she was crazy. Not anymore. The heat feels good to my bones these days."

"Is your wife enjoying it as much as she thought she would?"

"She did, but she passed on about six years ago."

"I'm sorry."

Sam didn't respond to that. For a moment he looked far away and sad, but then he shook himself out of memory and looked at the two detectives.

"We talked to you last week, didn't we?" Seamus asked him.

Sam nodded. "I told you I didn't see or hear anything."

"Just like everybody else in the neighborhood."

Sam shifted uncomfortably. Gil took a gentler tone. "What is it you wanted to tell us, Mr. Hollister?"

"I heard something, but I didn't look."

Gil and Seamus exchanged glances.

"What did you hear?" Seamus asked, dropping the role of bad cop. This guy wasn't going to need it.

"I heard gunshots. Four of them."

"About what time?"

"It was about two-thirty in the afternoon. I was on my back patio, watering Daisy's ferns. She loved those plants, and I figured she'd want me to keep them alive."

"I'm sure she would."

There was a silence as the man fell once again into memory, but then he stirred. "Four gunshots. I knew it wasn't a backfire, because they don't come close together like that. I'm not proud of it, but I just kept on watering the plants. I didn't want to know what happened."

"Why not?"

Hollister lifted his cup in a shaky hand and sipped coffee, as if taking time to consider exactly what he would say. "It's a good neighborhood," he said finally. "I've lived there nearly twenty years now. Would you believe I'm almost eighty-five?"

Seamus would have. He didn't think the years of widowhood had been kind to Sam Hollister. "I'd have guessed seventy," he lied.

Hollister smiled. "Well, I am. And at my age you don't want to get involved in things you can't do anything about. There's not enough time left."

"I can understand the feeling."

Hollister nodded, then abruptly shook his head with a sigh. "No, that's just an excuse. At my age you start feeling old and helpless and scared. You start to realize there's a lot of ways you can't take care of yourself anymore. That's why so many people my age have bars on their windows."

"You start to feel vulnerable."

"And selfish," Sam said flatly. "Too many of us get so damn selfish. Guess I've been doing that like all the rest."

Seamus nodded. "So you heard four shots."

"Yes, sir, I did. And I didn't want to say anything because . . . well, we've been having trouble with drug dealers lately."

Seamus felt his heart kick. This quiet neighborhood where nothing ever happened? "I thought you had a relatively crime-free neighborhood." That's what Rico had said.

"We did up until about, oh, six, eight months ago. Then these young hoodlums started showing up, selling their drugs on the street as bold as you please in broad daylight. Got so folks was afraid to look out their own windows, never mind go outside. We called the police, and everybody was all hot on starting a neighborhood watch. Except the first time we tried to patrol the streets like we were told, the hoodlums threatened us and we went back inside. And nobody even dared call the police again because of the threats. Everybody was afraid that someone might get hurt if we did. I don't know but what the police thought the problem went away."

"But it didn't," Seamus said.

Hollister shook his head. "No, it let up for a few days while the police patrolled a lot. They never did catch anybody. Then the police stopped coming as often, and the dealers came back."

"So you think this was a drug killing?" Gil asked.

Hollister shook his head. "I saw that boy's picture in the paper. Mark my words, he was no dealer. I may not get around the way I used to, but my eyes are still as good as any eagle's, and I'd have recognized the boy if he was one of the dealers hanging out."

Seamus looked at Gil. "Curiouser and curiouser."

Gil nodded. "Could you take a look at some photos and see if you recognize any of the dealers? Say tomorrow at the station?"

Hollister hesitated. "Let me think about it. I probably could, but . . ." He looked away, and his hands were trembling in earnest. "Something's wrong in that neighborhood lately. I'm not saying I know what it is, but everybody's as nervous as a cat on a hot stove since the killing."

"That would make anybody nervous, wouldn't it?"

"Not like this. Most especially since the dealers have gone away since then, most likely because the police are coming around too often. Seems to me they ought to be relieved, if it was just a case of one drug dealer killing another."

Seamus's respect for the man's intelligence increased greatly. "So what do you think is going on?"

"I don't know." He looked at the two of them from his reddened eyes. "I honestly don't know. But I got two things to tell you. First off, there was some unpleasant talk back about a month ago, about how we had to protect ourselves if the police wouldn't do it. I thought it was all bluster, but, well, you know. And another thing. I know I'm not the only one heard those shots."

"So why aren't his people talking?"

"I can't say for sure. It's not like anybody is telling *me* why. Maybe it's just what Rico said to us, that it was street justice, and we don't need to get involved if we don't want."

"Rico said that?"

Sam nodded. "He said nobody can force us to be witnesses if we don't want. And I know folks are scared. Thing is, I'm not really sure what they're scared of."

Seamus looked at Gil, then asked, "Mr. Hollister, do you think one of your neighbors took the law into his own hands?"

Hollister looked down. "I don't know," he said finally. "But I tell you, ever since I saw that boy's picture in the paper, the possibility has been something I haven't been quite able to get out of my head."

CHAPTER 12
14 Days

IT WAS NEARLY ELEVEN BY THE TIME SEAMUS LEFT the station. Glancing at his watch, he decided to head over to the radio station, and see what Carey was up to. He rationalized it by telling himself he just wanted to make sure she got home safely. The lie didn't work; he knew perfectly well that he just wanted to see her.

He turned the radio on as he drove, listening to her read an Otis poem over the air, as she had done last night, wondering if she was going to close her show every night with one of the poems.

Not that it mattered. It was her show, the poems weren't bad . . . and he was beginning to get a bit of an itch about Otis himself. Especially since the preliminary autopsy suggested that Harry Downs had been slashed to death with a razor or a scalpel.

Carey was coming out of the station when Seamus pulled into the parking lot. The off-duty cop who'd be hired by the station was helping her carry a large box ward her car. Seamus pulled into an empty slot near Carey's car and climbed out.

He recognized the cop. "Hey, Lou. When did you get turned into a mule?"

Lou laughed the deep belly laugh that made him one the best-liked cops in the department. "Hey, what's a guy to do when a lady staggers by carrying something this heavy?"

Carey flashed a smile. "There's something to be said for machismo after all."

"Right," said Lou. "I get the sore arms and shoulders tomorrow." When Carey opened her tailgate, he shoved the box into the Jeep. "Well, since Rourke is here, I'll just say good night. Gotta get back to my coffee."

"Thanks an awful lot, Lou," Carey called after him. He waved back at her.

Then, shocking Seamus, she opened her purse, pulled out a cigarette, and lit it.

"You don't smoke," he said.

"You're right. I don't. Except for the last week."

"Put it out."

"Mind your own business, Rourke. I'll go to hell any way I want to."

He sighed and leaned back against his car, folding arms.

181

The shore breeze was whispering in the trees, givibg the balmy night a sweet, soft feeling.

"What do you want?" she asked.

"To make sure you get home safely."

She puffed on the cigarette and blew a plume of smoke into the night. In the light from the streetlamps, her skin had an unhealthy color, and her eyes looked sunken. He remembered she had probably had even less sleep than he had.

"I talked to the IRS about your dad today," she said finally.

"And?"

"And they're prepared to negotiate. If you want, I'll see what I can do."

"I wish you would. You're apt to keep your cool better than I could, given that he's my father."

"That's why people hire lawyers." She flicked an ash, folded one arm beneath her breasts, and held the cigarette up near her shoulder.

It was an unconsciously provocative pose, and he felt his erotic daydreams suddenly spring to life again. This was stupid. He needed to get out of here while he still could. But he stayed, his feet planted on the pavement as if they were glued. "Thanks," he said.

"No problem. How is your dad?"

"Okay, I guess. Tomorrow's the first day they'll let me visit him. They wanted to get him through the DTs first, I guess."

"You must be looking forward to that."

He shook his head. "Sometimes I wish he'd just go away."

She looked at him, took another drag on the cigarette, then tossed it to the pavement and ground it out with her toe. "You blame him, don't you?"

"I blame myself."

She sighed and tipped her head back, looking up at the night sky as if she could find the answer to a riddle there. "You blame everyone," she said finally. "You blame yourself because you weren't there—although exactly how you were supposed to know your kid was going to get seriously ill beats me. You blame your dad because he was driving, you blame your wife because she didn't use the car seat, you blame her for killing herself, and you blame yourself for not reading her mind and knowing she was going to—"

"Carey . . ."

She shook her head and looked at him. "You even blamed me for trying to make you happy. Or maybe you blamed me because I almost did, and you couldn't live with it because you've got some crazy notion that you need to pay for what happened for the rest of your life."

"Carey . . ."

"But mostly you blame yourself, Seamus. For everything. Did it ever occur to you that sometimes things just happen? That sometimes you can't be in control? That you weren't even there, for God's sake, so how could you have affected anything? And as for not being there . . . Christ! You're a cop. You were on the job. Nobody can be two places at the same time."

He felt the black lash of hatred for her. He hated it when she cut him open in her surgical way. He hated her for saying all the things he couldn't say himself.

"Go visit your dad tomorrow, Seamus." She turned and headed for the driver's side of her car. She opened the door and turned to look back at him. "And try to remember that your father, your wife, and your baby were the victims of a drunk driver."

He wanted to strangle her.

"In fact," she continued in the same hard voice, as if determined to drive a point home, "you might even remember that no matter what your father did or didn't do, he probably couldn't have avoided the accident. Drunks drive right into headlights, remember?"

She climbed in, started her car, and drove away, leaving him standing there overwhelmed by an impulse to violence so strong that it scared him, But as soon as he felt the fear, the anger seeped away.

She hadn't said anything he didn't already know. The problem was, he knew it with his head. It was his gut that wouldn't listen.

Carey kicked herself all the way home. Her attack on Seamus had been unforgivable, and she knew it. It wasn't as if she'd said those things out of some desire to help him. No, she had said them to protect herself. Seamus was getting too close again, involving himself entirely too much in her life, and his showing up tonight for no good reason had been like setting a match to a fuse. Every self-protective instinct she possessed had kicked into high gear.

But that wasn't fair to him. She had no idea why he was suddenly spending so much time in her life—wanting to see that she got home safely struck her as an excuse, not a reason—and she, was afraid of the toll if she started to care for him again.

As if she had ever stopped caring. The gloomy realization struck her just as she was pulling into her driveway. It wouldn't hurt this much, she admitted, if she didn't care.

She should never have called him about Otis in the first place. Getting him involved hadn't done a damn thing to help. All it had done was pull the pin on the hand grenade that was her love for him. If she didn't keep a safe distance, her whole life was going to blow up in her face all over again.

"Shit." She said the word quietly, but with feeling, as she sat in her car. She had turned the ignition off, and the only sound in the stillness of the night was the tick of her cooling engine and the distant sound of traffic on Roosevelt Boulevard.

Maybe she ought to take a long drive across the bay. It had been a while since she had done that, and it always soothed her nerves. And maybe, if she drove far enough and long enough, she could put things in their proper perspective.

She leaned forward to shove the key back into the ignition, but just as it slid home, headlights pulled into the driveway behind her.

Her heart climbed into her throat, making it nearly impossible to breathe. She stared into the rearview mirror at those headlights and tried not to think about just how thin the canvas top of her Jeep was. It was no protection at all against a knife or a bullet, and locking the doors would be no help at all. God, why hadn't she just bought an ordinary car?

The headlights turned off and someone climbed out of the car. Twisting in her seat, she tried to decide if she should make a run for it. Then she recognized Seamus.

"Shit!" Suddenly furious, she grabbed the door handle and wrenched the door open. "Son of a bitch! You scared me to death!"

He froze a couple of feet away. "Sorry," he said. "I just wanted to make sure you got home safely."

She was shaking in reaction to the adrenaline pumping through her veins, mad enough to spit but afraid that her legs would give out if she tried to stand. She fumbled for her purse and lit another cigarette.

This time Seamus didn't say anything about it. All he said was, "I'll wait until I'm sure you're safely inside. Would you like me to check the house?"

She drew a deep drag of smoke and looked at her trembling hand, watching the way the glowing tip of the cigarette bobbed wildly. "Nobody's going to try to kill me," she said finally.

"Probably not. The Harry Downs thing put me on edge."

"Yeah, but there's a difference. If the murder was really related to Otis, then the whole damn Bay Area knows I think he might be innocent. I don't think I'd be real high on the victim list."

"You can't know that." Then, after a moment, "Want me to carry that box inside for you?"

Finally she climbed out of the Jeep and faced him. "You're crazy, you know that?"

"It's been rumored."

"After the way I talked to you down at the station, what the hell are you doing here?"

He shrugged a shoulder. "What you said was true. Anyway, I'm crazy. So I'm here."

Giving up, she opened the tailgate and let him heft the box.

"What is this?" he asked.

"Sally Dyer got me a bunch of press clippings on the Otis case. I haven't had a whole lot of time to look at it, but I wouldn't have thought the *Sentinel* had printed so much about it."

She unlocked the door, and they stepped inside. Seamus put the box on the lowboy at her direction, then insisted on checking out the house. She waited for him with a feeling of impatience, wishing him gone *now*. He didn't seem to be in any mood to oblige.

When he came back downstairs, she decided to apologize. Maybe then he'd go away, and she wouldn't have to keep feeling bad about the way she had jumped on him. "Look," she said. "I'm sorry about what I said. I had no business giving you a hard time."

"Like I said, it was all true."

"That doesn't give me the right to say it."

"Why not?" It was a rhetorical question, and his smoky eyes said he didn't expect a response.

She gave him one anyway. "You're crowding me, Rourke. I see you everywhere I turn."

"Hey, you were the one who called me."

"About *Otis*."

"And Otis is what has me turning up so often. You've had death threats because of your shows about Otis."

"I get death threats all the time." Well, actually, only rarely, but she wanted to sound as if she didn't give a damn, because if she let him know she was scared to death, he'd *never* go away. Having him play watchdog was *not* good for her sanity.

"But you don't get calls all the time from a guy who may well be a murderer."

He had her there. She glared at him, but couldn't think of a good argument. Her brain was fried after three hours on the air, and exhaustion was rapidly catching up with her. Memories of awaking this morning with Seamus beside her were beginning to waft around the edges of her thoughts like the fleeting fragments of nearly forgotten dreams.

"Look," he said finally. "I'll admit it. I've got you in my blood like cocaine. I keep remembering the high, and I keep wanting more of it."

"Cocaine isn't any good for anybody."

"Exactly." The smile he gave her was almost sad. "I'd

like to have sex with you again. But I'm afraid of the price tag. So hey, it's out in the open, now we can ignore it and concentrate on business. If John William Otis didn't kill the Klines, we're getting awfully close to running out of time."

It was like a one-two punch, and she nearly gasped for air. He'd like to have sex with her? Seamus had never been that crude. Like most men, he wasn't comfortable with terms like "making love" but he'd never, ever referred to just "having sex."

And then following it right up with the reminder that they had only two weeks left before Otis would die, and absolutely nothing at all that might help save him, left her feeling almost KO'd.

But then she was struck by something else. "You believe he's innocent?"

"I didn't say that. Let's just say I'm keeping an open mind about it. But having an open mind is making me awfully nervous."

She nodded and decided to forget everything else he'd said. It was the easiest way to deal with it, and the quickest way to get back to a safe distance while pretending normalcy. "Want some cofee?"

He shook his head. "You need some sleep, and so do I. If I hang around, neither of us is going to get any."

She didn't have to ask why not. She knew. He walked out the door and closed it behind him with finality.

But nothing was final, she realized. Her entire body was aching with a longing that hadn't been fulfilled in five long years. And all because the jerk had said he wanted to have sex with her.

Wrenching her thoughts away from those dangerous paths, she picked up the box and carried it into the kitchen, determined to read the stuff Sally had given her until she was too tired to do anything but fall straight to sleep.

The next morning Carey went to visit Evan Sinclair at the State Attorney's Office. The new criminal courts complex had been opened just after she'd left the State Attorney's Office, so it wasn't a familiar place she was coming back to. Somehow it still managed to have the same look and feel, though. Or maybe it was just the number of familiar faces, some of whom greeted her in a friendly fashion, others of whom looked quickly away. She decided some of them must have their noses out of joint over her coverage of Otis. It wasn't like there could be any other reason now that she was spending so little time in the practice of law.

Evan greeted her warmly enough, and even got her a cup of coffee. He closed his office door, though, before they started talking.

"I'm getting cross-eyed looks since I asked for this file," he told her. "I figure now that you've come to see me, my stock around here is going to be zero."

"Why should it matter? You're not the one making the ruckus.

"Nobody's real keen on having this case reopened."

"There isn't enough time to do that."

He shrugged. "You know what was really interesting? It usually takes three or four days to get old files out of the storage."

"I know." She looked at the folder on his desk. "It wasn't in storage, was it."

He shook his head. "Even more interesting. Harry Downs asked for it last week."

"Oh, God." The thought made her queasy. Could Harry have had some doubts, too? He'd certainly been gung ho during the trial.

189

"Yeah," he said, "that was kind of the way I felt. Oh, God." He looked at the folder. "But there's nothing in it, Carey. I read it over yesterday afternoon. Briefs, pleadings, motions, orders . . . it's a complete record of public documents. No trial notes, no interview notes, nothing. You could have pulled this record together from the clerk's office, except for the police reports. Those are still here. And the depositions and trial transcripts." He pointed to a stack of blue-bound court reporters' books nearly two feet high.

Carey realized she was chewing her lip, and stopped. "Could Harry have taken them out?"

"It's possible, but I can't imagine why he would have done that. You worked on the case. There weren't any glaring omissions or great big secrets, were there?"

"I didn't think so."

"So maybe some zealous secretary purged the file way back when. Or maybe Harry kept them in a personal file that never got stored. I don't know. I just know there isn't a damn thing in here to help you. But you're welcome to run through this stuff. Me, I've got to get to court or Judge Franklin's going to send the bailiff out to find me." He glanced at his watch. "Yeah. Jury selection in three minutes. I'm outta here."

She didn't need to bother reading the depos because she'd gone over them with a fine-tooth comb five years ago and hadn't been able to find anything other than the evidence that was used to build the circumstantial case. As for the trial transcript—well, she'd been in court every day. No surprises there.

But she opened the file folder and began to scan the motions and responses that had been filed by both sides. All of that had been reviewed by the courts, some of it had even been appealed, and everything had stood up.

190

Nothing there, but she looked anyway.

The police report hadn't changed any, either. No weapon had been found, no sign of forced entry . . .

The thought trailed off as she considered that. No sign of forced entry. Which most likely suggested that the killer had either had a key—which John Otis had—or had been known to the Klines. Neighbors and acquaintances had all been checked out, and all had alibis which stood the test.

Even John Otis's younger brother had been cleared, not that he'd ever been a serious suspect, since he lived in Atlanta. But given that he was related, and that he'd been present at the killing of their father, the cops had felt bound to check him out. An affidavit signed by James Henry Otis's foster mother, and forwarded by Georgia authorities, said her James had been at home in Atlanta at the time of the Kline killings.

The investigation hadn't been slipshod by any means, and with the elimination of each possible suspect, John Otis had become the most likely perp. The jaws of circumstance had closed tightly around him until no one else was left.

By the time she finished reading, her neck was stiff, and she had the beginnings of a headache. And that was all she had. The distance of time hadn't made one thing clearer than it had been five years ago.

It was a little after noon, and she debated whether to go somewhere for lunch or head home for the few hours before she had to go to work. Home, she decided. She could take some aspirin and maybe lie down for a couple of minutes, then dive back into the incredible volume of material Sally had given her.

Scenting a good story, Sally had gone above and beyond what Carey had hoped for In addition to stones from the last five years that were on computer disk, she'd sent a

191

huge volume of photocopies not only of *Sentinel* stories going back to the original murder of John Otis's father, but copies of clippings from other papers and the wire services. Getting through all that was going to take time, no matter how fast she read.

After an hour's nap to get rid of the headache, she settled at the kitchen table with coffee and a sandwich, and her laptop. The easiest way to do this, she decided, would be to go backward from the present.

Reading the information on the disks proved to sound easier than it really was. Sally had apparently stripped all the formatting from the articles so that they were straight text files, densely packed text that covered her entire screen.

Sighing, she started to read. This was going to take days.

And days were the very thing John William Otis didn't have to spare.

CHAPTER 13
9 DAYS

"Shit, I don't believe it," Seamus said.

He looked at Gil, then they both looked at their boss, Ed Sanchez. Ed, a dark-skinned man with fine features, always looked as if he had stepped off the pages of a menswear catalogue. No day was too hot or too long for him; he was always impeccably dressed. Seamus, who started to look rumpled by early afternoon, sometimes wondered how Sanchez managed it.

"Last night," Ed said. "It looks like the same MO, so I'm turning it over to you guys. If you need help, let me know. I can probably put Turanchek on it, too."

Gil and Seamus exchanged glances again. "We'll manage," said Gil. "The two of us are as good as four."

"Right." Ed gave them a sour smile. "Turanchek may be a pain in the butt, but he's got a good nose, and politically speaking, you may not have a choice about it if you dawdle too long."

Seamus arched a brow. "Threats?"

"Nah," said Gil. "Promises."

"Get outta here." Ed waved them away as if they were annoying gnats swarming around his face. "And give me something soon."

Back at the table, they opened the file.

"Beatrice Barnstable," said Seamus. "Housewife. Mother of five. Volunteer on the literacy project."

"Well, there goes the Otis theory," Gil said. "Our slasher must be picking them at random."

"Maybe. Maybe not." Seamus stared down at the Polaroid photo clipped to the report, apparently a family photo someone had given to the cops. In the background he could see a birthday cake and a stack of gaily wrapped presents. He flipped the photo oven. It had been taken three weeks ago, on Beatrice Barnstable's forty-ninth birthday.

The victim had been discovered by a neighbor, apparently within hours of the killing. The neighbor said she and the victim always had breakfast together before they went grocery shopping on Saturday morning, but this morning she had found the back door open and no sign of the victim. Thinking Beatrice might have overslept, the neighbor had entered the house and discovered the body in bed.

The ex-husband had picked up the children for the weekend the night before as usual, so the victim had been home alone at the time of the killing.

"The husband," said Gil.

"Could be." It usually was. On the other hand, the MO was the same. "But why would he kill Harry Downs first? Downs was a prosecutor. Does the husband have some kind of record?"

"Maybe the vic was having a relationship with Downs." Seamus nodded, considering. "Maybe. Approximately the same age."

"So maybe that's all it is."

"Yeah, but how does it tie in with the nightgown at the Summers place?"

"Maybe it doesn't tie in at all. Maybe that's just a whole different case. After all, nobody was killed at Summers place."

"But we have the caller to the radio station who said he did the Summers thing, then killed somebody."

"Maybe we're connecting the wrong victim to Summers."

"Christ." Seamus put the file down and rocked back in his chair. "Consistency. I could do with a little consistency across the board here."

"Hey, consistency is the hobgoblin of small minds. Maybe our perp has a large mind."

"He's sure as hell got a large knife. Or razor."

"How about the Barnstable killing isn't connected at all to the Downs killing? Maybe it's a copycat."

Seamus shrugged. "We'll have to take a look at the prelim and see."

One corner of Gil's mouth lifted. "Straws."

"Exactly. Well, where do you want to start?" He took another look at the file, scanning the rest of the police report and transcribed notes. "Well, fuck me," he said finally. "She had sliding glass doors."

"Hell," said Gil, leaning forward to look over his shoulder. "Sliding doors, no sign of forced entry, slashing . . ."

Then Seamus's heart stopped. Beatrice Barnstable had been nude when she was killed. But across the foot of her bed had been a pink silk nightgown.

He looked at Gil and saw the same knowledge in his partner's eyes.

"That screws the pooch," Gil said.

Twenty minutes later they were on their way to speak to the victim's ex-husband.

Talking to the bereaved was the least enjoyable part of the job, as far as Seamus was concerned. He could handle the murder scene a whole lot better.

Jerry Barnstable was at home, taking time off work to stay with his now-motherless children. When the detectives arrived, he sent the children out back to play for a little while. They went with heads down and gathered out back, sitting on the patio, looking listless and miserable. Seamus could see them through the sliding glass doors, and his heart went out to them,

Jerry Barnstable was a corporate manager with a local drugstore chain. He smoked one cigarette after another and stubbed them out in an overflowing ashtray while he talked with Gil and Seamus.

"Bea and I split because we'd gone our separate ways," he said. "All we had in common anymore was the kids. I work anywhere from sixty to eighty hours a week, and she's got her own life. It happens. I think it was dead before either of us knew it was dying, you know?"

Gil and Seamus both nodded understandingly, although neither of them had experienced anything similar.

"I'm divorced," Gil said, as if that made them members of the same club, although his own marital breakup had been over his wife's affairs.

Jerry's hand was trembling as he lit another cigarette.

"At least I thought it was dead." He shook his head and gave a short, unsteady laugh. "This hurts more than I would've thought. Anyway, I let her keep the kids because she's home more than me. This isn't gonna be good for them, having only me. I need to find a way to cut my hours . . ."

He trailed off and looked out toward the patio, where his kids were sitting like sorry little statues. "I don't know what to tell them. It's so crazy! They'd understand better if it was a car accident."

He looked at them again, his eyes reddened as if he was fighting tears. "You don't want to hear about my problems. And honest to God, I don't know why anyone would want to hurt Bea. She had a good heart. Everybody liked her."

"Did she work?"

"No." He shook his head. "We both felt that until the kids were a little older she should be home with them. But she was going to school over at USF, studying to be a teacher."

"So you were supporting her?" Seamus asked.

Jerry Barnstable shrugged. "Only until she got her degree. I'd be paying the child support anyway. She could have lived on that."

"Did she happen to know Harry Downs or Tricia Summers?"

Jerry's eyes widened, but he shook his head. "I don't think so. Why? Do you think there's a link to what happened to them?"

"We have to check everything out, sir," Gil said. "It's just a routine question."

"What about John Otis?" Seamus asked.

Jerry thought a moment. "I don't know. She never mentioned any Otis. Why? Do you think he did it?"

Seamus hesitated. "I'm talking about the John William Otis who is on death row."

Jerry started and paled instantly. "My God," he said hoarsely. "*That* Otis? She was on his jury five years ago!"

Seamus felt as if he'd just been gut-punched. He hardly heard Gil's last few questions, and was glad when it was time to escape.

"Bingo," said Gil, as they stepped out into the sunshine. They paused under the magnolia that shaded the driveway and shed their coats before getting into the car.

"So okay," Seamus said, as they opened the car doors and let the blast-furnace heat out before climbing in, "that makes two links. So what the hell does it mean?"

"Beats me. Revenge? Copycat? Robin Hood?"

"Robin Hood?"

"Yeah, somebody trying to get Otis off."

"The caller to the radio station said Otis didn't do it, *he* did."

"Meaningless," said Gil. "You know that. Give me some *proof.*"

Seamus looked at him across the top of the car. "Doesn't it give you just a little qualm that the wrong guy might die in a little more than a week?"

"You're spending too much time with that radio lady, Seamus. The jury convicted him. They said we got the right guy. And that's the way it's gonna be unless somebody gets some proof otherwise."

"So maybe I ought to ask the M.E. to compare the Kline autopsy report with these."

"Be my guest. But all it's gonna do is say we got us a copycat. And take my word for it, the chief isn't gonna be happy if you run around trying to solve a five-year-old closed case when we got a murderer running around right now."

"I know, I know." But he was damned if he was going to let it go.

Carey was just getting ready to leave for work when the phone rang. She picked it up with one hand while she continued to put the articles she'd read back into the box. There was still a stack waiting for her attention, but it no longer looked so overwhelming. in fact, she was beginning to get disheartened because she hadn't found anything yet that caught her attention. Basically, everything was a rehash of what she already knew

The tension was beginning to kill her. A little more than a week remained. Time was getting so short it felt like a constant pressure on the back of her head, driving her to exhaustion. And now, making it worse, she was beginning to have dreams about John Otis, dreams in which she watched him being strapped into the electric chair, all the while protesting he was innocent. Dreams of him screaming and burning when the chair was turned on.

Dreams that she was throwing the switch herself.

God. She had a constant tension headache that no aspirin could touch. Her stomach hurt all the time, and she was so much on edge that she had to keep biting her tongue to keep from biting someone's head off.

And nothing. Absolutely nothing. Why had she ever thought that she might find something in all this media rehash of the events? Why had she thought the press could point her to something that the cops and the entire investigative team of the prosecutor's office hadn't been able to find?

Hubris, pure and simple.

She put the phone to her ear, expecting to hear some cheerful salesperson's voice offering to sell her credit-card insurance or ask her for a donation. Instead she heard Seamus's voice.

"Carey?"

Shock kept her silent for a moment. He hadn't called, and she hadn't seen him since the night when they'd had it out. She had figured she would never hear from him again unless their paths crossed by accident. "Yes?"

"Be on your toes tonight. You might get a call from the killer."

"Why?"

"I'll meet you tonight after your show. We need to talk."

"Seamus, what's going on?"

"You know I can't discuss a case. Have you seen today's paper?"

"I didn't even open it."

"Take a look at the front page of the metro section."

"Now?"

"Now."

"Hang on a minute."

She'd tossed the paper on the lowboy in the foyer. She went to get it, heading back to the kitchen as she tried to pull the metro section out. It was wrapped around all the others, though, so she had to open it on the kitchen table to get the section out. Once she had it in her hands, she picked up the phone and tucked it between her shoulder and her ear. "I've got it."

"Look below the fold, front page."

She flipped the section over and saw a vaguely familiar woman's face beneath the headline *Woman murdered in bed.*

Scanning quickly she came to the woman's name, and a gasp escaped her. "I know her!"

"Tell me how."

"She was the jury forewoman on the Otis trial."

"I'll see you at eleven."

With a *click* he was gone, leaving her to listen to the dial tone and stare at the face of Beatrice Barnstable.

Seamus got home that night around eight-thirty, feeling like he'd been dragged behind a tractor. He was sticking to his clothes, and he stripped gladly, tossing the summer-weight suit into the dry-cleaning pile, the shirt into the hamper along with his underwear. Then he stepped into a cold shower, which around there meant the water was tepid. He soaped every inch of his body, washing away the sweat and the grime that had stuck to it.

When he had toweled off, he dressed in khaki shorts, a PAL T-shirt, and Top-Siders without socks. Florida chic, someone had called it, but he was damned if he could remember who. Chic or not, it was necessary for comfort in the subtropical climate. He knew it got hotter up north and many places out West, but Florida's dress code had been developed before air conditioners and by tourists. Shorts could take you just about anywhere.

He ransacked the refrigerator and finding nothing that he felt like cooking, he opened up a bag of precut salad, dumped some into a bowl, and poured bottled Caesar dressing on it. Then he opened a can of Vienna sausage and called it dinner.

He turned on the radio to Carey's show. She was at the Otis thing again, hammering on it to the apparent irritation of many callers who wanted to know why she was so obsessed. Carey held her ground, arguing right back and refusing to change topics.

Guilt was going to ruin her, he found himself thinking. He wondered if she even realized what she was doing to herself. Too much of this would kill her show. As near as he could tell, Florida was a rabidly pro-death penalty state.

People around here were likely to tell you that you had to break a few eggs to make an omelet, and that if an innocent person happened to get in the way, that was just too damn bad, because it was important to execute murderers.

Retribution, pure and simple.

As the thought crossed his mind, he found himself feeling suddenly uneasy. He'd always supported the death penalty himself, even though he'd long ago figured out that it wasn't much of a deterrent. It had always just seemed to him that the punishment had to fit the crime. Burglars and thieves had to pay restitution. The death penalty was as close as society could get to restitution for murder.

But it wasn't the same, he found himself thinking now. Would he have felt any better if the drunk driver who killed his baby had gotten death instead of five years?

No. Sometimes it bothered him a little to realize that while Mary and Seana were gone for good, the man who had killed them was long since back on the streets. But nothing would be any better if the guy were dead. It sure as hell wouldn't ease his pain any, or bring Mary and Seana back.

And in this case, there wasn't even any doubt about who had been driving the car that had caused Seana's death. Otis was different. There was doubt, because it was a purely circumstantial case.

Christ, he was beginning to think like Carey.

He rose from the table, his meal only half-eaten, and went to the back door, where he threw on the back light and looked out at the oak tree that had taken away the last of his dreams. His heart squeezed and his eyes prickled with tears he would never shed. God, the world was so empty sometimes.

But that tree didn't deserve to die. It deserved that even less than the drunk driver. Reaching for the phone, he called the tree-removal company and left a message canceling the appointment for next week, telling them he'd decided to keep the tree.

Then he called the real estate agent he'd bought the house from nine years ago and left a message on her voice mail, telling her he wanted to list his house.

It was time to move on, he thought. Time to go.

But first he had to make one last visit to the past.

Turning, he went to the back of the house and opened a door he hadn't opened in seven years.

Seana's room.

Dust layered everything thickly, and cobwebs grew in all the corners and on the windows, but he saw it as it used to be. Her crib mattress, still covered with a cotton sheet decorated with tiny rosebuds that were invisible under the dust now. The little quilt in yellows and greens that Mary had made with her own hands, still crumpled in the corner of the crib where Mary had left it the last time she had lifted their baby out of the bed.

He stood there, making himself look at it, forcing himself to accept the pain that tightened his throat and constricted his breathing. Promises made and broken, he thought. A baby was a promise made by life, and this time life had cheated.

Nothing could make that any better.

Carey's voice still reached him from the living room, distant but argumentative. Another promise made and broken. But he wasn't sure he could blame life for that one.

Taking a deep, unsteady breath, he walked into the room and began to strip the crib, bundling the linens into a pile. He considered throwing them away, then decided that sdome other child might need them, so he took them to the washer and threw them in. Maybe they were salvageable and he could give them to Goodwill.

He got some cardboard boxes from the garage and filled them with Seana's clothes and toys. Each little piece carried a sweet memory that stabbed him with a yearning so deep he thought the ache might kill him. He had to pause often and fight for control.

He took the crib apart and carried it out to the garage, along with the changing table and small chest of drawers. All of it was going to Goodwill, where it might make someone else smile.

By the time he finished, he felt as if he were hanging by a precarious emotional thread, breathing as hard as any marathoner as he battled the crushing tightness of grief in his chest.

He took a break, drinking a glass of ice water, and listening to Carey lambaste a caller who had dared to say that it was just too damn bad if Otis was innocent, he'd been convicted.

She was getting almost rabid, he realized. Too emotionally involved. This wasn't entertainment, this was turning into a bloody on-air fight. He wondered if she'd have a job tomorrow.

Guilt, It was amazing what it could make a person do.

Then, unable to help it anymore, he closed his eyes and let the tears squeeze out from beneath his eyelids, let the crushing grief depive him of breath, let silent sobs wrack him.

It hurt, and that was the one thing he hadn't allowed himself to really do in all these years. He'd flogged himself with guilt and anger, but he'd never let himself hurt.

He let it happen now, and half hoped the pain would kill him.

It didn't, of course. Grief might kill the soul, but the heart kept right on beating.

CHAPTER 14
8 DAYS

"CHRIST, CAREY," TED SAID AS HE CAME INTO THE studio just after she cut away to the news break, "I can tell what my show is going to be about tonight."

She shrugged.

"You sure got people mad."

"Well, I'm sure you'll soothe their ruffled feathers."

He shook his head and changed places with her at the console. "I'm not worried about *their* feathers, Bill might be harder to calm."

"He said he was going to support free speech."

"I'm not sure he wanted to go this far."

Carey shrugged again. "There's always work available for a lawyer." *Work that would do more good.*

She found Seamus waiting for her in the small reception area. Apparently Lou had let him in, even though only employees were supposed to be allowed in after business hours.

He didn't look good, she thought. There was something weary about the way he stood, and his eyes looked funny. Puffy.

"Do you want to get something to eat?" he asked.

"You look awful," she told him frankly.

He gave her a crooked half smile. "Gee, thanks."

"What's wrong?"

"Nothing new."

Back when they'd lived together, she'd gotten increasingly frustrated by his unwillingness to enjoy much of anything, as if he felt he weren't entitled to joy or pleasure. But never had she seen him looking as if he'd reached the end of his emotional rope.

"Seamus . . ."

"Look, it's *my* shit, and I'll deal with it, okay? Now do you want to get something to eat or just go somewhere we can talk?"

The wise thing would have been to go to some public place, but she was rapidly getting past the point of being wise about much. Time was goading her to the edge of irrationality. She knew it, but didn't know how to control the desperation that was dogging her. The more she read of John William Otis's poetry, and the closer the execution drew, the less caution she was able to exercise.

"Let's go to my place," she said. "Or your place. More privacy."

"Your place," he decided. "I've had enough ghosts for one night."

She didn't ask what he meant. His ghosts were nearly as real to her as they were to him. And now that she knew the full story, she better understood how they had twisted his life. Not that it made it any easier to be around his gloom, she reminded herself. There had been times when she thought his barely masked depression was going to smother her.

She had ordered a pizza that afternoon, and there was plenty left, so she stuck the remains into the oven to reheat and started a fresh pot of coffee.

"Cofee and pizza:' he remarked. "You've got to be thirty-something to think that goes together."

"I have cola if you want it."

"I was joking. Coffee's exactly what I want."

"So what did you want to discuss?"

"I want to know if you've found out anything I can use. This latest murder has got me really concerned. Did the guy call tonight?"

She shook her head. "I told my producer to make sure

he got through if he called, but he didn't. Not a peep."

"Shit." He ran his fingers through his hair, an impatient gesture she well remembered. "Can I talk to you off the record? Will you promise that nothing I say will go any further?"

"Sure." She didn't have any problem with that. In the first place, she didn't consider herself to be a newshound. In the second, she was more concerned about helping Otis than getting some kind of scoop to put on the air. And finally, she was first and foremost a lawyer. She knew how to keep confidentiality.

"Okay. I'm beginning to think you're right that this caller may have also killed the Klines. I'd be a lot more reluctant to think that if he hadn't drawn the connection himself, but given that he did, and given the new murders, I'm inclined to think he isn't just a crackpot. But there's no way on God's earth I can prove he did the Klines without a confession from him. I reviewed the record, Carey, and there's nothing there."

"There never was anything there," she said, pointing to the box of papers that was still on her table. "I've been over the state's file, and most of the clippings Sally Dyer gave me. It was a thin case against Otis to begin with, and I can't find a damn thing that would tie anyone else to it."

"So there's no way I can reopen that investigation," he said. "I don't even need to ask. They won't let me do it."

"So what now?"

"Damned if I know. Do you think there's some way you can get him to call your show again?"

"And do what? He's already said Otis didn't do it, that *he* did. You need more than that."

"Maybe you can get some details out of him that might prove he has more than ordinary knowledge of the crime."

She cocked her head. "Was there anything that wasn't

presented at trial as evidence? Anything you guys withheld that could be useful?"

He closed his eyes and squeezed the bridge of his nose. "Damned if I know," he said finally. "It's been five years. All I can rely on after all this time is what's in the file. I don't think anything was kept back, once the charge was filed." He opened his eyes suddenly and dropped his hand. "Christ! There's got to be something!"

"It would sure help if John would talk. I've got the strongest feeling he knows who really did it."

"Yeah? Then it would have to be someone he knows." He perked up a little then, and Carey could almost see the wheels spinning. "You told me that, didn't you. Christ, it's as plain as the nose on my face. Why didn't I check it out before?"

"I've got to say," Carey said after a moment, "that Otis hasn't been real helpful from the git-go. Just once, he said he didn't do it, then he clammed up. He wouldn't suggest anyone else, wouldn't cooperate with investigators, and now he's sitting there on death row with only a few more days to live, and he still won't say anything. So he's protecting somebody—although at this point you'd think he'd be getting scared enough to reconsider."

"Guilt makes people do funny things," Seamus said.

Carey straightened. "Guilt? What made you say that? You think he's guilty?"

"I don't know why I said it, and no, that's not what I meant. It's something I was thinking about, and it just popped out."

The oven timer *dinged,* and Carey turned to pull the pizza out. The mozzarella was bubbling, and the delicious aroma filled the kitchen.

"I just got hungry,' Seamus said.

"Me too." She put three pieces on a plate for him, and one on a plate for herself.

He poured the coffee for both of them, and carried it to the table, then removed the box of clippings to the window seat for the time being.

"I've got crushed red pepper," she offered.

"Not this late at night."

She grinned at that. "So I'm not the only one with an aging stomach?"

He surprised her with a genuine laugh. "I'm not sure whether it's age or abuse. Too many fast-food meals and too much coffee. Some jobs'll kill you before your time."

"No kidding."

They ate for a while in silence, their thoughts following separate paths. Then Seamus startled her by asking, "You ever think of having kids?"

That came from so far out in left field it took her a few seconds to understand his meaning. "Well, yes. I guess. The way people do who aren't married. Someday. Eventually. My biological clock isn't ticking mercilessly yet."

"I cleaned out the baby's room tonight."

She looked at him, waiting, not really certain what he meant.

"I haven't touched it since she died." He looked away from her and sighed. "Everything was just the way it was the night she was killed. I cleaned it all out, got it ready to take to Goodwill."

"And that's what got you thinking about guilt?"

He nodded and returned his gaze to her. "Exactly. For seven years I never even opened that door. Do you know how much dust accumulates in that time? I looked at it, and saw the way it used to be; but I saw the dust, too. It said something to me."

She nodded, wanting to encourage him to talk, and afraid that if she said anything he might shut up. This was something he'd never talked about before in any depth.

"I've been thinking that my life is like that room, frozen in time, and disappearing under a ton of dust."

She wanted to reach out and take his hand, but didn't dare.

"Anyway, I called a real estate agent. I'm going to sell the house. And all of that got me thinking about guilt. It's amazing what guilt makes us do. Look at you. You're risking your job."

"I'm risking my job to try and save a man's life."

"Come on, Carey. You know that nothing you say on your show is going to save Otis. There's no need to risk your job."

She shook her head. "That man is not going to go to his death without somebody speaking up for him. And this society is not going to execute him without someone standing up to say it's wrong."

"Why *you?*"

"Someone has to do it."

"It's guilt, Carey. Guilt because you had a hand in it. Guilt because you feel responsible. You're destroying your life just the way I destroyed mine, and for no more reason."

"You're one to talk."

"I'm one who *can* talk. Just take it easy on the air. What needs to be done isn't going to be done there."

"Unless I can get Bob from Gulfport to confess in detail and turn himself in."

"Anything's possible, I guess. But anything else is just going to get you fired."

"That's my problem."

"I care, Carey. That makes it my problem."

She didn't know how to take that. She stared at him, feeling irritated and strangely hurt. She didn't like him saying that he cared, not after all this time, but there was no reason it should hurt.

"Okay," he said after a moment. "It's your business, not mine. But it wouldn't hurt to reconsider. That's all I'm asking."

She wanted to stop this discussion, so she took the easy way out. "I'll think about it, okay?"

"Okay." He rose and started clearing the dishes. "So you haven't found anything in the press."

"I haven't finished looking."

"Want me to help?"

They picked up the to-be-read stack of clipping copies and divided them. It was well after midnight, but neither of them especially cared if they were dragging in the morning. Some things were more important.

At some point, Carey realized the words were swimming before her eyes, and that her mind wasn't even absorbing them. "I've got to stop," she said. "I can't see straight, and if I found something, I probably wouldn't even recognize it."

"Me too," he said. But he didn't move immediately.

He looked every bit as tired as she felt, but she had the distinct impression he didn't want to go. Thinking about how he said he had spent his evening, she guessed she could understand that. She felt an ache of sympathy for him, but didn't know what she could do to help.

"Time to go," he said, appearing to shake himself out of reflection. Without looking at her, he rose, carried his mug to the sink, then headed for the door.

She followed him, feeling a mixture of things she didn't care to identify. Feeling *anything* about Seamus Rourke was like testing a tooth that ached. There was no telling when the wrong touch might cause unbearable pain to flare.

At the door he turned to say good night, but he never spoke the words. Their eyes met, and something shifted in the air, making it electric—like the calm before the storm.

He felt it, too; she could see it in the way his pupils dilated, and his face seemed to take on a drowsy expression that had nothing to do with sleep.

Her heart began to beat heavily, and her mouth opened slightly. *No*, said some sane portion of her mind. Don't do this. Don't let this happen. The pain had nearly torn her apart last time. Hell, she'd hardly even dated for fear of an involvement that could cause her that kind of pain again.

Now here she was, her entire body suddenly straining toward Seamus as if she were a flower and he the sun she so desperately needed.

But desire was spiraling deep within her, building a whirlpool that was about to draw her in. Heaviness was filling her limbs, making her feel soft and pliant, and the screaming protests of her common sense seemed far away and muffled, and unimportant.

And he hadn't done a thing except look at her with that slumberous expression she remembered all too vividly. That look had always been a promise of exquisite pleasure and complete forgetfulness, a call to join him in another world where no one and nothing existed except the two of them. It had always been a promise that for a little while she would be the center of his universe, everything else forgotten.

But only for a little while. That hard-learned lesson held her back now, hovering over the whirlpool of need that was making her throb in every cell.

Afterward, memory always returned, and she was always once again the forbidden fruit, the sin he shouldn't have committed, the pleasure he didn't deserve. How many times had she seen that transformation grip him, turning

211

him from ardent, laughing lover into guilty widower?

She couldn't bear the pain again.

She started to turn away, to save herself. At least she thought she did. She felt the muscles tense in preparation, even though her feet, glued to the floor, didn't move at all.

But before she could escape, before she could even try to, he reached out and drew her into his arms.

She was lost then. In an instant she weakened, grew pliable, rediscovering the warm, soft place deep inside her that only he could reach. Everything else slipped away but her awareness of him and how he made her feel.

His chest was hard yet welcoming, and she fit against him with a comfort that she had felt with no one else. It was as if their bodies were matching pieces of a puzzle.

And the strength of his arms around her back answered some long-buried yearning, filling an emptiness—and making her feel safer than she had felt since the last time he had held her this way.

"Carey . . ." He barely whispered her name, then bent his head and covered her mouth in a deep kiss that wasted no time heading straight for her soul.

Her palms spread on his back, feeling his heat and strength through the thin layer of cotton, and her hips instinctively sought to press against his. And today and yesterday and tomorrow all slipped away as she spun dizzily into a maelstrom of need.

"God, I've missed you . . ." His words were husky, broken, as he lifted his mouth from hers and dragged air into his lungs. "Carey . . ."

Her name on his lips had sometimes sounded like a curse, but right now it sounded like a prayer. She dug her fingers into his back, hanging on for dear life, wondering how she could have survived for so long without this wild, heady, *warm* feeling he gave her. How could she have forgotten . . .

His mouth covered hers again, his tongue took possession of its hot, wet depths, driving away thought. His hands stroked her back, memorizing her slender contours, awakening nerve endings to forgotten pleasure, fueling the heavy ache between her thighs.

More . . . oh, she needed so much more! Impatient anticipation gripped her, causing her to hold her breath in hope that his hands would move to touch her aching breasts, or to draw her up more tightly against him. Every cell in her body was aching with the need for more and more . . .

And suddenly an icy tendril of fear wormed its way into her awareness, freezing her.

What was she doing?

Her hands gripped his shoulders and shoved, tearing her away from him. Breathless, aching, hunched almost as if she expected a blow, she stared at him, and said hoarsely, "No . . . no."

His hands had already begun to reach for her again, but they froze in midair. He closed his eyes, drew several deep, ragged breaths, then nodded.

When he looked at her again, she could see hurt, disappointment, and yearning. But she could also see determination.

"Good night," he said, and walked out, closing the door behind him.

She cried into her pillow before she fell asleep, probably the best reminder of why she didn't want to get involved again with Seamus Rourke. He was the only person in the world who could do that to her.

She *had* done the right thing by breaking it off. Even though her entire body, which had long since turned off any strong sexual impulses she might have felt, felt almost raw with aching need. Even the brush of the sheets on her skin seemed to have an erotic effect, reminding her of what she had just turned away, reminding her that she hadn't made love in five years, and that a young, healthy body wasn't happy being celibate.

But she knew where it would have led. For her, sex could never be divorced from emotion. If she invited Seamus into her bed, she'd be inviting him back into her heart, and the price on that was too high to bear.

So she tossed and turned restlessly, and took aspirin for the headache that crying had given her, and sucked on a lozenge to soothe a throat sore from sobbing, and wondered why life seemed to have turned into a living hell.

For a while she stared at the darkened ceiling and played a what-if game with herself. What if she'd never met Seamus? Would she be happily married to some other lawyer right now, with rugrats sleeping in the next room?

But she couldn't imagine a life wherein she'd never met Seamus Rourke. He was too large, too significant, too much a part of the person she had become. He overshadowed any possible image of a life in which he'd never played a part.

And John William Otis was beginning to shadow her in the same way. In fact, if she didn't find a way to save that man, there was going to be a blight on her life.

Men. Sometimes she wished she'd gone into a convent.

By four, Carey was out of bed again, smoking a cigarette and drinking a glass of milk in the hope that it would soothe her enough to let her sleep. Absently, she pulled the stack of clippings toward her and started scanning them again. She read four of them, found nothing she didn't already know, and decided she was probably wasting her time by reading the rest.

She was about to toss them all back into the box when she saw that there were several in the stack from an Atlanta newspaper. Otis's brother lived up there, she remembered. It would be interesting to see what spin they had put on the murder and trial.

More of the same, basically. She was beginning to yawn seriously and rub her eyes about the time she pulled the next one toward her, but the headline snapped her wide awake again.

> *Killer's brother committed.*
>
> *The younger brother of Florida killer John William Otis was committed to Channel Mental Hospital last week, sources close to the family say. James Henry Otis, 18, of Atlanta, apparently suffered a nervous breakdown in the wake of the sentencing of his older brother to death.*
>
> *The Otis brothers were involved in a previous murder trial eight years ago when John was charged with murdering their father The older Otis was acquitted on grounds of self-defense when it became known that the two brothers had suffered years of physical and sexual abuse at the hands of their father*
>
> *James Otis was adopted at the age of eleven by a Florida family who subsequently moved to Atlanta. "Jamie," said one source, "has been torn up by his brother's trial."*
>
> *Since coming to Atlanta . . .*

Committed. The word seemed to swim and grow before Carey's eyes.

Committed.

Unstable. And caring enough for his brother to suffer a nervous breakdown when he was sentenced.

And it had happened *after* the sentencing, when the verdict was already in, when no one would have been looking for any new information.

Her heart slammed, hard, and she stared blankly across the room. But James Otis had an *alibi*. There was a sworn affidavit in his brother's file. He had been home in Atlanta the weekend of the Kline murders. Worse, he had been just a kid. How could a kid have come all the way down here?

But who else would John Otis be so determined to protect?

And who would be more likely to lie to provide an alibi than James Otis's adoptive mother?

CHAPTER 15
7 DAYS

SEAMUS DECIDED THAT LACK OF SLEEP HAD MADE HIM crazy. So crazy that he was glad to stop tossing and turning and get up and go to work. So crazy that he actually hatched a lunatic plan. He tried to tell himself it was all Carey's fault, but he knew better. *He'd* been the one who'd kissed *her*

He hadn't planned what had happened in the foyer with Carey, and he'd have been a lot happier if it hadn't occurred. He hadn't really thought about it before, but it was beginning to seem that he lacked the promiscuity that appeared to characterize the rest of the males he knew. That might have been a blessing if his marriage had survived, but it was proving to be a curse instead.

Where was the constant searching for greener pastures that most men seemed to experience? Carey was a familiar pasture to him, yet she could still light a fuse of desire in

216

him that hadn't been lit since they split up.

For the first time he thought about the fact that he hadn't seriously dated a woman since her, or even thought of bedding a woman since her. He had thought he'd reached some plateau of maturity where he didn't respond to just anything in a skirt. Now it seemed he didn't respond to anything but Carey, and his response to her was as strong as any he had ever felt.

And he didn't like that at all.

The two of them couldn't get along for any length of time, no way, no how. Sooner or later they were at each other's throats. There was his guilt that drove her crazy, and her obsessiveness that drove him crazy, and there was no way in hell they were going to change their basic natures. They were both the types to get fixated on something and not be able to shake loose of it. That'd be okay if they got fixated on the same thing, but otherwise it could be maddening.

So, as the guy once said, the thing you most dislike in other people is the thing you most dislike in yourself.

Peas in a pod, too similar to live together, that's what he and Carey were.

But all the rationalization in the world didn't ease the need that was crawling along his nerves now, a need that only she could assuage.

He figured that little scene with her qualified him for the jerk-of-the-year award. Hadn't his dad always told him that it was best to let sleeping dogs lie?

And this was one sleeping dog with a hell of a bite.

So it was a relief to go to work, and lack of sleep had made him crazier than usual. Only craziness would have made him come up with this idea. Lack of sleep had his mind following paths it didn't ordinarily tread.

He knocked on Ed's door and was told to come in.

"Got something for me on the Barnstable case?" Ed

217

asked.

"Not yet." He certainly wasn't going to tell the man what he was thinking about that, not until he had something to hang his suspicion on besides a string of coincidence. "I want to talk to you about the Mayberry case."

Ed pointed to a chair. "Well, that's good, too. You get a break?"

"Maybe." He sketched his and Gil's conversation with Sam Hollister the other day. "The thing is, Hollister seems to think there might be some neighborhood involvement in the death."

"He got any proof?"

"Just the way people were talking. The thing is, there's too little information in that neighborhood. People were home at that time of the murder, yet nobody heard or saw a thing? I'm not buying it, and neither is Gil. Put that together with what Hollister said, and you get the feeling that we need to scratch the surface a little harder."

"Just how are you planning to scratch it?"

"That's what I wanted to talk to you about. I want to ask a few of these good citizens to come into the station for questioning."

Ed looked as if he'd just experienced acid reflux. His expression soured. "Won't that look good in the papers."

"None of them are going to talk to us if their neighbors see cops coming to the house."

"Shit."

"Well, there's another way to handle it. We could leak something to the papers about a suspicion of community involvement in the murder, then deny it when the media ask about it. That might scare somebody into talking."

Ed leaned back in his chair and closed his eyes. "Worse and worse. You do this just to drive me nuts, don't you,

Rourke?"

"That's a side benefit."

"I always suspected it." His dark eyes snapped open, "Let me think about it. I'll need to discuss it with the brass. They'll be the ones taking the heat."

"That's why they have the brass."

Ed almost betrayed himself with a smile. It showed faintly around the corners of his eyes. "What about the Barnstable case?"

"She was the forewoman on the Otis jury."

Ed's mouth opened just a little, but he didn't say anything.

"Yup," said Seamus, rising and heading for the door, content that all his little bombs had been dropped, "I kinda felt that way myself."

He made it back to his chair before he heard Ed swear.

"What'd you tell him?" Gil asked.

"Nothing he wanted to hear."

"I already figured that out. I got us interviews this afternoon with two people who volunteered with Barnstable at the literacy project. And the neighbor who found her said she'd be glad to see us at noon. I'm still trying to find out who she might have hung around with at USF."

"Probably nobody. At her age she was Pretty much a fish out Of water socially On campus, don't you think?"

"Maybe. But she wasn't the only middle-aged woman going to school. We might dig up something."

Reaching for his messages, Seamus started leafing through them. The real estate agent had called, could he please call back around noon? Might be tough, Seamus thought, considering the appointments he and Gil had scheduled.

The M.E.'s office had called. The prelim suggested that

the same or similar weapon had been used in both the Downs and Barnstable killings. He passed that one over to Gil to read.

"No shock," was all Gil said.

A message from forensics about an unidentified partial print lifted from the glass door at Barnstable's place. "Our guy may be slipping," he said, passing that one on to Gil, too.

"Jeez, no size fifteen hand-made Italian shoe print?"

"Sorry." He picked up the phone and called Oslo Mankin in forensics. "I got the message about the partial in the Barnstable case, Os. What can you tell me?"

"It looks like it was transferred through a surgical glove."

"Oh, I love it when they mess up."

Os laughed. "You and me both. I figure he had an itch to scratch and got some skin oil on at least one fingertip. There's some latex powder mixed in the oil, and it's a little bluffed, but it would be enough to hang the guy if you find him."

"I can't thank you enough."

"So you buy the beer."

"Anything else?"

"Just the usual bloody shoe prints. They match the ones at Downs, but the shoe is a size nine, with a rippled synthetic sole. Your typical cheap import, sold by the thousands at discount stores. No question the perp is the same guy, though. There's a distinctive cut across the left sole that matches in both cases."

"I love ya."

"I'll let my wife know. She's looking for somebody to take me off her hands."

He hung up and looked at Gil. "Os wants to marry me."

"That's not the way I heard it. So what's up?"

"We got a partial that'll link our guy to Barnstable, and a shoe print that links Barnstable and Downs."

"Major progress."

"I thought so. Now all we have to do is figure out who all this belongs to."

"Don't remind me.

The phone rang, and Seamus answered it.

"Seamus," said Carey, "what would you say if I told you that John Otis's younger brother was committed to a mental hospital for a nervous breakdown right after Otis's sentencing, and that the guy has spent the better part of the last five years in a mental institution in Atlanta. He was released just one month ago."

Seamus gave a low whistle and felt the back of his neck start prickling. "I'd be very interested indeed."

"Well, dont tell anybody I had to impersonate a lawyer to find this out."

"I wouldn't dream of it."

"I'm going to Atlanta to talk to his family."

"You're not going alone. Give me some time to get a couple of days off."

"We don't have any time!"

"I didn't mean days. I meant twenty minutes. Where are you?"

"At home. I spent the last two hours on the phone trying to find out this little bit."

"I'll call you back once I clear this." He hung up and looked at Gil, trying to decide how much to tell his partner.

"You're not leaving me?" Gil said.

"Just for a couple of days."

"Hell. Now? What's so damn important?"

"You don't want to know. Plausible deniability."

Gil regarded him steadily. "Otis."

"I didn't say that."

"It's printed in neon on your forehead. Okay, I don't know anything. What can I do?"

"See if James Henry Otis has a DMV record here or in Georgia. I'd kinda like to know his address."

"I'm not asking why."

"Smart move."

"Where are you going?"

"You don't want to know."

Gil sighed. "So call once in a while, so I don't worry. And bring me back a surprise."

Now, thought Seamus, rising, he had to convince Sanchez to let him go.

"What now?" Ed asked as Seamus reappeared.

"We've got a definite link between the Barnstable and Downs homicides."

Ed put down his pen. "And?"

"And a partial print that will link the perp to the scene."

"Better and better Got any ideas who to look at?"

Seamus hesitated. "Trust me on this one, Ed. I need to go to Atlanta for a couple of days. And believe me, unless I'm right, you don't want a whisper of what I'm doing to get around."

Ed frowned, his dark, patrician face looking uneasy. "What wild hare have you got now?"

"Call it a personal problem."

"I've got to have something more than that to put on a travel voucher." He shook his head. "Talk, or don't go."

Seamus hesitated, knowing he was about to put his foot in it. "Otis."

"Otis?" Ed looked as if he were about to launch for the moon. "Tell me you're shitting me! You're hanging

222

around too much with that radio bitch."

Seamus shook his head sharply. "Wait. Both Barnstable and Downs were involved in the Otis trial, Ed."

"So were a lot of other people."

Seamus blew an impatient breath. "Look. John Otis has a younger brother. That younger brother spent the last five years in. a mental institution. He got out just one month ago."

Ed stared at him for a long moment. "You're sure?"

"My source is solid. Tie that in with the calls to the radio station, and you've got a definite possibility that this younger brother is out for revenge." He didn't mention the possibility that James Otis could have committed the original murders. This sell was tough enough without convincing Ed he was haring off on some wild-goose chase that would do nothing but bring the department bad publicity. Nobody, but nobody, wanted to hear that John Otis might be innocent, not without a hell of a lot more proof than this. But as a suspect in the Downs and Barnstable killings, James was prime.

He decided to add a little more incentive. "I'll front this myself. Call it a vacation for personal reasons. If I'm right, I'll submit a bill when I get back."

"Two days?"

"Probably. Certainly no more than three."

"Go. Just bring me back something."

Carey waited impatiently for the phone to ring. She could go to Atlanta by herself, but she was glad Seamus wanted to go along with her. It would lend her visit an official capacity that might open more doors than simply going as herself. The family would probably be a whole lot more willing to talk to a cop than to a radio talk-show host.

For the first time, she seriously missed the badge she

had once carried.

She was wound as tight as a top, eager to leave for Atlanta, afraid to go, and afraid of what traveling with Seamus might mean after last night.

But Otis loomed larger and more important than getting mixed up again with Seamus. A man's life was certainly more important than her minor emotional crises.

And she was surprised to discover that she was having mixed feelings about talking to James Otis's family. Now that she had something more than a mere wisp of intuition to go on, now that she might actually find something factual, she was terrified.

God, why couldn't she have just left this alone? Seamus was right. The jury had made the determination, and it wasn't her responsibility.

But what if she got up there and found out something she really didn't want to know? What if she got up there and found something that proved that John Otis really had killed the Klines?

It was an odd thought to be having at this point, after so many days of beating her head on a brick wall over the man's innocence. Why was she all of a sudden worried that he might turn out to be guilty?

After all, if it turned out that he really had killed the Klines, she had nothing more to worry about. Did she?

When the phone rang, she practically jumped at it.

"I can go," Seamus said. "When do you want to leave?"

"I need to talk to the station. I'd be surprised if they can let me out of tonight's show, but I'm sure I can arrange to get away in the morning."

"Then let's go in the morning. I have some interviews to do this afternoon anyway. Make the reservations for us both, will you? And find out if the family is in town. I'd hate to get up there and find out they've moved to

Timbuktu."

"They're still there. I called this morning."

"You didn't tell them we were coming?"

"No, of course not. I just wanted to make sure they were there."

"Good. I think it'd be better to surprise them. I'll get back to you later to finalize the details."

She hung up the phone and wished to God she could shake the feeling that this was a major mistake.

When she got to the station, the first thing she did was tell Bill she was going out of town.

"You want to *what?*" Bill asked disbelievingly.

"I need to go to Atlanta," Carey said firmly. "Two days is all I need, okay? Maybe not even that much if I can get everything done in one day, but make it two to be safe."

"And I'm supposed to yank somebody in to cover for you on twenty-four hours' notice?"

He could do it, she knew. People got sick sometimes, and he had to juggle things. This was no major deal. But trust Bill to act like it was. "Ted would love to do my show, and you know it. Then there's the weekend hosts."

"And you've got a syndicated program. Did you consider that?"

"Use some of my old tapes then." That was one of the benefits of syndication. The tapes of the best of her old shows were still available. Some of them were even for sale.

"Do you think Rush Limbaugh just takes two days off at the last minute?"

She shrugged a shoulder. "I'm no Rush, and you know it. My absence won't even cause a ripple in the cosmos. Do you want me to call in sick?"

Almost in spite of himself, he laughed. "Jesus, you're something else. I'll make you a deal. Tape me two shows without call-ins and you can go."

"One show," she argued. "I'll do one show. That'll give you time to cover the next."

"Okay, okay. One show. Just tell me this trip you're taking will give us something good to use when you get back."

"Maybe."

"Maybe." He sighed and threw up a hand. "Okay. Get me that show. And it better not be another one like last night, because I'm already singed from covering your butt. You went way out there, Carey."

"I was angry."

"Most everybody who tuned in last night figured that out. I understand that you're passionate on this subject, but you need to remember this is a business. We need to make money. And we don't make money if people are turning us off. Got it?"

She nodded. "Actually, if the calls are any indication, getting angry is making people listen."

"I wouldn't count on that. Give me something else, Carey. Something I can use to reassure people you aren't just going off the deep end."

She did better than that. By two o'clock she had lined up five people to tape a show at four on the subject of sexual harassment. There was a man who'd been accused of harassment and the woman who had sued him, both of their attorneys, and the retired judge who had presided over the trial. The U.S. Supreme Court had agreed to review the case, and both sides apparently had a lot they wanted to say.

She didn't have any trouble filling up the three hours without any calls, and it turned into a damn good show, with the two attorneys shouting across the conference table at one point, the woman crying, the man accusing her of being a lying bitch, and the judge remarking that he wouldn't have tolerated these histrionics in his courtroom. The show ended with the judge giving the listeners his ruling in plain English that anyone could understand.

And from that, she went to her regular broadcast. Once again she opened with her countdown, reminding her listeners that John William Otis had exactly seven days to live.

Saying it out loud was almost like a punch to the stomach. Seven days. Only seven days. Panic fluttered in her stomach, and it was only with difficulty that she forced herself to concentrate on the subject she had chosen for tonight, the Americans with Disabilities Act.

As she had expected, *everybody* had an opinion about that, most of them negative, and most of them based on misconceptions about the law. The show moved quickly through the first two hours, but by the time she took her last newsbreak, she was feeling exhausted. The home stretch had rarely looked so good.

She slipped out back for a cigarette, hating herself for the weakness, and sat on the bench, petting Peg. She was getting more and more uptight about Atlanta, she realized, as the cat's soft fur tickled her palm. The closer the trip came, the less she wanted to do it.

Maybe it was because she was terrified that she wouldn't find anything there to help John Otis. She took a deep drag on her cigarette and thought about the small man sitting in a prison cell in Starke, about the man who had written the sometimes wise, sometimes naive, and always surprisingly gentle poems she had read. The man who dreamed of New England winters he would never see and who had worn out his Bible. The man who had never been allowed to be a child, the child who would never become a man because his life had followed such a tortured, twisted path.

If he died, how would she live with his death on her conscience? If she came back from Atlanta with nothing, there would be nothing left she could do, and that possibility *did* terrify her. In the back of her mind, the clock never stopped ticking.

She wondered what he was feeling tonight, with just seven days left in his life. Was he scared? Did he rail against fate? Did he feel hate for his tormenters? Had he found the peace he had been tying to project when she had visited him?

The back door of the station opened, and she looked up, startled. Seamus stepped into the buttery light of the security lamp.

"Lou told me where to find you."

She nodded and kept stroking the cat. "An open-door policy to the police department."

"Something like that. It's the badge." He came to sit near her on the bench. "So we're leaving in the morning?"

"We have an eleven-thirty flight. There was nothing available earlier."

"That's okay. Maybe I'll actually manage to catch up on some sleep tonight."

"I sure hope I do."

They sat in silence for a minute, but when Carey realized he hadn't come out here to tell her anything specific, she glanced at her watch. "I need to get back in. I'm on the air in two minutes."

He nodded and followed her. To her surprise, he didn't leave when she returned to the studio, but instead waited outside, watching her as she put on the headphones,

Scooted up to the mike, and looked at Marge for the countdown. And with the ease of long experience, she slipped right into her on-air persona, hardly even thinking about the words that passed her lips.

"This is Carey Justice, and you're listening to 990 WCST . . ."

"You know, Carey," said the first caller, "you're just another one of those liberal jerks who think all the rest of us should pay for people who can't take care of themselves."

"How's that?" she enquired.

"This ADA thing is just another example of the crap you're putting out. You could put a positive spin on just about anything. Look, it isn't a business's fault if some guy is in a wheelchair. It's not like they put him there. So why should they have to spend their hard-earned money to put in a ramp so he can get in the front door? And look at all this special handicapped parking. Parking space costs money."

She fielded his comments with only half her attention and moved on to the next caller, hoping for something she could really sink her teeth into. But Seamus's presence disturbed her concentration, and she found herself wishing she could just get out of here and let all these idiots go hang. Where ordinarily she enjoyed the interplay with her callers, tonight she just felt impatient, as if she were wasting her time.

Which, of course, she was. Nobody's mind got changed by anything she said. That thought, which plagued her from time to time, suddenly came over her with a vengeance. It was all she could do not to pull off the headphones and just walk away.

At least in court her speeches and arguments had had a chance of making a difference.

The errant thought was unwelcome, and it annoyed her. She cut off a caller earlier than she might otherwise have, trying to drive the traitorous thought away, and jabbed the button for the next caller without even looking to see who it was.

"Caller, you're on the air."

"Carey. Did you get the message?"

She recognized the voice instantly. Bob from Gulfport was back. Quickly she signaled to Marge to get the phone number, then waved to Seamus. Moving quietly, he came into the booth.

"Hi, Bob," she said into the microphone. "I figured you would call last night."

"You did?" He sounded almost pleased.

"Well, after the Barnstable killing, I figured you'd want to talk about it."

"So you knew it was me?"

"Of course I did." She looked at Seamus, saw him look back with the same sense of urgency. "What are you trying to do, Bob?"

"I told you, John Otis didn't do it. I did."

"You've said that before. The problem is this, Bob. It's not enough to say John Otis didn't do it. Anybody could say that."

"I'm proving he didn't do it."

"How's that?"

"I'm proving that I really did it."

"You could just be a copycat. So you see, killing people isn't going to get John out of prison."

Marge came into the booth with the phone number, and Carey motioned her to give it to Seamus. He took it and headed out. Marge went back to the control booth.

"They'd better listen," Bob said. "They'd better listen, because I'll just keep on killing people."

"How is that going to fix anything? Do you think they're going to stay Otis's execution because some guy threatens to kill more people? I need more than that, Bob.

A lot more if I'm going to stop the execution."

"They have to listen!" His voice was rising, and he was beginning to sound hysterical. "They'd better listen, or the killing is never going to stop! If they kill Johnny, I'm going to kill so many people that they'll be sorry! I will!"

"Bob . . . take it easy there, guy. Getting mad isn't going to fix anything. Just take it easy and talk to me." She hadn't a doubt Seamus was trying to get the number traced so that he could send out a car to pick up this guy. She *had* to keep him on the air, "Tell me what you want me to do."

"Save Johnny! You have to save him!"

"I want to. Believe me I want to."

"He doesn't deserve to die. He never did anything wrong."

"I know that. But I need some kind of proof. You've got to give me something that proves he didn't kill Linda and Harvey Kline."

There was a brief silence, then Bob said too calmly, "Look at the body." There was a click followed by a dial tone.

She wanted to swear, but her mike was open. She looked at Marge, who had hastily loaded a cart and now cut away to a commercial.

A breather. Not that it would do her much good. This guy was a lunatic, and she was scared to death that he was going to kill someone else before they could find him.

Seamus stepped back into the studio. "A car is on the way."

"He's gone."

"I know. But maybe they'll see him running away from the phone."

"It was a pay phone again?"

"This one was in Gulfport."

231

She looked at Marge and saw they were just about to come out of the commercial. She motioned Seamus to silence, then spoke into her mike.

"This is Carey Justice, and you're listening to 990 WCST. Well, folks, that last caller—it's getting to be too much, don't you think? If this guy is telling the truth, if he really did kill Harvey and Linda Kline, then he needs to step forward and take the rap before John William Otis goes to the electric chair. Because if Bob from Gulfport really did kill the Klines, and he doesn't step forward, then he's going to be personally responsible for the death of John Otis. Not that this guy seems to care much about human life.

"It's creepy. Do me a favor, people. Lock your doors and windows tonight, and don't let anybody in that you don't know. In fact, don't even answer the door unless you know the person on the other side. The body count is already high enough."

She looked at Seamus and motioned him to sit at the table in front of the guest microphone.

"With me in the studio tonight is Detective Seamus Rourke of the St. Petersburg Police Department. Detective, do you have any suggestions to make to our listeners about ways they can protect themselves?"

He shot her a sour look, then leaned toward the microphone. "Thank you for asking, Carey. People need to be especially aware of sliding glass patio doors. Use something—a broomstick, a piece of wood—and fit it so the door can't slide open. The locks on most of these doors are easy to bypass, so don't count on them to do the job."

He sat back, giving her a satisfied look, and throwing the ball back into her lap.

She questioned him for a few minutes about security,

avoiding the subject of the murders, even though she knew her listeners wanted to hear something about them, because she was aware that he could get in trouble for discussing an ongoing investigation without permission from higher-ups.

Then she made a point of thanking him and bidding him good night. He took his cue and left the studio immediately.

Now he couldn't be put on the spot.

And now she had to deal with an increasing number of callers who, for a change, were on *her* side in the matter of Otis. Most of them said the same thing: If Bob really wanted to save John Otis, then he needed to be a man and step forward.

She hoped Bob got the message.

Seamus was waiting for her when she left the station.

"You're getting predictable," she told him.

"It's age. It's turning me into a creature of habit."

"Did you guys get him?"

He shook his head. "He was long gone by the time they started looking for him. He either lives in the area, or he has friends where he can go to ground. We're going to watch the phones when you're on the air, though."

"If he's got half a brain, he'll use a different phone next time."

"Probably." Lightning flickered somewhere up north in Pasco County, a silent light show just above the horizon. Cicadas shrilled noisily, making the night seem alive. "Have you had any more death threats?"

"Nary a one. No more graffiti, either."

"Chickenshits."

An errant laugh escaped her. "Maybe they don't want to get caught and arrested."

"That assumes they have more brains than they

233

probably do."

"Well, it couldn't have made them happy when the station stood up to them. It wasn't the outcome they wanted."

"Nope." A gust of cool air blew over them, heralding the storms building to the north. "I'm going home with you."

Her heart stopped. Memories of their kiss had been plaguing her in unguarded moments ever since, and her body felt like a violin tuned too tight. If he plucked her strings, she was going to snap. "Why?" she managed to ask.

"I don't like the idea of this Bob running around killing people who were involved in the Otis case. You were involved."

"I'm also involved in trying to get Otis out. We've been over this, Seamus. There's no reason to think this guy win come after *me*. At least I'm giving him the attention he wants, if nothing else."

"And maybe this guy hasn't connected the prosecutor Carissa Stover with the air personality Carey Justice. You can't know for sure. Since I want to get some sleep tonight, I decided it would be easier to do it on your couch than at home worrying."

She was tired to the point of exhaustion, and maybe that's why she suddenly felt like throwing a temper tantrum, stomping her foot and telling him to quit wedging himself into every corner of her life. It was bad enough to find him creeping into her dreams, but she sure as hell didn't want to find him there every time she turned around when she was awake.

He'd insinuated himself so far that she couldn't go into her kitchen without seeing him sitting at the table, she couldn't walk into her foyer without remembering the stolen kiss that had left her almost too weak to stand, and every night when she crawled into her bed she remembered him stretching out beside her.

Now he was going to be her watchdog?

Her expression must have betrayed her, because he lifted a hand. "No funny stuff, I promise. But I couldn't square it with my conscience if I let you go home alone. Not with this guy on the streets."

"Damn your conscience."

He arched a brow. "Funny, but I thought you had one that was every bit as big and aggravating."

She couldn't deny it, not when she kept riding the edge of getting her show canceled because she couldn't allow a miscarriage of justice. But she didn't like being lumped in with him, primarily because *his* damn conscience had turned her life into hell.

"Fine," she said finally. "Do what you want."

"Don't I always? Let's get something to eat on the way to your place. My treat. Where do you want to go?"

She suggested Roof's because it was one place they'd never gone together in the past. Unfortunately, it didn't strike her until he was pulling into the parking lot behind her that now she would have another one of her retreats marred with a memory of Seamus Rourke.

Roof's was busy, but quieter than usual tonight. They had no trouble finding a booth, and for once there was nobody from the station there. She ordered a club sandwich, and Seamus ordered a steak. Country music washed over them, and Carey found herself listening with more than ordinary attention to "My Heroes Have Always Been Cowboys."

And suddenly she found herself aching for the days when she'd been a prosecutor and they could sit over a midnight meal and talk about their cases freely. Now there

235

was a gulf between them that couldn't be bridged. She couldn't ask him the questions most pressing on her mind about the killings, and he couldn't share any significant details of his day. She was an outsider now, and never had she felt it more acutely.

Their meals were placed before them, and Seamus reached for the steak sauce, pouring a little puddle of it on the edge of his plate.

"You could eat anything with that sauce on it and not know what it is," she remarked.

He flashed her an unexpected, breathtaking grin. "That's the point. Ever try a slice of fresh Vidalia onion between two pieces of bread with a dollop of steak sauce?"

She shuddered, and he laughed.

Willie Nelson gave way to Hal Ketchum and a song about the Trail of Tears. It was a sad, wistful piece that did nothing to help Carey's mood. Nor did it help her mood any that Seamus appeared not to have a thing on his mind except the steak he was devouring with obvious gusto. One section of her sandwich had left her feeling as if she'd swallowed lead.

Seamus looked up suddenly, his expression serious. "You ought to go back to the State Attorney's Office, Carey."

"I'd be about as welcome as a case of herpes."

He shook his head. "I think you're wrong. I think you were in a tough position the last time you were there, and you didn't have the self-confidence to push back when the system was steamrolling you. I also don't think the justice system is as cockeyed as you say. But it *does* need people like you to keep it on the straight and narrow. If you couldn't stomach being a prosecutor again, go with the Public Defender's Office."

"I'd go broke."

He cocked a brow.

She shrugged, suddenly feeling old and tired. "Okay, so it's not the money. I could manage. But I don't have the fire anymore, Seamus. It got water dumped on it one too many times."

"No fire?" He looked disbelieving. "You're charging ahead full tilt on this Otis thing, and thumbing your nose at all the powers that be. Don't tell me you've lost the fire. That's nonsense."

She shrugged a shoulder and looked down at her sandwich, trying to find a way to end this conversation. It was making her too uncomfortable. "What do you care, anyway?"

"You're a damn fine attorney. You shouldn't waste it. Besides, that passion in you isn't going to be satisfied by arguing with idiots on the radio and you know it. I don't get the feeling that you're really happy with your life now."

Her head snapped up, and she glared at him. "Ever think *you* might have something to do with that?"

He spread his hands and dropped the subject, going back to his steak and baked potato.

Leaving her to feel like a jerk. But she was always a jerk around Seamus, it seemed. He had just tried to say something nice and express concern for her, and she had thrown it back into his face.

"I'm sorry," she said

He looked up. "That s okay. But it would really help if you and I could learn to have a personal conversation without going to war."

She wanted to ask what it would help, then decided that was a discussion that might prove to be dangerous.

So she let it lie, and tried to eat, and tried not to think about just how right he was.

CHAPTER 16
6 DAYS

THEIR FLIGHT WAS DELAYED BY THREE HOURS, OWING to severe thunderstorms in Atlanta. Then, after they boarded, they were kept waiting for another hour. By the time they were rolling down the runway toward takeoff, it was nearly four in the afternoon, and Carey was beginning to feel seriously restless. She'd brought a novel to read, but it turned out to be less gripping than she had hoped. Giving up, she turned her attention out the window.

Seamus slept. Sometimes she thought he could sleep anywhere, anytime, and she envied him. His large frame overfilled the narrow coach seat, and every time she moved, she felt his shoulder brush against her She wouldn't have minded, except it got her to thinking about the other ways she'd like to have him brush against her.

Irritations aside, they did finally make it to Atlanta. Seamus woke just as they were touching down on the runway. He turned to look at her, his expression sleepy and relaxed, and she felt her heart squeeze with an urge just to burrow into his arms. She quickly averted her face, wondering if she was losing her mind.

He spoke. "I guess, considering how late it is, we should just call these folks from the airport and take a cab over to see them before we do anything else."

"Sounds good." At least he hadn't read her face. Sometimes it could be unnerving how much he could read in her expressions.

They waited until nearly everyone else had deplaned before taking their bags out of the overhead rack and making their way out. By the time they reached a pay phone another half hour was lost.

"Do you have the number?" Seamus asked as he dropped his carry-on on the floor beside hers. "I think I should make the call. At least you won't have to impersonate anyone."

She quite agreed. She searched her purse until she found the scrap of paper she had written the name and number on. Waiting impatiently, she watched him dial.

"May I speak with Mr. or Mrs. Wiggins, please?"

She tried to read his face as he waited, but Seamus had always been unreadable when he wanted to be.

"I see," he said. "Thank you very much. No, no message necessary. I'll just call back in the morning." He hung up.

"What?" she asked. "What?"

"They went out for the evening. I gather James wasn't the only child they had. It sounded like a playground in the background. Anyway, they won't be back until after eleven."

Carey felt her shoulders slump as expectation slipped away. She had thought her waiting was over at last but apparently it wasn't. Time. They had so little time. Six days now.

"Hey," Seamus said almost gently. "It's okay. We'll see them tomorrow."

"What if they're not home?"

"I'll catch them. You're talking to a cop, remember? I catch people who are actually trying to hide from me."

She felt a smile lift the corners of her mouth, but it didn't quite reach her heart. "Time," she said, and let the word hang.

"I know. Believe me, I know."

Bending, he picked up both their bags. "Come on. Let's get a car and get a hotel. There's nothing else we can do right now."

They got adjoining rooms at a motel not too far from the subdivision where the Wigginses lived. They left the door between them open, but separated anyway. Carey paced her room trying to control the anxiety that was making her skin crawl. *Six days.* Time had grown terrifyingly short.

She heard Seamus on the phone in his room, but she couldn't hear what he was saying. Probably calling work to see if anything was happening, she thought.

Nerves kept her moving, her mind spinning at top speed as she tried to find some way to pass this evening usefully. The thought of sitting around with nothing to do until morning made her want to scream.

Finally, desperate to find some relaxation, she went to take a hot shower. The heat *did* have the effect of relaxing her muscles, but it did nothing to slow down her mind. It was going to be a long, long night.

When she came out of the bathroom, wearing a robe and toweling her hair dry, she found Seamus sitting on the end of her bed, reviewing some notes on his ever-present pocket notepad.

He looked up and smiled at her. "Dinner in the room? Or would you prefer going out?"

Neither option really appealed to her. "Let me think about it." Opening her suitcase, she looked for her hair dryer and brush.

"Sure." He leaned back on his elbows, watching her paw impatiently through her belongings. "Getting uptight isn't going to help, Carey."

She threw up a hand. "I know that. I'm uptight anyway."

"No kidding."

She could have screamed at him; she was certainly irritable enough, feeling as if everything was rubbing her the wrong way. But when she looked at him, reclining there with a pleasant, almost hopeful smile on his face, something inside her lot go.

Plopping down beside him on the bed, she held her blowdryer in one hand and her brush in the other. "I'm sorry," she said. "I'm so on edge right now that everything is just irritating me past belief."

"I got that feeling. Is it just that you're worried about Otis's execution? Or is there something else going on here?"

She looked at him, taking in his rumpled hair, the unbuttoned collar of his white shirt, the way his shoulders stretched the fabric. Broad shoulders. He'd always had broad shoulders, both physically and emotionally. Even in the midst of all his guilt about his wife and daughter, he'd been willing to shoulder as much of her burdens as she was willing to share.

Why hadn't she realized that before, when it would have mattered? Why had she insisted on focusing on his guilt and grief, as if they were somehow an offense to *her*?

"God," she said suddenly, "I'm such a selfish twit!"

His brows lifted. "Huh? What did I miss?"

"Never mind. I'm just reflecting on my own shortcomings."

"What good will that do—except to evade my question?"

"You damn cops. You never forget a thing."

"Same goes for you damn lawyers." he said it jestingly, but there was real concern in his gaze. "Carey, just tell me. You're about to fly right off the handle, and I don't think it's just that we're running short of time. It's getting close, but tomorrow morning still isn't too late. It's just a little dicier."

"I know." She looked down at her hands. "I know."

"So tell me what's really eating you."

When she didn't respond, he sat up and took the blowdryer and brush from her, leaning over to put them on the nearby chair Then he drew her down so that she lay with her head on his shoulder and his arms around her. He didn't even seem to mind that her hair was wet.

Nor did she feel any danger in the embrace. He was holding her to comfort her, and it had been a long time since anyone had wanted to do that. She let herself relax into his embrace, and soaked up what comfort she could.

"Tell me," he said.

His voice rumbled deeply in his chest, and the sound of his steady heartbeat was reassuring against her ear. "I don't know how," she said. "It's too stupid."

"So tell me," he said, "are you more afraid that we won't find anything useful at all, or that we'll find something that incriminates John Otis?"

Shock stiffened her. "How did you know?"

"I know you," he answered, his hand running soothingly down her arm, stroking her as if she were a cat. "You've had too many illusions destroyed, haven't you, sweetheart?"

He shouldn't call her that. She tried to marshal a protest, but the words wouldn't come past a throat that was suddenly tight with tears she didn't want to shed. It was all she could do to breathe and hold it all in.

"When I met you," he continued, "you still had ideals left. It was one of the things that drew me to you. You believed in justice, in truth, in rightness. You thought you could make a difference. Your belief was wavering—I could see it—but you hadn't lost it all yet. I watched it get stripped from you in the time we were together. I watched you get crushed by your job—and by me. I take my full share of the blame."

He was laying her soul bare and she wanted to crawl away into some dark place and hide, but somehow she couldn't make herself move. She needed his comfort too much.

"Part of you still wants to believe," he continued in the same deep, slow tone. "Somewhere inside you that idealist still exists. You've developed a good shell of cynicism, but a true cynic wouldn't care whether John Otis is innocent."

She pressed her lips tightly together, unable to deny it.

"The way I see it, you crawled out of your shell when you got word Otis was going to be executed. You crawled out, and you dared to believe again, just one fragile little hope. You went to see him, and you came away daring to believe he was innocent. That takes a lot of faith, sweetheart. A lot of faith."

"It's nuts," she said thickly.

"Most people would say so. That doesn't make it wrong But now you're in a real bind, aren't you?"

She sat up suddenly, looking down at him. The tears she didn't want to shed, tears that came from an aching, frightened heart, hung on her lower lashes. "No kidding," she said thickly.

He reached up and touched one tear with a gentle fingertip. "Seems to me you've got as much to lose here as Otis. What if we find out he's guilty? You'll never believe in anybody again, will you? And what if we can't find anything at all, and he gets executed? Will you ever believe in the justice system again? I doubt it. You're close enough to that already. And the worst possible outcome of all is that we find out to our own satisfaction that he's innocent, but we can't save him. How are you going to live with that?"

She shook her head, looking away, her vision blurred by tears.

"You've put an awful lot of your hopes and dreams in one leaky little basket, Carey And that's why you're coming apart now. Because we're getting so close to the death of the last little flickering hope that's never been quite stamped out by life."

She dashed away her tears with the back of her hand and drew a shaky breath. "I'm an open book, huh?"

"Not exactly. For some reason I've been doing an awful lot of thinking about what happened between us before. What you told me recently about what was really going on when you were having all that trouble at work—well, it made me start reevaluating my perceptions of what had happened. Things are always clearer in hindsight, aren't they?"

"Seems like it."

"I wasn't fair to you."

She turned her head and looked at him. "What do you mean?"

"We were both hanging on by a thread, weren't we." (It wasn't a question.) "But I had no business getting involved with *anyone* while I was still in the grip of survivor guilt. And that's exactly what it was—and is. I was so fucking involved in my own guilt trip that I didn't have anything to give you."

"That's not true. You were always there for me . . . at least until the end when everything started to . . . fracture."

"I only *seemed* to be there. I wasn't really And I think you knew it. I couldn't handle the really important stuff, like the emotional hell you were going through at work. I didn't have anything left for it. So I blew you off and didn't listen as carefully as I should have. I know that, so don't bother denying it."

She twisted so that she was sitting cross-legged beside

244

him, looking at him. "Where is this postmortem going?"

He pushed himself up on an elbow. "Simple. The guilt trip you're on right now made me realize what kind of guilt trip I've been on—and how destructive it can be. It made me look back at what I've done—mostly to you. It's ugly, Carey. It's real ugly."

"Are you saying that what I'm doing is ugly?"

"No. Not at all." He reached out and brushed a damp tendril of hair from her face. "What you're doing is beautiful, actually. Beautiful and caring and admirable. But the guilt you're feeling isn't. Guilt is an ugly thing when it haunts us day and night, and drives us to do irrational or hurtful things. Guilt has one purpose: to make us realize when we've done something wrong. But when it consumes us it becomes a disease."

She sniffled. "I never thought I'd hear you say that."

"Sometimes even my thick head gets the message. I've let guilt eat up a significant portion of my life. Worse, I've let it cause me to hurt somebody I care about, namely you. I don't want to see it do the same thing to you."

She shook her head. "What can you do about it? It's something you feel."

"That's what *I* said." He sighed and flopped back down on the bed. "Talk is cheap. I'm just flapping my jaws. All I can see is that you're heading for a major emotional wreck, and I'd do anything in my power to prevent it."

She didn't know what to say to that. He was right. All her mixed feelings were rising like floodwaters behind a weakening dam.

"One thing I do know," he said after a while. "You've got no cause to feel this guilty. You didn't single-handedly put John Otis on death row. It's *his* life, and he's not doing a damn thing to prevent this. He clammed up from the very start, and wouldn't give us a thing to go on that might have gotten him off. You said it yourself—he knows who did it.

"Well, if *he* knows and won't do anything to save himself, how can you carry the entire burden? Give yourself a break, Carey. Even if you'd had no part in the trial, the outcome would have been the same."

She nodded slowly, but she didn't see how that really exculpated her Because no matter what he said, she *had* played a role.

Closing her eyes against the anxiety that was eating her alive, she suddenly remembered the book that had been lying in John Otis's cell: *A Tale of Two Cities*. And just as suddenly she remembered the famous quote from that book, "It is a far, far better thing that I do, than I have ever done; it is a far, far better rest that I go to, than I have ever known." Was that what Otis was thinking?

"Son of a bitch," she said suddenly. "He has no right to do that!"

Seamus sat up. "What?"

She told him about the book and the quote.

"Christ," he said, following her reasoning. "Self-sacrifice? How can you stop that? And what do you mean, he has no right to do it?"

"Because he's not just sacrificing himself! He's making all of us *accomplices* in his suicide by forcing the state to kill him when he's innocent. He's making us all into murderers by doing that. He has no right to do that to anyone. He has no right to do that to *me!*"

"No," Seamus agreed after a moment's thought. "Last year some guy got suicidal and didn't have the guts to pull the trigger himself. So he pulled a gun on a cop. The cop's still in therapy."

"But even if he doesn't see it as suicide—and maybe he doesn't—he's wrong in thinking he's committing some noble act of self-sacrifice. If his brother were innocent, that would be one thing. But the guy is evidently a multiple murderer. Saving James has already cost three people their lives. How many more are going to die if James stays free? Where is the nobility in allowing a murderer to kill again? God, Seamus, John has this all twisted up in his head!"

Seamus rubbed his chin and sighed. "You're probably right."

"I'll tell you one thing, I'm not going to let him make me a party to this. If I do nothing else, I've got to make sure that James never kills another person."

"I'm going to order room service," he said after a while. "We both need the rest. Besides, I'm expecting a call."

"From who?"

He gave her a crooked smile. "Local law enforcement. You never know what you might find out."

She looked down at her restlessly twining fingers. "I don't think I can eat, Seamus."

"Okay. I won't order. We'll go out later."

Then, without so much as a by-your-leave, he reached out and pulled her down so that she lay half across him, her breasts pressed to his chest, her face inches from his.

"I'm starved," he said, his voice rumbling deep in his chest in a way that reminded her of a huge cat. "I haven't eaten since breakfast, and you know my appetite."

Yes, she knew his *appetites*. They were all large, and not all of them were for food. She was feeling almost giddy, being this close to him, reading the slumberous heat in his eyes. Food wasn't all he wanted. A slow, deep pulsing began between her legs.

It was as if all the air had been sucked from the room, and the entire universe had narrowed to this man. Everything else seemed to recede into the distant reaches of space and time. Her entire being hummed with yearning just for him, and not even the last fading voice of sanity could stop her. She needed him. She needed the forgetfulness he was offering.

There was an almost painful sense of awakening somewhere inside her, as feelings she had long ago put to sleep began to stir to new life. She had never stopped wanting this man, she realized. They were doomed, but she had never stopped wanting him anyway. She had only pretended that she didn't care anymore.

Because care she did. She felt as if she were being painfully yanked out of some warm dark place and forcibly thrust back into reality, and with the emergence all the anguish returned. The scars on her heart, so tender yet, burst wide, revealing the gaping wound that had never healed.

It hurt. It hurt almost too much to bear, to realize she still loved this man. But no matter how much it hurt, she couldn't make herself turn away, because that would hurt more.

Just then, the phone in his room rang. His eyes closed briefly, and he drew a deep breath.

Freed of his hypnotic gaze, she rolled away quickly, grabbed the blow-dryer and brush, and locked herself in the bathroom. Tears came then, and she bit a towel to stifle her sobs. She didn't want him to know how much he still touched her. She couldn't bear for him to know that she was still completely and totally vulnerable to him.

Because she didn't want him to know just how totally crazy she still was. Because it terrified her. Because she didn't think she could survive another broken heart.

An hour later she had dressed in a green sheath and low-heeled pumps, ready to go out to dinner. He was in his room, behind the closed adjoining door, and she could hear him talking still. Finally, growing impatient, she opened the adjoining door and walked into his room.

He looked up from the phone still welded to his ear, and smiled, raising a finger to indicate he'd be just a minute.

When he hung up, he let his gaze travel slowly over her with obvious appreciation. "Changed your mind about going out?"

Anything was better than spending any more time alone with him in the vicinity of a bed, she thought. "I need to get out of this funk. It isn't doing anybody any good. Worse than not doing any good, it was putting her in danger. She felt so at sea, so frightened, that she was apt to sail straight into the port of Seamus's arms. Only she knew it wasn't a safe port.

"Good." He stood up and began buttoning the top buttons of his shirt. "I hope you don't mind, but I said I'd meet a detective from the Atlanta police in about thirty minutes at a place not too far from here. If we don't have dinner with him, we can go somewhere afterward, okay?"

"Sounds good to me." In fact, it sounded infinitely better than being alone with Seamus anywhere. "Going to trade war stories?"

"We already did some of that. But it seems he was acquainted with James Henry Otis."

Carey forgot her emotional crisis as her heart jumped. "Really? What does he know?"

"That's what we're going to find out. It could be interesting. Then again, it may be nothing but ordinary childhood pranks."

"Not if it needed a detective."

"I don't know if he was a detective then." He glanced at his watch, then unbuttoned his shirt collar again. "Let me wash up a bit. Traveling always makes me feel as if I've got layers of dirt everywhere."

He disappeared into his bathroom, leaving her to wonder if at last they were really onto something.

They met Detective Gordon Shanks at a pub about twenty minutes from their hotel. He was a tall, lanky man, with skin the color of coffee and a ready smile and handshake. He looked tough, but his voice was surprisingly gentle from a man so big.

They sat together in a leather-padded booth with highbacked benches that effectively cut them off from the world. A waitress brought crackers with the menu and took their drink orders. Everyone ordered coffee, but Shanks added a double order of potato skins.

"I don't know about y'all," he said, "but I'm famished. I figure we can share the skins, and order dinner later if you want."

"Sounds good to me," Seamus agreed, and Carey nodded her approval.

"So," said Shanks, looking at Carey, "Seamus tells me you were with the prosecutor's office down your way."

"Yes, I was."

"And now you're a radio talk-show host. I think I've heard you. Carey Justice, right? You're doing all those shows on John William Otis."

She nodded. "That's me."

"Bet you're taking some flack."

She had to smile. "You could say that."

"Well, just as long as my name doesn't get on the air, I don't mind. And we're talking about juvie records here. I shouldn't be discussing it at all."

"I have no intention of putting any of this on the air. We're just following a lead."

Shanks nodded. "That's what he told me. Well, I gotta

say if the brother you have down there is anything like the brother we got up here, you're wasting your time. This kid was born to be trouble."

Seamus leaned forward alertly. "How so?"

"One scrape after another. You know, when you've got a juvenile who, gets into trouble once or twice you can think maybe it's just a kid feeling his oats and not thinking too clearly. But when you got a kid who does it again and again, you know you've got real trouble."

"What kind of trouble?"

"Well, it started with joyriding. Then he got involved in shoplifting. Five or six incidents, as I recall, but his family had money, so they made restitution and the kid got probation. He was in and out of court from the time he was twelve until he was sixteen or so. And in and out of counseling, too. Given his background, the courts didn't have any difficulty believing this was a seriously troubled kid who needed help."

Seamus nodded, scribbling notes on his pad. "Nothing violent, though?"

"I wouldn't say that. It never got charged, but I heard he popped a teacher and was suspended for a while. The school didn't report it because he was on probation for a car theft at the time, and the judge would have slammed his butt in jail. The parents apparently paid off the teacher, and got Jamie into a new counseling program. I heard he threatened other kids with a knife, but again, nobody pressed charges or called the cops."

"How'd you hear this then?" Carey asked.

He smiled. "I was on juvie detail back then. I had ears to the ground all the time. When I found a kid who was going bad, I started checking on them from time to time, you know? I know other kids were scared of him, but it wasn't like he was out-of-control violent. It was like they

251

liked him but they knew he had a problem with his temper, so they kind of tiptoed around him."

"Not a serial-killer type then."

"I don't think so." Shanks sat back to let the waitress put the two platters of potato skins and three plates in front of them. "Dig in, folks. Help yourselves. There's more where this comes from." He took his own advice, lifting two of the large, stuffed skins onto his plate.

Seamus and Carey each helped themselves, and for a little while no one talked as they ate.

"No," said Shanks, as he reached for a third skin, "I wouldn't have figured him for that type at all. He had an impulse-control problem. That's how he kept getting into trouble. He'd do whatever fancy took him without thinking about it. And he *did* have an anger-control problem. A serious one. I always figured we'd be locking his butt up for a long time one day when he lost his temper and really hurt somebody. Why? Do you see turn doing something different?"

Seamus filled him in on the murders in St. Pete and the radio-station caller who was linking them to John Otis. Shanks nodded, eating as he listened.

"Well, it could be, I suppose," he said. "Can't say I know the man at all now. It's possible he's got himself worked up into some land of emotional frenzy Or maybe something happened to him in that mental hospital, and he's turned into a cold-blooded murderer."

"What do you know about his institutionalization?" Carey asked. "Anything at all?"

"I checked on that after Seamus and I talked. Jamie was on probation at the time, and the thing wound up in a courtroom, so he wouldn't be charged with a violation. The doctor said it was a stress-induced nervous breakdown, that given the boy's past, he had a lot of unresolved stresses and problems, and that it might take years of therapy to get him sorted out. So he's out now huh?"

"As of a month ago," Carey supplied.

"I guess they figured they straightened him out."

Seamus and Carey exchanged glances but didn't say anything. Carey found herself wondering if James Otis had really gotten better, or if he'd just gotten smarter.

"Good question," Seamus said several hours later, as they were heading back to the hotel room. They'd had an enjoyable evening with Shanks, trading war stories. "He probably just got smarter. I've seen people who've gone through endless counseling before. They learn what to say and what not to say. It doesn't seem to take them long to psych out the shrink—if that's what they want to do."

"Exactly what I thought. But what did you think of what Shanks said? Does it sound like Jamie could be our guy? I mean, he seemed to limit himself mostly to little stuff. I've seen plenty like him who never graduated to murder."

"And I've seen some like him, with an anger problem, who discover the first time they kill somebody in a fit of rage that it isn't so damn difficult at all."

"But why would he have been angry at John's foster parents?"

"That, m'dear, is the all-important question."

When they got to the motel, they went their separate ways, closing the door between their rooms. Carey hung up her dress and steamed it in the bathroom, to get out the wrinkles for the next day. Then she changed into a short cotton nightgown and curled up in front of the TV, watching a late-night movie, some ridiculous science-fiction tale from the fifties.

And somewhere about the time the inevitable nuclear

253

weapon was coming to the rescue, she dozed off.

Sometime later, a sound disturbed her and she opened her eyes to see Seamus standing in the doorway between their rooms. He was wearing pajama bottoms and nothing else. He had a gorgeous chest, she thought drowsily.

"Sorry," he said. "I heard the TV and thought you were still awake."

" 'S okay," she said, pushing herself up on the pillow and rubbing her eyes. "What's wrong?"

"Nothing. I was just thinking."

"So pull up a seat." For some reason she didn't want him to go away.

"It's nothing major." But he came to perch on the edge of the bed anyway. "I was just thinking about what Shanks said tonight, and then I remembered that affidavit that James's adoptive mother signed, saying he was home the entire weekend of the Kline murders."

She nodded. "I read it over. Nobody really suspected James though, because he lived so far away and didn't have a relationship with the Klines."

"Right. I remember. It was just to plug a possible defense loophole."

"Exactly. Pretty much *pro forma*. I read it over the other day, and there's nothing in it. Cut-and-dried."

"Yeah . . ." He drew the word out. "Except that I was remembering what Shanks said about how many times the Wigginses apparently bought James out of his trouble. And what he said about the kid being on probation at the time of the murders."

Carey sat up straighter. "It would be a powerful motivation to lie, wouldn't it?"

"Exactly what I was thinking. Maybe we ought to delve into that a little. Not just ask about the guy's whereabouts now, but see if we can rattle her alibi for for him."

Carey felt a sudden leap of hope. "My God, Seamus!"

He smiled. "It'd wrap the whole thing up in a nice little bow, wouldn't it? But don't get your hopes up. We might not be able to shake the Wigginses. And we don't have time to try to question everybody who knew James about a weekend five years ago. Most people probably wouldn't even remember."

"But if we can shake her. . ." Hope was suddenly shining in her eyes, and singing in her heart.

"If we can shake her, we're on our way."

And then, without further ado, he bent over and kissed her soundly.

CHAPTER 17
5 DAYS

CAREY WAS ALREADY RIDING A WAVE OF EXULTATION over the hope that they might learn something truly useful in the morning, but when Seamus kissed her, she felt that exultation rise even higher

Memories mixed with present sensations, giving her a surreal feeling. She knew him so well. The smell of him, the feel of him, the way he held her and kissed her—all of these had never been forgotten, and she had never stopped missing them. She felt like Penelope upon the return of Odysseus.

It was as if every cell in her being, and every fiber of her soul, found home port. The loss she had never stopped mourning was suddenly gone, replaced by relief and satisfaction so profound they defied description.

This was where she belonged.

It was illusory, and some part of her knew it. Five years, she was sure, had made them into different people. The

255

love they had once shared and frittered away did not belong to the people they had become. All they had was a memory, and a need they had never managed to slake.

With no hope of a future with this man, she should have backed away. The memory of pain was as strong as the memory of love. But it was not as strong as the hunger that filled her now, and that drove her to return his kiss with all the need she felt.

Love between them had died, but passion had not. Its ember remained burning in her heart, a hurtful presence that had kept her from moving on. So let it burn, she thought recklessly Let it burn and flare into an almighty conflagration, and soon enough, nurtured by nothing but itself, it would burn out and leave her free at last.

Seamus lifted his head, supporting himself on his elbows to either side of her shoulders. He looked down at her for what seemed a long time, as if memorizing her face.

She stared back at him, soaking up every detail of how he looked. His face was careworn, speaking of the dark paths he had trod in the past five years, but there were no shadows there, she realized. So often in the past she hadn't been sure whether he was really seeing *her,* or whether he was seeing his demons. But tonight she could tell he saw only her.

He spoke, his voice husky. "God, I've missed this."

She had, too, and she was in no mood to quibble about what he had missed. Lifting her arms, she twined them around his neck, enjoying the sensation of his warm skin against her. There was nothing, she thought, as exquisite as the feeling of skin on skin.

"Remember the magnolia tree?" he asked.

She nodded, feeling a smile tug at the corners of her mouth. A trip down memory lane might be dangerous, but she understood his need for it. This feeling, this moment here and now, needed to be put in perspective. "I remember."

The first time they had kissed had been at the end of a very long day. They had planned to go to a movie that evening, but work had interfered for them both, and finally, around eleven that evening, they had managed to meet at her old apartment.

They had decided to take a walk down the dimly lit streets, and had come to a huge old magnolia that spread its sheltering branches over the sidewalk. Seamus had turned to her and drawn her into his arms, giving her a kiss at once hungry and gentle. From that moment she had been his. And to this day, whenever she smelled magnolias, she thought of him.

He spoke. "There's one outside the hotel. I was walking out there earlier when I found it, and I was standing under it remembering . . ."

"We made a lot of mistakes, didn't we?"

"Every one in the book." He looked at her mouth. "Are we about to make another one?"

"I don't give a damn." And right now she didn't. She had been needing him for five long years, and she wasn't about to let fear of tomorrow stand in her way now. There was something to be said for the Scarlett O'Hara approach to life.

If he smiled, she never got the chance to see it. He seized her mouth in a deep, ferocious kiss, as if by will alone he could make the past and future vanish, leaving them with now and only now

And now was more than enough. His lips were warm and firm, his tongue was hot and wet as it pillaged her mouth. The heady scent of him. was evocative of all the pleasures she had known with him, and her body responded instantly, giving fun rein to the hunger he had always awakened in her.

His weight bore down on her as he shifted so that he lay over her, crushing her aching breasts, fitting himself to her so that she could feel the heat of his manhood at the apex of her thighs. It was a sensation so exquisite that her desire pooled instantly there, a heavy, throbbing weight of need. She opened her legs, wrapping them around him, trying to bring him closer yet.

Long, lonely nights were driving them too fast, and for an instant she feared it would all be over before she could savor these long wanted moments.

But then, as suddenly as he had become fierce, he gentled, lifting his mouth from hers to trail butterfly-soft kisses across the arch of her cheekbones, over her eyelids, and down her throat. She tipped her head back, encouraging, and drew a sharp breath of pleasure when the moist heat of his mouth found the pounding pulse in the hollow of her throat.

He nibbled her earlobe gently, the whisper of his breath in her ear causing her to shiver and arch with delight. Then he pulled away, just long enough to pull the nightgown over her head and expose her to his view.

Long ago, he had taught her to be proud of her body. She was proud now as his gaze trailed over her, followed by his hands, stroking her from head to toe as gently as if she were a cat pausing to linger over the aching, yearning places just long enough to drive her to the edge of madness.

Then he followed his hands with his mouth, sprinkling kisses and gentle licks of his tongue over her shoulders, her arms, her belly, her thighs, her knees, and her ankles. Each gentle caress fueled her longing until she felt as if she was a vessel full of throbbing, aching need.

"Seamus . . ." She heard herself groan his name as his tongue touched the arch of her foot. He lifted his head and smiled at her, waiting.

"Seamus, please . . ."

He returned to her side, drawing her full-length against him. "What do you want, sweetie?" he asked huskily. "Tell me."

She rubbed against him like a cat, trying to ease the ache in her breasts and between her thighs, seeking touches he had not yet given her. Something near desperation drove her to push him onto his back and straddle him. As she rose above him, he at last gave her some of what she wanted, reaching up to cup her breasts tenderly in his palms.

She let her head fall back, reveling in the exquisite shocks of pleasure that shot from her breasts to her center, adding to the heavy weight between her legs. Reaching down, she found his nipples and plucked them gently, the way she wanted him to pluck hers.

He knew. He had always known. From the instant he had first touched her all those years ago, he had known her body better than she did. But even as he groaned in response to her touches, and arched his pelvis toward hers, seeking the warm place inside her, he denied her what she wanted.

But she knew how to push him past this teasing game he was playing. Pushing his hands away, she bent down and took one of his small nipples in her mouth, lapping at it with her tongue, nipping gently with her teeth. She felt him jerk sharply with reaction, and heard his groan with deep satisfaction.

He was hers. The thought gave her a heady sense of power, as it always had. And for now the desire to torment him as he had tormented her overtook everything else.

But just as she moved to his other nipple, prepared to torment him as fully as he had tormented her, he rolled her onto her back and rose over her.

In an instant he was buried inside her, filling a place that had been empty far too long. For a moment, she hung suspended on the wonder of their union, glorying in the overwhelming satisfaction of having him deep within her.

Then he bent and took her breast into his mouth, tormenting her exactly as she had tormented him, with gentle nips and licks that each sent fresh shocks of passion racing through her. She writhed against him, but his hips pinned hers, denying her the satisfaction she sought.

She loved it. But finally, when she could stand it no longer, she called out his name. He answered with the strong thrust she had been waiting for, carrying them both on the climb to completion.

With a wrenching cry, she reached the top and tumbled over to the peaceful place beyond. A moment later, he followed her.

They fell asleep twined together, replete at last.

When Carey awoke in the morning, Seamus was already gone. For a few minutes, she didn't move, allowing herself to relish the way she felt, allowing her body to remember all that had happened.

But reality didn't leave her alone for long. Finally, she could no longer ignore the fact that he'd left her, and could no longer pretend that it didn't matter. He was putting distance between them, and that was a good thing, she told herself. They had to keep away from this precipice.

But she didn't believe it. She had the worst urge to curl up and cry into her pillow, because she had lost Seamus all over again. God, how could she have been so stupid? Had she really believed that she would wake up this morning and feel no pain? Had she really convinced herself that it would "burn out?"

She turned over, hugging the pillow, smelling the scent of him on the sheets, and felt her eyes burn and her throat tighten, and her chest ache so hard she could barely breathe. Oh, God, she couldn't stand this again! It would rip her apart, and she didn't know if she had enough strength left to put herself back together again.

But as quickly as the impossible grief surged through her, she squeezed her eyes tightly shut and forced herself to sit up and pull the sheet around herself. No. She was absolutely not going to give in to this. She couldn't afford to. Grief and loss were things she'd learned to put away in some dark, dusty corner of her heart, and she was going to put this new wave back in its place no matter what. She absolutely was not going to do this to herself again.

Pawing through her purse, she found a battered pack of cigarettes and lit one, her first in two days. Her hand was shaking, and she could barely see, but the act of drawing a deep breath of smoke steadied her a little. Quitting was something she would deal with when she got Seamus safely out of her life again. Until then, she was going to use any crutch she could find, and not apologize for it.

She smoked half the cigarette, forcing herself to think about John Otis and the people they were going to meet today. Think about the really important things, she told herself. The really essential things. Her own emotional catastrophe could be dealt with later.

The adjoining door opened, and Seamus stepped into the room, wearing his pajama bottoms. Around his neck was a towel, and his hair stood up in wet spikes.

"Damn," he said with a smile, "I was hoping I could wake you up."

She gave him a fleeting smile and took another drag of her cigarette, sure that if she tried to speak she was going to fly apart into hysterics. She could feel him looking at her, but she refused to meet his gaze.

"I'm sorry," he said after a moment. "I figured, as late as we were up, that I could shower before you woke."

"No problem," she managed, and flicked her ash into the ashtray.

"You shouldn't have been alone when you woke up," he said gently.

She shrugged a shoulder, holding on to her self-control as desperately as a drowning man clinging to a raft. Her voice held an edge. "It doesn't matter. We need to get started, don't we?"

"Okay." Now *his* voice had an edge. She dared to glance at him from the corner of her eye and wondered why he looked angry.

He opened the adjoining door wider and turned to go back to his room. "Breakfast is here," he said over his shoulder. "We've got a ten o'clock meeting with the Wigginses."

My, she thought almost bitterly, he *had* been busy. She stubbed out her cigarette, pulled on her robe, and followed him.

Breakfast was laid out on the small table in one corner of the room. Lifting the covers, she found he'd ordered steak and eggs for one, and fruit and French toast for one. He remembered her morning preferences, she realized with an aching twinge. She poured herself a cup of coffee from the insulated carafe and sipped it until he came back out of the bathroom this time with his wet hair combed and a pajama shirt on.

"Is it okay?" he asked. He didn't sound as if he really cared.

"Great," she said.

They sat across from one another, and ate in a silence that was almost stony. She didn't want to admit how much she hurt, and he wasn't going to ask her what was wrong.

Typical, thought Carey. Their relationship had ended this way, with long, stony silences interrupted by flaming arguments when things built up too much. How could she possibly be missing *this*?

Finally, her appetite killed by tension, she went to shower and dress. And to hell with Seamus Rourke!

Gerry Wiggins was an accountant who worked out of his home, so they met in his office. He sat behind his large cherry desk, and his wife sat nearby. Seamus and Carey took the two green leather chairs facing the desk.

Gerry Wiggins was an athletic-looking man of about forty-five with a car salesman's smile and a pair of very dark, intelligent eyes. His wife, Marcia, was about fifty, with short auburn hair and green eyes. She looked frazzled and worried, and more tired than her husband.

"Yes, we adopted Jamie Otis," Gerry said in answer to the first question. "Marcia felt so sorry for him after she read about him and his brother in the paper. We didn't want the boy who'd done the killing, of course. Couldn't be sure he wouldn't do it again." He gave a brief, humorless smile. "Apparently he did."

Seamus merely nodded.

"We've adopted a lot of children, though. We have three right now, still in school. And there were two before Jamie."

"That's remarkable," Carey said. "Do you always adopt older children?"

He shrugged a shoulder. "They're the ones most in need of a loving home. One of our boys has muscular dystrophy, and one of the girls is mildly retarded. These are the kids that nobody else wants, but we've got plenty of room for them here, and plenty of love, too."

Marcia nodded agreement. "It's the right thing to do."

"You're to be congratulated," Seamus said.

"I think so," said Gerry Wiggins. "We feel very blessed. And never a moment of regret, have we, Marcia?"

"No, never." She said it with a determination that indicated she suspected where this might be heading.

"But you wanted to talk about Jamie," Gerry said, leaning forward. "Is he in some kind of trouble?"

"I really don't know," Seamus said carefully. "I heard he was released from the hospital around a month ago."

"That's right. Unfortunately, Jamie was our only disappointment. After he was institutionalized, he didn't want to see us anymore, and after he got out—well, we're still hoping he might call or stop by, but he hasn't."

"Do you have any idea where he might have gone?"

Gerry shook his head. "None at all. It really surprises me. I never thought he was an ungrateful child, and I paid for all his hospitalization—I hate to tell you how much it cost—and he still wouldn't see us. And now this. Well, maybe once he's had a taste of life, he'll come back. We're the only family he has left now."

"You're very generous people."

"Just trying to do what's right. I'm sorry we can't be more help. But I wish you'd tell me why you're interested in him."

But Seamus changed tack. "I understand that Jamie had some trouble in high school."

"Just some scrapes. He did some things he shouldn't have That all pretty much cleared up, though, by the time he was sixteen. We never had any more trouble after that."

Seamus nodded, making a note in his ever-present notebook. "I also understand that you occasionally . . . made monetary settlements to keep him out of trouble."

Gerry Wiggins bridled. "If you're suggesting I bribed anyone—"

"No, of course not," Seamus interrupted hastily. "The thought never entered my head. I apologize. I was just trying to get a complete picture."

"Well, I made restitution, if you will. That's all I did. His teachers and the school were very understanding about what might happen to Jamie if he violated probation. Everyone understood that he was a difficult child, and that he had a great many problems to overcome."

Carey decided this guy must be made out of money. Seamus made another note before he continued the questioning.

"Now," he said, "I'm sure you know that Jamie's brother John is on death row in Florida for killing Linda and Harvey Kline."

Gerry nodded. "Which just goes to show I was correct in not taking both boys, doesn't it, Marcia?"

"Yes, dear."

Seamus favored her with his best smile. "Now," he continued, "you may remember just before John's trial you were asked to confirm Jamie's whereabouts the weekend of the Kline murders."

"Yes, of course," Gerry answered. "My wife said he was home all weekend."

"But you didn't make an affidavit?"

Gerry shook his head. "They never asked me. I was out of town at the time they approached Marcia, and while I expected them to get in touch with me, they never did."

"Mm." Seamus looked down at his notebook, as if he were reading something there. "Was he really at home?"

"Now wait one moment!" Gerry nearly came out of his seat. "How dare you imply—"

Seamus looked at him with hard eyes. "I'm not implying anything. I'm asking."

"If my wife said—"

"Look," said Carey, intervening. "I was the prosecutor on the John Otis case. I saw the affidavit. I know what your wife said."

"Well, then." Gerry settled onto his chair. "Before we go any further, I want to know why you're asking these questions. Otherwise, this interview is over."

Carey answered. "There have been a couple of murders in the Tampa area. Slashing murders just like the Klines. Both the people who were killed were involved in the John Otis trial."

"That doesn't mean—"

"It wouldn't necessarily mean anything at all, except that a man has been calling me, telling me that John didn't do it, that *he* did, and that he's going to keep killing people unless we stop the execution."

"Anyone could say that!"

"Perhaps. But we can't imagine who else would be killing people to try to save John Otis, and frankly, we've got only five days left before the execution. We're looking for anyone or anything who can help us find this killer before he kills again, and if this person really *did* kill the Klines, we need to know it as quickly as possible so we can keep the execution from going through."

"Basically," said Seamus in a hard voice, before Gerry Wiggins could reply, "if you know anything at all that you've been keeping back to protect Jamie, and it turns out that he is indeed the person who's been doing these killings, then you may be responsible for the deaths of other innocent people. And you will most certainly be responsible for the death of John Otis."

There was a silence so long that Carey found herself listening to her heartbeat. She didn't think the Wigginses were bad people. Maybe a little full of their righteousness, and proud of themselves, but their intentions were the best.

Finally Gerry spoke. "I can give you the names of some of Jamie's old friends. Maybe he contacted one of them. But after all this time. . ." He shook his head again. "I don't think you'll find out much. And since I know most of the families, I think I would have heard about it if Jamie had seen or called any of them."

"It's worth a try," Seamus said.

It was then that Carey looked at Marcia. "I understand why you want to protect your son. Truly I do. I'd feel the same way if I were you. But if there's anything you know, you might save lives."

Marcia darted an uncertain look at her husband.

Seamus spoke. "Did Jamie have a driver's license?"

"Before he was hospitalized," Gerry answered. "Obviously, I don't know if he's gotten one since. But he had his own car then. I saw to it."

"Why?" Seamus asked.

Gerry gave a crooked smile. "I always believed that making sure children had their own pocket money, and later their own transportation, helped keep them from life's temptations, you know?"

Seamus nodded. "I see your point."

"I even make sure they have credit cards from the time they're sixteen. You don't need to steal what you can buy, or what you already have," Gerry continued, looking more comfortable now "And our children have already been deprived of so much. Marcia and I want to make it up to them, don't we, dear?"

Marcia nodded, casting another uncertain look, this time at Carey.

"So," said Carey, keeping her gaze on Marcia, "Jamie, could have driven to Florida when he was seventeen. If he had wanted to. Or he could have bought a bus ticket."

Gerry shrugged. "I suppose. The thing is, he *didn't*. He was here."

"Gerry," Marcia said tentatively.

Carey took advantage of the moment, the way she so often had as a prosecutor. "Where *exactly* was your son on the day the Klines were murdered?"

"Exactly?" Gerry said blankly. "What in the world . . ."

"I mean, was he *here?* In this house? In his own bed? Did he have dinner here and breakfast here, with you? Did you actually see him with your own eyes?"

"Look . . ." said Gerry angrily, rising to his feet.

But Carey pressed on. She'd pressed on even in the face of irritated judges. No accountant was going to stop her. "Was he here, or did you lose track of him, say between noon on Saturday and noon on Sunday? Did he tell you he was going to stay with a friend? Or did he call and say he'd be out late, and then claim the next day that he'd left early? What *really* happened? In detail!"

Gerry raised a finger, his face twisted in. anger, but Marcia never took her eyes off Carey. Something in her face seemed to crumple.

"I don't know for sure," she said finally, her voice quavery.

"Marcia!" her husband barked. "You don't have to say anything at all. You gave them a sworn statement five years ago, and they have no right to anything else."

Marcia did look at him then. "Yes, they do, Gerry. I

268

told them he was at home. I told you he was at home. And I really thought he was. But you were away that weekend, remember? And I never thought Jamie would *lie.* He had never lied to me before, even when he'd done something really bad. So I just assumed what I said was true, that he was here in Atlanta, and that saying he was at home simply kept Kevin Rutland out of it. You know how you feel about the Rutlands. They'd have been appalled, and you would have been appalled, if we did anything that dragged them into that mess in Florida. So I hedged the truth just a tiny bit."

"Marcia. . ." Her husband's voice had grown quiet, almost disbelieving.

"Until this very minute, I honestly believed he was right here all the time. But when Miss Stover said all that about the car and was he really here every minute or did I lose track of him . . . And then, thinking of what they said about what's happening in Florida . . . Gerry, maybe I was wrong! Maybe he lied to me! Maybe he didn't really go to spend the weekend with Kevin after all!"

CHAPTER 18
5 DAYS

THE MAID BROUGHT TEA AND COFFEE FOR EVERYONE, giving Marcia a chance to calm herself. Her hands trembled so badly that the bone china cup rattled against the saucer as she held them. Her husband ignored the beverages and stared at nothing in particular, a man stunned.

Finally, he looked at Seamus. "You're not going to charge Marcia with perjury, are you?"

"I don't see the point," Seamus answered. "She said

what she thought was true at the time. I'm just glad she had second thoughts about it now. I would like Kevin Rutland's phone number, to confirm whether Jamie was there, if you don't mind."

Gerry nodded wearily. All his anger was gone, and he looked whipped.

"And credit cards. You said you give the children credit cards. Did Jamie have one?"

"Yes, he did. A small limit, naturally. One doesn't want to give a child too much money."

"No, that wouldn't be a good idea. I don't suppose there's any chance you would have kept the bills from so long ago?"

"Well, of course I kept them." He grimaced. "I'm an accountant. I keep everything for at least seven years."

"Would it be possible for me to see Jamie's?"

Marcia was considerably calmer now, and while Gerry left the room Carey turned to her. "Was there anything Jamie was upset about right before that weekend? Anything to do with his brother?"

Marcia's eyes teared up again. "I was just thinking about that. Friday night, John called. Apparently he'd had a terrible argument with his foster parents and had been thrown out. Jamie thought he'd been thrown out for good, but I told him no parent would do that, not for real. I don't know whether he believed me or not. But I do know that Jamie was upset about it. He said something about the Klines not deserving a son like Johnny."

Meanwhile, Gerry had returned with a file folder. He sat at his desk and flipped it open, leafing through a stack of credit card bills. When he was about halfway through, he froze. "My God," he said.

"What?" asked Seamus.

Now it was the accountant's hand that trembled as he passed a receipt to Seamus. Carey leaned over to look at it.

James Henry Otis had spent the night of the murders in a cheap motel in Tampa.

"Didn't you notice that when you paid the bill?" Seamus asked him.

Gerry's face was ashen. "I didn't pay the bill. The children pay their own credit card bills. It's their responsibility."

"Do you have a picture of him you could give me?" Seamus asked.

Gerry nodded.

And Marcia began to sob.

Ten minutes later they departed, photo in hand.

"Well," said Carey, as they walked out to their rental car, "we now have motive and opportunity."

"It's not enough. Not by a long shot."

She paused to look at him as he unlocked the car door. "It's enough to give me a lever if he calls the station again this week."

Seamus opened the door for her. "Maybe. Jesus, we've got to get our hands on this guy before it's too late!"

"Maybe Kevin Rutland has talked to him."

"God, I hope so."

Seamus drove to a pay phone and placed the call to Kevin Rutland, who was these days working in his father's corporation. He was put through almost immediately.

"Mr. Rutland, my name is Seamus Rourke. I'm a detective with the St. Petersburg, Florida, Police Department."

"Oh. I've never been there," said a young man's cultured voice with Georgia's tentative drawl.

"Well, that answers one question I was going to ask you. But you *do* know James Henry Otis?"

271

"Yes. At least I used to. We went to school together and hung around together a lot back then."

"Have you seen him or heard from him since he was released from the hospital a month ago?"

There was a pause. Finally the young man said slowly, "I haven't seen Jamie since his brother was convicted of murder years ago. Even if he hadn't gone to the hospital, my family wouldn't have approved. We don't associate with that sort. I don't know anything about him."

"I see. Mr. Rutland, I really need your help here, so if you could stay with me a few moments?"

"Sure."

"Do you happen to remember the weekend when Jamie's brother committed the murders in Florida?"

"Vaguely. It stuck in my mind because that was when Jamie started to have his breakdown. At least I think it was. It was months, of course, before he got bad enough to be hospitalized, but that's when he started acting strangely."

"What happened?"

"He was terribly upset because his brother had phoned and said his foster parents had thrown him out. I know we spent most of the evening together after the call. Jamie could hardly talk about anything else. He was very upset. Too upset, I thought at the time."

"Why is that?"

"Well, Johnny may have been his brother, but Jamie hadn't seen him much in years. Johnny came up to visit once or twice, I recall, and a couple of times Jamie went down to visit Johnny, but there wasn't a whole lot of contact between them, other than occasional phone calls. Besides, I'd had fights with my parents like the one Johnny had. Or at least I thought I did. Maybe Jamie didn't tell me everything. Anyway, I remember getting bored with it and telling him to cut it out, that it wasn't his problem."

"How did he feel about that?"

"He got mad at me and went home."

"Would he have gone to visit anyone else?"

"I doubt it. It was late. Besides, I was his best friend. Most of the other kids wouldn't put up with him for long."

"When did you see him next?"

"At school on Monday."

"How did he act?"

"He wouldn't talk to me. I thought he was being extreme, so I blew him off. After that, he didn't have any friends at all, especially after we heard Johnny had been charged with murder. Some of us really wondered about Jamie. He'd been in trouble with the law, and there were a couple of times he went over the top, hitting a teacher and pulling a knife. Up until then, we kind of ignored it, because we'd all heard how tough it had been for him as a kid, and our parents thought we should make allowances. But after Johnny was charged—well, we all kind of wondered if Jamie was any better."

"So he was ostracized?"

Kevin Rutland hesitated. "I don't know that I'd say that, exactly. People were polite to him. It's just that nobody wanted to be alone with him after that. Besides, he pretty much dropped out of everything himself. He used to be fun, at least, but after that, he just got dark and quiet. Brooding. He even got so he didn't answer when anyone talked to him."

"When he was talking to you that night after his brother called, did he say anything about going to Florida?"

There was a long pause. Finally, "You don't think he murdered those people, do you?"

Seamus looked out at the steady flow of traffic, tying to decide how to answer that. "I'm just clearing up a few details. Did he say anything about it?"

"No. Not to me. But he did say they ought to be killed."

"Damn it!" Carey said after Seamus related the conversation. She slapped her hand on the dashboard. "Damn it, I should have come up here to take Marcia Wiggins's statement myself!"

"Hindsight," Seamus said shortly. They were approaching the airport, and traffic was getting thick. "You had an affidavit that confirmed his alibi."

"No, I was a fool. People lie. People lie all the damn time, and I knew it even then! I should have questioned the affidavit! I should have talked to his mother myself. My God, who had a better motive to lie than his mother?"

"Carey, nobody was seriously looking at James Otis as the killer. Why should we have? He lived all the way up here, he was just a kid—who was going to suppose he could even get to Florida? How many seventeen-year-old kids do you know with their own cars and credit cards?"

"These days there are a lot of them."

"Right. And we never see them because they come from good families, and if they ever do wind up in trouble, it's usually because of underage drinking, drugs, or DUI. Not because they crossed state lines in their own cars, using their own credit cards, in order to kill somebody they hardly know. It was such a long shot nobody even seriously thought about it. You know that."

"It doesn't make it any better."

"Besides, we had the problem of no forced entry. It had to be somebody with a key, or somebody the Klines let into the house. That pretty much pointed to John."

She laughed almost bitterly. "Right. Except now we know that Jamie knew the Klines well enough that if he had shown up on their doorstep unannounced, they'd probably have let him in because he was John's brother."

"We know that now. We didn't know that then."

"Yeah." She shook her head and wrapped her arms tightly around herself, trying to hold in all the feelings that were roiling inside her. "God, what a lousy investigation!"

Seamus pulled into the rental car return place. "I'll be back in just a minute. Quit beating yourself up, Carey. It's not going to help."

But she couldn't stop. She'd been one of the people on the team that had dismissed James Otis too quickly and too easily. But she had believed John was innocent, so why in hell hadn't she looked more closely at his brother?

It was all well and good to say that it appeared Jamie was too far away, and they did have an affidavit from his mother saying he was home all weekend, but that didn't ease her conscience any now.

And worse, she believed that John had known his brother had committed the murder. Who else would he stay silent for all this time except the little brother he had once killed to save? Damn, it was as obvious as the nose on her face! Why hadn't she seen it back then, when it would have saved so much grief? So much death.

It was Friday. John Otis would be executed early on Wednesday. Time was running out, and now they had the weekend in front of them, a time during which it would be almost impossible to do anything to stay the execution.

Not that they really had enough yet. God, they needed more!

They arrived at the gate just in time to board their flight. Carey sat in the window seat and wondered if

Seamus was going to sleep all the way, as he had last time. She didn't know which would drive her crazier, being left alone with her own thoughts, or talking to Seamus for the next several hours.

As they were taxiing down the runway to takeoff, Seamus reached out and took her hand. She felt contradictory urges to yank it away and keep it there forever.

"Carey?" He leaned toward her. "Remember what you told me about my guilt trip over my wife and daughter?"

She looked at him, not knowing how to take this change of subject. "What do you mean?"

"You told me I'd done the best I could, and that's all anybody can do. I'm finally starting to believe that. Maybe it's time you took your own advice. You did the best that you could."

Carey looked away, staring out the window as the runway began to pass by in a blur. Acceleration pressed her back into her seat, and finally she felt that heart-stopping bob as the plane took flight.

Her best, she thought bitterly, hadn't been enough.

Carey was the one who dozed off on the flight, and awoke as they were approaching Tampa with a stiff neck and a headache. Seamus was reading the book she had brought along. Apparently he had pulled it out of the side pocket of her carry-on when he realized she wasn't going to be much company.

When he felt her stir, he turned to look at her. "Get a good nap?"

"I was out like a light, but now my neck is stiff and my head is killing me."

He reached out and put his hand on the back of her neck. "Let me rub it."

At his merest touch, her body felt shivers of delight that

her brain resented, but she couldn't bring herself to pull away. His fingers were working the tension out of her so quickly that she could feel the difference, and with the tension, the headache began to let go.

"Better?" he asked after a few minutes.

"Yes, thank you."

He removed his hand, leaving her feeling ridiculously bereft. "How's your guilt trip?"

"Vicious."

He nodded and leaned his head back against the seat. As the plane made its approach, the ride was growing bumpier.

"Are you really over yours?" she asked.

"I'm beginning to think so. At least the worst of it. I realized the other night after I cleaned out my daughter's room that I've been hanging on to the guilt to avoid feeling the loss. Their deaths left a great big hole in my life, and I filled it with guilt. Make sure you don't do that."

She looked down at her hands, feeling moved in a way she couldn't quite identify.

"About this morning," he said, catching her unawares. "Are you going to tell me what it was I did that pissed you off?"

In the past, he wouldn't have asked. And it was only now that she realized that his failure to ask had always left her feeling unimportant. Feeling as if he didn't care. She turned her head, feeling the residual stiffness in her neck protest. "It doesn't matter."

"Yes, damn it, it *does* matter. You were angry with me, and I want to know why. I apologized for not being there, so it has to be something else. I'm not a mind reader, Carey. I can't fix it if I don't know what it is."

She felt as if a hitherto closed door in her life had

277

suddenly opened. He was trying to bridge the silence that had once helped cause the end of their relationship. And she was in danger of falling into the old pattern of not telling him how she was feeling and why. She'd come a long way from the girl who had once had an affair with him. In the intervening years she'd become downright blunt about anything and everything she had an opinion or feeling about.

Except now, with Seamus. Being with him had her walking on those old eggshells again because . . . because at the very bottom of it all, she feared that if she expressed the less pleasant things he made her feel at times she would lose him.

She was still looking at him, but she hardly saw him as she understood something about herself. The icy silence across the breakfast table had reminded her of all the times their relationship had been silent. Times she had forgotten because the memories of their flaming fights were so much quicker to spring to mind.

But the silences had probably been as deadly as the fights.

It amazed her how difficult it was to explain what happened, but she tried. "It was . . . it was that I was feeling . . . well, raw. And you weren't there, so I thought you were regretting what happened."

"But I explained."

She nodded. "You did. And then I didn't want to admit how vulnerable I was feeling . . ." Her voice trailed away, and she averted her face. She wouldn't have believed it could be so difficult to admit such a simple thing.

Seamus reclaimed her hand, and he squeezed it. "That's always been hard for you to admit, hasn't it."

She nodded, still unable to look at him.

"Well, for what it's worth, I feel vulnerable as hell."

Then she *did* look at him. "You do?"

"You better believe it. You twist me up in ways no other woman has ever done. You think I'm not worried about what happened between us last night? You think I didn't consider looking for a place to hide this morning? But regardless, there's one thing I can tell you for an absolute fact. I never once regretted our lovemaking last night."

In that moment, she felt as safe as she had ever felt with him. Before, she had never considered that he might have as much to lose as she did. In fact, she had believed him to be emotionally removed from their relationship, so bound up in his guilt and grief that nothing she might do would affect him at all.

In retrospect, she could see that she had believed she was the only one with anything to lose. And fear of her vulnerability had kept her silent when she should have spoken, leading to a tension that had inevitably resulted in fights where she attacked him, rather than just expressing her fears and insecurity. And naturally, he had responded in kind, leaving them both bruised, bloody, and distrusting.

She had never trusted his feelings for her. Worse, she had never believed he had any. It was a little shocking to realize that she had engaged in a six-month relationship with a man she thought didn't care a damn for her. And worse, that she had been so afraid of losing him that she had almost lost herself.

"What?" he asked, watching the shadows flit across her face.

"I've been a fool," she said. Funny, but that was a lot easier to admit now than it would have been five years ago. There was a bump as the plane's tires hit the runway, and she felt her hands tighten on the armrests.

"How so?" he asked.

The reverse thrust cut in with a roar, making it impossible to speak. Only when it quieted again did she look at him. He was waiting expectantly.

"Seamus?"

He nodded encouragingly.

"Did you ever really love me?"

He nodded slowly, holding her gaze. She couldn't doubt him.

"Hell," she said finally, and looked away. "I never believed you did."

Neither of them spoke again until they were docked at the gate. While passengers stirred around them, jamming the aisle and reaching for luggage, they sat quietly in their seats.

Seamus turned and looked at her as the crowd began to thin. "That was my fault," he said. "I felt so damn guilty about what I felt for you that I resented it."

She nodded, feeling a wave of sadness wash over her. "What a mess we made of it."

"We could do better this time, if we try."

She thought about that all the way home. He drove her over the Courtney Campbell Causeway and dropped her at her town house.

"I've got to get back to work," he said. "See if I can get the ball rolling on the Otis thing. Get some sleep, sweetheart."

She shook her head. "No. I'm going to call the governor and see if I can't get him on my Monday show. Even if we don't come up with anything else over the weekend, maybe what we have will be enough to convince him to stay the execution while we continue the investigation."

He shook his head. "Good luck. If the man wants to get reelected, he's not likely to do that."

"I have to do everything I can, Seamus. Everything."

"Yeah." Leaning over, he brushed a kiss on her lips. "I'll be in touch."

She climbed out, pulled out her suitcase, then stood in her driveway in the hot Florida sunshine and watched him drive away. He'd be in touch. It wasn't a whole lot to cling to, but here she was, clinging again.

Either she was a fool or she was a saint. And either one was a pretty miserable thing to be. She might as well wear a sign saying "kick me."

Then she went inside to tackle the governor

Gil Garcia was at the table making phone calls when Seamus arrived at work. He raised his eyebrows questiongly as he saw his partner walk into the room.

Seamus came over, pulled out his familiar chair, and sat, reaching for his own messages. They'd stacked up, he saw, even though Gil had probably handled any calls that had to do with their active cases. He scanned them quickly, while he waited for Gil to get off the phone, then set them aside to deal with later All of them could safely wait.

Gil hung up the phone. "How'd it go? Did you bring me anything?"

Seamus passed him the credit card statement and his notes. "Take a gander at that."

"And here I was hoping for roses." But Gil opened the notebook and began to read. "At the very least I was hoping you could learn to write legibly . . ." His voice trailed off. "Jesus Christ." He looked at the credit card statement. "Jesus" he said again.

"It's pretty obvious, isn't it?"

"Motive and opportunity. Christ, Seamus, it's a stronger case than we had against John! At least we can positively prove James was in the same town at the time of the Kline murders. That's more than we were able to do with John."

Seamus nodded and leaned back in his chair, loosening his tie. "If this were a routine investigation, I'd be leaping for joy."

"So what's wrong?"

"In five days the wrong man is going to die for the Kline murders. It's not enough time unless we can find James and get him to confess." At this late stage, nothing less could halt the process. The law had already made its decision on John's guilt.

"I ran his name through DMV in fifty states. The guy doesn't have a license, at least not under his own name."

"Shit." Seamus drummed his fingers on the table. "Well, I've got a picture of him. Let's flood the streets with it and see what we can turn up. We know he's been calling from Gulfport, so the logical assumption is that he's somewhere within walking distance of the pay phone he's been using."

Gil nodded. "Time to talk to Ed."

Ed looked up as they entered his office. "Back from the missing, eh? Was it a nice little vacation?"

"That's what I want to talk to you about."

Ed cocked his head. "I take it this means the department is going to pay for your trip?"

"Considering I found a strong suspect in the Downs and Barnstable killings, I should hope so."

"What have you got?" He listened, nodding from time to time as Seamus went over the details, and expelled a long breath when he finished. "Shit. It's not enough."

"It's enough to try to find the guy."

"I know that." Ed grimaced. "I was just thinking of John Otis. We might not have enough time."

Gil laughed. "Have you been listening to Carey Justice, too?"

"Of course I listen to her. When she isn't crapping on the legal profession, she's scalding cops. It never hurts to know what kind of press we're getting. Did you hear that thing she did last night on sexual harassment? Good show. I especially liked the part where the lawyers were threatening each other." He flashed a grin. "Okay, so let's get the picture out on the streets. We'll need to coordinate with the Gulfport PD. I'll talk to them."

St. Petersburg surrounded little Gulfport on two sides, divided by a line only a surveyor could see. To the uninitiated, it all seemed like one town. To the cops, however, that dividing line was a crucial one that had to be observed in favor of good intercity relations.

"Oh," Ed said as they were about to leave, "the Mayberry case. You've got the go-ahead to call in some of the local people for questioning. The chief just wants it to be quiet and gentle, okay?"

Seamus held up a hand. "No blackjacks and rubber hoses, I swear."

"Try not raising your voice," Ed said sourly. "Gently, Rourke. Gently."

"The first one I want to talk to," Seamus said to Gil as they headed back to their places at the table, "is Rico."

"Rico? Why?"

"You know that thing Hollister said about him, that he told those people they didn't have to be witnesses if they didn't want to?"

"Yeah, I remember. So? It's true."

"It's true, but what cop tells a witness something like that?"

"He's studying prelaw."

"Ahh. That might explain it."

"Maybe."

He and Gil exchanged looks, then both of them shook their heads at the same time, and said, "Nah."

They took the picture over to get it copied and distributed, then went Rico hunting.

CHAPTER 19
5 DAYS

RICO WAS ON PATROL. BUT THEY LOCATED HIM TAKING a break at a convenience store. He was standing outside, leaning against his patrol car, eating an ice cream sandwich and talking to some ten-or eleven-year-old kids. The kids were fascinated by him, by his uniform and all the things on his belt. Ice cream in one hand, he used the other to point out each item he was carrying.

A good neighborhood cop, Seamus thought. It didn't make him feel any better. He suddenly had the cowardly wish that he were up in Feather Sound, with his arms and legs wrapped around Carey's naked body, instead of here in the sweltering heat, about to make life difficult for a guy who was probably basically a good cop.

"Let's get an ice cream," Seamus suggested to Gil.

"Good idea."

They climbed out of their car and waved to Rico as they entered the store. He waved back and returned his attention to the children.

"How many kids did you count?" Seamus asked as they stood at the ice cream freezer.

"Five."

"Popsicles or ice cream sandwiches?'

"Buy the sandwiches. We're wealthy enough."

Seamus picked up seven ice cream sandwiches and paid

for them at the checkout. Outside he and Seamus approached Rico and his cluster of admirers.

"Well, look what we have here, kids," Rico said. "Two detectives."

The kids looked around with interest that quickly faded when all they saw was two men in slightly rumpled suits. Rico was a far more interesting figure—until Seamus started handing out ice cream sandwiches. The children retreated to the cool grass in the shade of a live oak with their treasures. Seamus ripped open his own sandwich and took a bite.

"So how's it going, guys?" Rico asked. He popped the last of his sandwich into his mouth and licked his fingertips.

"Why do they always make these with vanilla ice cream?" Gil asked. "I wish they had strawberry."

"They've got some Neapolitan ones in there," Rico said. "Didn't you see them?"

"Guess not."

"Don't mind him," Seamus said. "He's never happy with anything.

"Born complainer, that's me."

Rico laughed. "So, you made any progress on the Mayberry case?"

Seamus looked at Gil. "I don't know. What do you, think?"

Gil shrugged. "Depends. Hollister had some interesting things to say."

To Seamus it seemed that Rico stiffened ever so slightly. Unfortunately, he was wearing sunglasses, and his eyes were invisible behind them. "Sam Hollister?"

"That's the guy," Gil said. "Know him?"

"He lives in the neighborhood. I've talked to him a couple of times."

"What's your impression of him?"

Rico hesitated. "You know how old folks get. A little confused."

"He didn't strike me as confused," Seamus said.

"Me neither," Gil agreed.

"He's better sometimes than others," Rico said with a shrug. "What did he say?"

"Just that he was worried the neighborhood watch might have gotten a little, um, forceful in their duties." Seamus spoke casually, as if he didn't really believe it, but there was no mistaking the tightening of Rico's jaw. He could tell Gil saw it, too.

"So what do you think Rico?" Gil asked. "Any of those old geezers capable of taking the law into their own hands?"

Rico looked down at the pavement, but didn't say anything.

Seamus spoke again. "Hollister said you told folks over there they didn't have to be witnesses if they didn't want to."

"Christ!" Rico's head jerked up, and his chin thrust forward. "Yeah, I said that. I said that when I was talking to them about neighborhood watch four or five months ago. Some of the women were worried about having to testify in court against drug dealers if they saw them up to something. So I told 'em nobody could force 'em to testify, that'd have to be their own decision. What the hell is wrong with that?"

"Not a thing," Gil said pleasantly. "So you were the one who told them they could claim to be blind, deaf, and dumb?"

"Basically. I was trying to reassure those old ladies."

"Well, they apparently learned their lesson well."

"Yeah." Rico sighed and looked down at the pavement again.

286

Seamus spoke. "So what about Hollister's feeling that one of his neighbors might have shot Mayberry?"

Rico expelled a long breath. "He might be right."

"Do you know?"

"Honest to God, I don't want to know," Rico said angrily. "They were a bunch of old people scared in their own homes and streets. When I first heard a guy'd been shot over there, I thought it was just street justice, and about damn time."

"But Mayberry was innocent of any wrongdoing. Just a young guy taking a shortcut home from the store on his bike."

"Yeah."

"So," Seamus pressed, "what if I were to ask you to speculate who would be the person likeliest to have pulled the trigger—if, by some wild chance, it *was* one of the residents."

Rico shrugged, as if he wasn't going to answer, then said, "Barney Wieberneit. Now I'm not saying he did it. Just that he'd be the first one to spring to my mind."

"Thanks a lot, Rico," Seamus said. Just then, the breeze gusted and wrapped his tie around his ice cream. He swore.

Gil started laughing, and finally even Rico smiled. After that he talked much more freely about the neighborhood. Satisfied, Seamus and Gil drove over to the site of the Mayberry killing.

"There he is," Seamus said to Gil forty minutes later. They'd pumped Rico for enough information about the neighborhood that they felt they knew which residents they wanted to question in addition to Wieberneit. It was early evening, now, and most everyone was home. Rico had said that Barney Wieberneit was fanatical about his yard, and came out every evening to check on it.

It was Seamus who had suggested they wait for Wieberneit to get outside before they approached one of his neighbors for questioning. They wanted the man to see what was going on, and maybe get nervous.

Barney Wieberneit was a solidly built man, still straight and powerful-looking in his early seventies. He had steel gray hair and a square, pugnacious jaw.

"I can see him as a Marine in WWII," said Gil. "Bet he was a gunny."

"Probably." Seamus, who'd done his own time in Marine green in his reckless youth, recognized the type. They sometimes got the notion they were a law unto themselves.

Herman Glowinsky was the man they were going to see first. Rico had felt that if Wieberneit had actually killed Mayberry, Glowinsky would be the one most closely involved.

"He's seen us," Gil said,

Indeed he had. Wieberneit had paused by the flower bed and was staring openly at them. Good neighborhood watch activity.

"Let's go." Seamus climbed out of the car first and stood on the sidewalk. He was about twenty feet from Wieberneit. "Excuse me," he called to the man. "I'm Seamus Rourke, St. Pete PD. Are you Herman Glowinsky?"

"No." The man continued to stare.

"Which house does he live in?"

"You got some ID?"

Seamus obligingly produced his shield.

"Over there," Wieberneit said with a jerk of his head. "He got a problem?"

Seamus smiled. "We just want to ask him a few questions. Thanks for your help."

Together he and Gil walked to Glowinsky's front door, feeling Wieberneit's gaze on them every step of the way.

The door was answered by a fragile-looking woman with thin white hair and a wide, warm smile. "Can I help you?"

Seamus showed his shield while Gil explained that they wanted a word with Mr. Glowinsky about the Mayberry murder.

The woman introduced herself as Mrs. Glowinsky and invited them inside. In a matter of two minutes, they found themselves comfortably seated with tall glasses of iced tea and a plate of cookies, and a view of a small swimming pool full of sparkling blue water.

"Herman's in the garage," she said. "He's building a cradle for our next grandchild, who's due in two weeks. He's built a cradle for each of the grandchildren, you know. They'll make wonderful heirlooms. I'll just go get him."

"Hell," said Gil, after she left them alone. "These are good people'"

"So was Mayberry."

Gil nodded, but Seamus suspected he wasn't any happier about this than he was himself If it turned out that the good folks of this neighborhood were the bad guys after all, it wasn't going to feel very good.

Herman Glowinsky joined them just a couple of minutes later. He was a small man, lean like his wife, and stooped around the shoulders, but there was no mistaking the vitality in his step, or the strength in his arms and shoulders. His wife brought him a glass of iced tea and handed it to him as soon as he was seated in a wicker chair. She sat beside him, her knees primly together, and her hands folded in her lap.

"We have a few questions about the murder that hap

pened here two months ago," Seamus said.

Glowinsky nodded. His wife's hands fluttered in her lap.

"We understand you started a neighborhood watch because drug activity was spilling over into this area."

The old man nodded again. "They were standing out there, at the mouth of the street, brazen as you please, and walking through our neighborhood as if they owned it. But it wasn't just the dealers. It was the kind of people they brought with them."

"It was terrible," Mrs. Glowinsky said. "It used to be so peaceful here. We hardly ever needed the police. Maybe that's why they came here in the first place."

"They move around a lot," Gil said. He sipped his tea and complimented Mrs. Glowinsky. "Once we start cracking down on them in one area, they move to another."

"That's what I said," Herman agreed with a nod. "I said all we had to do was stay on the streets so they knew we were watching, and ask the police to come here more often, and they'd move on. The whole reason they came here in the first place was that it got too hot over on Twenty-second."

"Probably," Seamus agreed with a nod.

"But it was scary," Mrs. Glowinsky said. "I didn't even want to drive by myself because they'd shout things at me when I drove past. At least after we started the watch, and started doing things in groups, they weren't as threatening."

Seamus set his tea down on the low glass table and pulled out his notebook, pretending to peruse it. "Unfortunately," he said slowly, "we've received some . . . information. It has been suggested to us that the neighborhood watch might have done more than watch."

The Glowinskys exchanged quick looks.

Herman spoke, his voice cracking. "I don't know what you mean."

"No?"

Gil leaned forward. "Really, we can understand why you might have felt as if you were under siege. People ought to feel safe in their own homes, and ought to feel safe on their own streets. And we know how intimidating these scum can be. Heck, you couldn't ever be sure one of them wouldn't pull a gun just because he didn't like the way you looked."

"That's right," Herman said flatly. He put his tea glass down sharply, for emphasis. "Do you know what it's like to know your wife is being terrorized by some young punk? And that man who was shot—well, I don't care what the papers say, he was probably one of them. He'd been around here a lot."

"Herman. . ." His wife reached out a hand and gripped his forearm. She looked apologetically at the detectives. "He has high blood pressure. Besides, we all feel awful about that young man. Maybe he wasn't the hoodlum who was hanging out on the corner all the time with his friends. But he *did* look like the one who was. Maybe one of the other drug dealers made a mistake?"

"Or maybe," said Seamus, "somebody in the neighborhood watch made a mistake?" He noted how Herman's face paled. "Someone like Barney Wieberneit?"

Herman's face was now chalky, and his breath sounded labored. "I don't know what you mean."

Seamus nodded and closed his notebook. "We're going to find the person who did this, Mr. Glowinsky. Rest assured. And I *do* understand why the neighborhood would want to protect him."

But Herman didn't say another word.

Outside, they found that Barney Wieberneit was still in his yard, watering the flowers with a watering can. They walked over to him, and he set the pot down.

"What can I do for you?" he asked.

Seamus answered. "We need you to come down to the station with us, Mr. Wieberneit."

He nodded, his jaw setting. "Can I tell my wife I'm leaving?"

"Sure. You won't be gone long. Only an hour, if that. We just need to ask you some questions."

Wieberneit looked at him. "You're not fooling me. I knew you'd find out it was me sooner or later. It was nice of my neighbors not to say anything, but I knew you'd figure it out. I didn't mean to kill him, you know. I only wanted to scare him."

It was well after midnight when Seamus got home. The long day and lack of sleep were definitely catching up with him, and he found himself thinking that if Mary hadn't died, she probably would have divorced him by now. No woman in her right mind would want to live with a man whose hours were as long and as unpredictable as his sometimes were.

Between one breath and the next, the thought caught him like a punch to the solar plexus, washing away his fatigue in a sudden flood of . . . what? Guilt? Pain? He couldn't even tell. All he knew was that something inside him felt as if it were on the edge of a major explosion.

He stood there shaking like a dog caught in a thunderstorm, and he didn't even know why. He couldn't move, he couldn't stand the feeling, and he didn't know what the hell to do about it.

Then he heard himself draw a gasping, ragged breath,

as the will to live reasserted itself over shock, and his brain started working again.

Mary would have left anyway.

The thing he had refused to admit for seven years was staring him in the face like a grinning death's-head.

Mary would have left anyway.

And that was why he felt so damn guilty. It was why he'd kept Carey at a distance that had eventually killed their relationship. No, it wasn't Carey's mouth, or the tough time she'd been having at the end there, or anything else she had done. It had been *him.* Just him.

Mary would have left anyway.

The signs had been there for months, starting just before Seana's birth. Mary had begun talking about how he could be anything in the world he wanted to be, that he didn't have to be a cop forever. She had started complaining about his hours. In a thousand little ways, she had let him know that she didn't like his job and that she wasn't happy with the way they were living.

She hadn't come right out and said it. She hadn't threatened to leave. She had just hinted in a woman's gentle way, like water dripping on stone, planting ideas as she tried to bring him around to her way of thinking. And he, not really catching on to the deep discontent she was trying to express, had laughed the hints off and said he was born to die a cop.

Her response had been that a dead cop made a lousy father.

And he hadn't caught it. He'd thought she was just complaining the way wives will. The way his mother had about his dad's long absences. But his mother had never left his dad, and so he hadn't taken it seriously.

Big mistake. An even bigger mistake, maybe, than not being home the night Seana was taken ill. He'd been blind to his wife's discontent.

But only on a conscious level, it seemed, for as the sewer of his unconscious opened up to show him exactly what he'd been steadfastly ignoring, he discovered that he felt guilty for Mary's death because he had ignored her. Because his selfishness might have directly contributed to her despair. Because he feared she had hanged herself not only because of grief over their child, but because of the way he had abandoned her emotionally.

Jesus. Oh, Jesus.

Grief gripped him, squeezing his chest so hard that he could barely breathe. But even as he gave in to the full realization of his part in the tragedy, some soothing wind in his mind whispered the truth: *Mary would have left anyway.*

And somewhere in the dark night of his soul, he understood something else. He had lost his daughter, but only because Seana hadn't been in her car seat, and because a drunk driver had hit the car. It hadn't been *his* fault at all.

He had lost his wife, but he hadn't handed her the rope she had used, or even suggested her suicide. She had made that decision herself. Instead of turning to him with her grief, she had turned away. He, too, had been swamped in the anguish of loss and guilt, but he hadn't killed himself. And while he may not have offered enough support to Mary after Seana's death, she had offered him none at all.

His wife had made her own fatal decisions, from the choice not to put Seana in her car seat, to the choice to end her life. And it was time to stop taking full responsibility for things over which he had had no control.

What he needed to do, what he had to do, was cure the fault that was under his control—the distance he put

294

between himself and the people he loved.

Sometime later, after he got a handle on his emotions and showered away the day's sweat, he pulled out the photo albums. Sitting in the lamplight in his living room, he looked at them for the first time since Seana's death and let himself relive it all, good and bad.

He would miss Seana forever, he realized. But Mary— Mary had nearly killed something in him by her actions, and he found now, as he looked at photographs of her, that he had long since let her go.

It was over.

At quarter to nine in the morning, freshly showered and shaved, Seamus called Carey. "Did you get the governor?" he asked.

"You're kidding, right? The best thing I got was a promise that somebody would call me back first thing Monday morning."

"You're doing okay. They wouldn't promise to call me back at all."

"What about Jamie? Have you got anything?"

"His picture's on the street. He'll have to hide under a rock to avoid notice."

"Thank God. Four days, Seamus."

He didn't respond to that. What could he possibly say? "I'm going to visit my dad this morning. Want to get together afterward?"

He heard the hesitation and couldn't blame her. He'd hurt her enough before. Why would she want a second round?

"All right," she said. "Let's go to the beach, okay? If I don't spend a little time getting some rays and unwinding, I'm going to have a nervous breakdown by Monday morning."

"You and me both. Listen, sweetie. Everyone's really serious about finding Jamie. Everyone knows what's at stake. It's all we can do right now."

"Yeah. Okay. When do you want to meet?"

"Say I pick you up at noon? Want me to bring a picnic?"

"I'll take care of the picnic, Seamus. You go see your dad."

Danny Rourke was sitting on the patio out behind the treatment center. A molded plastic chair seemed almost to swallow him. He'd shrunk, Seamus thought. He'd shrunk even more since being admitted.

But for the first time in years, Danny's eyes weren't bloodshot, and his hands weren't trembling. He was wearing pajamas and a robe, despite the warmth of the morning, and had found himself a patch of sun to sit in.

Danny probably spent a lot of time out here, Seamus thought. His dad had lived most of his life outdoors, and hated being cooped up.

"Seamus."

"Dad." He pulled up another molded plastic chair and sat facing his father. "You look good." Better than he had in a while. In fact, for the first time in a long time, he looked into Danny's eyes and saw a spark of the man his father had once been. "They treating you well?"

"Well enough." Danny smiled. "I don't remember much about the first few days."

"Probably just as well. How are you feeling?"

Danny nodded. "Better, son. Better. The IRS thing. . ."

Shit, thought Seamus, he had completely forgotten about it. "Carey was talking to them about negotiating a settlement. She'll come up with something more reasonable."

"Nothing would be reasonable," Danny said drily. "I

ain't got a thing left."

"You've got me, Dad."

The older man looked straight at his son and asked, utterly without self-pity, "Do I?"

Seamus felt his throat clog. He had to look away and breathe deeply to steady himself. Finally, he was able to look at the old man again. "Yeah, Dad," he said. "You do."

Danny nodded and turned his attention to something off in the distance. After a bit, he said, "I wouldn't blame you if you forgot you ever knew me."

"I'm not gonna do that. Not ever. I've been . . . kind of crazy the last few years. Ever since . . . ever since Seana and Mary died."

"We've both been kind of crazy since then. I sit up a lot of nights wondering why I didn't ever tell that woman to put the child in the car seat. I finally got to drinking so I wouldn't think about it anymore."

"You didn't think about it then, Dad. Hell, she was Seana's mother. If she didn't think about it, why should you?"

"They didn't have those car seats when you were little," his dad said as if he hadn't heard. "I guess I just never thought a thing about it. Your mom used to carry you on her lap all the time in the car."

"Yeah."

"And the baby was so sick. . ." Danny swallowed hard, and when he looked at his son again, his eyes were wet. "I never told you how damn sorry I am that I was driving . . .that I didn't do enough . . ."

Seamus reached out suddenly and gripped his father's frail hand. "Dad, I've been blaming you, and I've been blaming myself. But I wasn't there, and anybody could have been driving that car. You didn't cause that accident

297

A drunk driver did. Hell, you weren't even speeding."

"But if I hadn'ta had that beer—"

"That beer wasn't enough to make a difference. I know that. I just needed somebody to blame. . ." His throat closed again, and he had to wait a moment before he could clear it and continue. "The simple fact is that there are some things that just happen. Some things you just have no control over, and nothing you do will make any difference His voice broke and he looked away.

He felt Danny's hand turn over beneath his, and then for the first time in years felt the comforting strength of his father's grip. He squeezed back, and tried to swallow the tears that blurred his vision.

Neither of them spoke for a long time. The sun rose higher, and a large egret strolled slowly across the lawn, ignoring them as it searched for lizards and bugs. A seagull landed on a nearby table, but realizing after a moment that the humans had no food, took flight again.

Seamus spoke finally. "I'm selling the house."

"Good. Good. Sometimes you need to make a clean break in order to get on with life. It's time you got on, son."

Seamus nodded. "I've been marking time for too long."

"That you have."

"So, when you get out of here, you'll come stay with me, right?" He thought he felt his father's hand tremble.

"Sure," Danny said. "For a while. Until I find me a job and a place of my own."

"You don't have to do that, Dad."

"Yes. I do. We both need to build a life for ourselves, son, and we'll never do that if we're hanging on to each other and reminding each other of the past. You need to find a good woman and start a new family for yourself. And so do I." A dry laugh escaped him. "The good woman part, not the family part. At my age, I want grandchildren, not babies of my own."

"You never know." He turned to look at his dad, and saw an almost-forgotten twinkle in the old man's eyes. To his own surprise, he laughed. God, it felt good to be free to laugh. "Yeah, right," he said, rising. "I'll stop by again in the next day or two, okay? But there's a case going on right now that I need to keep an eye on. And don't you be bothering those young nurses."

Seamus walked away, followed by his father's chuckle. And then he heard Danny say quietly, "I love you, son." He made it to his car before the tears reached his cheeks.

CHAPTER 20
2 DAYS

CAREY JOLTED AWAKE, HER HEART POUNDING IN terror, and stared into the inky black of night. She had been talking to John Otis, had watched him turn with a sad smile and begin the long walk down a narrow corridor from which he would never return. She screamed that he was innocent, she tried to run after him, but no one had listened, and no matter how hard she ran, she hadn't been able to catch him.

Now she was sitting in her bed, drenched with sweat, her heart pounding wildly.

"Carey?" Seamus's sleepy voice came out of the darkness beside her. "What's wrong?"

"Nightmare."

"You okay?"

"Yeah." Part of her wanted to turn toward him and feel the comfort of his arms around her, but she knew she wasn't going to be able to go back to sleep. Less than forty-eight hours remained. She patted his arm reassuringly. "I'm just going to get something to drink."

"Okay." His breathing slowed and deepened. He was already back asleep.

She envied him. Easing out from beneath the covers, she rose from the bed and felt around for her bathrobe. It was four in the morning, and her body felt chilled, even though she kept the house at eighty degrees. She found the robe and slipped it on, wrapping it tightly around herself.

The lights were still on downstairs. She felt almost guilty as she remembered the laughing chase through the house that had ended with them both sprawled on her bed. How could she have had fun when a man was about to die?

The question struck her foggy brain as puerile. Of course she had fun. And she would go on living and having fun no matter what happened. She couldn't seriously think that she was going to spend every minute of her life in mourning over something she couldn't stop.

It was like seeing somebody in front of a train, she thought as she pulled out the milk and poured herself a glass. All you could do was try to save them. And if you failed, you couldn't spend the rest of your life tying to atone through self-flagellation. That's what Seamus had been trying to do for the last seven years, and she couldn't see that it had done a damn bit of good.

But all this reasoning did little to ease the panic that kept her heart fluttering. She was afraid to look at the clock, for fear that she would count the minutes that were slipping away.

She stood at the patio doors and looked out into the moonlit night. With the kitchen light off, she could see her garden, frosted in silver, looking deep and mysterious in the quiet of the predawn hours.

She wondered if the governor's office would call this morning, or if she would have to make some kind of threat to get his attention. She wondered if Jamie was out there somewhere, prowling, looking for another victim to make his point. She wondered if John Otis was sleeping tonight, or if he was sitting awake, afraid to relinquish even a few of the last precious minutes of his life to sleep.

The flutters of panic intensified, making her heart pound until she wondered if it would hammer its way out of her chest.

All weekend long, all the law enforcement agencies in Pinellas County had been looking for Jamie Otis. They'd had only minor success. A convenience store operator in Gulfport thought he'd seen him a couple of times. A pizza shop thought they'd sold him pizza once, and maybe a sandwich another time. A grocery clerk in South Pasadena, which bordered Gulfport on the west, thought he'd bought a few groceries there. None of the apartment houses in the area recognized him as a tenant, but that didn't mean much. He could be crashing with a friend. Or, at this time of year, before the snowbirds returned, there were an awful lot of vacant houses where he could be hiding.

Given that the only photo they had of him was five years old, he might look so different now that he could walk the streets right under the noses of the police and never be recognized.

Shit. Her heart gave a big lurch, and she turned from the window, wondering how hours could seem at once so long and so short. She couldn't wait to get to the station this morning and start working on the governor again. It was their best hope at this point, and a very poor one at that. She knew the political climate in this state too well to believe that the governor was going to order a stay based on what they had. But she had to try. Trying was all she could do.

"Can't sleep?"

Seamus must have moved as quietly as a cat, because she didn't hear him until his shadowy figure filled the kitchen doorway.

"I'm having a glass of milk."

"You're worrying."

"Better yet," she admitted, "I'm having a panic attack."

"Thought so." He crossed the room and took the milk from her cold hand, putting it on the table. Then he wrapped her snugly in his arms and held her against the warm, solid strength of his chest. "I wish I could help."

"There's only one thing that can help."

"I know." He squeezed her tighter. "Why don't we go for a walk?"

"I'd rather run."

"Fine. Go get your stuff on."

"You don't have anything to run in."

"I can run in my Top-Siders."

"You'll kill your knees."

"They died years ago. They'll never notice. Come on, let's go change."

Ten minutes later they stepped out into the moon-silvered world. The air was calm, humid the way it always was in the early morning. The night was quiet enough that they could hear the whine of individual vehicles over on Roosevelt.

Carey turned and headed the way she always went when running. She ran as fast as she could go, not caring whether she made her full three miles, and Seamus kept pace.

The only sound now was the slapping of their soles on

the pavement and their labored breathing.

And the taunts of the demons on their heels.

At ten o'clock, when the governor's office still hadn't called, Carey called them.

"I'm sorry, Ms. Justice," the press secretary said, "but Governor Howell has a function to attend this evening. He won't be able to call your program."

"I'm sure he can steal five minutes to talk to me. I have information that John William Otis may be innocent of murder, and I'm sure the governor would prefer to hear about it *before* the execution."

There was a brief pause. "Ms. Justice, if there had been any evidence to exonerate Otis, it certainly would have turned up by now. All the man's appeals are exhausted. The courts have spoken, and the governor is going to let justice take its course."

"Well, you tell the governor for me that if he doesn't think a man's life, even a *guilty* man's life, is worth five minutes of his time, then I'm going to use my entire three-hour program this evening to discuss his campaign-funding problems and the recent cuts to the education budget. I might even get around to remembering the incident in Ocala six years ago." When Howell, not yet the governor, had gotten drunk at a State Bar Association meeting and had shoved his hand up her dress. She'd had to sock him in the jaw to get him off.

"What incident in Ocala?"

"Trust me, he'll remember. I've never mentioned it to anyone, but you never know when the urge to talk about it might overwhelm me." She'd never mentioned it because Howell had been drunk, and then so abjectly apologetic the next morning. However, Otis was important enough that she was willing to use every tool in her arsenal.

"This sounds suspiciously like extortion."

"No, it's a statement of fact. He can give me the five minutes so I can discuss the subject I want to, or I will have to discuss something equally attention-getting."

"But your program isn't about politics, it's about the law."

"Amazing, isn't it, how politics and the law get tangled up—especially when politicians make the laws?"

There was a sigh from the other end of the phone. "Very well, I'll give it another shot. But I'm not making any promises. I'll call you back in an hour."

She didn't have to wait that long; he called back in just under twenty minutes.

"He'll give you five minutes just after ten o'clock tonight."

"Make it 10:10, and give me seven minutes."

"Ms. Justice—"

"Seven minutes," Carey repeated. "I've got to intro him and cut off any previous callers."

The press secretary sighed. "Seven minutes. No more."

"Good. I'll start promo-ing his call on the air." Which was a nice way of saying the governor had damn well better not bail out.

Fifteen minutes later she had taped a thirty-second promotion for her show that highlighted the governor's call. Twenty minutes after that, it was being slotted into the newsbreaks and commercial breaks for the rest of the day.

Bill Hayes decided he was pleased. Carey thought it took him a minute or two to make up his mind, especially since she was going to be dealing with the Otis thing again, but having the governor call was a plus that apparently outweighed his other concerns.

"Just tell me," he said to her, "after this guy is executed, are you going to keep harping on it? Because if you are . . ."

He shook his head.

"I promise I'll drop it." If she didn't cut her own throat first. "But I want to do a show tomorrow night that runs through the execution, Bill. I want to be on the air until after they flip the switch."

"I don't know. I'll have to talk to Ted. That's his show."

"He'll want to do it. Especially if you suggest that he join my show earlier in the evening. We can cohost the execution watch."

"Jesus." He rubbed his chin. "I don't know about this. Let me think."

She let him think while she went out back to have a cigarette. Running this morning had burned her lungs in a way that it hadn't in a while. She was letting herself go to pot these last few weeks, and she knew it. She had to start running every day again, and give up the cigarettes.

Later. Once she found a way to live with this goddamn mess.

When she poked her head back into Bill's office, he sighed. "Okay," he said. "Ted's agreeable. You cohost from nine until one. The execution is set for 12:01 Wednesday morning, right?"

"Right. Can we send someone out to do phone-ins from outside the prison?"

"Why?"

"Well, you know. There's always a group holding a candlelight vigil against the death penalty, and there's always a pro-death penalty crowd to cheer when the execution is carried out. Man-on-the-scene interviews."

He put his head in his hands. "Why do I let you do this to me? What do you want? A three-ring circus?"

"No. I just want to be sure that the state-sanctioned

murder of an innocent man doesn't slip by without a single peep."

He raised his head, and the look he gave her was different from before, as if something in him had shifted away from considering all of this a nuisance. "You really believe that, don't you?"

She nodded, and came into his office. Reaching for his pack of cigarettes, she handed one to him and lit one for herself. As an afterthought, she closed the door, then paced the six feet of empty space in front of his desk. "I didn't tell you what I found out in Atlanta."

"I figured you were planning to tell the whole world tonight."

"You're right. I am. But let me tell you right now. Maybe you'll see why this is so damn important. John William Otis has a younger brother, Jamie."

"Right, I know that. Everyone knows that."

"What everyone doesn't know is that Jamie got out of a mental institution just a month ago. And he was here in St. Pete the night of the Kline murders. The cops have the credit card bill to prove it. Jamie is the one who's been calling my show and saying John didn't do it, that *he* did. And the cops are looking for him right now in connection with the Downs and Barnstable slashing murders. They also think he did the Klines."

"Jesus." Bill lit his own cigarette and tipped back in his chair. Swiveling suddenly, he opened the window behind his desk. "Damn smoke. One of these days somebody around here is going to complain about me to the air police. You're a bad influence."

"You're the one who keeps an ashtray in here."

"Shut up and let me think. Christ, this is going to gut the news budget."

"You can just have someone call on the telephone."

"Fuck that. If we're going to do a three-ring circus, I'm not going to be relying on phones and phone availability in outer nowhere. Jesus." He flicked ash into the ashtray and took another drag.

"Okay," he said a few minutes later. "I'll send a remote van out tomorrow morning. I can probably talk Ed into doing it as straight news from that end."

"Thanks, Bill. Thanks an awful lot."

"You need to quit smoking. You're going to ruin your voice."

"Hey, it just gets more sultry with abuse."

He snorted. "Just tell me one thing."

"What's that?"

"How in the hell did you get the governor to agree to call tonight?"

"I promised not to ever tell—unless he doesn't call."

Bill looked up at her, a faint smile playing around the corners of his mouth. "God, what I'd give for that story."

"The governor's willing to give me seven minutes. How much is that worth?"

He shook his head. "Get out of here so I can do some work, will you?"

At four that afternoon, Seamus called her. "Jamie's going to call your show tonight."

Her heart quickened, and her mouth went suddenly dry. "How do you know that? My God, don't tell me someone else is dead!"

"No. But there was an attempted break-in last night. The perp tried to get through the sliding glass doors, only the vic had electronic security. The whooping sirens scared him off, and woke the entire neighborhood."

"Who was the victim?"

"John Otis's trial attorney."

"Ben Webster?"

"The same."

Carey sank back in her chair. "My God," she whispered.

"Anyway, if he follows his usual pattern, he's going to call you tonight. I'm putting a cop at the station in your producer's office. If he calls, I want the number the minute you guys pick up the phone, not after he gets through to you on the air, okay? Every second is going to count."

"Okay. Sure. The station shouldn't object."

"Tell 'em to not even bother. I can get enough paper out of a judge in the next half hour to bring a whole damn squad of cops in there."

"I'll be sure to tell Bill that. But I don't think he's going to object."

"Good. And when Jamie calls, keep him on the phone as long as you can."

"Sure. I'll do my best."

"Did you get the governor?"

"He's giving me seven minutes of his precious time at ten minutes after ten tonight."

"Well, if the gods are smiling, maybe Jamie'll call first and we can wrap up this whole damn case and give it to Howell with a ribbon on it when he calls."

Carey found herself crossing her fingers, and she closed her eyes against a sudden wave of fear and almost unbearable hope.

"Are you okay?" Seamus asked suddenly.

"On the edge of my seat, ready to scream from tension, but yeah, I'm okay."

"Hang in there, sweetie. I'm planning to move heaven and earth in the next thirty-six hours, if I have to."

"I know."

"Gotta go. We're getting ready to blanket the streets

tonight to watch the pay phones. I'll meet you after your show."

"Okay."

Then, after the briefest pause, he said quietly, "I love you, Carey."

With a click, he disconnected. She took the receiver from her ear and stared at it, wondering how he could drop a bomb like that at a time like this.

Then, deciding that she had to think about something else or lose her mind completely, she called the IRS. It only took a few minutes to persuade them to accept Danny Rourke's confiscated boat as full payment of his tax debt and penalties.

But when that was done, there was nothing left to do except stare at the clock and watch the irretrievable minutes slip away forever.

In her heart, she believed John Otis must be doing the same thing.

At last the clock was creeping toward 10:10. Because she couldn't be sure the governor would call exactly on time, Carey let the jerk on the phone spin out his version of legal utopia a little longer. Through the window to the control room, she could see Marge sorting carts and answering calls in her headset Beside her stood a uniformed St. Pete police officer, looking bored to death. Jamie still hadn't called. What if he didn't call at all?

She said something reasonably noncommittal to the caller, inadvertently getting him wound up all over again. There were no back-up calls for her to replace him with, though. Apparently, the Bay Area was waiting for the governor's call.

But then the idiot said something which revealed him to be a pseudo-Nazi. Within fifteen seconds, her board was lighting up with calls. She hated the idea of keeping all these people on hold when they were undoubtedly upset over her current caller's opinions.

Marge apparently had the same thought. She spoke to the callers on hold, and one by one they went away.

Carey punched the button that allowed her to talk to Marge without being heard on the air, while Aryan-Nation-junior continued to rant. "What are you saying?"

"I'm telling them to call back in ten minutes, that we're holding for the governor's call."

"Thanks." She punched the button, and decided she'd had enough.

"Look, jerk," she said into the microphone, "I don't know where you get the idea that God is a white male. It seems to me that if God created life, he or she created *all* life, whether black, white, brown, yellow, red, or purple with pink polka dots. And while we're on the subject, Jesus was a Jew. So spare me your ugly little diatribes."

She cut the caller off. "Man, oh man," she said to her audience, "people like that give me the willies. And since the governor should be making his promised call any moment now, I'm going to stop taking calls for a few minutes. But those of you who want to respond to this last caller, stick around. You'll get your chance."

Even as she spoke, a line lighted up and a message appeared on her screen: *Governor Howell.*

"Well, talk about timing. The governor is with us now." She put him on the air. "Governor Howell. Thank you for taking time out of your busy schedule to be with us this evening. Can you hear me all right?"

"Good evening, Carey. I hear you just fine. It's a pleasure to be with you this evening."

"I don't know whether you heard our last call, but I won't waste your time by asking you to respond to it."

"Oh, I heard it, Carey." Dave Howell's voice took on

the rounded speech-making tones that were always so impressive. "It's appalling that any civilized man could hold such opinions. I'm glad to say that he does *not* speak for the state of Florida."

"But you *do* speak for the state of Florida, Governor, and that's why I asked you to call this evening. Some evidence has come to light recently that suggests that John William Otis, who is scheduled to be executed Wednesday morning at 12:01 A.M., may well be innocent. Now, we sent you a fax earlier today detailing this evidence. I'm not sure you've had a chance to review the fax yet, but since I haven't yet shared the information with our listeners, I'll just run over it quickly again."

"Certainly."

What else could he say with a quarter million people listening at this very moment, Carey thought cynically. "You may remember, sir, that no one was able to prove that John Otis was in town the night of the murders, that he did in fact have a hotel room in Daytona Beach that entire weekend."

"I remember," said Howell. "I also remember that no one recalled seeing Otis in Daytona Beach during the critical time frame."

"True. But, as you may also remember, Governor, John Otis has a younger brother, Jamie. In the past four days, the police have developed evidence which puts Jamie Otis in St. Petersburg at the time of the murders for which John was convicted. They have also uncovered evidence which points to a motive for Jamie to have committed the murders. Even as we speak, the police are combing the area looking for Jamie Otis in connection with two murders which have occurred in the last few weeks."

"Interesting," said Howell noncommittally.

"It's more than interesting, Governor. In less than

twenty-six hours, John William Otis will die, and yet the police believe that the wrong man may well be on death row. So I'm here to ask you, sir, if you can't find a way to stay the execution of John William Otis. Just for ten days, a week. Just enough time for the police to complete their investigation and settle the matter beyond any shadow of a doubt. Please, sir, is there any reason the state should deny John Otis this one last chance? Is there any reason we should execute a man when there is a distinct possibility he may be innocent?"

There was the briefest silence from the governor, so brief that Carey thought most of the listeners didn't notice it. She did, however, and felt an instant of exultation before he started to speak.

"That's very interesting, Carey. But you have to keep in mind that as governor I only interfere with the judicial process when I have incontrovertible evidence that there has been a miscarriage of justice. What you've given me here is unconfirmed circumstantial evidence."

"John Otis was *convicted* on circumstantial evidence."

"So he was. His case was presented in court, he was adequately represented by counsel, and twelve men and women—handpicked men and women, I might add—heard all the evidence and judged him guilty. The courts have upheld that conviction as legal through the entire appeals process, right up to our state supreme court. Now, I have the greatest respect for the judicial system in our state. I have the greatest respect for the men and women who reached this agonizing verdict. I cannot, and will not, interfere with our judicial process based on a supposition."

"It means nothing to you that the police believe the wrong man is on death row?"

The governor's tone became almost indulgent. "I'm sure you don't speak for all police officers in the state.

312

Some of them may agree with you. But their opinions don't constitute legal proof. Bring me a confession from this brother, and I will most certainly stay the execution. But right now all you're giving me is a single fact—that Jamie Otis was in town at the time of the murders. There were a lot of people in town at the time of the murders. Only one of them was convicted for the crime."

"Twenty-six hours, Governor. That's all we have left to prevent a miscarriage of justice. Why can't you at least stay the execution for a week, to give the police time to do their job? Is it so essential that this man die on Wednesday morning? How can it harm the state to take a week and see?"

"It would be executive interference in the judicial process, Carey. That's not something I, or any governor, can do without much better reason than you've given me. I'm sorry, but I have to remain firm. The courts have spoken. You, and the police, have twenty-six hours to bring me a signed confession, or incontrovertible proof that John Otis didn't kill these people. Until then, I have to believe that the judicial system knows best.

"I'm sorry," he continued. "But our time is up. Good night to you and all your listeners."

Son of a bitch! Carey thought as she punched him off before the dial tone could go out over the air.

"Well, you heard it here," she said into her microphone. "The governor says that unless there is incontrovertible proof, John William Otis will die. What do you think of that? Our number here is . . ."

Automatically, she went through the numbers and the station identification, then signaled Marge to give her a break. A commercial started going out over the air, some offensively happy jingle about air-conditioning repair. She pulled off her headphones for a minute and rubbed the sides of her head before putting them back on again. Forty

313

minutes left to go, and all she could hope for now was that Jamie Otis would call.

She looked out the window, saw that it was raining again. All of this had started on a rainy night just three weeks ago. God, it felt like a whole miserable lifetime.

Turning back to the console, she took a deep breath and prepared to deal with the next caller Marge was giving her the countdown. Three, two, one . . .

"This is Carey Justice, and you're listening to the Talk of the Coast, 990 WCST, Tampa Bay's number one talk radio station. For those of you tuning in late, we've just had a call from Governor David Howell . . ."

The words kept coming, but she no longer heard herself. In the control booth she could see Marge making gestures, then suddenly the cop went outside. Glancing down, Carey felt her heart stop. Bob from Gulfport was on the line.

Keep him waiting. Staring at the screen, she talked about the governor's call, about what she'd said and what Howell had said, encouraging her listeners to call and express their opinions. And then she knew she couldn't keep Jamie waiting any longer. He would know that he'd gotten through during a commercial break, and the longer she made him wait, the more likely he was to get suspicious. Her hand hovered over the buttons, trying to decide whether she could risk making him wait a little longer, while she took another call. He must have heard what she said to the governor. He must know they were looking for him. Oh, God, she shouldn't have mentioned him by name . . .

She put her finger on the button, but before she pressed it, the light went out. He was gone.

She got through the rest of the show somehow, but she was never able to remember it. She clung to the hope that the cops had interrupted Jamie's call, and had apprehended him.

Forty minutes later, that hope was dashed, too. Jamie had slipped the net. No one knew where he was.

CHAPTER 21
TWENTY HOURS

CAREY AWOKE CRYING FROM ANOTHER NIGHTMARE. Seamus rolled over and hugged her tightly until the tremors began to ease. He hadn't been sleeping at all. His mind was running overtime, trying to find some way to prevent the execution at midnight, trying to find some little link that might lead him to the real killer. And absolutely furious at the officer who'd wandered away from his post to find himself a cup of coffee right in the critical time frame. But for him, they would probably have Jamie right now.

"It's okay," he murmured to Carey. Useless words, but the only ones he could offer. "What did you dream about?"

"I don't want to talk about it."

"Carey . . ."

He felt her turn her face away in the dark, and heard her sniffle. The sheet rustled as she wiped her wet face. "I dreamed that they both did it," she said finally.

"What?"

"I dreamed that John and Jamie killed the Klines together."

"Christ." The thought sent an icy trickle down his spine.

Carey sat up suddenly and switched on the bedside lamp. A moment later she lit a cigarette. He didn't say anything, although he promised himself that as soon as this was over he was going to ride her butt about it.

"What if it's true?" she asked, her voice shaking.

He looked at the slender line of her back and wondered how it was that she always took so much on herself. "So what if it's true," he said finally. "What earthly difference does it make? We've still got to find Jamie. And we will."

"But . . . what if this is all a scam? What if they did it together and now Jamie's trying to muddy the waters so much that both of them get off?"

"You can't really believe that."

She puffed on her cigarette, and finally sighed. "No. But what if they did it together?"

He moved over so that he sat beside her. "There comes a time when you just have to believe in something, Carey. Even the worst cynic among us believes in something, even if it's only the misery of the human estate. You've believed in John Otis this long. Don't desert the ship now."

"But what if . . ." She couldn't say it again.

"If that's true, we'll deal with it when we know for sure. And somehow You'll learn to live with the fact that you were misled by a convicted killer. You wouldn't be the first person who was. But what's the point of worrying about it now? It won't change a damn thing. We've got to find Jamie so we can prevent the execution. Then we can sort it all out."

A shudder ran through her, so strong that he felt the bed tremble. She turned a gaunt face to him and looked him dead in the eye. "I don't know if I can handle being wrong about John Otis. I think . . . I think I would never believe in anything again."

"What do you want me to do? Stop trying to solve this case? Sorry, Carey, but I won't do that. I can't do that. I'm going to find that s.o.b. and let the chips fall where they may."

She nodded and looked down at the burning cigarette in her hand.

He sighed in frustration and ran his fingers through her hair. "Carey, honey, you've believed for five years now that this guy didn't do it. Now you've got me and half the St. Pete PD convinced he didn't do it. And it's all because of you. All because you listened to your instinct when the whole damn world thought you were crazy. Don't flake out on me now. Remember the evidence."

"What evidence? That Jamie was in town? Like the govenor said, there were a lot of people in town that night."

"Not that." He reached out and took her hand, squeezing it gently while he watched her take another drag on that damn cigarette. "Not that," he said again. "You're forgetting the evidence from the first trial. Bloody footprints."

"They were never matched to any shoes."

"I know that. But they also indicated there was only one killer. One set of footprints, not two. And there sure as hell would have been two sets if two people had been in the room when the Klines died."

She sat very still for the longest time, so long he began to wonder if she'd heard him. But finally she looked at him, and there was the tiniest easing of the strain on her face. "You're right," she said.

"Of course." He flashed a smile. "I'm always right. Jamie killed those people, and we're going to find him. Before it's too late."

"I wish I could believe that."

So did he, but he didn't want to tell her that. He wanted her to believe, at least for today, that right would triumph. If anybody deserved to believe that, it was Carissa Stover.

But the simple fact was, if Jamie didn't call the station tonight, and they didn't catch him at the pay phone, in less than twenty hours, John William Otis was going to be dead.

Carey went to the station early. She couldn't stand the misery of her own company any longer, and she'd given up hoping the phone would ring with the news that Jamie Otis had been caught.

At least at the station, she had other people to talk to, and other things to think about. The station was hyping the hell out of the "death watch" program, which made her feel sick to her stomach, so she stayed away from the speakers where she could hear the promotions. She picked a few stories off the wire for the first half of her show, then wandered into Bill Hayes's office.

"The owners aren't real happy about this remote," he told her the instant he saw her.

She shrugged.

"I figured you'd feel that way. Close the door."

She did as he bid, and wasn't surprised when he lit a cigarette and tossed the pack to her. Turning, he popped open the window and let in the warm, humid air and the incessant sound of traffic.

"They think it's a waste of money," he continued. "It's been done to death, was how one of them put it."

"Not for an innocent man, it hasn't"

"Well, this guy is no Ted Bundy. They don't figure the interest is going to be all that high, you know?"

"So what did you tell them?" Giving in, she lit a cigarette, and took a deep drag of the welcome smoke.

He swiveled his chair around and looked out the window. "See that live oak tree out there?"

She leaned forward. "The one beside the royal palm?"

"Yeah. You see that itty-bitty little limb sticking out at the top? The one that looks like it isn't strong enough to support a squirrel?"

"Yeah?"

"I crawled out on that limb for you."

All day her face had felt heavy, unwilling to smile, but now one corner of her mouth tugged upward. It was almost painful to give him the smile. "Thanks, Bill."

He shrugged. "I told 'em what you told me yesterday, and told 'em they'd be a lot happier if they were on the side of the angels on this one."

"I thought they were on the side of profits."

"Well, of course, but think what advertising hay they can make out of being right if the cops catch the real killer."

"And if they don't?"

"Well, then they can fall back on the old disclaimer: Opinions expressed in this program are not necessarily those of the management." His eyes twinkled.

"Thanks, Bill."

He waved her gratitude aside. "However, Ed wasn't as happy about having to go up to Starke. He, too, was of the opinion that this has been done to death, and he wasn't keen on interviewing the weirdos who show up for executions. He called them lunatics, if I remember correctly."

"They are."

"Well, of course they are. Both sides. But the ones who give me the willies, are the ones who cheer. It's all well and good to support the death penalty, but I don't see an execution as a reason for jubilation."

"Families of victims might not agree with you."

"Yeah, I wonder about some of them, too. But, thank God, I've never been in their position, so I'll keep my mouth shut. If something happened to one of my kids, I might be every bit as bloodthirsty."

"Me, too." She blew a cloud of smoke across the room and tipped back in her chair. "I haven't been thinking about much else lately. Part of me still supports the death penalty, you know? Some crimes are just so awful, it's as if the perp has lost the right to be considered human. But on the other hand . . ." She shook her head. "I don't know. I keep wondering if there can be any justification for doing something so irrevocable when there might be a possibility, however slim, that the convicted person is innocent."

"I heard you hammering that. It made me think." Sighing, he put out his cigarette. "I don't think there are any good answers, Carey. But I'm no longer going to buy into the 'you've got to break eggs to make an omelet' approach to this."

"Yeah. Like Blackstone said a couple hundred years ago, 'It's better that ten guilty men go free, than that one innocent man be punished.' "

He flashed a grin. "I don't know if I want to go that far."

"Most of us don't seem to."

His expression sobered. "Are you going to be okay? I realize a guy should never tell a woman this, but you look like hell, Carey. You're losing weight, you've got these great big circles under your eyes, and you're as jumpy as a cat."

"I haven't been sleeping well. I'll get over it, Bill."

"I hope so. And for your sake as much as anyone's, I hope they catch this guy before it's too late."

The rest of the day both dragged and sped by too fast. At times Carey's nerves seemed to stretch to breaking as she kept waiting for the phone to ring with news that would save John Otis. At other times the hands of the clock seemed to crawl as she wished for this interminable day to end.

By nine o'clock her hands were trembling. At the break, she stood out behind the station and chain-smoked. Less than three hours to go, and John William Otis would be no more. In less than three hours, his only appeal would be to God.

Three hours. The thought kept hammering at her in time to her pulsebeat. Three hours . . . three hours . . . Hope was dying a painful death in her breast. She'd waded through the first two hours of her show feeling as if she were drowning in the depths of the sea, crushed by the pressure of thousands of tons of water above her. Somehow she had managed to talk, and even laugh, with her callers about the quirks in maritime law that had gotten two scalawag teenagers off a theft charge.

But now she couldn't pretend any longer that it wasn't happening. In a few more minutes she was going to return to the studio to begin the death watch in the company of Ted Sanders. Ted was unabashedly pro-death penalty. It would make for lively discussion. It would cause ratings to soar. And she felt guilty for that even as she felt it was absolutely essential not to let the final moments of John Otis's life slip away in silence.

Swearing under her breath, she ground the cigarette out beneath her heel and went back in.

"How do you want to start?" Ted asked, as she sat at the console and reached for her headphones.

"I'm going to read one of John Otis's poems. Then I'm going to make an appeal for his brother to call the station."

Ted nodded.

Carey glanced at the control booth. Marge was shifting carts and talking to the cop who was there again tonight. If Jamie let his brother die without making at least one more call to her in an attempt to save him, she was going to tell the world exactly what a scumbag he was. And when they caught him, she was going to spit in his eye.

Yeah, right.

Marge gave her the countdown.

"This is Carey Justice, and you're listening to the Talk of the Coast, 990 WCST, Tampa Bay's number one talk radio station. Tonight we're going to do something different. Ted Sanders is with me in the studio, and we're going to host the next four hours together. Ed Rich is on location in Starke, right outside the walls of Raiford Prison, and will be giving us updates from the scene, as we broadcast the death watch for John William Otis.

"Those of you who have listened to my show over the last few weeks know that I think John Otis is innocent. Those of you who were tuned in last night heard that there's new evidence in the case, and that the police are even now seeking the man who they suspect really killed Harvey and Linda Kline. And those of you who listened to the governor's call last night know that even *that* is not enough to stop the justice train once it's rolling.

"In two hours and fifty-three minutes, innocent or guilty, John William Otis will die. And when we wake up tomorrow morning, or the next morning, or next week, and read in the papers that the real killer of Harvey and Linda Kline has been found, we're not going to be able to give John Otis his life back.

"The justice train is rolling, and it stops for no one. No one, unless the real killer steps forward and confesses before midnight tonight. Jamie? Do you hear me? If you want to save your brother, this is your last chance. Call me. Now."

She swallowed and reached for the notebook containing the Otis poems. "Right now I'm going to read to you a poem written by John Otis. Call it his epitaph, since it's the only one he'll probably ever have. It came in the mail to me today, and I think he wanted me to read it. It may well be the last poem he'll ever write."

"Lawrence"

Lawrence brought a book today.
Dusty cover, cracked and worn,
Yellowed pages, marked and torn,
Just because he's nice that way.

Lawrence checked my cell last night.
Aching legs, stomach flu,
Raspy throat, coughing too,
Stopped to see was I all right.

Lawrence told me, face set hard.
Fists clenched, misty eyes,
Lips drawn tight, muffled sighs,
Had to say goodbye, my guard.

Lawrence left to do his job.
Shoulders sagged, walked away,
Cycling night, cycling day,
I thought I heard a quiet sob.

Carey let a moment of silence go out on the air. "How many of us would be thinking of others this way a few days before we were to die? Two hours and forty-seven minutes left in the life of John William Otis."

They cut away to Ed Rich, who was outside the prison. He reported on the usual cluster of anti-death penalty advocates who were holding a candlelight vigil and praying, and on the group of partying pro-death advocates who considered execution to be a matter for jubilation.

He spoke to a couple of the participants and embarrassed one pro-death guy by asking if he was in favor of abortion, too.

Ted smothered a laugh, and even Carey smiled faintly as the man protested that abortion and the death penalty were two different things. An anti-death activist immediately chimed in that either life was sacred or it wasn't.

Old, old arguments that changed no one's opinion.

Then she and Ted debated the issue for a couple of minutes, and Ted surprised her by saying that the Otis case was giving him his first doubts about the death penalty. "I know I've always been foursquare in favor of it," he said. "But this is the first time I really thought it was possible that an innocent man was going to die. I'm rethinking the whole issue now."

Then they opened the phones to callers, a majority of whom seemed to be of the opinion that Otis couldn't fry quickly enough.

All too quickly, they were at the ten o'clock break, and Jamie still hadn't called. Carey paced the yard behind the station and managed to smoke two cigarettes in five minutes. Tension had gripped her head in a vise, and her heart was beating rapidly, unwilling to slow down. She wished she could just crawl out of her skin and be done with this.

But she was back in the studio on time. Ted opened the hour with his own monologue on tonight's execution, finishing with a plea to Jamie to call, and a reminder there were less than two hours remaining.

They started to get calls from the victims of violent crime, moms and dads who had lost a child to murder and couldn't bear the thought that in only a few years the killer would be walking free while their child lay in a cold grave. The discussion shifted toward a life sentence without possibility of parole as a viable option to replace the death penalty.

A couple of people called in to cheer the upcoming execution. Ed did two more reports from the prison, where the waiting crowds were growing as the hour approached.

When Carey took time to glance at the clock again, it was almost eleven.

Then she glanced down at her screen and felt her heart stop.

Bob from Gulfport. Johnnie didn't do it.

She looked at Ted who was listening to a caller who had addressed her remarks to him. She caught his eye. "Take the next two calls," she whispered. "Leave Bob for me."

He nodded.

Carey hurried from the booth, nearly colliding with the policeman who was barreling out of the control booth. "That's him," she said.

"I know. I'm radioing it in right now."

She entered the control booth and found Marge frozen over the commercial and news carts. "Marge."

Her producer turned. "It's him."

"I know. Listen, skip the newsbreak. I don't want to lose him. And get the governor on the line right now and give him a live feed. I don't care how many bells you have to ring, or how many whistles you have to blow. Mention me and Ocala, tell him I'll drag his butt into court on a sexual-assault charge—I don't care what you have to do. And when you get him, tell him he's got to hear this right now because he's not going to want to read about it in tomorrow's paper. Got it? Tell him I'm going to get an onair confession, and I've got a quarter of a million live listeners."

Marge's eyes were huge. "Sexual assault? Are you sure?"

"He'll know exactly what I mean, and yes, I'm sure."

She hurried back to the booth, where Ted was fielding a call from some bleeding heart who didn't understand why everyone was so upset about a murderer dying when people killed innocent animals all the time.

She sat at the console, put on her headphones, and drew her finger across her neck, telling Ted she was going to cut off the caller. He nodded and signaled it was hers.

She switched lines. "Bob from Gulfport. Are you there?"

"I'm here."

"What do you want to say tonight?"

"Johnnie didn't do it. I did." His voice was laced with anguish, as if he were on the edge of tears. "Johnnie didn't do anything wrong. I did it. *I* did it."

"Jamie? Jamie Otis, is that you?"

She was answered by silence, and panic hammered her as she wondered if she had lost him. But no, she could still hear the sounds of traffic in the background over the phone. "Jamie? Are you still there?"

"Yes . . ." It was almost a whisper.

"Jamie, did you hear the governor last night?"

"Yes."

"Did you hear what he said? We can't stop this unless someone else confesses. You just did that, didn't you? Why don't you turn yourself in right now—"

"No! But if they kill Johnnie, I'm going to make them pay! Do you hear me? I'm going to make every one of them pay, just the way I made the others pay!"

Carey caught her breath, stilling an urge to tell him that she knew exactly what he had done. She had to draw this out, keep him on the phone as long as possible so the police could reach him. "What did you do, Jamie? What

326

others are you talking about?"

"You know what others! You know! I heard you say the police are looking for me. Well, they'll never find me. I'll just keep on killing people, and I'll never stop unless they let my brother go."

"Jamie . . . Jamie, we've got less than two hours. In fact, I'd be willing to bet we've only got a little over an hour to stop this execution. It'll take time to get the governor, and time for him to stop the execution. So don't give me any crap, okay? Just tell me what you've done. Then maybe everyone will believe what you say you're going to do."

There was another silence. Then Jamie said quietly, "I killed Downs and the Barnstable woman."

Seamus had Carey's show playing quietly on the radio as he sat with Gil, and they waited for the call. His hands were clenched into fists so tight that they were cramping.

"Come on, come on," he muttered tautly. "Let's go, dammit!"

"They'll let us know as soon as they have the location," Gil said.

"We don't have all goddamn night."

"No shit, Sherlock."

"Did anyone ever tell you you're short on sympathy?"

Gil shrugged a shoulder. "I don't have as much wrapped up in this as you do. You could give a damn about Otis. It's Carey you're worried about."

"Tell me something I don't know. Besides, I do give a damn about Otis. I helped put him there."

"Just one of the job perks."

Just then the radio squawked. "Suspect is calling from a phone at Sixty-sixth Street and Thirty-eighth Avenue

327

North. Move in cautiously. We don't want the bird to fly the coop."

"Christ!" Seamus slapped his hand on his thigh. "We don't have anybody all the way up there! He's never called from up there before."

But Gil didn't answer. He just put the light on the top of the car and headed for Sixty-sixth.

Governor on the newsline.

The message popped up on Carey's screen and Carey looked up to see Marge giving her a thumbs-up through the window. Bill Hayes was there, too, and he looked ready to chew his tie.

"Tell me about Henry Downs, Jamie," Carey said into the mike. "He was a friend of mine, you know."

"I know. I saw you there. You helped get Johnnie convicted."

The announcement made her heart lurch, but she kept her voice steady. "So, are you going to kill me, too?"

"No. I thought about it. But I decided you're okay. You're trying to help him. But if they kill him were tonight . . ."

He didn't complete the thought. He didn't need to. Carey suddenly had a vivid image of spending the rest of her life being stalked by a murderer. She suppressed a shudder. "So tell me about Henry Downs, Jamie. Why him? He was only doing his job."

"That's what the Nazis said, too. They were only following orders. But he said terrible things about Johnnie in court. He said Johnnie murdered our dad for no good reason! He lied! He was a liar, and he deserved to die. Johnnie killed Daddy because he was . . . he was. . ." Jamie's voice broke. "He was going to hurt me. Johnnie told him to stop. He told Daddy it was a sin

328

before God, and Daddy hit him and made Johnnie's nose and ears bleed, and then he grabbed me and started pulling my clothes off and then Johnnie got Daddy's razor. . ." He trailed off, panting heavily. "Johnnie saved me," he finally said plaintively.

Carey gentled her voice. "He didn't save you so you could go around killing people, Jamie."

"I didn't have any choice! I didn't! Those people hurt him. They threw him out and told him never to come back. Nobody treats my brother that way. He saved me, and I had to save him. So I killed them."

"Who did you kill, Jamie?" She asked the question gently, but as an attorney she knew how important it was to pin down the specifics. "Who did you kill to save Johnnie?"

"Linda and Harvey Kline," Jamie said, sounding weary. "It was easier than slaughtering pigs. I went to their house with Johnnie's key. They were asleep and I just cut their throats first thing. Bang bang. Better than a gun. Quieter."

"I see." Carey's stomach was rolling over as she remembered the murder scene. It was far too easy to imagine all that had led up to what she had seen the following day in the Kline bedroom. "So you killed the Klines to save Johnnie. And you killed Downs to save Johnnie, and because he lied."

"That's right. They deserved it, too. All of them deserved it."

"So what about Beatrice Barnstable?"

"Bitch. She was a bitch. She was the one who stood up in the courtroom and said Johnnie had to die. So I killed her. What goes around comes around. That's what they say. It sure came around on her. I *ex-e-cu-ted* her. I let her know what was going to happen. I just

329

wish I could have made it last five years, the way she did to Johnnie."

"But what about Ben Webster? Ben defended your brother. He did his best in that trial to keep Johnnie from going to jail."

"I didn't kill him."

"No, but you tried to, didn't you. You tried to break into his home Sunday night."

"I wish I'd made it."

"But why? He tried very hard to save Johnnie."

"No, he didn't. The Klines left everything to Johnnie in their will. Everything. I thought when I killed them that Johnnie would have a home even though they'd thrown him out. But Webster took it all. He took it all to pay for Johnnie's defense. At least that's what he said. Thirty thousand dollars!"

"He earned the money, Jamie. He represented your brother for a long time."

"Until the money ran out. Then so did he."

"I see." Glancing at her console, Carey saw that the phones were absolutely silent. Whoever was listening to the program right now was listening on tenterhooks, just as she was. Nobody wanted to interrupt.

She looked at the clock and saw that more precious minutes had ticked away. Panic began to climb into her throat.

It was then that she decided to take a chance. She might cause Jamie to hang up, but she had to take the risk. Hardening her voice, she changed tack.

"Jamie?" Carey said. "You still there?"

"Yeah."

"Let me see if I have this straight, okay? You killed the Klines, but you're letting your brother take the rap for it?"

"I'm trying to save him!"

330

Carey made her voice as hard as she could. "It doesn't look that way to me. You could have confessed five years ago and saved him all of this!"

"You don't understand!"

"Oh, I understand perfectly. Johnnie knows you killed the Klines, doesn't he?"

Jamie was silent. Panic lodged in Carey's throat making it almost impossible for her to breathe. Then he said uncertainly, "I . . . think so."

"So there's your brother, whom you profess to want to save, sitting on death row in your place. What's more, he knows you did it, Jamie. But he loves you so much that he's willing to die to save you. Isn't that right?"

"I . . ." Jamie's voice broke, and he drew a ragged breath. "I . . . don't know!"

"You do know. You know he's giving his life to save yours. You know that he loves you enough to do that. But you don't love Johnnie enough, do you, Jamie? You don't love him as much as he loves you!"

"Yes, I do! Yes, I *do*! That's why I killed those people! Because I love Johnnie, and I want to save him!"

"If you really loved him as much as he loves you, you'd turn yourself in to the police, and you'd confess, and you'd do it right now. *Right now,* Jamie. Because your brother is going to die in less than an hour if you don't do it *right now!*"

The silence on the phone was so long that Carey would have feared she'd lost him but for the background traffic sounds that told her the line was still open. She held her breath, and felt as if most of the Tampa Bay area were holding its breath along with her The phones remained utterly silent. Everyone was listening.

"Jamie?" she said finally. She heard him sob. "Jamie," she said gently, "you know what you need to do. You know how to show your brother you love him as much as he loves you. You know how to save Johnnie right now. Will you talk to the police?"

"I . . . I . . ."

Suddenly there was a loud bang, as if the phone receiver hit something. There were voices, some of them raised in the background, and the sounds of a scuffle.

"Jamie?" Carey called his name. "Jamie?" Oh, God, what had happened? Had he run?

But then she heard the rattle of the receiver again, and moments later a familiar voice saying, "This is Detective Seamus Rourke of the St. Petersburg Police Department, Ms. Justice. We have apprehended James Otis. Thank you for your assistance." Then with a click, he was gone.

Carey didn't even blink. She hit the governor's line and put him on the air. "Governor Howell, you're on the air now You heard the live feed we were sending you?"

"Uh . . . yes. Yes, I did, Ms. Justice." His voice, at first sounding shocked, rapidly strengthened. "It was . . . interesting, to say the least."

"You'll stay the execution of John William Otis then?"

"I can't do that."

"Oh for God's sake," said Ted Sanders, jumping in on his microphone. "Let's not be asinine about this, Governor! You just heard a man confess to the killings for which John Otis was convicted. Don't tell me—and don't tell our quarter million listeners—that you're going to let this execution go through!"

"I need more than this to pardon a man. All I have is some verbal claims made on the telephone."

"Then don't pardon him," Carey said sharply. "But at least stay the execution until we have a signed confession. Don't kill an innocent man because the *paperwork* won't be there on time!"

There was a pause. "Well, of course I'll stay the execution. I couldn't do anything less under the circumstances. You'll have to excuse me now, because I need to make the call to Raiford Prison."

Carey glanced at the clock. It was now eleven twenty-seven. God, had she been on the phone with Otis that long? "Thank you, Governor," she said. "Thank you very much."

The phones were all lit up now, and messages from Marge filled her screen. She looked at them, then took her headphones off and rose from her chair. "It's your show now, Ted."

Bill caught her outside in the hallway. "You can't leave! Everyone is going to want to talk to you. My God, what a program' But you can't leave."

She looked him dead in the eye. "I'm leaving. My show was over a half hour ago. And you know what, Bill? I'm not sure I'll be back tomorrow."

"Carey . . ." He called after her, but she just kept walking.

She couldn't say why, but she didn't feel jubilant. She felt . . . ill. And all she wanted was to get out and never come back.

EPILOGUE

TWO DAYS LATER, SEAMUS AND CAREY DROVE UP TO Starke, and were waiting outside Raiford Prison when John William Otis emerged into the free sunlight for the first time since the death of his foster parents.

333

There was no fanfare, no press of reporters to plague him. At his request, the prison had not revealed the time of his release.

He stood blinking, as if the light was brighter outside, somehow. Or as if he didn't quite know what to do. The prison had given him a bus ticket back to Tampa, and would have transported him to the terminal, but when Carey had called the prison and offered to come get him and take him home, he had jumped at the chance. For him it was just that many minutes sooner that he would be free of the last physical reminders of the nightmare.

When Carey approached him, he smiled and offered his hand, shaking hers with surprising strength for a man so small. He remembered Seamus from the investigation after the murder, and from the courtroom, and he looked uneasily at the much larger man.

But Seamus pumped his hand warmly. "I'm glad it all worked out."

John turned and looked back at the prison. "Did it?" he asked.

Seamus and Carey exchanged uncertain looks. But then John squared his shoulders and gave them both shy smiles. "Thanks for coming for me. Thanks for . . ." His voice trailed away, and Carey had the distinct impression he didn't know how to thank them for saving him at the expense of his brother.

"I'm sorry about Jamie," she said.

John nodded. He looked down at his toes. When he spoke, his voice was infinitely sad. "Jamie doesn't know how to love," he said. "He never had a chance to learn."

"He could have learned from you."

John's face somehow seemed to crumple in on itself, as if the pain was almost too much to bear. "Maybe he did," he said quietly. "Maybe he did."

There was another silence, and they stood in a frozen tableau, as if none of them were sure what to do next.

"Well, we'd better go," Seamus eventually said. "I'd like to get back before dark."

John nodded, and they started moving toward the parking lot.

"We got you a plane ticket, John," Seamus continued. "It's open-ended. You can use it whenever you want."

"Where to?" John asked.

"Boston. We figured you'd like to go up there and see the autumn colors in a couple of weeks."

"And then you can see the snow. Real snow," Carey added.

He nodded and paused to look back once more at the prison. There was a haunting, wistful tone in his voice.

"I just wish Jamie could go with me."

"Are you feeling the way I'm feeling?" Seamus asked Carey that night as they strolled beside the water at St. Pete Beach. Ahead of them rose the exotic spires of the Don Cesar Hotel. Beneath their feet, damp sand resisted, then gave way. The gulf was quiet tonight, gentle waves rolling in with a lullaby rhythm. They held hands, their fingers clinging.

"How do you feel?" Carey asked.

"Letdown. Sad. I don't know. I thought I'd feel on top of the world, but I don't."

"It was sort of a Pyrrhic victory. John isn't jubilant either."

"I can understand what he feels. It's his brother, after all. But I can't understand what I feel. It's as if I didn't save anyone at all." Seamus kicked up a shower of sand, expressing his frustration.

"Maybe that's what's wrong with the death penalty."

"Maybe."

They walked until they reached the hotel, then turned around and started back.

He squeezed her hand. "Are you going back to radio?"

"I don't know. It seems so pointless right now. But I don't have to decide yet." Bill had given her two weeks off rather than lose her. Time to think, he'd called it. She planned to use every minute of it.

"Well, if you don't go back, I'm going to miss hearing your voice every night."

Her heart squeezed, whether because he apparently felt they weren't going to see each other again, or because she had never guessed he listened to her show, she couldn't say. "You listen to me?"

"Every night, unless I'm working." He gave a quiet laugh. "I was like a starving man in need of food. I needed to hear your voice. It didn't matter what you said, just that I could hear you."

She caught her breath, and some of the sorrow she'd been feeling seemed to be lifting from her shoulders. The night sky suddenly held more stars than she could ever remember seeing, and the water looked as if it were strewn with diamonds. "Really?"

"Really." He gave another laugh, this one almost embarrassed. "I told you the other day that I love you."

She stopped walking and turned to face him, hardly aware that the warm water lapped over her feet, ruining her shoes. "I remember. Your timing sucked, Rourke."

"I know. It usually does." He rocked back on his heels and looked up at the heavens as if seeking guidance. "The truth is, Carey Stover, in all these years I never stopped loving you. Sometimes I almost hated you for that, but I never once stopped loving you."

"Then where the hell have you been?"

He looked down at her, and in the starlight she could see his almost-rueful expression. "A gentleman hopes that a lady will not respond that way to the declaration of his deepest feelings."

"Cut out the malarkey. I'm not Gil. Talk to *me*, Seamus."

"I'm trying. You're not being very helpful."

"So try again, and I'll shut up."

"That'll work. Okay. So where have I been? I've been hiding from my feelings because I felt so guilty for the way you made me feel. I had some stupid notion that I had no right to be happy."

"And now?"

"Well, you could say I realized just how idiotic I'm being. I mean, when the universe is kind enough to shower you with the best gifts life has to offer, only a jerk would turn them away. Which I did. And I was. A jerk, I mean."

Carey nodded.

"You don't have to agree with me."

"I didn't say a word."

He felt the stupidest smile stretching his cheeks, as he realized she was enjoying this. She was enjoying watching him squirm. His heart took an upward leap. "Then, the universe gave me a second chance with you. It dragged me kicking and screaming back into your proximity."

"I didn't hear any screaming."

"That's because you couldn't read my mind the night you called about the death warrant. Trust me, I was screaming. Silently."

"You hid it well."

"Thank you." He took a little bow. "Anyway, all of

this is leading up to the fact that I've never stopped loving you, and after the last few weeks I love you more than ever. I've put away my demons, for better or worse, and I want to know—do we have a chance?"

She looked away, pursing her lips, and he felt his hopes plummet. She wouldn't have to think about it if she felt the same way he did.

"A chance for what?" she asked.

"A chance for me to strangle you if you keep doing this to me! You know very well what I mean. Can we try to build our relationship again? Can we make another stab at it? You know. The marriage thing. The kid thing. The minivan, picket-fence, diapers thing."

She tilted her head back and looked up at him. And there was no more playfulness about her. Her heart seemed to have climbed into her throat. "You want that . . . with me? After . . . after what you've been through? Seamus, are you sure?"

He nodded. "I'm sure. I can't hide forever, Carey. If you want anything in life, you have to take risks. I'm ready to take this one again."

Her heart squeezed, and she felt tears tremble on her lashes. He had more guts than she did. "But we made a hash of it last time, Seamus."

"I know. Look. I made mistakes. You made mistakes. A lot of it was just bad timing. I was running from grief. You were hiding from shattered illusions. I didn't appreciate you, until you were gone." He paused for a moment, watching the waves. "I wanted a lifeline, not a partner."

"Maybe I did, too. But I remember all the fights, all the anger, all the ways we grated on each other's nerves. I want to love you, Seamus. I *do* love you. But I don't want to hurt that way again. I don't want to hurt you again that way."

338

"History is not destiny," he said. "Otis proved that. The world did everything it could to break him, and what did he do? Write poetry. Love his brother. He was stronger than the bad stuff that happened to him. And so are you. I think I am, too."

He reached over to take her hand. "For all these years, you've been the light at the end of the tunnel. Now we're at the end of the tunnel. Don't take away the light. I love you, Carey."

Something inside her felt as if she had tumbled over a precipice, but instead of falling into the pit below, she took wing and soared toward the stars. She reached for him, and felt his arms close around her, the safe haven she had always sought. She blinked away tears. "So this minivan, picket-fence, diapers thing. You're serious about this?"

"The past is past, Carey. I have to look to the future. And when I look at the future, all I see is you. Will you marry me?"

"Can I have a big wedding with all the trimmings?"

He laughed, lifting her off her feet and swinging her in circles. "We can get married on the moon if you want."

"Well, in that case, yes. I've always wanted a fancy wedding . . ." But the teasing tone of her voice faded away, and as he set her on her feet, she gripped his upper arms, looked straight into his eyes, and said, "Forever, Seamus."

He nodded. "Forever."

She leaned into his embrace and closed her eyes, feeling his warm solidity, hearing the timeless beat of the waves.

And hearing the timeless words of the Frost poem John Otis had kept on his cell wall.

And miles to go before I sleep,

And miles to go before I sleep.

Suddenly, the words didn't sound wearying and sad to her. They were a promise. And she was going to cherish every one of those miles with Seamus.

Dear Reader:

I hope you enjoyed reading this Large Print book. If you are interested in reading other Beeler Large Print titles, ask your librarian or write to me at

Thomas T. Beeler, *Publisher*
Post Office Box 659
Hampton Falls, New Hampshire 03844

You can also call me at 1-800-251-8726 and I will send you my latest catalogue.

Audrey Lesko and I choose the titles I publish in Large Print. Our aim is to provide good books by outstanding authors—books we both enjoyed reading and liked well enough to want to share. We warmly welcome any suggestions for new titles and authors.

Sincerely,